ZRADA

A DEWITT AGENCY ADVENTURE

By Lance Charnes

WOMBAT GROUP MEDIA — ORANGE, CALIFORNIA

Wombat Group Media
Post Office Box 4908
Orange, CA 92863
https://www.wombatgroup.com/

First Printing November 2020

ISBN 978-1-7333989-1-6

Cover design by Damonza.

This is a work of fiction. Names, characters, businesses, places, events and incidents are either the products of the author's imagination or used in a fictitious manner. Any resemblance to actual persons, living or dead, or actual events is purely coincidental.

No animals were harmed in the writing of this novel.

Printed in the United States of America

For Betty

Who's glad this keeps me busy

OTHER BOOKS BY LANCE CHARNES

The DeWitt Agency Files:
The Collection (#1)
Stealing Ghosts (#2)
Chasing Clay (#3)

Doha 12
South

For bonus chapters from ***Zrada***, a downloadable cast list and
map, reading group questions, and an interview with the
author, check out https://www.wombatgroup.com/zrada/

ZRADA

A DeWitt Agency Adventure

ZRADA CAST OF CHARACTERS

The DeWitt Agency

- Carson / Tarasenko: *Former Toronto Police Service detective sergeant; associate #126 at the DeWitt Agency*
  - Ron Carson: *Carson's ex-husband, a TPS inspector*
  - Lisa Carson: *One of Carson's cover identities*
  - Genadiy Rodievsky: *Pakhan of the Solntsevskaya Bratva in Vienna; Carson's sometime employer*

- Abram Stepaniak: *Principal Agency associate in eastern Ukraine (#113)*
  - Stas: *Stepaniak's driver/henchman*
  - Vadim: *Stepaniak's henchman*

- Allyson DeWitt: *Carson's employer; "fills needs" for wealthy/powerful clients*
- Olivia: *Allyson's major domo and fixer; a voice on the phone*

Assisting Carson

- Galina (Galya) Lukayivna Demchuk: *Smallholding farmer outside Olhynske*
  - Bohdan Iliyovych Demchuk: *Her missing husband*

- Matt Friedrich: *American ex-architect, ex-gallery assistant, ex-convict; Carson's sometime Agency partner (#179)*
- Dieter Heitmann: *Kunsthistorisches Museum Bonn chief curator*

Makiivka Brigade (separatist militia in eastern Ukraine, fighting for the rebel Donetsk People's Republic [DNR])

- Col. Dima Artemovich Mashkov: *Brigade Commander*
  - Sr. Sgt. Lenya Vasilenko: *Senior brigade NCO; Mashkov's assistant*
- Lt. Col. Evgeniy Shatilov: *Mashkov's Chief of Staff*
- Sr. Lt. Dunya Fetisova: *Senior brigade medic*

Russian Army

- Lt. Col. Edik Gregorivich Rogozhkin: *Officer of the 45th Guards Spetsnaz Brigade (Russian special forces); military advisor to the Makiivka Brigade*
  - SFC Oleg Yartsev: *Spetsnaz* starshina *(senior sergeant); Rogozhkin's assistant*

All action takes place 11-19 May 2016.

For a downloadable, printable cast list and map, go to https://www.wombatgroup.com/zrada/bonus-material/

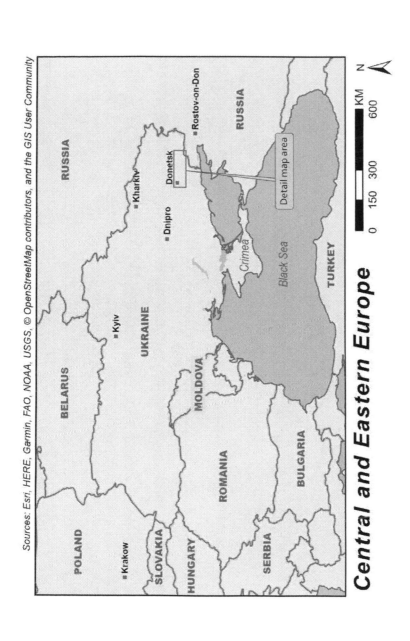

Sources: Esri, HERE, Garmin, FAO, NOAA, USGS, © OpenStreetMap contributors, and the GIS User Community

POLAND
Krakow
SLOVAKIA
HUNGARY
SERBIA
BELARUS
UKRAINE
Kyiv
MOLDOVA
ROMANIA
BULGARIA
RUSSIA
Kharkiv
Dnipro
Donetsk
Rostov-on-Don
RUSSIA
Crimea
Black Sea
Detail map area
TURKEY

Central and Eastern Europe

KM
0   150   300   600

N

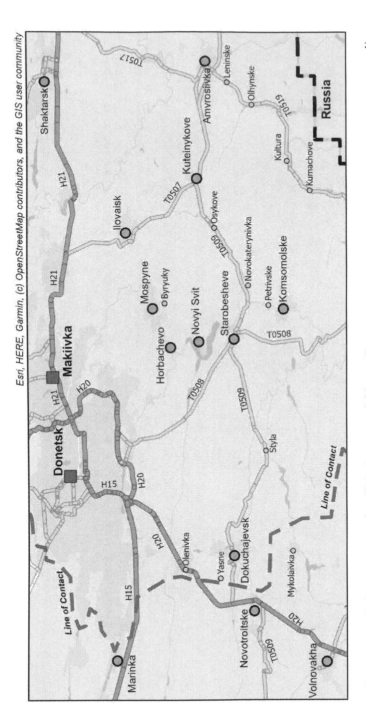

Central Donetsk Oblast, Ukraine
May 2016

CHAPTER 1

"Touch me again," Carson growls in Ukrainian, "you lose the hand."

The hand caresses the top of her ass. Its thumb taps the bottom edge of the ballistic vest beneath her slate-blue, long-sleeved polo.

Stepaniak chuckles. After Carson turns to glare—not before—he peels his left hand off her and holds it up, palm out. A playful smile splits his close-cropped black beard. "Dear Carson," he purrs. "Don't be that way. You used to like having me touch you, I remember."

"Used to like lots of things that're bad for me."

She uses the window reflection to pat the hood-head out of her hair, then stalks away with two Zero Halliburton aluminum attachés—eight kilos of dead weight at the end of each arm—to the middle of the gravel road carving a slot between two long, low concrete-block buildings. It's good to be outside and on her hind legs again after being strapped into the Range Rover's back seat for over four hours with a black canvas sack over her head. Bad road, checkpoint, bad road: rinse and repeat.

The familiar noise of squabbling chickens and the familiar smell of chicken shit leaks out the narrow windows sheltered under the eaves of the corrugated metal roofs. The first thing she'd ever killed was a chicken. Her mom had tried, but she was drunk, as usual, and botched it. Carson had to finish the job. She was nine? Ten? She'd cried over the dead bird she'd helped feed and raise, the next-to-last time she remembers crying.

She turns a slow 360. Ten hostiles—no, eleven, one on overwatch on the north coop's roof—split into two groups: one by the olive-drab cargo truck ahead of the two Range Rovers, the other arced around the back end of the matte-black Toyota technical behind the SUVs. Smoking, chatting. Three different camouflage patterns on their utilities, at least two different types of boots, four types of headgear, black or olive balaclavas. Mostly AK-74s or AK-105s.

And she's not armed. She'd tangled with Stepaniak when he told her to leave her sidearm at the Volnovakha hotel this morning, but he won. He'd said, "Our hosts get nervous when people they don't know bring weapons to a meeting." He gave her his slickest smile. "Don't worry, dear Carson. I'll protect you."

Fuck that. That's when she ducked into the toilet and stashed her collapsible steel baton in her body armor. She hates bringing a club to a firefight, but it's the best she can do today.

Stepaniak's muscle—Stas and Vadim—stand smoking by the second Range Rover. Vadim has a slung Ksyukha; Stas a suppressed Vityaz-SN submachinegun. *Hostiles? Hard to tell.* Vadim leers at her knees. Not because he can see them (they're covered with black denim), but because the handles on the Halliburtons are there.

The other militia troops stare at her. Yes, she's the only woman there, but really? *They're way hard up if they're checking* me *out. Or is it the luggage? Do they know, too?*

She spins toward the rattle of nearby gravel. It's Heitmann, crabbing toward her with two large black portfolios slapping his calves. He'd been in the second Range Rover with Stas and Vadim. He's one reason she's here (the cases being the other). "*Fraulein* Carson?"

"Yeah?"

Heitmann's a curator for a German museum and looks the part: fine-boned face, rimless glasses, careful graying middle-brown hair everywhere except on top. A short, over-neat beard and mustache compensate. "Do you know where we are?"

"You don't?"

He shakes his head. "No, I am sorry. In the negotiations, the solicitor never told us where the militia held our artworks." His English carries a soft German accent— "v" instead of "w," hard esses—and he speaks carefully, like the words might break. He glances around like a bird looking for cats. "We can hope this is the place."

Yeah. Hope. "We're probably still in Donetsk Oblast. Locals call it the 'Donetsk People's Republic,' or 'DNR.' Can't tell how deep we're in, though." Stepaniak took both their phones, so there's no way to look it up. For all she knows, they're in Russia now. It's only fifty straight-line klicks to the nearest border from where they'd crossed the contact line. But as shaky as Heitmann looks, he doesn't need to hear that.

"We drove so long." Heitmann seems to be developing a bad-car-crash fascination with the militia troops by the cargo truck. "Who are these people?"

"Militia. Rebels."

"What do they rebel against?"

Carson cocks an eyebrow at him. "Figured you'd know all about this."

He shrugs lightly. "Our news is full of Syrians, for obvious reasons."

The "obvious reasons" being the million refugees who crashed into Germany last year. "Well…short version is, late 2013, the president of Ukraine killed an agreement with the EU. Most of the country wanted it." Good thing she read the agency backgrounder. "Yanukovych—the president—was from here, the Donbass. Basically a crook and a Russian stooge. Hear about the Maidan?"

Heitmann nods. "Yes, I think. The big protests in Kyiv?"

"Right. Basically a revolution. Protesters kicked out Yanukovych. That pissed off the Russians—the ones living here and the ones in Moscow. He was their boy. Putin used the Russian Army on the down-low to 'help' the locals take over Crimea. Then he started a civil war here. That was two springs ago." She thumbs toward the militia troops. "They're supposed to be fighting it. Guess the Russian Army's doing most of the fighting now."

"I see." He edges closer. "Your man"—he glances toward Stepaniak—"is he…reliable?"

Is he? Carson doesn't need to look at him to see him, but she does anyway. Stepaniak had liked making an impression when they first met four years ago, and apparently nothing but colors have changed. Back then he wore all black; now it's all blue—the leather car coat, the dress shirt open at his throat, the sharply creased slacks. His black hair should have some gray by now, but doesn't. Dye, not good genes.

"He's agency lead here. They vouch for him." *I won't.*

"I see."

A shout from behind her: "*Pora!*"

It comes from a third low building, this one just east of the southern chicken coop and about a third as long. Three rusty roll-up metal doors. The Kapitán stands in the open middle doorway in his pristine digitized green camo utilities —the latest Russian pattern—fists on hips, like recess is over and the kiddies need to come back to class.

The Kapitán rode in the SUV with Carson and Stepaniak. She doesn't know who he is, but guesses this is his 'hood; he wears the same patch on his left shoulder (a blue-and-black shield with a rising yellow sun) as the other troops. Every time they stopped at a checkpoint, his was the only voice she could hear clearly.

She hefts the Halliburtons and jerks her head toward the open door. "You heard the man." Then she marches off, the gravel crunching under her boots.

She checks her watch: 1:52 p.m. All goes well, they're out by 2:30 and back to Volnovakha—on the Ukraine side of the line—by six. She wants this to go well, meaning done. Babysitting isn't her favorite chore. Neither is being a bagman.

Carson stops at the open roll-up to let her eyes adjust. What she sees looks like vehicle maintenance: three service bays, workbenches, tools, floor jacks, a stack of snow tires in the southwest corner, two 200kg barrels against the east wall. Other than the roll-up doors, a standard door set into the west wall to her right is the only other way out.

Something about the setup tweaks her gut. A lot of people are filing into a not-large space. Most are heavily armed. *If shit goes south...*

She jerks away from a hard grip on her shoulder, then spins to find Stepaniak's face just inches from hers. She growls, "What'd I just tell you?"

Stepaniak hisses in English, "Make sure *nemyets* does his job." *Nemyets* is Russian for a German. He brushes past her to catch up with the Kapitán.

By the time the roll-up door slams down and the fluorescent strip lights blink on, Carson counts ten people with her in the center bay: Heitmann, Stepaniak, the Kapitán, Vadim, five militia troops, and a dark, semi-handsome man in a shiny charcoal pinstripe suit and no tie.

They gather around an old wooden trestle table holding two side-by-side rectangles, each maybe half a meter by two-thirds, wrapped in midnight-green plastic. Heitmann sucks in a sharp breath when he sees them.

The paintings.

Carson lays the Halliburtons on the table next to the paintings, handle side toward her. Everybody in the room starts to drool. It's like watching a pack of coyotes ogle a rabbit.

Heitmann fidgets next to her at the table, breathing fast. His eyes skate from one assault rifle to the next. He whispers, "So many guns."

Carson has two jobs here. One is to carry and guard the attachés; the other is to keep Heitmann breathing regularly and focused on his job. That second part's harder.

She leans her lips toward his ear. "Relax. Nobody's drunk yet." That's always a good sign for her. The startled look Heitmann gives her says it's not working for him.

Stepaniak and the Kapitán take places on the other side of the table from Carson, their backs to the bay doors. The suit frowns at the end of the table to her right. Four militia troops fan out behind her; the fifth stands beside the center roll-up door. They're looking both more alert and more nervous now. Vadim hovers in the bay to Carson's left, watching everybody else.

Six hostiles still outside, plus Stas. Keeping others out…or us in?

"Carson, *nemyets*, friends. Please." Stepaniak's English lugs a heavy accent, but his cadence sounds like a TV chat-show host. He points at Heitmann, then toward the two plastic-wrapped rectangles. "Look at pictures. They are right? Say yes."

Heitmann leans the portfolios against the nearest table leg and fumbles with the rectangle farthest to the left. He'd work faster if his hands didn't shake so much.

The adrenaline rush starts to dilate time. Carson's rational mind tells her she's not scared, just careful. Her rational mind isn't usually the one that keeps her alive, though.

She flashes to the first time she walked into a room full of shady men with weapons. She was a patrol cop in one of Toronto's crappier neighborhoods, fresh off her probation, less than a month working solo shifts. A prowler call took her to a supposedly empty storefront that was full of biker types doing a bootleg cigarette deal.

Her supposed brothers in blue slow-rolled their response to her backup call—girls still weren't supposed to be street cops—so she had to face down seven hardened felons carrying long weapons and submachine guns with only her Glock, buckets of adrenaline, and a big dose of attitude. It wasn't until backup finally showed and she was safe that she realized she'd pissed herself. Thank God for navy-blue trousers.

The green plastic—a trash bag—rustles to the floor. The painting's gaudy, with messed-up perspective and figures that look like dolls. An angel with a blond perm and red-and-gold wings blesses a praying woman in a blue gown while a glowing pigeon hovers over them both.

Carson whispers to Heitmann, "Museum's paying money for this?"

He shoots her a look usually used on rude children and crazy homeless people. "It is an Annunciation," he whispers. "By Lucas Cranach the Elder, in 1515. Please, have respect."

Whatever. Carson isn't an art expert.

Heitmann pulls a white three-ring binder from a portfolio. It's full of pictures of the painting. He flips to a page, then peers through an old-school magnifying glass at the real thing and compares it to the photo.

Someone grumbles in Russian, "What does he do?"

It takes Carson a few moments to narrow down the voice. It's the first time she's heard the suit speak. His Russian's coated with a thick accent she can't place. He's dark with almond eyes. From one of the Stans? The Caucusus?

Stepaniak says, "He's checking that it's real."

The suit snarls, "Of *course* is real. What do you say?"

"Nothing, Ruslan, nothing." Stepaniak's in calming-the-mad-dog mode. "The museum wants to make sure, that's all. It's a condition."

"They say I cheat? I not cheat. I am honest man."

The Kapitán mutters, "You're a fucking *brodyaga.*" A street-corner black-market dealer. Not a compliment.

Ruslan stabs a finger at the Kapitán. He booms, "*I am fucking brodyaga? You pay fucking brodyaga. What are you?*"

Shit. Now the dick-waving starts.

The Kapitán growls, "Look, *cherniy*—"

Stepaniak darts between the men, holding up a hand to each. "Friends, friends, please. All is good, yes?" He smiles at the Kapitán. "You get your money..." Then at Ruslan. "...*you* get your money..." Then both. "...everyone gets what they want, yes? No need to fight, yes?"

Carson checks on Heitmann while the trash talk spirals toward the roof. The German's frozen at the table, his magnifying glass vibrating in midair. She hisses, "You done?" He shakes his head. "Get done before this comes apart. Move."

Ruslan's slipped into whatever his native language is. It's not hard to tell what he's shouting. The arm he stretches toward the Kapitán over Stepaniak's shoulder says a lot. She's already heard at least two militia troops running their rifles' bolts. Carson hopes Stepaniak spotted the pistol in Ruslan's waistband—not because she cares much about Stepaniak, but because if it comes out to play, the militamen will go kinetic on everybody.

Heitmann's abandoned the first painting and is stripping the bag off the second one. Sweat runs down his forehead. He's breathing like he just finished running up a cliff.

Carson switches focus to the fight. A militia troop has Ruslan's arms pinned. Stepaniak's huddled with the Kapitán, who's holding the pistol he'd had in his shoulder holster. Good news: it's still aimed at the floor...for now. Carson really, *really* misses her Glock.

The yelling and rustling suddenly switches off. Everybody—*everybody*—stares at the table. *What the...?*

It's an icon, old enough that the paint's cracked and faded and the faces have turned dark. It looks like the same idea as the other painting, but totally different. The angel and woman are stretched, almost boneless. The flat, fake buildings behind them are a stage set, not a place.

The Kapitán crosses himself the Orthodox way, right shoulder before left. A couple other militiamen do the same. Even the suit shuts up for a minute. Someone behind Carson murmurs what sounds like a prayer.

Heitmann looks behind him, then all around, then dives into comparing the icon to the pictures in the binder. Carson whispers, "This famous or something?"

"The artist is. This came from Dionisy's studio. He and Andrei Rublev founded the Moscow School, the style of icon you see here."

None of those names mean a thing to her. "Shouldn't there be more gold?"

"This is very early. They used not so much gilding then." Only the halos shine in the strip lights. "The fifteenth and sixteenth centuries were very difficult for the Church."

Okay. She checks the room's temperature. The Kapitán's all folded arms and stormy face. His eyes toggle between the icon and Ruslan, who's pacing a small circle at the end of the table like a caged hyena waiting to kill something. The militia troops keep shuffling their feet and fingering their weapons' trigger guards.

Stepaniak's back at the table. When his eyes aren't glued to the attachés, they follow every twitch the German makes. He's watching her, too. He smiles. "Is like old times, yes?" he says in English.

Carson grumbles, "Keep telling yourself that."

Heitmann stands straight, shuts the binder, then faces Stepaniak. "I am satisfied these works are the pieces stolen from our museum."

Stepaniak puts on a big grin. "Ah, *nemyets*. Very good, you please me." He shifts to Russian. "Dear Carson, please show the men"—he sweeps his hand around the room—"the gift you brought them."

Everybody's watching her now. "I need Heitmann's phone."

"Why?"

"The combo's on it." A security measure. The museum gave her the cases locked.

Stepaniak grumbles, then dips his hand into his car coat's left pocket and brings out a newish Galaxy S7. He hands it to her; she passes it to Heitmann. He opens it with his thumbprint, fiddles with the screen, then turns it so she can see. In Notes: "829."

She draws a deep breath. Once she does this, her value to these men goes to zero. She turns both cases on end and twiddles both locks to the key code. Lays them down, pops the locks, swivels the cases so they face Stepaniak and the Kapitán. "Go ahead."

Stepaniak lifts the lids on both attachés. His smile turns sharkish. The Kapitán's jaw sags. Ruslan steps around, peeks, palms his mouth.

They're looking at a hundred straps of used €200 notes with

non-sequential serial numbers. Ten thousand yellow-faced bills. Two million euros in untraceable cash.

Carson considered taking it herself. That's why the German had the combo.

Stepaniak grabs a random strap. He riffles the hundred banknotes with his thumb, then tosses the bundle into the case. He steps back two paces.

"Dear Carson." His grin practically glows. "Very good. You please me."

He cross-draws a pistol from under his car coat.

He shoots Carson.

CHAPTER 2

No air.

Carson lies gasping on her side. It's like an angry draft horse kicked her in the ribs. She tries to suck in a breath but her diaphragm doesn't work, her lungs won't fill. She can hardly make a sound. Not that she could hear it if she did.

Bullets rip apart the air above her.

Who's shooting who? She can't tell. The four militia troops who used to be behind her are now flat on the slab, their blood oozing toward the floor drain. Heitmann's down, dark red spreading over his polo. Carson can't move well enough to see anything else. If she can't start breathing again, she won't see anything at all in a couple minutes.

For an instant, Carson's in a hockey game, sprawled on the ice after a bad body-check. Draws her knees toward her chest to relax her gut. (Doesn't work; hurts like hell.) Tries to force her stomach out when she inhales to kick-start her diaphragm. But her vest, her jeans, even her compression bra are trying to keep everything *in*.

Black fringes her vision. She wants to scream but has no air to do it.

The ringing in her ears is so loud, she almost doesn't notice the shooting's stopped. Not that that's her worst problem right now.

Carson's fingers scrabble for her fly. Top button open; unzip. A little room to shove her stomach downward in time with a stunted inhalation.

That works, sort of: a trickle of air sneaks into her lungs. It's like a snort of coke.

A single gunshot. *Why? Not important.*

Stomach up, stomach down. More air. The black edges around her vision melt away.

She's breathing again. *This shit never gets easier.*

Another shot. Closer.

Carson flips on her back, recovers from the effort, then turns her head toward the sound. Just in time to watch Vadim put a round in a fallen militiaman's head.

Shooting the wounded. Wonderful.

Gunsmoke fills her nostrils. The coughing bucks her upper body off the concrete, then slams it down.

Vadim watches Ruslan drag himself a meter. Aims his pistol, fires.

He looks toward Carson with bored eyes.

Oh, no, you don't.

Her right hand fumbles under her shirt. She'd clipped her baton to the vest's left-hand Velcro side strap this morning.

It's not there.

Vadim's busy pulling cash out of Ruslan's pockets. A man's gotta have priorities.

Carson's fingertips trip over something round and rough just inboard of the side strap. It's metal and warm and sits where an invisible someone is going at her body with an auger. Stepaniak's bullet.

I love my vest.

Vadim's done with Ruslan. He stands, draws his pistol, then steps over Ruslan's blood trail to head her way.

Where's my baton?

Something metal and cylindrical under her digs into her ribcage. She rolls flat on her back so her fingers can grab it.

Vadim stops a foot away to watch her.

She rasps, "What're you doing?"

Vadim shrugs. "Cleaning up." His gun hand swings forward to aim.

Carson's right arm arcs up and out. There's a *zzzzzzip* sound. Her baton extends an instant before it smashes into Vadim's hand. His scream and the reflex gunshot mask the crunching of bone as Carson follows through her backhand.

Her forehand swing destroys his left knee. She manages to roll out of the way before he crashes onto the slab where she'd been.

Standing is a challenge—every move shoots lightning bolts out of her ribcage into her eyes—but Carson manages. She zips her jeans, retracts and shoves her baton into a hip pocket, pants for a while, then hobbles to where Vadim's pistol landed next to a dead militia troop. A Heckler & Koch P30; nice weapon. She drops the magazine to check its load. Five rounds left out of fifteen.

She happens to glance at the table.

One briefcase is gone. So's the icon. *Fuck!*

Carson shuffles to Vadim. She searches him roughly, confiscates his stubby Ksyukha assault carbine, three more magazines for the HK, the wad of cash he took from Ruslan, and a Russian tactical knife and its ankle sheath. Vadim swears and groans, often at the same time. Then she crouches behind his shoulders and grinds the pistol's muzzle into his temple. "Listen," she growls in Russian. "I hurt like hell and I'm pissed. Answer my questions or I make you hurt worse than me. Understand?"

Vadim keeps swearing, but there's more groaning. He eventually nods.

"Where's Stepaniak?"

He breathes hard for a few moments, then shakes his head.

"Stupid fuck." Now that she's not suffocating, she has time to get mad. Stepaniak tried to kill her and this idiot tried to finish the job. She jabs her pistol into the back of his right knee and pulls the trigger.

People in Berlin can hear Vadim scream.

She reacquaints the muzzle with his temple. "Let's try again. Where's Stepaniak?"

Vadim pants for a while. "Driving. Get away. Rings. Tells me. Where to go."

"What was the plan?"

More panting. "Take money. Paintings. Ask for. More money."

Of course. *Asshole.* "He tell you to shoot the wounded?"

He nods once.

"He tell you to shoot *me?*"

He nods again. Of course he would. If he said *no*, owned what he was about to do, he'd have to figure she'd blow his brains out. Which she might do anyway.

No. Too easy. "Guess what, Vadim. Just for being an asshole, you get to live...until the militia gets here." Something occurs to her. "What militia is this?"

He pauses. She can't tell if it's because the pain's caught up with him, he's pissed and has stopped talking, or he's thinking about what happens when the militia arrives. "Makiivka Brigade."

Which means nothing to her. Militias are ten a penny here. Still, it could be useful to know.

Carson groans to her feet and staggers toward the roll-up door. There hasn't been a peep from outside since Stepaniak shot her (*that asshole*). She circles the table, steps over the Kapitán's legs—it looks like he caught a round in the side of his head, probably from Stepaniak—then peeks through one of a line of bullet holes in the door.

Bodies cluster around the cargo truck. They're also draped over the second Range Rover's hood (Stepaniak's is gone, of course) and scattered around the technical. All in uniform. Stas must've gone with Stepaniak.

Jesus Murphy. They were serious.

When she turns, she almost stumbles over the fifth militia troop. He sits with his back against the door, clutching his side with both hands. Tears streak his cheeks as he watches her. He's so damn young.

"Hold on," she tells him in Russian. Her voice is still husky and rough. "Help will be here soon."

Heitmann's still when she kneels beside him. No pulse. He took three rounds in the center of his chest; if he wasn't dead when he hit the floor, he was soon after.

Carson braces her hands on her thighs and hangs her head. *Fuck.*

She had two jobs here and she failed at both. The icon and half the money are gone. And Heitmann's dead.

She hardly knew the guy. Still, he was her responsibility and she hadn't protected him. The frozen pain on his face makes her want to barf.

You couldn't even protect yourself.

She gently closes his eyes and carefully replaces his glasses. "Sorry. I'll get the other one." Then she pats him down until she finds his wallet. His German driving license goes in his front hip pocket so they'll know who he is and where he belongs. She stares at a snapshot of an average-looking woman in a floral dress staring back. The wife? Carson let her down, too. She pockets his wallet, watch, and wedding ring so the local vultures don't steal them. The least she can do is get them to his museum.

His phone's on the floor by his feet. The top-left corner's

chipped, but the screen still works. She presses his right thumb against the button, turns off the passcode, then enters her left thumb as a second print. At least now she has a phone.

The militia kid's sobbing by the time Carson gets back to him. The right side of his utility blouse is solid rust. She checks her watch: it's been fourteen minutes since she walked through this door. She needs to get out of here. This kid isn't her problem.

But he's *so* young. A boy. Jug ears and a fuzz of dark stubble where hair should be. He reminds her of her kid brothers. He won't last until help comes if she doesn't do something.

Sigh. "Wound kit?" she asks. He nods toward his right thigh pocket.

Carson does what she can with the basic supplies in the little medical pouch, using his belt to strap a gauze dressing against the ragged wound near the bottom of his ribcage. He probably won't bleed out as fast. No matter what she does to him, he doesn't make a sound other than crying. *You're wasting time* fights with *why can't I do more for him?* in her head.

When she's done, she lays the wound kit and his canteen on his lap. The utterly lost look he gives her almost breaks her heart. She strokes the puppy hair on his scalp. "Stay there. Don't move. Help will come."

Now what?

She can't get caught in a roomful of dead people. Nobody'll want to listen to an explanation.

Find Stepaniak. Get the icon. Fuck him up for shooting me.

Carson swipes a not-too-bloody tactical belt off a dead militia troop. It holds four thirty-round magazines that'll fit the Ksyukha—the AKS-74U she'd swiped off Vadim—a Russian-pattern canteen, and a larger version of the kid soldier's wound kit. It's heavy but useful. She closes and locks the Halliburton and tosses the painting into one of the black portfolios.

Call for help? Of course, there's no cell reception in this concrete box.

An engine sounding like an asthmatic lawn mower clatters into earshot outside. Tinny doors slam; men yell; gravel crunches.

The adrenaline hit that Carson had when she left the Range Rover less than half an hour ago returns for an encore. She rushes to peek through the perforated door. An olive-green Jeepish UAZ with two blue bubble lights on the roof crouches near the Toyota technical and its sprinkle of dead men. Two men in peaked caps and sky-blue shirts race from body to body. One's on his phone. (*He gets reception. Figures.*) Ukrainian police, or more likely, rebels in police uniforms. Nobody Carson can afford to meet.

   She has no idea where she is or which way to go.

   But she goes anyway.

CHAPTER 3

Mashkov stops at the line of six dead men laid side-by-side, shrouded with their own ponchos. He whispers, "*Bozhe moy.*"

Vasilenko stalks down the line toward Mashkov. The senior sergeant's face is as dark as the rain clouds smothering the sky.

Mashkov exits his UAZ Hunter—the Russian answer to the Toyota Land Cruiser—and meets Vasilenko near the last dead man in line. No salutes; they're in the field, and it had taken ages to teach the men to not salute and show the enemy snipers who to kill. "How many?"

"Eleven dead."

Worse than I thought. "What happened?"

"Still working it out. Three shooters, as far as we can tell."

"And the money?"

"Gone." Vasilenko shakes his head like it's made of uranium.

Damn it! Mashkov allows himself a long growl of frustration, then stows it. He can't start screaming and kicking the Hunter's tires; he's the commander and he has to set an example. "Stepaniak?"

"Also gone, along with that scarecrow Stas. The one with no neck? Vadim? He's still here."

That's promising. "Has he told you anything yet?"

"He hasn't come to yet. Somebody got to him before us. His right hand's smashed and both knees are chopped meat." Vasilenko shakes his head. "Think it's bad out here? Just wait until you see in there." He jerks a nod toward the smallest of the three structures around them.

This was supposed to be easy, Mashkov grumbles to himself as he follows his brigade's senior NCO toward what looks like a storage or maintenance building. His men snap to as he passes, but his brain's too busy to react. *Swap money for a couple of paintings. Everyone wanted this to happen—the museum, us, the Chechen. What in God's name happened?*

The stink hits him the moment he passes through the right-hand steel door: blood, piss, shit, gunpowder. He's smelled all this before, though not usually so concentrated. Maybe the close quarters are making his stomach heave.

Two of his troops shuffle past with a body slung in a black tarp. Three more of his men sprawl in a lake of blood at his feet. Stepaniak's man is closer to the table. A civilian—a balding man with graying hair—lies on his back nearby. "Who's that?" Mashkov asks, pointing.

"A German. Dieter Heitmann. Probably the museum's man."

"Oh, Colonel." Dunya—the brigade's lead medic—pops up from behind the table. Her utilities are at least a size too big for her. "This man's awake now."

"Thank you, Lieutenant." Mashkov skirts the table, then halts when he sees Fedak crumpled on the floor with a hole above his ear. Mashkov's hand slams the tabletop before he can control it, startling every living person in the room. *My best captain. That bastard Stepaniak's going to pay for this.*

The medic's kneeling beside a bloody, pale soldier. The young woman wears running shoes. Mashkov used to be the "Donbass boot tsar," and now his troops can't get proper footwear.

He crouches next to them. The wounded soldier's face is another punch in the gut. It's a child's face turned old by agony. A schoolboy. *Bozhe moy.* "What happened to him?"

The medic's face is also young and aged by pain—other people's, but a constant burden. She backhands a drift of brown hair from her forehead. "One entry wound here, exit wound here. It hit his lung or liver, I can't tell. But…"

"Yes?"

She bites her lip. "Someone tried to patch him up." She waves toward the soldier's discarded olive web belt and a pile of bloody dressings. "He couldn't have done it, not in his state. It probably saved his life."

Would Stepaniak have done something like that? Mashkov doubts it. He leans close to the boy and strokes his cheek with his fingertips. "Son? What's your name?"

The boy's breath rasps. His big brown eyes try to focus on Mashkov but can't quite pull it off. "Artem. Sir."

"My father's name. Can you tell me what happened?"

Artem's body bucks under a spasm of hacking that bubbles blood from his mouth. The medic quiets him, wiping sweat off his forehead with what looks like a dishrag. She nods to Mashkov.

"Artem?"

The boy wrestles with his breathing for some while. "Man in blue. He shoots everyone. Runs away. He takes the icon. And money."

"All the money?"

"One suitcase."

That son of a whore. "What happened to the other suitcase?"

"The lady took it."

"What lady?"

More coughing. Mashkov feels the pain that twists the boy's face. *What have I done? He shouldn't be here. He should be in school. He should be with his mother.* But the veterans—the men who joined the brigade in 2014—are either dead or retired to their farms or fled to the West. There aren't enough men to replace them.

So he recruits boys. And the boys die.

"Son?"

"She had…the money. Came with…with the man in blue."

A woman with Stepaniak? "Did she shoot people?"

"No. He…shot her."

But clearly didn't kill her. This makes no sense to Mashkov. "Who helped you?"

"The…the lady." Artem's voice is slowly fading.

Dunya takes the boy's pulse, then faces Mashkov. "Sir, you have to stop. He's very weak."

"Can't you help him?"

"No, sir. I have no supplies, no drugs. He needs to go to a hospital." Her face crinkles. "I'm sorry."

Not that the hospitals are much better off. The boy may have important information, but Mashkov won't risk killing him with questions. He gently kisses Artem's forehead and strokes what little hair he has. "Rest, son. We'll take care of you. You've done well." He squeezes Dunya's shoulder. "Thank you, Lieutenant."

He has to leave quickly before he loses control.

Mashkov stops once he's outside again. He stares at nothing as a familiar anger slops up from his gut.

"What do you want to do, sir?" Vasilenko's next to him.

Mashkov pivots and grabs the sergeant's arm. "I want that bandit Stepaniak hanging from an electric pole. I mean that literally. Understand?"

"Yes, sir. The GLONASS bug on his Range Rover is still working. We'll find him."

"See that you do. Take whatever resources you need. We need that money, Lenya. That's fuel for the brigade and the troops' back pay, yours and mine included. Keep me posted."

Vasilenko gives Mashkov his usual saw-toothed smile. "Yes, *sir*. The woman?"

The woman. On the one hand, she took half the money, so she may be in with Stepaniak; on the other hand, the bandit shot her, so perhaps not. And she helped the boy. "Find her. It shouldn't be too difficult. Bring her to me if you can. I want to hear her story."

"If she resists?"

Mashkov marches toward his Hunter. "Do what you need to. That *suka* doesn't get to escape."

CHAPTER 4

Carson watches the Hunter drive off to the north.

The man who'd climbed into it was clearly some kind of senior officer. He walked like he was in charge, straight and confident, and the troops he passed snapped to attention.

Carson's in the northeast corner of a ruined hundred-meter-long chicken coop surrounded by trees and bushes. The briefcase with the money and the portfolio lean against the wall next to her. About seventy-five meters northeast is the road that runs to the maintenance building. She's safe-ish for the moment.

She stares at the portfolio. The painting inside caused this whole mess. The backgrounder said that one night in 2009, a burglar broke a window next to a fire exit at the Kunsthistoriches Museum Bonn, or KMB, and walked away with the two closest artworks. They vanished until last fall, when the KMB director got a photo in the mail showing them next to a TV playing a current program. Lawyers and the insurance company took the next six months to work out the ransom. That's why she's here.

Carson massages the throbbing in the lower left part of her ribcage. Nothing seems to be moving in there—maybe her rib isn't busted—but the only way to tell for sure is to take off her shirt and vest and poke around. The last thing she wants to do when she might have to run or fight *now*.

She pulls a strap—€20,000—from the briefcase and riffles the notes. It may be only paper, but a hundred sheets of A4 just doesn't feel like this. She stashes the bills in her jeans pockets, her bra, and in a Velcro pocket she'd had sewn on the belly band of her U.S. Armor ballistic vest. It's not the most cash she's ever had on her, but it's the most that she doesn't have to answer for. Whatever she doesn't spend will be her tip for putting up with this shit.

Time to find out where she is. Carson turns on location services and brings up Google Maps. Two flaky bars of reception make for a long map download.

She's about a klick southwest of Amvrosiivka. Nineteen klicks from the Russian border. A hundred three klicks from Volnovakha by foot on main roads.

Shit.

She could walk it in Alberta or Ontario. It would suck, but she could. Here? It doesn't take a tactical genius to figure out the nearest highway—the T0509 according to the map—is the quickest supply route from Russia to Donetsk. Tons of Russian trucks and troops. The gamble is, would she be raped and killed before she makes the next town, or only raped?

Carson's not scared yet. She probably should be, but right now she's mad. Scared will come when she can think again.

She came away from the massacre convinced she needed to track down that asshole Stepaniak and take him apart. But he knows the area and he has wheels. He can move farther and faster than she can. How will she find him? Maybe Olivia can track his agency phone...*if* he still has it, *if* it's on, if, if, if.

You got a picture.

Yeah.

You got half the money.

Yeah. So?

Call it good. Get the fuck outta here. Let somebody else kill Stepaniak.

Heitmann died why?

Not your problem. Half the swag and you alive beats the shit outta no swag and you dead.

Carson has these debates with herself now and then. The voice sometimes sounds like her, sometimes like her dad. Not that he made the best choices; she wouldn't be here if it wasn't for his shitty decision-making.

This time the voice sounds more like her, so she listens more (not the best decision-making on her part). She may have a local name and speak the languages, but this place is more like Mars than anything her parents talked about. Moving will get hard once the militia starts looking for the people who popped half a platoon of troops. Vadim and that kid soldier will talk about the broad who ran off with half the money.

Even though it'll slow the phone's map download, Carson punches in the only agency number she knows by heart—the only one she needs to.

A posh English voice answers. "Good afternoon."

"One-Two-six." Carson's employee number.

Olivia makes a *hmm* noise. "You're not using your mobile. What number is this?"

The DeWitt Agency's named for Allyson DeWitt, the owner, but Carson talks to Olivia most. She takes care of the associates in the field, makes sure they're paid, and straightens them out when they need it. Olivia's helped Carson more times than she can count and straightened her out more than once.

"One-Thirteen's gone rogue."

Silence on the other end of the line, then a keyboard clicks. "Oh, dear. Go on."

"Fucker shot me, took half—"

"Do you need medical attention?"

"Had a vest. He took half the money and one of the pictures." Deep breath. "He and his playmates shot fifteen people, including me. *And* the client's rep."

Olivia's hard sigh tells Carson she's pissed. Her end of the line goes dead for a couple seconds, then returns. "I'll notify the client. Are you mobile?"

"Mostly."

"Do you know where One-One-Three might be?"

"No. He's got his phone and mine. Can you track him?"

"I'll see to it. What do you need?"

"Extraction."

The keyboard clicks in bursts for the better part of a minute. "Sadly, this is spring, our busy time. Our clients allow their problems to fester over the winter, then demand we sort them once the snow melts." More clicking. "I have a Russian associate coming available on Friday, but he's in Kazakhstan just now. It may take a spell for him to reach you."

"Nobody in Ukraine?"

"We have three other associates there, but One-One-Three recommended them all. In light of recent events, I'd rather not rely on them for this. Can you hire a car?"

"Out here in East Podunk? Think of the most rural part of England, then empty it out more. Avis ain't here." Carson's getting pissed again. One of the unwritten contracts the agency makes with associates is that it'll never strand them downrange. The agency fills clients' needs, but apparently not hers. "How many Russians are on the payroll?"

"Several. I believe I mentioned this is our busy time. Our closest idle associate is in the south of France. However, he doesn't speak Russian or any other Slavic language."

Carson's neck and cheeks heat up. She snaps, "I'm a hundred klicks from the front. *Alone.* No car. Hauling a million euros in a suitcase. Maybe Step—One-Thirteen's looking for me. Maybe the militia too. What…the *fuck*…do I do?"

Dead silence. Then, "One-Two-Six." Olivia's voice is as hard as Carson's ever heard it. "I share your frustration. If I could do anything at all to help, I would do. I can't simply conjure resources from the air. I suggest you make your way toward the frontier in the safest manner possible and keep me informed of your progress. The very moment I can provide assistance, I shall. Do you understand me?"

Carson mentally slaps herself around. She'd gone off on Olivia, one of the worst ideas ever—Olivia could send her to Siberia, then cancel the return ticket. She tries to shove her anger down her own throat before she says anything else.

As she waits for her steam to vent, two camouflaged trucks with olive-drab canvas cargo covers grind to a stop next to the two big chicken coops. Troops spill out the back. *Oh shit oh shit…*

"Olivia…? Sorry." Her voice has melted. "My ribs hurt like hell. Can't describe it."

"More or less than childbirth?"

"Can't say. Never had kids. Look, this has been a bad day. I know you'll help when you can. Militia's coming after me. More troops just got here. I gotta go." She swallows. "Thanks."

"Of course." Olivia's voice has turned back into a warm blanket, something she does really well. "Please be careful. I wish I could do more. And…you're not alone. I'm here. If you need to talk, please ring."

"Sure." Carson hangs up before she can say anything else stupid. After letting her mind clear, she checks the GPS. She's in for a long, long walk.

CHAPTER 5

Rogozhkin stares across the old gray-steel desk at Mashkov, the commander of this sorry excuse for a fighting force. "How in *hell* do you lose a dozen men when you're not even fighting?"

Mashkov stares back. Bad move: Rogozhkin's locked eyes with Abkhazian rebels, Chechen warlords, Kosovar guerillas, Moldovan *mafiya*, and Night Wolves biker thugs. A Ukrainian factory manager in a uniform isn't even a challenge.

At least Mashkov looks the part: tall (at least, taller than Rogozhkin, no great feat), square shoulders, a strong face, regulation hair. He wears the uniform well. So many of these militia types look like gangsters playing dress-up. Then again, many of them are.

After a few moments, Mashkov folds his arms and breaks off to look toward but not exactly at the shabby office's only window. The blinds are down; he's not admiring the view. "They were ambushed."

"Ambushed?" Rogozhkin barely keeps a laugh stuffed in his gut. "By who? Partisans? The fascists are eighty kilometers from here."

Mashkov examines the desk blotter, half a meter square with a yellowed calendar page from September 2014. "Bandits."

"*Bandits?*" This time, he laughs. Mashkov's face tells him the man doesn't even believe his own lie. "Bandits killed a dozen armed soldiers and didn't lose anyone? Good God, we need a brigade of your bandits instead of..." He doesn't finish the thought. He doesn't need to. "What were your people doing out there, anyway?"

"Training exercise." Mashkov covers another obvious lie by turning to pour hot water from his cherished electric kettle—a gift from his wife, he never tires of mentioning—into a glass holding a thumb's-width slick of *zavarka*. Rogozhkin hopes Mashkov won't offer him any; the man's tea tastes like paint solvent.

Rogozhkin shifts stiffly while he waits for the Ukrainian to stop fiddling with his teapot. A demon from Hell—an unwanted souvenir from the Balkans—stabs his left leg. "What aren't you telling me, Dima? I can't advise you if you hide things from me."

Mashkov worries at his tumbler of tea. He shrugs. "You usually just advise me not to fight."

Rogozhkin barely avoids rolling his eyes. *Not this again.* "Look what happens when you do. You'll get your chance, don't worry. What concerns me now is that you launched an operation without telling me and ended up with half a platoon in body bags—in a pacified area. Was it a training problem? A recon or intel failure? We need to know so we can fix it. What happened?"

Mashkov snorts. "'Pacified.' What an interesting word." He turns to glare at Rogozhkin. "We're not invaders." He points to himself. "*We're* not invaders. *We* live here. It's 'friendly.'"

The man's been like this lately. Subtle and not-so-subtle digs about who belongs in this dump and who's a "guest." In a way, Rogozhkin can't blame him; Mashkov was born here and was in this so-called "revolution" from the beginning. Still, if Rogozhkin and the other "guests" hadn't stepped in two years ago, the Donbass would be just a failed part of Ukraine and Mashkov's bones would be swinging from a streetlight. "Not friendly enough, apparently."

"Well, maybe if you came up with the supplies you promised us—"

"You know that's not as easy as it sounds. The OSCE observers—"

"Don't slow down *your* resupply any, just what you give us. We're living off the land. You know what that makes us? Locusts. No wonder there's grumbling—"

"Dima—"

Mashkov slashes the air with his free hand. "Or maybe we can just go fight and get out of these poor people's way. Join that operation next Monday by Dokuchajevsk, for instance. Be heroes of the Donbass again instead of...*nasekomyye.*" The Russian word for *insects.*

I wanted this job. I volunteered to advise this brigade. These are the good ones. God help us. "I've told you—we can't simply drive a convoy of lorries through your front gate and dump supplies here. We can't be seen as the only reason you're still in the field, even if we are. If *your* people provided for—"

"How? Where do they get modern weapons? Where do they get armor? The economy's flat on its back. They can't provide for themselves. *Moscovia* promised us so much—"

"Stop." Rogozhkin swallowed the first two things he wanted to say. *Moscovia*, indeed. He'd heard the men here grouse about the *Kacápskyi*—something like the English word *Russkies*, but used like the Russian *svolotsch*, for asshole or scumbag—and felt their eyes carve him up while he passed. "Other militias would be happy to get what we give you. Look, we've gotten away from the real issue. I need to know what happened today. You know I have to report it to Command." Not that General Tulantyev cares about what happens to these people, so long as he gets another star on his shoulder boards.

Mashkov shakes his head, gulps down the rest of his tea, then thrusts a manila folder at Rogozhkin. "Here."

Rogozhkin scans the operations report. Then he laughs. "Seriously. You want me to tell them this?"

Mashkov plops into his desk chair and leans back with a squeak. "I don't give a damn what you tell them. Your 'people' aren't useful to this brigade. When they start keeping their promises, maybe I'll be grateful." He waves toward the old wood-and-glass door. "You're dismissed."

Dismissed? Rogozhkin should let it go, but this jumped-up clerk needs his attitude adjusted or there'll be more disasters like today's at Amvrosiivka. He shoves the folder under his right arm—there won't be any saluting here—and gives the man another dose of his warlord stare. "Dima Artemovich. We've discussed this. I know the tab on your blouse says you're a colonel, and the one on mine says I'm a lieutenant colonel. But…what did I tell you about rank in a militia?"

"Something about whores." Mashkov's face is turning a delicate shade of purple.

"Close enough. You people have an old saying. 'A crow will never be a falcon.' Sometimes the *babushki* are wise." He turns a crisp about-face and marches to the door.

"My *babka* had another saying," Mashkov growls. "'The devil always takes back his gifts.'"

Rogozhkin stalks away from the squat concrete-block building into the heart of the abandoned grain mill on the edge of Kuteinykove. Gravel, cement, and tin roofs as far as he can see, with the derelict grain silo thrusting up like a huge monolith in the center. He makes as quick a circuit as his leg allows and finds Yartsev, his *starshina* or senior sergeant, drilling a gaggle of junior militia sergeants in clearing a building. This may be a miserable base, but it makes a fine urban-warfare training ground.

He stands off to the side, watching, until one of Yartsev's pupils notices him and calls the squad to attention. Yartsev spins and snaps a salute. Rogozhkin returns it, then pulls the sergeant out of the troops' earshot. "Any hope?"

Yartsev's lean and wiry, with a pinched face and a perpetual squint. He's stripped off his utility blouse to expose his *telmyashka*, the blue-and-white striped undershirt that, along with his sky-blue beret, marks him as a *spetsnazovets*—a member of Russia's elite fighting force, like Rogozhkin. The locals still fear Moscow's trained killers more than the regular ground troops. As well they should.

He glances over his shoulder at his class, then shrugs. "Not as bad as some, sir. I'll take them over the Ossetians."

For the first time in an hour, Rogozhkin smiles. "That's a low bar." He hands over the folder. "Look into this. They're hiding something. I want to know what."

"Yes, sir."

"Stay around the Ops Center for the next few days. Let me know if they do anything...off. Call it training the support staff if you need to. I'll talk to the battalion commanders." He shoots a glance toward Mashkov's office. "They may be trying to grow a brain. If they are, we need to stop it."

CHAPTER 6

Carson leaves the chicken farm just as the militia forms up to do a sweep. She hides in one stand of trees or another for the next three hours, racking up close calls and near-disasters seemingly every five minutes until her pursuers finally pass by. She tells herself that she's not being a coward; singlehandedly fighting two dozen soldiers with automatic weapons is just a damn stupid thing to do. It doesn't always sink in.

It's still daylight by the time the troops disappear into the dusty string of farmhouses passing for a village to her west. She should get going, but she'll stick out like a horse in a herd of sheep while she tromps around the countryside. She grudgingly takes cover in a small wooded area until dusk.

She's been going on adrenaline and momentum until now. With no visible threats, sitting in her little blind robs her of both. The constant tension left her drained. She didn't sleep much last night—jet lag, irritation at being thrown at Stepaniak again, and the usual pre-project can't-turn-off-her-brain thing. Holding her eyelids open is harder than bench-pressing her own weight. She catches herself drifting off. It's the last thing she can afford with random military vehicles roaring back and forth on the gravel road a few meters in front of her.

There's nothing but plowed fields north and south of her. A few sprout green fuzz that'll turn into crops by fall. The dirt beneath her is almost black. *Chornózem*, the famous Ukrainian soil that can grow nearly anything. The same kind that belts Alberta, the reason so many Ukrainians migrated there over the past century. Like her parents.

Not that they were farmers. City people from Kharkiv, around three hundred klicks northwest of here. Her older brother Bo told her that when they washed up in a little nothing of a place called Clive in central Alberta, the neighbors suggested they raise chickens behind their trailer. Her mom was pissed that she had to ask them how. If she'd wanted to be a farmer's wife, she'd have married a farmer, not a cop.

The first home Carson remembers is Elk Point, up by Alberta's Cold Lake tar sands. This place reminds her of there: flat, green, lines of trees for windbreaks, an endless sky.

Get out of your fucking head. Pay attention.

Hours grind by. She'd forgotten how far north Ukraine is; Kyiv and Calgary are at roughly the same latitude (she looked it up). In May, it's light until well past eight at night. Traffic on the road—most of it still military—keeps her head down until the clouds finally fade to black.

Two a.m.

At last, it's only drizzling. It started raining at roughly the same time Carson started walking and stayed steady most of the time since. The farmers probably like the free irrigation. She's soaked to the skin. Only walking keeps her warm.

There hasn't been a moon all night; the cloud deck's blotted out the sky. Everything's a shade of dark gray until car headlights go by. It's actively dangerous to walk on the broken pavement—she's gone down a couple times after stepping in potholes or tripping on frost heaves. The muddy fields are like swamps.

She'd headed south from the chicken farm down a two-lane country road that passes several villages. She'd bet her life on the idea that farm folk everywhere turn in early. She's winning the bet.

Cars are another thing. This semi-paved country road turns out to be officially a highway. A lot of people must want to stay away from the truck convoys and patrols on the big highway, even at night. She's been scrambling from the blacktop into the mudholes on either side to stay out of their headlights.

Progress has come hard.

She hadn't expected battle damage out here in the sticks, but it's there. Even Leninske (maybe two hundred people on a good day) has shot-up or shelled-out houses and a scorched hulk of a six-wheeled truck instead of a "Welcome to..." sign.

Wet. Bone tired. She's been up for nearly twenty-three hours straight. Her eyes burn like somebody's poured coal dust into them.

She stumbles on the road even when there's nothing there to trip her up. At least the car traffic finally trailed off around one.

She staggers past a blue-and-white Cyrillic sign reading "Olhynske." Stops to find it on the GPS. Squeezes her eyes shut to try to focus.

She's come to several hard realizations over the past few hours. It will never stop raining. Moss will start growing on her soon.

Her Ariat steel-toe paddock boots are soaking wet and caked with about five kilos of mud each. She grew up in paddock boots—they were the only thing she couldn't destroy in days, and they helped her blend in with the farm and ranch girls at school—but she'd expected to have to kick men in the nuts, not hike long distances in a monsoon. Her socks are like sponges, and her feet are wet and cold and hurt almost as much as her ribs.

The painting and the briefcase full of money both weigh about the same now: a hundred kilos each. She has to set them down every few hundred meters to work the kinks out of her shoulders and hands. She would literally kill someone for a backpack.

She hasn't eaten since noon, when Stepaniak stopped the Range Rover and stuffed a sandwich and a bottle of water into her hands. She's been burning calories like crazy ever since. There's nothing left in her stomach and it's pissed off. That adds to her pounding headache.

The real potential show-stopper: Heitmann's phone had eighty-one percent charge when she picked it up. It's now at fourteen percent, nagging at her about "low battery charge," like she hasn't noticed. The phone's her map, her light, her connection to the world…and it'll die in way less than an hour.

She stutters to a stop at the T-intersection that defines Olhynske. Through the gloom, she can just make out the dark bulk of a stand of mature trees and underbrush at her two o'clock. It looks dense enough to shield her from the two nearest farmhouses.

Good enough.

Carson squelches into the trees, finds a semi-sheltered place, sets down the briefcase and the portfolio, then slowly eases herself onto the ground. Sitting feels better than any sex she's had lately. She listens to water dripping on the leaves over her head.

She closes her eyes to wash out the grit. Just for a minute.

CHAPTER 7

Carson wakes up wet.

Wet's not a surprise. The surprise is, she was asleep.

She pries open her eyes. There's pearly gray light between the tree trunks—not a lot, but enough to see what's around her. The trees aren't as dense as they'd looked last night in the dark. No visible threats. She finds a clean part of a sleeve to wipe the crap out of her eyes, then sucks some moisture from the cloth. Her head hurts as much as her ribs and feet. Her mouth tastes like a baby dragon shit in it.

She'd fallen asleep hunched over, propped against a tree trunk. Someone replaced the whole left side of her body with petrified wood while she was out. She crawls up the trunk until she can more-or-less stand, swearing most of the way.

Carson starts her morning stretching routine with the hope that it'll break loose her left side. She grits her teeth with every twist and bend. As she lets the muscle memory take her through the movements, she sizes up her situation.

She'd covered eight whole klicks overnight. Half what she'd expected, and it knocked the shit out of her. Of course, what she'd expected was based on a full night's sleep, enough food and water, a daypack, and a clear trail. At this rate, she'll make it to the contact line in two weeks...*if* she survives that long. It'd be quicker to walk to Russia.

What's your next bright idea?

Ten minutes of stretching starts busting up the stiffness. She stops for a moment to rotate her left shoulder, then twists left and right at her waist.

Craaack.

At first she thinks it's her back. *Too far away.* It could be nothing: a dog or a pig, or just a branch snapping in the light breeze. She returns to her exercises, faster now, bigger movements as her muscles warm up.

Snap.

She stops instantly, cocks her head, and listens hard, breathing slowly through her mouth so she doesn't have to filter out the sounds of her sinuses. She doesn't know what she's listening for, but her gut's telling her *pay attention, dammit.*

The wind tickles leaves far above her head. Two branches squeak against each other. A bird twitters to her four o'clock. Pigs grunt and bicker way off her one o'clock.

Tink.

Not a natural sound. Metal on metal, a few meters to her ten o'clock. *Militia? Someone freelancing for a reward?*

Carson glides carefully toward her tree, sliding her feet so her toes push away the deadfall instead of stepping on it. The way her dad taught her after she'd asked, "How do you sneak up on bad guys, Daddy?" Eight-year-old her: junior crimebuster.

She hefts her Ksyukha like it's made of blown glass and eases down the safety to its second detent. Semiautomatic mode. Wraps the sling once around her left bicep. Takes a kneeling firing position behind the tree.

The *tink* happens a couple more times, each a bit closer. Her right ear's straining to pick up something other than the bird. If she hears it, she's in the shit.

A car drives by a couple dozen meters away on her left. Not a threat, but it wrecks her sound picture.

"Dear Carson! I want to talk with you. I know you are there." Ukrainian; Stepaniak's voice.

Of course. Had to be that asshole. But she's confused; his voice is coming from her three o'clock, but the metal-on-metal noises are off her eleven. *Answer him?* If he has any doubts where she is, that'll give him her position. She needs to know what's happening up ahead. "Is Stas in here with me?"

"Of course. He will not harm you if you stay in place. Before we talk, you should know that we know exactly where you are. Stas! Show our dear Carson that you've found her."

A bullet *thwaps* into her tree. No weapon sound; it must be suppressed. She fires a couple rounds toward the muzzle flash.

Stepaniak yells, "Carson! Dear Carson, stop! *Please* don't make this unpleasant."

"It's already unpleasant. Give me a good reason not to shoot your ass."

He sighs loudly. "Why are you so angry with me?"

Really? "You fucking *shot* me, asshole!"

"I...yes, I did. I am very sorry I had to do it. Where did I shoot you?"

"Under my left tit. Hurts like hell."

"But your vest stopped the bullet, yes? There is no extra hole in you?"

She won't give him the satisfaction of agreeing with him.

"I knew you were wearing body armor. I made sure when you got out of my car."

"When you groped me?"

"I did not. I gave you a friendly pat." He waits, maybe for her to concede. "How can you blame me, dear Carson? You have an irresistible *dupu*. So solid, so—"

"Think that's a compliment? Think that's helping? Wrong, both counts." Carson wants to empty a magazine in his direction. She probably wouldn't hit him, but it would feel *so* good. "You killed Heitmann."

"The German? I did not do that. That was Vadim, I think. Do you know what happened to Vadim? Was he shot?"

"Yeah." *By me.* "You tell him to kill the wounded?"

"It seemed to be so important to him. I could not say no."

This isn't helping Carson's headache any. "You tell him to shoot me?"

"What? Of course not. If I want you dead, I will kill you myself. I owe you that. I wanted you out of the way so no one else will hurt you. I do this because I like you, dear Carson, and I do not want any harm to come to you, yes? You see?"

Carson likes to think she has a good bullshit detector. Unfortunately, it overloads around Stepaniak. "Whatever. You fucked up the deal. Why?"

"Yes, yes, we must talk about business." Another sigh. "Do you ever plan for the future? This work we have, it is for young people. Do you want to be doing this five years, ten years from now? No, of course not. I too have to look ahead. Do you remember the club in Kyiv? *Chervonyy?* Where we celebrated the end of your very first project?"

She remembers: a Eurotrash hypermart. "Where you got me drunk?"

Stepaniak laughs. "There is not enough liquor in the world to make you drunk, dear Carson!" His voice drops into vodka-and-velvet range. "You know we both wanted it. You only needed to relax just a little to let it happen."

The hell of it is, he's mostly right. "Always had shitty taste in men. What about the club?"

"I have an opportunity to become a co-owner. You remember what I told you, yes? I have always loved running restaurants, cafés, clubs. I love to make people happy. And now I can own part of the hottest club in Kyiv! This is...what do you say?" He switches to strongly-accented English. "Big time. Is big time for me. Like you, when you go to big city in Canada to be police. You can be police in small town on steppe, and—"

"We call it the prairie."

"Yes, yes. You do that, maybe you are still police. But you go to big city. Be big police. Is big time for you. Same for me. We are same."

"No, we're not." Again, he's partly right. She could've been a community peace officer in Cold Lake. They wanted to hire her. But no, that wasn't good enough. She wanted to be a *real* cop. "Let me guess—you want the money I've got."

"*Zvychayno.*" He's back to Ukrainian. "I need one million and a half euro for the club. The rest I need for a home, clothes—"

"Booze. Hookers."

"No, no. Well, maybe a little. But yes, I do need that money." Pause. "Dear Carson. Leeeesa. Do—"

"Not my name."

"Yes, I know it is not your name." For the first time, he sounds tetchy. "Carson is not your name. You never tell me your name. What else can I call you but 'Carson'? Unless you prefer..." he purrs "...*lyubyy.*"

Darling? Hell, no. "Stick with Carson."

She squats and massages her temples. She doesn't care who gets the money. She wasn't supposed to go home with it anyway (though she wouldn't mind). She hates to hand Stepaniak a win. If things had gone the way she'd planned last night, she'd blow him off. But they didn't, and right now she's more interested in scraping up a win for herself than she is in making him lose. "Hey, Stepaniak."

"Yes, dear Carson?"

"Still got that icon?"

"Of course."

"How's this? Give me the icon, I give you the cash, we're done. Call it 'me buying the icon.' Deal?"

The ground vibrates under her. She really needs to eat something. *Please say yes.* Please *say yes. I want this shit over with.*

Stepaniak clears his throat. "You are serious about this?"

"No. I just say random shit, like you. Of *course* I'm fucking serious. I want to go home." *And not be a complete failure.* "Yes or no?"

The vibration isn't her imagination. There's a mutter some distance away to the north. It doesn't sound like artillery. Carson stands, cocks her head. *A train? Tanks?*

A voice behind her yells "Abram!" then rapid-fire something she doesn't understand. Must be Stas. Stepaniak shouts back. Whatever's happening, neither of them is happy about it.

Stepaniak shouts, "Dear Carson! Your offer interests me. We will talk later. Be safe!"

"*Later?* What do you mean, *later?*"

No answer.

Car doors slam, an engine starts, then a boxy black shape blurs past the tree trunks west of her.

To the east she hears the rumble of heavy vehicles. She trots to the copse's edge and peeks around a tree trunk.

A BTR—a giant olive-drab armored cockroach on eight wheels—rattles and squeaks toward her on the highway. Two cargo trucks follow. The BTR's close enough that its tan-and-black camouflage reveals the rough brushstrokes of a broom. It roars past. There's a crest on the side: a blue-and-black shield with a yellow rising sun.

The Makiivka Brigade has arrived.

CHAPTER 8

Stepaniak holds on for dear life as the Range Rover charges west on the dilapidated road leading away from the highway and the militia.

Was that a coincidence? He doesn't usually believe in that. Not believing in it makes him weigh the other possibilities. He doesn't want to believe in those, either.

"Were you seriously going to take the bitch's deal?" Stas growls in Georgian.

"The turn is up here. Slow down." Stepaniak uses Ukrainian. Georgian gives him a headache.

"Fuck slowing down." Stas drifts them onto a northbound gravel road—Stepaniak grips the grab handle and armrest so hard, it hurts—then stomps the gas. The gravel scouring the underside and rocker panels sounds like hail.

"Thank you, Stas, for drawing attention to us. I *love* attention. When the militia gets here, they will hear all about the crazy men in the fancy black car playing *Fast and Furious* through their part of town."

Stas concentrates on the place where the gravel turns into dirt, about five seconds away. Just as well.

"Yes, I'm seriously considering Carson's offer."

The gravelstorm stops; mud speckles the windows. At least it's not removing the paint.

Stas snaps, "That wasn't the plan."

"I *know* it isn't the plan. I *made* the plan. The plan didn't work as well as I wanted. Now I am making a *new* plan."

Stas glances at Stepaniak. He snarls—not for the first time, Stepaniak's reminded of the unwrapped mummies in the British Museum—then focuses on the road again. "Sell the paintings, you said." Even when he's not growling, he growls. Too many cigarettes. "Get another half-million for them, you said. That means another quarter-million for me. Like hell we give that up.

Kill the bitch and take it all."

Stepaniak doesn't like Stas assuming he'll get half now that Vadim's out of the picture. Those two were supposed to *split* half. Also, Stepaniak never likes it when Stas comes up with his own ideas. They're usually impractical or involve lots of dead bodies; either way, bad for business. "Were you paying attention back there? Did you see what happened? The militia found us *again*. How did that happen? We were clear of them last night."

"Lucky. Coincidence."

Hard to imagine how the man's still alive, believing that nonsense. "They almost found us at the meeting point yesterday. Tell me, Stas, how lucky are those people? How many *coincidences?* No. Once we get the money, we can go to the West and be rid of those militia idiots forever. Carson's offer is a good starting point. If we kill her, the DeWitt woman may send someone looking for us. Or Carson's *mafiya pakhan"—godfather—*"will object. She owes him moncy."

"But...we give up the icon? I thought you had a buyer already."

He does. Flexibility is key. "Patience, dear Stas. I said 'starting point.' I need to think how we can turn it our way. Turn right up here."

"Right?"

"We will go south, then west. We need to leave the militia's neighborhood."

Stas's mouth hangs open. "We'll go right past them."

"By the time they get all their chickens in the coop, we'll be far away." He hopes.

Stas drifts the corner and tears east along the edge of a reservoir. He grumbles something Stepaniak ignores. "Did you fuck her?"

Stepaniak chuckles. Nothing gets by Stas...eventually. "Of course I did. We had a lovely weekend together in Kyiv four years ago." Now that Stas isn't trying to kill them both, Stepaniak can lean back into his very comfortable black-leather seat. "Have you ever stayed in the Eleven Mirrors Design Hotel? The best hotel in Kyiv. TripAdvisor says so. It was...*superb*. You must try it sometime."

Stas rolls his eyes. "You fucked...*her.*"

"Is that a problem?"

"Did you look above her tits?"

"Don't be typical, dear Stas. Yes, she has an *honest* face. Yes, she may be *plain*. But..." He leans toward Stas. "When the clothes come off? She is *amazing*. And she's a lion in bed. A *lion*. Have you ever had sex with a lion?"

"I don't do animals."

Metaphor is lost on the man. Stepaniak pulls his phone from his car coat's inside pocket and brings up the tracker app. Carson and the painting are still where he left them. He hopes she'll be careful. He doesn't want the militia to find her...yet.

CHAPTER 9

Carson, flat on her stomach, watches as two militiamen walk along the ruts the Range Rover's tires left in the wet grass ten meters away.

She's screened by the underbrush in the stand of trees she's colonized since two that morning. The militia senior sergeant and corporal are in the field west of it. If they know she's watching them, they're hiding it well.

While her eyes follow the militiamen around, her brain puzzles over two very important things she learned a few minutes ago.

One: Stepaniak can find her wherever she goes.

Two: the militia can find Stepaniak.

She doesn't feel good about either of them. The only way Stepaniak can track her is by using some kind of GPS bug on something she's carrying. *Did he have enough time to stash something in the briefcase? Did he plant something on me when he groped me? Is it on the picture?* She'll have to check that out when she's not knee-deep in militia.

One important thing she didn't learn: can only Stepaniak find her, or can the militia, too?

The longer those two out there stomp through the calf-high weeds, the more likely the answer is *no*. If they could, they'd have come for her by now. Not that that's super comforting. Any of those bored soldiers milling around on the road just east of her could wander in here to take a leak and stumble across her.

Those two very important things she learned? They killed off the idea of walking out. She'd be an easy, slow-moving target for Stepaniak.

Can she really make a deal with him? He didn't blow her off. When they first met in Kyiv, he talked about owning a string of restaurants and clubs until the dumb bastard crossed a local mobster and ended up in prison. He seemed to miss that life. His story about why he shot her at the exchange made some twisted sense. Stepaniak and his lapdog were obviously trying to pin her down here, not kill her. They had plenty of opportunities for a head shot and didn't take any.

Do I trust him enough to do a deal?

She never actually trusted him very far—he's too much of a player for that—but their interests sort-of align right now. He wants cash, not art. She has cash and wants that icon. Can they both win? There's only one way to find out.

If he's scamming her, she can kill him later.

Olhynske is split into two parts. Half is strung out along the so-called highway for over a klick south. The road just north of Carson's trees stretches west toward a low rise. Roughly half a klick west of the highway, the rest of the town starts to line both sides of that road.

She's done hiking the highway. When the militia roars south, she heads west.

There's not a tree or building to hide behind for that first half-klick. Carson walks it like she belongs there. It's a bit of bravado she learned a long time ago as a junior patrol cop walking through neighborhoods where cops were game animals and were always in season.

Knots of trees mark the edge of the western part of town. Carson ducks into the densest grove to watch and prepare for what's next. The Halliburton and the portfolio are dangerous to her now: they occupy her hands when she needs them free, and they make her look like she has something worth taking. She buries them in the underbrush and leaf litter. After a lot of internal debate, she also hides the Ksyukha. She still has Vadim's pistol and her baton tucked away. Being obviously heavily armed won't help her make friends.

She'd counted eleven checkpoints on the way into Amvrosiivka with Stepaniak. Even the Kapitán seemed to have trouble getting them through some of them. She can steal a car and the GPS can show her which roads to take, but it can't tell her where the checkpoints and roadblocks and blown bridges are, or who to bribe and how much. By herself, she probably won't make it past the first couple of checkpoints.

So she needs a local guide...preferably one who won't sell her out first thing.

A scruffy older man leads an equally scruffy medium-sized dog through the middle of this part of town, away from her. Carson waits for them to get a long way away. She takes a deep breath. *Can't be worse than Moldova.* She steps into the middle of the road, straightening her shirt. Then she strolls into town to find a car and a driver.

A string of concrete utility poles carrying a single electrical cable traces the road's south side, where most of the development is. A stork's nest perches on a pole up ahead. Most properties are compounds, not single houses: a house or two, a barn or storage building, sheds, tumbledown fences. A couple look empty, with busted windows and tall weeds. One of the first she passes—faded pink stucco behind an arbor—looks like a giant hand punched through the roof, grabbed everything inside, and scattered it over the yard.

And there are flags and bumper stickers. *Lots* of them. Black, blue, and red horizontal stripes: the DNR. White, blue, and red: Russia. An American Confederate flag without the stars: the battle flag of Novorossiya. Militia flags and stickers of all kinds.

Carson's agency backgrounder said only about forty-five percent of the people in the Donbass—mostly the Russian-speakers—support the rebels. All she has to do is find someone from the other fifty-five percent. *No problem.*

People stare at her from their front yards. Old women peek from behind lace curtains or printed-pattern drapes that look like bedsheets. An old guy stalks to the road's edge holding a double-barrel shotgun. An old woman's voice rasps "Go home!" in Russian.

The last time Carson got this much hostility from a whole neighborhood, she was in Toronto's Moss Park area and the locals were reacting to her uniform. *I get it, I'm a stranger. But what's with these people?* Whatever it is, she wishes they'd stop. Staying on constant alert is exhausting. Sooner or later, she'll read a reaction wrong and do something that'll *really* piss them off.

A skinny, muddy stray dog trots out from a driveway, sniffs, then follows Carson, barking. Not "Are you my friend?" barking; the "I'm gonna rip your legs off" kind. *Even the dogs hate me.* Its attitude's way bigger than its body, so Carson tries to ignore it.

Her reception doesn't improve as she moves on. People must be leaving the fields to come give her the stink-eye. She hears muttered curses, hissing, the ever-popular *suka*. *Go back to the West. Leave us alone.* She'd be more afraid if there were able-bodied, fighting-age men here, but there aren't. The only guy in his twenties is missing half an arm; he spits on the ground when she passes. The few youngish women look as old and shopworn as the middle-aged women who are probably their moms.

The western part of Olhynske stretches over a kilometer until the road dead-ends into a plowed field. Carson turns to take stock. Despite the heckling, nobody except the dog approached her, though she'll be gossip fodder for the next month. She doesn't care. She'd counted four cars or trucks at houses without rebel or Russian flags. With any luck, one of those will get her out of here.

Three of the four candidates are south of the road. Carson skirts the nearest farmhouse and counts off as she heads east through what passes for back yards.

The "back yards" are mazes of bleached-out wooden sheds, chicken coops, vegetable gardens, wire fences, beehives, rabbit hutches, chopping blocks, sawhorses, and busted junk. And mud. And the occasional wanna-be watchdog with too much time on its paws.

The fifth house from the west end is the first with a possibly useful car. Carson winds through a collection of rusty green and red oil drums. She finds a *babusya* sweeping her back step with the kind of straw broom Carson's seen in pictures from a century ago. The granny's less than five feet tall and shaped like a concrete block, a symphony in clashing floral prints.

Carson's sure she looks like she swam across the Black Sea to get here. She finger-combs her shortish brown hair as best she can, makes sure her shirttail covers the butt of her pistol, then clears her throat. "*Dobri ranok, babka.*" Ukrainian for *good morning, grandmother.*

The old woman's head jerks up. She smells prey. Her eyes are like cinders from a wildfire—small but hot and bright. Her face prunes when she sees Carson. She changes up her grip on her broom so she can swing it like a baseball bat. "Get away from me! Get off my land! You young people always bring me trouble..."

Carson retreats. She knows when she's overmatched. Not that it's a high-speed chase; she can walk briskly and still outpace the deadly broom as the granny hobbles after her, screeching curses. The ninja granny's parting shot: "You young girls are nothing but trouble!"

It's been years since anybody called Carson a "young girl."

The second candidate car sits five properties down the road. A peek through a rear window reveals dust and mold invading a tiny, abandoned bedroom. The puke-green Lada she'd seen from the street is on blocks and has no engine.

She slogs through the mud past angry geese, snorting pigs, and nosy dogs. *What if I can't use any of the four cars? Try the other part of Olhynske? Go back to Amvrosiivka? Jack a car and try my luck on the road solo?* None of those options sound great.

The last possibly useful car on the south side of the road is nine farms down. The house is small compared to its neighbors—squarish, whitewashed brick, peeling green window trim, and a corrugated iron roof crusted with moss. The weathered clapboard storage building behind it looks like it'll fall over the next time a big truck drives by. Its door is open; Carson can't tell if there's somebody inside or if the hinges are busted. There's not as much crap in the back yard as there was at some other houses, but there's still a lot. She skirts a disintegrating chickenless chicken coop, squeegees her hair flat, then knocks on the back door.

No answer. She tries again. Nothing.

Someone pumps a shotgun behind her.

CHAPTER 10

A woman stands in the storage building's doorway seven or eight meters away from Carson. Wear on her square face. *My age? Hard to tell.* Shorter than Carson. Sturdy but not overweight. Her darkish hair's under a kerchief that's faded to a non-color. Her work shirt probably started life as red or brown, but it's turned a warm gray from too much sun and harsh washing.

The shotgun's steady. The woman holds it like she knows how. The eyes boring into Carson from behind the sights are almost as dark and motionless as the shotgun's muzzle.

She's serious. Watch yourself.

Carson rests her palms on the fronts of her thighs so the woman can see that her hands aren't up to anything. She says "Good morning" in Ukrainian.

"What do you want?" Also Ukrainian; possibly a good sign. Hostile, though.

A glance shows Carson there's nobody else in the field. Nobody answered her knock on the door. If there's a man, he'd have shown up by now. She'd planned to appeal to a guy's greed and vanity. She hadn't expected to find a woman on her own.

How do I play this? She lives in a war zone. Who knows the kind of shit she's put up with. She won't trust some random stranger just because we both have vaginas. What does she need to hear?

Something she's probably said to somebody else. "I need your help."

The woman shuffles a couple meters across the gravel paving her yard. She moves well with a weapon; the shotgun never wavers from Carson's head. "Who are you? *What* are you?"

"My name is…Tarasenko." Carson's real last name. She hopes that being a fellow Ukrainian will score some points. It doesn't extend to first names, though; a few minutes with Google would turn up all kinds of shit that won't help the trust issue any. "I'm from the West. I'm fighting a terrorist militia in this area." The Ukrainian government calls the war here an "anti-terrorist operation"; she hopes the woman will make that connection.

Trust her? Trust isn't a huge part of Carson's mental toolkit. She hasn't found a lot of people she can trust even if she's inclined to. Call this wrong and this woman could just bury Carson in the field and get on with her life.

No flags, no bumper stickers, no decals. If she believes in anything, she's hiding it. That means only one thing around here. Carson takes a deep breath. *Time to commit.* "This militia stole two expensive paintings from the West. I have to rescue them before the militia sells them. I got one. Bandits stole the other, an icon, and killed my associate. I need to get it back, then take it and the painting to the West."

Yeah, it sounds like a bad spy novel. It's the best she can do. If she had a usable phone, she could call Matt, her partner in a couple big projects last year. He's good at making up stories.

The woman hasn't shot her yet. "Where is it? The painting you have?"

"Edge of town." She'd point, but hand gestures and sudden movements aren't a good idea.

"Are you alone?"

Carson hesitates. *Yes* is the truth, but it gives this woman a clear road to make her disappear. But if she's not alone, what does she need here? "*Tak.*" Yes

The woman pulls her face away from the shotgun's stock so she can look at Carson through both eyes. The shotgun's still aimed, just lower. She stares at Carson for a short eternity. "What do you want?"

"You have a car?"

"Yes."

"Drive me to where the bandits are, then to the line of contact. I'll pay you."

The woman's eyebrows arch. "It isn't that simple."

"I know. It's simpler than walking."

"There are many checkpoints. I will have to pay bribes."

"I'll pay them."

"Petrol is expensive and hard to get."

"I'll pay for it."

The shotgun's muzzle sinks a bit. It's now pointing at Carson's gut. "Which militia?"

"The Makiivka Brigade."

The woman's face clouds over. "You are sure of this?"

"Blue-and-black shield with a yellow sun?"

The woman's lips—none too lush to begin with—turn into lines. "When you took that painting, did you kill any of them?"

Carson hopes the woman's reaction means she's sick of the militias, not that she thinks Carson is a bandit. "Would that be a problem?"

"For them, not for me."

Good answer. "Between me and my associate, about a dozen."

Another long stare. Then the woman nestles the shotgun's barrel in the crook of her left arm. The ghost of a smile revives her lips. "Not nearly enough."

Exactly the reaction Carson hoped for. "What do I call you?"

"Demchuk, Galina Lukayivna. How much will you pay?"

Good question. The backgrounder said that the average monthly wage in the rebel areas is a bit over 5,700 hryvnia (around €200), the Ukrainian currency nobody in the East wants. Pensioners get less than €80 a month. What the agency pays Carson in a day would be an unimaginable fortune here. "Two thousand euros for you and your car, plus all your expenses."

Instead of shock, gratitude, or amazement, Galina gives her disappointment. "That's not enough. I need eleven thousand."

What? That's crazy talk. "I'm paying in euros, not hryvnia."

"I know. I need eleven thousand. No less."

Carson recognizes the set to Galina's face; it's the same expression Carson uses when she digs in her heels. Looking at Galina is almost like looking in the mirror. Sometime she'll get a chance to think about that. "Why?"

"What you ask for is dangerous. I could lose my car. I could be shot. You have to pay for that. It seems that you need me more than I need you. So." Her tone's completely even, like she's haggling for turnips in the local market.

If Galina was pulling a number out of the air, it would more likely be a multiple of five or ten. Eleven thousand is a specific number. *She wants something. She's motivated.*

But agreeing means violating the first rule of effective graft: never pay more than the going rate. If she overpays, she signals that she either doesn't know the local market, or she spends her money foolishly. Either way, she makes herself a target.

Galina's right about one thing, though—Carson needs her if she's going to get out of this dump.

It's not your money. It's not the agency's money. Who cares?

It's the principle. I hate being extorted.

You don't get to stand on principle, you dart.

Carson's internal voice pisses her off sometimes. She grits her teeth. "Twenty percent in advance. Thirty percent when we get the other picture. The other fifty when you get me across the line. Don't even try to counter—that's as good as it gets."

"Hmpf." Galina points to the ground in front of Carson. "Put the money there, then back away."

Carson counts out bills by feel in her left pocket. They're soggy, of course, like the rest of her. She drops them on the gravel, then steps back three paces.

The half-hearted rain doesn't seem to bother Galina. She lunges forward, scoops up the notes, then retreats well out of Carson's reach to count them. "You gave me too much. Here." She holds out a bill.

"Keep it. I'll take it off your progress payment." It's interesting that Galina would offer to give back the overpayment. Maybe she's semi-honest. *That'd be a nice change.*

Maybe this will work.

Galina shoves the money into one of her work shirt's breast pockets. "You have a deal, Tarasenko. I will take you where you want to go. But if you cheat me…" She hefts the shotgun.

CHAPTER 11

Carson sits on a wood-plank bench set on two overturned plastic buckets on what passes for Galina's back porch. She's barefoot and down to her underwear, a ratty towel, and Vadim's HK. Galina let her wash her shirt and jeans in the kitchen sink (mostly mud removal); the water drizzling from the tap didn't look much cleaner than what went down the drain. Whatever. It's *so* good to be rid of the body armor for a while. She wishes she could dump the longline Cheata compression bra too—twenty-seven hours in the thing is about fifteen hours too long—but walking around topless sounds like a bad idea right now. Besides, she needs someplace to hide the money she took from the briefcase.

She took advantage of being mostly undressed to check her clothes for a GPS bug. Nothing. It must be in the briefcase or the painting. She'll look when Galina isn't snooping around.

Heitmann's phone got nearly thirty minutes of charge inside. Enough to call Olivia.

"I worried for you," Olivia says after the normal greetings. As usual, her voice's warm and calm. "When I lost your mobile's location, I feared you'd come to harm."

"Battery died." It's good to hear that somebody's worried about her. Carson doesn't have many friends left—most were in the Toronto Police Service, and nearly all of them ghosted on her after she got chucked out. "Find One-Thirteen's phone?"

"Sorry, no. He may have switched it off. But I did find yours."

Yes! "Where?"

"Let's see…it's passed Vyshneva and appears to be approaching Novozarivka." She says the names slowly, like she's sounding them out.

Carson brings up the GPS and finds the towns southwest of Olhynske. "Great. Text me updates? I'm gonna follow him."

"Of course. Are you well?"

"Enough." Carson won't bug Olivia about stuff she can't fix.

She watches gray clouds march across the gray sky. "Text me One-Seven-Nine's number. I might have an art question." One-Seven-Nine is Matt, the only guy she knows who knows anything about art.

"Of course. Do be careful. If you think your mobile is about to die, please send a message so I don't try to muster the SAS when I lose your signal."

"You can do that?" *That's worth killing the phone.*

"We shall see."

The ZAZ Slavuta liftback is a scabby five-door that looks like an escapee from the '90s. It once was dark blue, but chalky white skin cancer's taken over the roof and hood. Gravel and salt scour from the winters has chewed away at the rocker and quarter panels. Silver duct tape patches splits in the vinyl upholstery. Galina had to work at getting it running. It sounds like an angry sewing machine and it's obvious there's not much suspension left. With all the stuff Galina packed in the car, it looks like they're going camping for a week rather than taking a few hours' drive.

Half an hour out of Olhynske, fields and the strings of trees between them pass by Carson's window as the car trundles south on the allegedly paved road. The rain's stopped for a while, but the sky's still overcast. Heat leaks out the front vents.

Carson glances behind her. The portfolio and her Ksyukha are on the floor behind Galina's seat. The money's behind Carson in an olive-drab rucksack Galina gave her. The Halliburton was a great piece of luggage, but it was heavy and incredibly obvious.

Carson's clothes are warm and damp by now instead of cold and dripping. Galina gave her a threadbare plaid flannel shirt—not unlike the one Carson sleeps in when it's cold and her bed's empty—to wear over her polo. "Your clothes are too nice for here," she'd said. It's a man's shirt. Galina wears a battered silver wedding band on her right ring finger. Carson remembered pictures of a decent-looking man at the farmhouse. Not the man himself, though.

Carson says, "Anybody taking care of your place while you're gone?"

"Yes. A neighbor." Galina also washed up and changed clothes before they left. The smell of strong soap replaces her previous scent of sweat and dirt. She's wearing jeans and a black sweatshirt with an elaborate red-gold-and-white geometric design on the chest.

"You trust him?"

"Yes."

Okay, Galina's not a talker. That's fine with Carson; neither is she. Still, she'd like to learn more about how things work here. "You don't like the Makiivka Brigade."

"I don't like any of them. Gangsters and criminals pretending to be soldiers. That one I hate more."

"Why?"

"Do you know anything about them?"

"No."

Galina nods like Carson just confirmed her worst suspicions. "They destroy houses and schools. They kill the wounded and people surrendering to them. They sell prisoners into slavery at labor camps. They steal from villages and take crops from farmers. They recruit children to fight for them."

Carson thinks back to the kid at the chicken farm. He was in his mid-teens at most. "They better or worse than the other militias?"

"There can be worse things?"

"Torture. Mass executions. Weaponized rape. Sex trafficking."

Galina glances at her, frowning. "You have seen such things?"

Carson looks away, staring at the muddy sky.

Some silence passes along with the plowed fields. Galina finally says, "These things happen here, too. I don't know if the Makiivka scum do them, but I wouldn't be surprised."

Carson's backgrounder said the war's "dirty," but didn't go into details. More and more, she understands Galina's shotgun "Why are you still here?"

Galina chews her lower lip for a while. "That farm is mine. My *babka* left it to me. We didn't want to leave it to these...*kolorady*."

"What's that?"

"There's an insect in America, in the state of Colorado. A potato beetle. It's a pest. It's black and orange, like the Saint George ribbon. The terrorists, the militias—they all wear this ribbon. More destructive *pests*."

Carson had seen the ribbon on the militia troops' utility blouses but didn't know what it meant until now. "You said 'we.' You and who else?"

"My husband."

"This is his shirt?"

"Yes."

"Thanks for the clothes."

"Now you don't stand out so much."

Except she does: even winter pale with no makeup, she looks healthier than anybody else she's seen here. "Where's your husband?"

"Away."

"Is he fighting?"

"Not anymore."

"But he's still alive."

"Yes. He hasn't come back yet."

Even Carson can figure out this is an open sore. "Should I stop asking?"

"Yes, please."

"Sorry."

"No. It's natural to ask. He will come home. I will bring him home."

That last remark—more a vow—gives Carson something to gnaw on for a while. "Must be hard, with so many neighbors supporting the rebels." No answer. "How long to get to the contact line?"

"How long do you think?"

"I don't know. It took us over four hours to get from there to Amvrosiivka."

"Hmpf." Galina shakes her head. "You had an official escort, yes?"

"Yeah."

"Now you don't. Nothing happens quickly here, except maybe death. We wait in queues everyplace now. Trips we used to finish in hours now take days. There's no point to even trying to predict how long we will be going from here to there." Galina glances at Carson. "You said you are from the West. Where?"

"Canada."

"Hmm." She gives Carson the side-eye for a beat. "Where did you get that gun?"

"The Ksyukha? From a dead militiaman."

Galina nods once. "Do you know how to use it?"

"Yes. Do you?"

"Be careful who you show it to. There are too many boys here who want to prove they are men."

What a surprise. Carson scans the simple medium-gray dashboard for a twelve-volt plug but doesn't find one. There's a working ashtray that takes her back a couple decades. "Do you have a charger in here?"

Galina flips open the glove box. It's full of junk—including a bunch of rolled-up rags and a big flashlight—but Carson immediately locks onto a twelve-volt socket with a USB adapter and a MicroUSB cable, flopping loose on the end of a pair of wires. "Perfect. Thanks."

Galina punches on the radio. What comes out sounds like Leonard Cohen singing disco with a backup girl chorus. She chair-dances a little. All cleaned up, she looks less weathered and younger than before, definitely within shouting range of Carson's age. She has a pleasant but unremarkable face; she shouldn't give up farming for modeling anytime soon.

They crawl through a town even smaller than Olhynske. Rust and weeds and potholes and planters made of old truck tires; wherever the money is in this area, it's not here. Then more fields. They're not setting any land-speed records, though that's smart given how rough the pavement is. They pass the rusted, burned-out wedge of a BMP infantry fighting vehicle. Its broken tracks trail across what passes for a shoulder. Galina doesn't seem to notice; Carson stares. *How many men were inside when it torched?*

Is Stepaniak chasing us? Olivia hasn't texted her lately, but cell coverage is crap out here. That Range Rover can travel these roads a lot faster than this little tin box. In one way, that would make things easier; they could finish their business and be done with the whole thing.

And what if Stepaniak and Stas come out shooting?

Carson's guilt about not mentioning the possible danger gets heavier with time. Is this the best time to tell her? Better now than when he catches up with them. "Galina…? Something I should've told you."

The song ends; so does the chair-dancing. "The bandits don't want to see you?"

"Maybe not. It's complicated."

"If they are bandits, I think it isn't so complicated."

"Maybe. They drive a black Range Rover. Two men. They know how to use their weapons." She watches tree trunks slide by. "Sorry. Should've told you before."

"Yes. I thought they might look for you. Anyone who pays so much money so fast must be in much trouble."

The Russian DJ cycles through several numbers. The performers are all from the Eurovision Song Contest, something like *American Idol* times ten for Europe. The semi-finals are tonight. Galina chair-dances or sings along silently to all but the Russian entry, a tenor over-selling a syrupy love song. The car sings along, too, with a collection of squeaks, rattles, thunks, and groans. Carson gnaws on raw carrots from Galina's kitchen as muddy fields drift by.

Then the traffic stops.

Carson sticks her head out the window. A line of cars and trucks stands still as far as she can see. People step out to stretch. One guy wades into the knee-high grass to piss; there aren't even any trees to go behind.

Galina sighs, turns off the engine, then leans back in her seat.

Carson waits until the soprano belting a power ballad segues into a man doing an R&B-ish dance cut before she says anything. "What's happening?"

"Checkpoint."

CHAPTER 12

Already? Carson shakes her head. "Whose checkpoint?"

Galina shrugs. "Can't tell yet. It could be anyone."

It could be the Makiivka Brigade. "How does this work?"

"We wait. When we get there, we pay the bribe and they pretend to search the car. Then we go."

Probably not that simple. "We went through eleven checkpoints between the contact line and Amvrosiivka. Why so many?"

Galina gives her an amused glance. "Only eleven? Every militia has them all around their land. It's for money. The police make them too, same reason. The *mafiya* does it. Sometimes bandits make them, though they do it to stop cars and steal from them." She sees something in Carson's face and laughs. "I told you what you want isn't easy."

"I know." Carson brings up the GPS on Heitmann's phone. "Where are we?"

"North of Kumachove."

Another country town, this one several times the size of Olhynske, sprawled along a jumble of two-lane roads. Carson shows Galina the screen. "Look. Can we take this road here and drive through town to get past the roadblock?"

Galina shrugs. "If they haven't blocked it. They probably have. You should go see."

Not what Carson expected. "Why me?"

"This was your idea."

"Fine." Carson steps into the gray morning.

Galina settles into her seat. "Be careful. You are worth a lot of money to me."

Safer to leave the money here or take it? Carson grabs the knapsack.

It's cool and humid outside with a steady west wind. Better than a lot of early May days Carson remembers from back home. The north sky is dark and dramatic; not her problem yet. She adjusts the straps on the knapsack full of money and hikes south past the traffic.

The string of stopped cars seems endless. New cars, old cars (lots of those), semis, box trucks. A pair of draft horses grazes on the shoulder, hooked to a flatbed cart with truck wheels and a load of lumber. People mill on the road, chatting, smoking, pacing, talking on their phones. A gang of little boys throws rocks at a turretless tank hulk rotting in a field about ten meters from the road. Tieless older men in suits, women in sweatsuits and scuffs, kids in pajamas, teen girls in short skirts and platforms huddled in knots to keep warm. A fortyish man with a missing leg swings down the road on his crutches with a string bag of groceries hanging around his neck. No fighting-age men or teenaged boys.

So these are Ukrainians.

They're not like the Canuck Ukrainians back home. Those don't look much different from the English or French except maybe for their cheekbones. These people look smaller, paler, hungrier. Their Eastern European fashion sense doesn't help: mismatched colors, clashing patterns, ugly shoes, those teenagers shivering in minis. Yes, Canada's rich and Ukraine's poor and the Donbass is even poorer. Carson remembers seeing lots of pretty people in Kyiv, but that makes sense—all the pretty people go to the big city. It's like natural selection. She thought about that a lot when she moved to Toronto and learned how tough the competition was in the dating game.

The southbound line of cars curves to the left. A stutter of northbound traffic rolls past her. The fringes of Kumachove dust the land to her ten o'clock: little farms, knots of trees, plowed fields. It's a walkable distance away. Can they drive it?

She reaches the road she'd seen on the GPS. It's blocked by a *Mad Max*-reject SUV with bolted-on armor, a heavy machinegun mounted on the roof, and the Makiivka Brigade's crest on the driver's door. The militiaman behind the gun and the driver behind the wheel watch her go by. *Because I'm female? Because they recognize me?* She tries to not pay too much attention to them and to not call attention to herself as she passes. That's hard. At five-nine she's the tallest woman she's seen out here, and as Galina pointed out, beneath the flannel shirt her clothes are nicer than most.

Militia troops eye her as she passes. Once again she walks like she belongs and knows where she's going, hoping that'll put them off. It may also help that between the body armor and her compression bra, she looks almost flat-chested. *Unless they like that here.*

Another half-klick of walking later, she can finally see the checkpoint. Two rows of concrete blocks form a serpentine across the traffic lanes. There's a BTR, a camouflaged truck for hauling troops, a couple Hunters, and a sandbagged machinegun nest. Militiamen are going through a little gray sedan with all its doors, trunk, and hood open, and stuff piled on the street.

Carson watches for a few moments, then turns and marches back to Galina's car.

"It's the Makiivka Brigade," she announces once she's in the Slavuta. "They're not pretending. Where are we trying to go?"

Galina scowls. "Do they look for you?"

"Don't know. They're taking apart a car like there's money in it for them." Carson points out on the GPS the crossroads where she saw the militia looting the sedan.

Galina growls something Carson doesn't try to translate. "We must go through there to here"—she moves the map with a blunt index finger—"then west to here, then north to Novozarivka. Much faster than the way the bandits went."

"Except now it isn't. What do we do?"

"What would you do?"

"If I knew, I wouldn't be paying you. You're the guide, so guide."

Galina rolls the Slavuta forward a few car lengths. "We go through it."

"You mean, let them search the car?"

"No, no. We don't stop. We run straight through."

In this piece of shit? Carson stares at Galina until her open mouth dries out. "You're crazy. They'll blow us to pieces."

"Ah, that's too risky for you. We can turn back and drive about seventy kilometers. It may take hours and we will have to go through at least two checkpoints. We may be able to pay to pass them. Maybe your bandits will be gone by then."

Stepaniak may go to the West if I don't catch up. "Safer's nice, but that'll waste a day."

Galina nods. "That's too slow for you. If you want to go fast here, you must take risks. If you want less risk, you go slow. Nothing is 'safe.' Now I know what's too slow for you and what's too fast. Give me your *mobilka*." She points at Heitmann's phone. Once Carson hands it over, Galina fiddles with it for a minute or so, then smiles. "We can go around the checkpoint here. We take this small road to the top of Kumachove, then go through the streets. The *tarhany*"—cockroaches—"will shoot at us when we go off this highway and chase us through the town, but if we are smart and lucky, we get away." She returns the phone. "What you say to that tells me who you are."

Wonderful. A test. Carson sorts through the options. It's not a suicide run like Galina's first plan; a beehive rather than a hornet's nest. But avoiding being chased and shot at was the whole idea behind hiring a driver. "Thought you were worried about your car."

"You bought my car."

She wants you to wimp out. It'll make her feel superior. I'm not gonna play that way. "Okay. Let's do the third one." *Watch her try to back out...*

"Good." Galina bobs her head. "We are a kilometer from where we turn. Look at your map and learn how the roads go. You can tell me where to go."

Huh. *Maybe that's what she wanted. Good thing I don't play poker.*

The farther the line creeps forward, the edgier Carson gets. The one thing she hates more than anything is not being in control. It's why she stopped doing drugs. She'd have already tried to take over driving if she wasn't so tired and hungry. And who knows how good a driver Galina is under fire? "If you want, I'll drive. I'm not a good passenger anyway."

Galina eventually says, "Okay. You drive. I want to see what you can do. Don't kill us."

It takes over thirty more minutes to move up to the place where Carson saw the checkpoint on her hike. Only the cars being ransacked have changed. Carson's finally got the driver's seat set so it's not too uncomfortable and is remembering how to work a stickshift. She's been trying to get a feel for what—if anything— the little car can do. Sloppy steering, same-day acceleration: not her first choice for running a roadblock, but it's all she's got.

The radio's launched into a marathon of winning Eurovision

songs from previous years. So far, she hasn't heard any she recalls or any winning singers she's ever heard of. Still, she needs the distraction as they creep closer to the roadblock.

Almost fifteen minutes later, Galina points to their ten o'clock. "There it is. Do you still want to do this?"

Carson can just make out a semi-gravel track branching off from the highway about a hundred fifty meters ahead. It's not on the GPS, but it crosses the road that is. Neither is guarded. Bright spots in the overcast reflect off puddles scattered across the area. She can't tell how deep the ruts are, only that they look like veins in an old woman's leg. "Any better ideas?"

A hundred meters. Carson opens a gap with the cars ahead. She and Galina watch two militiamen at the checkpoint hustle a man into the back of a cargo truck. *That could be us next.*

Fifty meters. She revs the engine. The track looks even worse now than it did; it's more dirt than gravel. A long mud slick, not a road.

Twenty meters. A militia Hunter slowly rolls by northbound. Its driver peers into every car. Galina crosses herself the Orthodox way.

Five meters. Carson yanks the steering wheel to the left and floors it. The Slavuta's engine screams like a terrified little girl. They churn across the gravel shoulder.

Carson swings onto the eastbound road leading to a long line of farmhouses. There's absolutely no cover for the next hundred forty meters—no trees, no walls, nothing. Once the militia sees what she's doing, they'll have no excuse for missing when they shoot at her. She risks a glance to the highway. "They haven't noticed yet."

Galina clutches the grab bar above her door. "They will."

Suddenly, even the pretense of gravel is gone. The path's not dirt anymore—it's a chocolate shake. There's hardly any tread on the tires. When they get stuck, they'll be an easy target.

Mud spouts to their right, ahead of the Slavuta. Troops scramble up the highway.

Carson's whole body works hard, wrenching the wheel back and forth, trying to absorb the car's leaps and lurches while zig-zagging to throw off the militia's aim. Maybe eighty meters to the houses.

"The BTR just started." Galina points toward the checkpoint. "The turret's moving."

Sixty meters. A line of mud geysers walks across the track ahead as tracers jet past them. Every tenth round is usually a tracer. A serious wall of lead is coming their way. Carson yells, "Hold on!" then swerves to their right.

"What—?"

More eruptions, this time to their left. The gunners are aiming at where the car was, not where it is. Carson slews across a mudhole. Thirty meters.

"A Hunter's going into town." Once again, Galina points out her window, not that Carson can actually look. "They will try to cut us off."

"One thing at a time."

The first *clang* from a solid hit makes Galina scream. Then a crunching sound: a ragged hole appears in the rear window. They're almost to the houses, but their speed's gone down by over half—not that it was all that fast to begin with—and the militia's finding its range. Carson swerves the car wildly. Her ribs scream at the abuse. She keeps her mouth clamped shut so she doesn't bite her tongue.

Then...gravel. They slew onto the southbound road. The Slavuta slowly throws the mud off its tires and picks up speed. It's like drag-racing a snail.

Carson yells, "Where are we going?"

Galina peers at the GPS. "Straight, then left!"

Trees and raggedy houses fly by. A dog bolts across the road. The car's getting dangerously close to eighty (kph); the engine whines, the front end shimmies like a belly dancer, and the steering's sloppier than a three-day drunk. The road's end grows larger by the second.

"Left! Left!"

Carson tries to drift the turn, but the tires aren't up to it. The car spins, skidding onto someone's scraggly front yard. They're facing west instead of east.

A Hunter lurches to a halt in front of them. The driver's jaw drops.

"Hold on." Carson shifts into reverse, hits the gas. The Slavuta leaps back. Still, there's no way they'll lose the Hunter driving backward. The moment the trees disappear from the roadside, Carson stomps the clutch, yanks the handbrake, and cranks the wheel all the way to the right. They're facing east again. Second gear; gun it.

The rear window disappears. Automatic gunfire breaks through the music. A quick glimpse in the rear-view: troops hanging out the Hunter's side windows, shooting. "Crossroads!"

"Right! Go right!"

The car bombs down the narrow road, swerving to avoid the barrage of fire coming from the Hunter close behind it. The passenger's side-view mirror explodes. Bullets clang into the bodywork. Galina can duck, but Carson can't and keep the Slavuta on the road at the same time. A tractor abruptly backs out from a farm; Carson just barely keeps control as she caroms around it, narrowly missing a tree.

"How much farther?"

"Keep going!" Galina twists in her seat, raises the Ksyukha, and squeezes off a long burst into the Hunter's front end.

Carson's ears shut down. "Fuck! That's loud!"

Galina cuffs her ear. "Don't swear!"

They reach a crossroads. To their left: a huge plowed field. Ahead: another swamp of a dirt road. To the right: the BTR from the roadblock, heading straight for them. The *what?*

Straight ahead it is.

Fat, slow tracers arc over the little hatchback. Fountains of mud burst just meters in front of it. Carson cuts to the right between two small stands of trees, jouncing over bumps and rocks. She's lost track of the Hunter, which is fine, because the heavy machinegun in the BTR's turret can tear them in half if it ever hits them.

"Keep turning!" Galina thumps into her seat. "The gunner turns the BTR's turret with a crank. Move fast and he can't aim at us."

They tear up a green field, slam over some washboard. The eight-wheeled monster behind them cruises over the mud like it's asphalt, spraying a brown rooster tail high in the air. A tracer streaks by Carson's window at head height.

And then…Celine Dion on the radio, singing a peppy love anthem. Eurovision winner in 1988. Carson remembers this one.

She cranks the volume.

The big field is gone; they're back on gravel. Carson's sure she'll dislocate a shoulder the way she's twisting and heaving. Her head bounces off the side window, fuzzing her vision.

Ne partez pas sans moi, laissez-moi vous suivre...

They lurch to the left; a line of dirt-and-gravel fountains spurts just to their right. Then to the right. There's a *bang* in back that sounds like a big rock hit them. More geysers to their left. A cemetery blurs past; not a good omen.

La plus belle aventure, les plus beaux voyages...

Galina yells, "Right! Right! Right!"

CHAPTER 13

Carson fishtails them around the corner, fighting to keep the Slavuta on all four wheels. She glimpses a large, ruined building to their right, partly screened from the road by tall weeds.

Galina thrusts her arm toward their one o'clock. "In there! Hurry!"

"In there" is a narrow, unpaved driveway crammed between two trees to the left of the ruins. Carson threads the needle, crashing over an exposed tree root.

Galina points out her window. "Go in there now! Between those trees!"

The gap looks about a meter wide. "We can't fit—"

"Do it!"

Carson swerves into a tiny clearing in the impromptu forest growing behind the wrecked building. The little Slavuta manages to fit almost exactly between two trees, hiding it from the road.

Galina slaps the dash with both palms. "Yes!" She looks pleased with herself.

Carson has to catch her galloping breath. "Why are we stopping?"

"Come with me."

They grab their weapons and pile out of the car. Carson follows Galina through a permanently open door into the building, which is little more than a shell with a skeletal roof and disintegrating plasterwork. They end up inside a large room, peeking out a sizable front window with no glass.

The BTR couldn't turn as fast as the Slavuta. It backs into the intersection, then pulls even with the building. A top hatch flies open; a trooper in a black tanker's helmet pokes his head and shoulders outside. He stares down the street through binoculars.

The Hunter stops behind the armored personnel carrier. The windshield's pocked with bullet-sized holes and the entire front is caked with mud. The Hunter's driver jogs to the BTR's nose and talks with its driver. Carson hears voices but no words. The hand gestures tell the story: *Where did they go? That way, I guess. You sure? Well, where else?*

Both vehicles eventually take off westward down the street. The BTR leaves behind a fog of diesel exhaust and ground vibration.

Carson settles on a rusting metal chair. "Now what?"

"We wait for them to go away."

Carson considers Galina. She knows that a BTR's hand-cranked turret is too slow to track a fast-moving target. She knows how to hide from patrols. "You've done this before."

Galina gives her a small, grim smile. "You did well. I'm impressed. You may be worth the trouble." She stands. "We fix my car now."

She digs a can of spray paint and a roll of heavy-duty packing tape from the depths of the trunk, then shows Carson how to patch the dozen-and-some bullet holes in the car. Carson says, "You just happen to have this."

"It's good to be prepared."

The paint matches the original color with enough squinting. The driver-side taillight is splintered and the rear window's entirely gone. Still, Carson hopes it'll be harder for the militia to spot them in traffic.

How did Galina learn to do all this? She can handle weapons, too. Carson finally asks, "Who are you?"

Galina deadpans, "Just a simple farmer."

Bullshit. The question bouncing around Carson's brain: *how bent is she?* Is Galina a bandit? A wheelman for a gang? A smuggler? Not that these are bad things in this context, but Carson would rather know now than find out the hard way.

Galina takes the wheel. She turns down the radio, then leans her seat back and closes her eyes to show she's not interested in talking. That leaves Carson to play sentry. Love songs and dance mixes are exactly the wrong soundtrack for the situation, but she doesn't dare change the station.

An hour later, Galina fires up the car. Starting is almost as much a cliffhanger as it was that morning in her driveway. She untangles the car from the trees and heads south to join up with the highway.

◎

Stepaniak's focus shuttles between the tracker app on his phone and Stas's grumbling under the Range Rover.

"Dear Carson, what are you doing?" he mumbles to himself. The red pip on his tracker shows her going northwest toward Novozarivka. *If she keeps that up...* "Are you following us?"

"Somebody else after us?" Stas drags himself out from under the SUV. He sounds more sour than usual.

"Carson may be. She's less than ten kilometers from Komsomolske."

"Almost closer than we are." Stas takes a big pull from Stepaniak's late-Art Nouveau silver flask. He waves it at the Range Rover. "Can't find a fucking thing. If they put a beacon on us, I don't see it."

Of course not. Stepaniak sighs and scans the ruins of the collective farm all around them. They're parked on what was the concrete floor of some kind of storage building; now it's just a slab surrounded by fragments of wall. The orderly grid of Petrivske takes up the Kalmius River's east bank about three hundred meters to the east.

It had been a hard slog to get this far. They'd had those militia idiots on their tail since they fled Olhynske this morning. That ridiculous technical—a Toyota Hilux pickup draped with sheet steel and sandbags—nearly ambushed them in Kultura; Stepaniak and Stas managed to dispose of the three-man crew without anyone noticing right away. They weaved around back roads until that five-kilometer-long wallow on dirt tracks to Petrivske. Stas swore and groused nonstop as he muscled the Range Rover through bogs and over rain-swollen creeks while they both expected the militia to shoot them at any moment. But they finally made it here.

Hoping the militia won't follow.

The road running southwest-northeast through Novozarivka— where Carson's driving— is supposed to be the western boundary of the Makiivka Brigade's area of operations. *Where did she get a car? She's resourceful that way, but still. Is she following us? How? Is she working with the militia?*

Stas hands back Stepaniak's flask. Empty, predictably. "Well?

What do you want to do?"

"Did you check inside?"

"Yes."

"Dear Stas, please think. They are not following us with magic. There must be something."

Stas sweeps his hand toward the SUV. *Look for yourself.*

"Yes, yes. It may not matter now if those militia fools stay where they belong. But Carson may be giving us an opportunity—we don't have to look for her if she comes to us."

"That shit deal again?"

"Perhaps." Stepaniak's been thinking about that ever since they left Olhynske. If Stas is satisfied with only a quarter of the money—not at all a certainty—that leaves Stepaniak with the bare minimum to buy into the club. He'll still have expenses to set himself up in proper style in Kyiv. That means he needs to get not only the money from Carson, but also the painting she has. It's definitely not the deal she proposed.

Stas shakes his head in disgust. "She's just a woman. There's plenty of those in Kyiv. Stop talking shit and kill her. You know you have to."

Stas is being predictable again. In this case, though, the man may have a point.

Rogozhkin finds Yartsev worrying a cigarette outside the brigade's concrete Operations Center. Rogozhkin marches past him, snaps, "With me" in Russian, then leads the sergeant some twenty meters down an alley between two long mill buildings.

Once they're clear of any eavesdroppers, Rogozhkin faces Yartsev. "What's happened?"

"There's been an incident near Kumachove. A local bypassed a checkpoint. Fire was exchanged. It's still confused, but I'm hearing three dead."

"What? Civilians?"

Yartsev shakes his head, then thumbs over his shoulder toward the Ops Center.

"Oh, for fuck's sake." Rogozhkin tears off his sky-blue beret and scrubs his fingers through his short salt-and-pepper hair.

"Who shot who?"

"I can't tell yet, sir. Their radio discipline's shit. They're yelling over each other, no call signs. But there's something else." Yartsev steps closer and lowers his voice. "They've got a patrol following someone. I don't know who, yet—they call him a bandit—but they've got a GLONASS beacon on him and they're chasing him all over to hell down there. He may be part of this. I've asked questions, but no one's answered them yet."

Rogozhkin won't even bother to ask why the militia's wasting its time in a backwater like Kumachove. They'll call it a "training exercise," like this bunch needs more practice stopping traffic. "Where's this patrol?"

Yartsev grimaces. "West of Novozarivka."

"*What?* That's outside their zone. Who authorized that?"

"I can guess."

So can Rogozhkin. "Which unit's down there?"

"Detached from A Company, Second Battalion."

Rogozhkin waits for his flare of anger to fade. "Goddamned Mashkov. That's deliberate."

The first and third battalions have Russian commanders, supposed ex-Russian Army "volunteers" supposedly working for the Wagner Group, Russia's answer to the American Blackwater company. They know better than to do anything without telling Rogozhkin about it first. Second Battalion's commander is still a local. It used to make sense: he was reasonably competent and it was useful for appearances. But it gives Mashkov a way to operate independently and leads to trouble like this.

He turns over the problem in his mind long enough for Yartsev, a slow smoker, to finish his cigarette. Then Rogozhkin makes a decision. "Are you getting enough intel to vector me toward this bandit?"

"Yes, sir. Most of the time."

"Good. I'll get a team from the 45th to help get to the bottom of this mess. Mashkov doesn't need to know where I am or what I'm doing. Tell him I'm at Command for a meeting if he presses you. Feed me whatever intel you get. These *hoholy*"—*idiot Ukrainians*—"are spending a lot of time and blood on something. I intend to find out what it is."

"Yes, sir."

"Did you ever get anything more about Amvrosiivka?"

"No, sir. They're playing it tight."

"Keep digging. I won't be surprised if all this is related. I swear, Oleg—if these morons are running drugs, some of them are going to end up hanging from that silo." He claps Yartsev's shoulder. "Good work. I'll check in when I'm on the road."

CHAPTER 14

Carson and Galina bribe their way past a roadblock and roll into Komsomolske by midafternoon. It's the largest town they've been through today, though that's a low bar.

They pull into a small parking lot surrounded on three sides by market stalls and smallish buildings. A dozen other cars share the lot. Most are in marginally better condition than the Slavuta, though no cleaner. Carson groans out the door.

It seems like they've been in the car forever, but the GPS says they've covered only forty-five klicks, less than half the distance to the contact line. Carson's ribs are kicking her ass. Not broken—she knows what that feels like—but probably cracked. She hobbles around for a minute, then braces against the car to stretch out her legs. "Is there someplace to eat here? Fucking starving."

Galina glares at her. "You have a filthy mouth."

Not even Carson's mother says that to her. "I bet *you* got dinner and breakfast."

Galina leans against the fender, folding her arms. She watches Carson work out her physical kinks. "I can tell you aren't from here. You get upset when you miss a meal." Galina looks her up and down. "You haven't missed many."

"You saying I'm fat?"

"You aren't thin."

Carson stands straight and shoots Galina a laser stare. "You should talk. Let's strip you down and see how many of *your* ribs we can count." Not fair, but her hangry's coming out. "Just so you know: I have this thing called fasting hypoglycemia." She uses the English words. "My blood sugar crashes if I don't eat regularly, or if I burn a lot of calories." It doesn't help that she drinks too much, but there's no point in overdoing honesty. "Want to see it get worse? If I have to wait until supper time, I'll probably break your fucking neck." She stalks off toward the market stalls before Galina can scold her for her language again.

Komsomolske's main shopping area is a jumble of repurposed shipping containers, pipe stalls, and tables set up under corrugated iron roofs, selling a little bit of whatever people can afford to buy. Her €200 notes are useless here; she could buy out a vendor's entire stock with one or two. Luckily, she still has Ruslan's bankroll: 11,220 Ukrainian hryvnia (roughly $620 Canadian), 765 euros, and 375 Russian rubles (about eight bucks), the Donbass' "official" currency.

She scores two dozen *pyrizhky* and a half-dozen bottles of Morshinska water at a string of tables piled with produce and baked goods. Forking over euros in small bills—at a very generous exchange rate—coaxes a grudging smile from the pickle-faced seller.

Carson finds a stool in an empty stall and wolfs down half a dozen pastries in record time. When she looks up, she sees Galina standing on the other side of the counter, watching her.

She looks thoughtful. "I didn't know you're sick."

Carson doesn't feel like explaining the condition-versus-illness thing. "Should've told you. I get headaches when it happens. Then I get mean. Then nobody's happy." She pushes the paper bags of *pyrizhky* to the counter's front edge. "Chopped chicken here, mushroom in there. They're good."

Galina nods her head for a moment, crosses herself, then takes a careful bite of a chopped chicken roll. "It is. Thanks."

"You're welcome. I remember these from when I was a kid. Mom couldn't cook for shit, but she could make these."

"Would you talk to your mother that way?"

"She talked to me that way."

Galina shakes her head as she finishes off the chicken *pyrizhky*. She picks a chopped mushroom pastry from the other bag. "Where is your family from? I mean, not in Canada."

"Kharkiv. Left in the '70s. You grew up in Olhynske?"

"No, in Donetsk."

Not what Carson expected. "You're a city girl?"

"I lived there. I didn't like it very much. My parents sent me to live on *babka* Yulia's farm in the summers. She was Father's mother. The air was better than in the city and she always had good food."

"Still, it had to be a shock."

Galina shrugs. "I liked it. Farm work is very honest. You have to do the right thing or your crops die or your animals die. You always have to do the right thing. Not like in the city."

Is packing a shotgun or knowing how to run roadblocks the "right thing"? She'll ask later if it becomes important.

Heitmann's phone bleeps. It's a WhatsApp text from Olivia: 113's signal disappeared between your location and Starobesheve.

"Fuck. We lost Stepaniak."

"Language. Who's Stepaniak?"

"The bandit. He stole my phone. My people are—were—tracking it. The signal died." She texts back, which direction?

North.

Wonderful. She hopes he just hit a dead spot in cell coverage. The alternative—that he figured out her phone was on and shut it off—means they've lost him maybe forever. If that's what happened, she might as well have Galina take her over the line with the job half-done. text if it comes back.

Of course.

Carson looks up Starobesheve on the GPS. It's less than twenty klicks northwest of here. "He was heading north to Starobesheve. Should we follow him?"

Galina considers this between sips of water. "Service is bad between towns. We should wait to see if his *mobilka* comes back. If it does, we will know where he's going."

Wait. The last damn thing she wants to do. There are still four hours or more of daylight left; it seems silly to waste them. Still, she gets why Galina wants to stay here for now—they could tear off after Stepaniak in one direction only to have him go the opposite way. "If we're gonna sit here, I'm doing some shopping. You can come or stay. Your choice."

Galina brings the surviving *pyrizhky* while Carson buys a toothbrush, toothpaste, a traveling hairbrush with a folding handle, hand sanitizer (she hopes it isn't acid-based), a tube of aloe (ditto), and more boot socks. Her mental clock sounds like her watch is surgically implanted in her ear. She checks Heitmann's phone every ninety seconds or so, but Olivia doesn't text.

An hour has dissolved by the time they dump another flat of

water in the Slavuta and Carson brushes her teeth in the parking lot (the toothpaste tastes like liquid chalk). Carson's tired of waiting. She pulls Heitmann's phone and thumbs in her number. Her thumb hovers. If her phone's off and he doesn't turn it on again, she'll leave a voicemail that he'll never hear. If Stepaniak somehow doesn't know yet that her phone is still on, this'll be a big clue. On the other hand, if Stepaniak's serious about doing a deal, there's no reason for him to not want to meet and get it done.

She hits the "call" button.

"*Slushayu*." Stepaniak's voice.

His voice startles her. She didn't expect him to answer. "Still interested in a deal?"

Lots of silence follows. "Dear Carson. I have been thinking about you. Where are you?"

Like you don't know. "Still want to deal?"

"I'm happy the militia didn't harm you. I worried for you, dear Carson, I truly did. I must apologize for leaving so abruptly, but I am not the militia's favorite person today."

"I wonder why. Answer the fucking question. Deal or no deal?"

"Carson. *Lyubyy.* Please don't be so hostile. I want nothing but the best for you. Yes, of course I am interested in your offer. It serves both our purposes."

A text from Olivia: 113 is in Starobesheve.

Gotcha. "Great. Where are you? Let's meet."

"Ah, dear Carson, I am sorry. As much as I would like to see you now, I have business I need to attend to. It will take me late into the night. Can you perhaps make time for me tomorrow morning? We will both be rested. It will be better for us, yes?"

Carson hates wasting three hours of daylight. "Why wait? You know the terms. We can be done in ten minutes, tops. Then we can both leave this…" she almost says *shithole* but remembers it's Galina's home "…place."

"Yes, yes, that would be ideal. Sadly, there are other people involved whose schedules I do not control. Tomorrow, early? You can be across the line in time for dinner. I would not ask this of you if it wasn't important. Please."

She could try to put a time limit on the deal. But what if he doesn't take it? She goes home with the job half-done. Heitmann's death is half a waste. "Where?"

"In Miskyi Park there is a café. Leto. Very easy to find. Tomorrow morning at seven. It is not open so early, but people will be nearby. Good for both of us. Do you agree? I look forward to seeing you again so soon. Wear something pretty for me, yes? I—"

"In your dreams. The body armor stays on. Come on time." Carson cuts the connection.

How did she ever fall for his bullshit? Easy: she was still angry and humiliated over getting turfed out of the force and hadn't gotten laid in months. Her standards went *way* down, not that they were so high to begin with. She'd married Ron, after all.

She looks at Galina, whose eyebrows kept climbing up her forehead as the call went on. "He's in Starobesheve. The swap's here tomorrow morning. You know someplace to stay?"

"There is a hostel." Galina's lips twist.

"That good, huh?"

"We are safer sleeping in the park."

Carson's stayed in places like that. Sleeping sitting up in a chair facing a barred door, a pistol in her lap. "Anything else?"

"I know a place." Shrug. "It has a roof. It maybe still has doors."

Carson and Galina case the town to find an alternative site for the swap. No way is Carson walking into a place Stepaniak chooses. They find a huge vacant lot north of the market, a hundred thirty meters by two hundred twenty with one tree on it. She'll call him a few minutes before seven in the morning to tell him things have changed.

Galina takes Carson to Viktoriia, a restaurant in a pink building a block east of the street market. It's basic but tidy. The Ukrainian supper is filling because it's rich rather than plentiful.

The dark sky's clouding over by the time they leave. Galina leads Carson to a nearby bar. It looks like a low-rent *biergarten*: wood-slab tables, benches, a freestanding bar counter at the end farthest from the front door. All the drinkers are men, and most look like they've had a lot of practice. The most modern things in the room are the two flat-screen TVs on the walls showing soccer.

Carson buys their first two Chernigivske ales from the bar and sits across a table from Galina. "How hard will it be to cross the contact line tomorrow?"

Galina shrugs. "If there's fighting or the checkpoints are closed, we maybe can't go. It's not like a real border. The crossings are open only if both sides want them to be. The *kolorady* are afraid of people going to the West and not coming back. The Ukrainian police are worried about *kolorady* going to markets to buy all the things we can't get here now. They come home and sell them for too much money. Then they give the money to the gangsters."

Wonderful. "How far to the nearest crossing?"

"Fifty kilometers to the one at Dokuchajevsk. It's highway almost the whole way. The crossing is open most of the time because it's big."

"When I came east, we entered somewhere near Staromarivka."

Galina shakes her head. A little silver Orthodox cross flashes on a chain around her neck. "No. That's not a real crossing. There are usually bandits there, and the roads are bad."

"You mean, worse than today's?"

"The ones we used today are good for here."

Supper had been quiet, but the stronger drink gets the women talking more now. Beer runs interrupt regularly. So do the come-ons by the local lushes.

Carson shakes her head as she watches a persistent one stagger to his table. "Are the men here more desperate, or are we hotter here than we would be in Kyiv?"

Galina laughs. It's the first time Carson's heard her let go. "Both. The young women went to the West, like the young men. Why stay here when the future's there?" She leans in, lowering her voice. "We are on the steppe. The men may *think* they want a pretty wife, but they know pretty women are a problem, yes?"

"I hear you."

"A strong, healthy woman who will work is a much better wife for the farm. She won't think she can win an oligarch in the city and be a princess. She won't lose her beauty when she gets old because she never had it. Is it that way in Canada, too?"

"It can be. Draft horses versus racehorses."

"Yes! I like that." Galina rests her chin on her folded hands, then smiles. There's a little gap between her front teeth. "It's my turn to ask about your husband. Do you have one?"

"Not anymore."

"Did he die, or did you kick him out of the house?" Sly smile.

"We divorced about six years ago."

"What kind of man was he?"

An asshole. No, she won't go there. "A police detective. We worked together. Getting married was a bad idea."

Galina cocks her head, puzzled. "You were in the police?"

"Yeah, in Toronto. Thirteen years. I was a detective sergeant when I left. My ex was an inspector."

"Why are you not together? Did you not love him?"

She did, once, for a while. Carson lets the flashbacks go by while she drains her bottle. "He couldn't keep his pants zipped. He'd come home smelling like perfume. I'd drink. We fought a lot. Big fights—hitting, throwing things, cops coming to referee. The sex was great, but we couldn't live together when we were vertical. We called it quits before we killed each other."

Galina nods. "The women he went with—they were pretty?"

"Go on, rub it in."

"Racehorses. As I said: pretty women are a problem." She gets distracted by swirling white circles on one of the TVs. "Oh! Eurovision!"

Carson's seen the Eurovision Song Contest only once, in a Berlin bar two years ago. It's a big deal over here, but she never figured out why. Now she gets a full dose with the second semi-final broadcast. She recognizes songs she heard on the radio today, performed with glitzy lights and lots of swooping cameras and audience reaction shots. Galina sings along silently (or sometimes not-so-silently) with each one. Much beer disappears. Even the drunks pay attention, though mostly they make rude comments about the male singers and semi-dirty ones about the women.

Over an hour into it, Galina shouts "Jamala!" and claps as a pretty brunette in a flowing blue gown sings something dramatic that for once isn't a love song. Apparently Ukraine made the semis. Galina applauds loudly at the end. The drunks mutter or hiss.

For the first time, Carson regrets giving in when Galina talked her into leaving her body armor in the car. Being free of it is a relief, but the drunks' reactions make her edgy.

She asks, "What was that song about?" Most of the words were English, but she couldn't figure out what they were trying to say.

"It tells of the Russians deporting the Tatars from Crimea in the Great Patriotic War. It's very powerful, even—"

A drunk starts singing in Russian in a rough tenor loud enough to drown out both Galina and the TVs.

Russia – our holy nation.
Russia – our beloved country.
A mighty will, great glory –
These are yours for all time!

His buddies join in using a couple slightly different keys. Carson recognizes the piece: it's the Russian national anthem.

Galina looks disgusted. She shoots an evil stare across the room at the men, who return it. Then she stands and belts in Ukrainian with a clear, strong soprano voice.

Glorious spirit of Ukraine shines and lives forever.
Blessed by Fortune, brotherhood will stand up together.

What? Carson doesn't know this one. She assumes it's the Ukrainian national anthem.

The drunks lurch to their feet and sing louder. They throw gestures—*gang signs?*—at Galina. She catches them and hurls them back.

Galina waves to Carson to get up and sing. Carson doesn't know the words. She looks them up on Heitmann's phone, stands, then flogs her wavering mezzo to keep up with Galina. A singer, she's not.

Both sides stagger to an end at roughly the same time. The drunks yell, "Fascists! Go back to Kyiv!" and other endearments. Galina shouts "*Sataná!*" and "*Kacápskyi!*" Carson tries to pull her down onto her bench but can't make her stay. The men edge toward them.

Carson's getting worried. She can take down a gaggle of old drunks with not much trouble. She doesn't know what the consequences might be, though, and doesn't want to find out. And her body armor's half a block away. She grabs Galina's arm. "Let's get out of here."

Galina yanks her arm away. "No! I am staying to watch the show." The way she sways says she may be a bit tipsy.

A fiftyish guy with a Molson muscle and seriously bad teeth is just a few feet away. He holds a beer bottle by the neck, like a club.

Carson scruffs Galina like she would a naughty dog. "Listen," she growls. "You threw rocks at the wasp's nest. The wasps are coming for you. We're done here."

"Ow! You're hurting me!"

"They'll hurt you worse. Let's go."

There are too many pissed and pissed-off men between them and the front door. Carson drags Galina toward the back door. The youngest lush—a wiry guy in his forties with a scar down his right cheek—tries to slip in behind them. *Fuck this.* Carson draws and cocks her pistol, aims at Scarface, and snarls in Russian, "Move or die."

He moves.

The women burst through the back door into a jumble of garbage cans, broken furniture, and cardboard boxes. Carson grabs a handful Galina's coat collar and hustles her toward the street as the men tumble outside after them.

By the time the drunks start throwing bottles, Carson and Galina are running down the street.

CHAPTER 15

Carson drives the kilometer and a half to the house on the northern edge of town. The streetlights don't put out much light and nearly all the windows are dark; she has to watch carefully for stray dogs and drunks.

She glares at Galina. "You had to do that."

Galina giggles. "It was fun."

"Fun?" She shakes her head. "You don't drink much, do you?"

"No. It's bad for you." Her arm slews around to point in the bar's general direction. "Look at them. Too much drinking. That's what happens." She speaks over-carefully in the way not-quite-drunk people do when they want to convince themselves they're not quite drunk.

There's hardly any traffic, so they pull into the abandoned house's driveway faster than Carson expected.

The squatters didn't clean up after themselves. The kitchen tap produces water the color of tree sap that smells like it could remove the linoleum floor. The two remaining light bulbs still work. There's a stripped double bed, some creaky chairs, an overturned table, and lots of empty beer bottles. Galina was right, though: it still has an intact(ish) roof and working doors.

It's in the low-teens Celsius and cloudy with a brisk wind that hurries their unloading of the car. A dim rumbling to the west seasons the sound picture without overwhelming it. Carson listens for a few moments. "Is that thunder?"

"No. Artillery. It's too far away to be a problem tonight."

All the lights die. A hush settles on the town around them. "You were saying?"

"Hmpf. This happens all the time. Someone shoots a power line or a generator and the lights go out. Or a powerplant breaks. All the engineers went to the West, so no one knows how to fix anything." Galina laughs. "It's very, very funny. Except tonight."

"Why tonight?"

"Eurovision! I want to see if Jamala goes to the finals."

Carson mutters "for fuck's sake" in English under her breath. "Why do you like that show so much?"

"Eurovision?" Galina's face turns serious. "I've loved it since I was a girl. But now? There's so much hate and killing and death all around. The water doesn't work, the lights go off. I hate the news. I miss my husband. But Eurovision is still the same. It's pretty, everyone is excited, the songs are fun. All the nations compete, but with singing. There's no war, no killing, no hate. It reminds me…" She sighs. "I remember what it's like to be human." She tugs on Carson's sleeve. "Let's listen to the radio together."

"Listen to what?" Carson's exhausted. She'd planned some quality time searching the painting for a tracking bug. After that, she wants to get the goddamn bra off, curl up in a sleeping bag, and turn out her own lights.

"*Eurovision*. Of course."

Oh, for God's sake. "It's not over yet?"

"No. It goes to midnight. After the singing comes the voting. That's the important part."

The battle-scarred bed is calling Carson's name. But she doesn't want to shit on Galina's fun or get into a fight with her. She still needs her. Being locked in a car for hours with someone who's pissed off at her makes for a very, *very* long day. "How drunk are you?"

Galina shrugs. "Maybe a little. Why? How drunk are you?" She sounds almost playful.

"Not." Carson's totally sober. Lots of practice. "Shotgun's still in the car?"

"No."

"Get it. We're not sitting in a dark car in a dark city without our weapons."

"Yes, Sergeant." Galina throws her a sloppy salute, then wanders to the bedroom.

Carson straps on her vest, sweeps the Ksyukha off the weary kitchen table—they'd set it on its feet after clearing the beer bottles—then trudges out the side door to make another circuit around the house. Just to make sure.

By the time Carson returns to the driveway and slides into the Slavuta's passenger-side door, Galina's already settled in and has the radio playing louder than necessary. A woman's singing what sounds like the title theme for a James Bond flick that hasn't been made yet. Galina leans toward Carson. "*Albania.*" She rolls her eyes in a way that says, *that explains everything.*

Carson doesn't pay attention. Her neck's tingling. It's *dark* out there in a way a city never is, even if the power's out. She hates not being able to see much more than a few meters away and wishes the side-view mirror wasn't missing. She keeps the Ksyukha on her lap and the flashlight between her thighs and peers out each window in turn.

The Bond theme gives way to a bouncy dance tune that starts vaguely like "Another One Bites the Dust." When that ends, talking heads take over.

Carson tunes them out. She'd been edgy leaving a million euros in cash and a painting worth seven figures or more buried in the trunk when she and Galina were at dinner and then in the bar. Having them in the house doesn't make her any less nervous. Knowing that Stepaniak can find her—more likely, find the painting—doesn't help. She'd thought about bringing the painting out here to search it while Galina does her fangirl thing, but she'd need lots of light to see what she's doing and that would kill her night vision.

The car's interior lights up. It's Galina's phone. Carson barks, "The fuck are you *doing?*"

"Language! I'm voting." Galina's thumbs hammer the screen. "Vote for Jamala! Come on, vote!"

"Turn. That. Thing. *Off.*" Carson reaches to grab Galina's phone. Her night vision's shot, spiking her tingling sensation.

Galina crams herself against the driver's door, holding her phone just out of reach as she tries to swat away Carson's hand. She freezes. "What was that?"

"What?"

"I thought I saw a light in the front window."

"Good try. Turn off the phone. *Now.*"

"No, truly. Look."

Carson glances toward the three six-paned windows in the street-facing wall. Galina's right: a blue-white glow bobs around behind the tattered lace curtains. *What the...?* She checks her watch—they've been in the car for almost an hour. Squatters?

Stepaniak? He's had more than enough time to finish his meeting and find them. "Stay here. Lock the doors."

"But…"

Carson quietly shuts the door on Galina's protest. She readies her assault carbine, then ghosts around the house. Moving lights: one in front, one in the back where the bedroom is.

There's two doors—one on the driveway side, closed, and an open one in back. A glow lights the bedroom through the open door. The cash and the painting are in there, hidden under the bed behind the duffels, the only place in the house that offers any concealment. Okay if she or Galina is sleeping on the bed, as she'd planned; not so good when they're both in the car.

Wait for them out here? Go in after them? Waiting has some merit; she can engage on her own terms, get some surprise on her side. However, "outside" means broadcasting a firefight through the whole neighborhood. It also opens more escape routes for the men inside.

Going in pins them in place. However, rooting them out means a nasty, close-quarters firefight.

Staying outside seems the best of two bad choices.

Carson steps back until she's a few meters from the house, then goes prone. She switches from the Ksyukha to the pistol so she can fire one-handed and sights in on the door. First one out gets a nasty surprise.

It doesn't take long. Both lights converge in the bedroom, then blink off. Nothing happens for a few minutes. *Getting their night vision back,* she figures. She crosses her wrists (pistol in her right hand, flashlight, off for now, in her left, both aiming at the door) and concentrates her ears on the doorway.

Boots rustle on a wooden floor. A shadow shifts in the back door.

She snaps on her flashlight, catching two men on the threshold. They freeze just long enough for her to try to double-tap the one on the left. He goes down after the first torso shot, grunting. The other guy crouches and swings up his weapon.

Carson douses her flashlight beam and rolls to her left just as he fires. *Phutphutphutphut.* A suppressed weapon. Bullets slam into the ground to her right, too close, spraying her with dirt. She fires twice at a point behind the muzzle flash. Her own gunfire fuzzes out her ears. If she hit anything, she can't hear it.

One's down, a solid torso shot. If these two really are Stepaniak and Stas—she couldn't tell in the few moments of light—they're wearing vests, so the best she can hope for is that whoever she hit is as out of breath as she was at the chicken farm.

She rolls to her feet and charges to the back corner of the house farthest from the open door. As she's moving, a blue-white beam floods the jumbled back yard. It sweeps across the decrepit storage sheds and empty chicken coop, then snaps off.

They know she's out here. The only surprise left is where she is now. Their next move should be to try the side door by the driveway. She needs to get there first.

Carson runs as quickly and quietly as her ribs let her around the house's front to the gravel driveway's edge. As she passes the Slavuta, she glances inside: dark and quiet. She assumes Galina's got enough sense to be head-down behind the dash. She ducks behind the front-left fender, aims her Ksyukha at the side door, and waits.

A black void replaces the door's dull gray. Carson ducks an instant before the tactical light skids along the car's hood, then slides down the driveway toward the back yard. When it disappears, she snaps to her firing position.

Movement in the doorway.

She fires a short burst into the void. A squawk; a *thud. A hit?*

Phutphutphutphut. Rounds clang into the Slavuta's hood, crash into a headlight. The side door slams shut.

So far, so good. She's hit one of them twice, or both once. Carson knows their dilemma: one shooter or two? They have to assume two, so they're pinned. She hopes.

They could stay in there all night, nurse their wounds. They could try to go out a window. The house has windows on three sides. She can't run around enough to cover them all; the little running she's done has her side screaming.

They're inside. They're hurting. It's her move, now.

She carefully twists the rusty doorknob, eases open the side door (thankfully, no squeaking), then slips inside the entry hall. Her heart's beating hard enough to warn the intruders.

She swivels right, then stops in the kitchen to listen. Rustling, the occasional squeak. She wishes she'd spent more time getting used to the layout in here. *Too late now.* She switches the Ksyukha to semiauto—full auto burns too much ammo—then glides slowly to her left toward the door to the front room.

Just a smidgen shy of the doorframe, something crunches under her boot.

A bright blue-white flood slams into her. She dekes to her left as a burst of suppressed fire fills the room. Plaster dust and breaking glass attack her. She rolls to the doorway and fires two rounds at whatever's behind the light, but that target's already moving. All she hears is plaster cracking.

Carson sidesteps into the front room. The bedroom's through the next door. The back door's in there. The laundry room-washroom thing is to the left through the bedroom, taking her to where she started. Will they try to circle behind her? Leave?

She stops at the door to the bedroom. She can hear whispering inside in a language she doesn't understand. The sharp tang of blood.

There'll never be a better time...

Carson pivots to aim through the doorway, flicking on her flashlight as she moves.

An orange flash of eyes surrounded by a balaclava. She gets off two rounds before a chorus of *phutphutphut* and bullets smashing off the walls drive her back into the front room.

Boots scrape on the wooden floor. She kills the flashlight, drops on her face, rolls onto her back, then sticks the Ksyukha into the bedroom. A shadow retreats into the entry hall. She fires twice into its center. She can't hear any impact; she can't hear a thing except static.

She crawls into the bedroom, using the bed for cover. Risks using the flashlight: nobody here. Up on her feet, fast to the entry hall. Before she can peek inside, the doorjamb disintegrates next to her, spraying her with splinters and chunks of wall. She throws herself between the bed and the back door.

Thunk. Something hard rolls across the floor.

Oh fuck oh fuck oh fuck...

She drags the mattress on top of herself. A thunderclap rattles the room an instant later. Plaster from the walls and ceiling cascades like white rain. The window above her disintegrates. Something heavy lands on her, but she doesn't dare try to see what.

All she can hear is static.

A grenade. A fucking grenade...

She wasn't scared before. Amped, hypervigilant, heart going like a squirrel on speed, but not scared. Now she's scared. The next step is for one or both these assholes to walk in and spray the mattress with bullets.

Carson tries not to breathe. Not to cough, though her mouth and sinuses are full of dust. Make them think she's dead. *I can't hear. I need to hear. Where are they? What are they doing?*

Seconds last hours. Nothing happens. *Where* are *they?*

Finally, Carson manages to wriggle out from under what's left of the mattress and the bed on top of it. Standing takes a lot of effort. Nobody's shot her. Yet.

The flashlight beam shows her a burned hole in the bedroom floor. Plaster scoured off the two walls closest to the door to the front room, exposing the concrete block. Nightstand fragments and the door. Shrapnel holes in the ceiling. The mattress's top is a tangle of tears and blooms of stuffing. The bed saved her. The heavy wooden frame soaked up the grenade fragments that otherwise would've gone straight through the mattress into her.

The backpack with the money is gone. So's the portfolio with the painting. *Fuck!*

She shakes her head clear(ish), staggers into the entry (empty), sweeps the kitchen and parlor. Nobody.

Outside, the Slavuta's empty. *Where's Galina?*

Boom.

It sounds far away but probably isn't. Her ears are still totally jacked up.

Boom.

Not a grenade. Not loud enough. She shines the flashlight into the car. Galina's shotgun is gone.

Gunfire cracks from down the street. Single shots, unsuppressed. Carson lumbers down the driveway and hits the asphalt in time to see the dark box of an SUV pull away from in front of the house two doors down. There's a *thump*. A shape falls away from the right side.

Carson automatically empties half a magazine into the retreating SUV's rear end. It swerves across the road several times before dissolving into the dark.

She tries to run toward the SUV, but the pounding in her head threatens to explode her skull. She slows to a trot. "Galina?" Her throat tells her she's yelling as loud as she can, but it sounds like her voice is a block away.

As she approaches the place where the SUV started, she can see the dark shape that fell away from it. A body, sprawled halfway off the street.

No no no no no no…

"Galina? *Galina?*"

CHAPTER 16

"Please don't let her be hurt." Carson doesn't even know who she's mumbling to. "Please let her be okay." *I don't wanna hurt somebody helping me...again.*

"Here." Galina's voice, dazed.

*No no no...*Carson crashes onto her knees next to Galina, who's trying to push herself upright. The flashlight reveals blood dripping down her forehead, mixing with the blood dribbling from her nose. "You okay? Are you hit?"

"They hit me with their car door." Galina sounds like she's half-asleep. She touches her hand to her upper forehead, then tries to focus on the dark smear on her fingers.

"You are *so* lucky." *Thank God it wasn't worse.* Carson's been hit by a car door a couple of times. It's no fun at all, but it's way better than a bullet.

"Hmpf. Lucky." Galina shakes her head. "It was him. The bandit. I shot the windscreen. There were two men. One carried a backpack and something that looked like that big black thing you had the painting in. He was helping the other one. How did they find us?"

Goddamn Stepaniak. Six hours before the swap and he decides to take everything. He never wanted a deal. *Asshole.* "The backpack and portfolio were from the bedroom. Why didn't you stay in the car?"

"I couldn't let you fight alone. I waited here for them to come for their car. An ambush." Galina squints up at her. "They took your money and your painting?"

"Yeah. They must've followed us from the bar." Or, more likely, followed the tracker. She'd never told Galina about that. Now's not a good time for extreme honesty.

"It's good I took what I did, then." She points toward a low wall screening a house from the road.

Carson skirts the end of the weather-beaten block wall. Behind it, she finds a Halliburton briefcase and a rectangular something wrapped in a plastic bag. "Where'd you get this?"

"From the car. It was behind their front seats. Silly men. They left it unlocked."

She opens the attaché. It's full of €200 notes. A wave of relief washes over the upwelling of doom she felt when she saw that Stepaniak got away with the Cranach and the money. *I can still fix this.* Carson trots to Galina, gives her a one-armed hug, then kisses the top of her head. "You're amazing. Let's get you inside and clean you up."

Carson half-leads, half-carries Galina to what's left of the house. She weighs more than Carson expects, not helpful as Carson comes crashing off her adrenaline high. She sets Galina on a battered wood-frame chair in the kitchen, then props up the flashlight to shine on the ceiling. Galina's first-aid kit is unusually well-stocked.

She quickly surveys the house before she goes to work on Galina. The painting and backpack are definitely gone. A blood trail leads from the side door into the bedroom, then out the back door. Did she shoot Stepaniak or Stas? How badly? How much she should care?

In the kitchen, Carson cleans Galina's head wound. "Quit wiggling." She grabs the top of Galina's head to hold it still. "This beats getting an infection."

"It's not so bad. Don't worry so much about it."

"I'll worry about what I want to."

Galina grimaces as Carson swabs more iodine on her wound. "What will they do when they see we have their painting and money?" Her voice is awake again.

"Louder. My ears." Carson's been asking herself the same question. "They'll be pissed off. Don't know what they'll do with it."

"They shot at you twice? Three times since yesterday? They shot at *us*. That makes me pissed off."

"Me, too." Carson steps back. "There. Butterfly strips should hold it closed enough to scab over. Don't fuck with them."

"Language."

Whatever. Carson sags against the counter. It's almost two in the morning. The day had ended the same way it started—with Stepaniak and his pit bull shooting at her—and she's beyond tired of that shit. The adrenaline's gone. Her brain's processing what happened. She's weak and vaguely sick to her stomach.

This time was different. The first time, at the chicken farm, she can almost buy as Stepaniak's dumbshit way of getting her out of the way. The second time, at Olhynske, was clearly a shakedown, not a hit. This time? They threw a fragmentation grenade at her. The dark and her ability to duck fast are the only reasons she's still alive.

Plus, Stepaniak conned her. He isn't interested in a deal. He wants everything and almost got it. Shame on her for not expecting this and not being prepared.

That's not gonna happen again.

An ache in her hands makes her look down. She's been throttling the thin blue towel Galina had pulled from a duffel when they unpacked.

"Tarasenko?" Galina leans forward, her elbows on her knees, staring at Carson.

Carson's brain is drifting. "Sorry about tonight."

Galina shrugs.

"You did good. We were both lucky. Maybe we won't be next time. I can't risk your life for this money or some old picture. They aren't worth getting killed over."

Galina leans back into the creaking chair, frowning. "You're quitting?"

"No. I'm done with Stepaniak. Bastard tried to kill me tonight. Nobody gets to do that more than once. I'm gonna find him and kill him."

"Good."

"But I'm not gonna risk your life to do it. It's not fair. My fight, not yours. Tomorrow—this morning, I guess—if you help me get a car, you can go home. You'll get your money and live to use it. Okay?"

Galina's eyes try to drill into Carson's head. Her mouth's a pucker. "I want to help."

"I know. Thanks. But…what I asked you to do before was dangerous enough. This is too much. You've seen these guys—

they're not amateurs. We got lucky. Could've turned out way worse for us."

"I understand. It's dangerous." Galina sniffs. "Living here is dangerous. Some Russian shell or bomb could hit my house tomorrow. I could step on a mine in a field." She reaches out to touch Carson's knee with her fingertips. "I still want to help. I know where things are, how things work. These *tarhany* are everywhere here. They made this place the way it is. I want to help stomp on a few."

Carson would rather not be alone when she hunts down Stepaniak. But... "A few years ago, when I was a detective? I had an informant. He fed me amazing stuff. Worked with him for almost a year. Kept telling him, 'You gotta get out, it's dangerous, they'll kill you.' He wouldn't. He had a grudge. He wanted to help put these Russian *mafiya* assholes away." Just telling this story bunches up her guts. "One day he disappeared. I went nuts trying to find him." Long pause; trying to get the words together. *Andrei, I'm so sorry...*"They sent me his head in a box."

Galina grimaces.

"I promised myself I'd never let anybody sacrifice themselves to help me again. Especially when it's just about stuff or money. Haven't changed my mind." She pushes off the counter, looking everyplace except at Galina. "I'm gonna run down Stepaniak and take him off the board. I like that you want to help. I do. But I can't let you. This isn't worth your life."

CHAPTER 17

Carson wakes up slowly. There's an overcast sky outside the busted-out window in the washroom. Her watch says it's past eight, far later than she normally sleeps. She must've needed it.

They'd barricaded the outside doors, dragged the shredded mattress into the mudroom, and huddled on it in sleeping bags. It wasn't an ideal situation, but it was more secure than sleeping in the car and they didn't have anywhere else to go. Carson took the first watch, switching out with Galina at five. She fell off fast and hard. Galina must've let her sleep in.

She's not there now. Carson feels for the other sleeping bag and doesn't find it. *Huh.*

She sits up carefully—her head's still vibrating from the grenade blast—and works out her left shoulder for a minute. That side of her body stiffened up again overnight. Before she turned in, she finally got the Cheata bra off and had her first good look at where Stepaniak shot her: a livid bruise bigger than a bread plate, already turning green around the edges. Nothing seems to be moving under there, luckily. Her ribs may only be cracked.

Carson pulls on her jeans and steps into her boots. The house echoes as she shambles around, trying to kick-start her brain and her body as she brushes the bedhead out of her hair. She's groggy from sleep and lack of sleep.

Galina's not there. The chair that barred the side door is in the kitchen. Rounding up breakfast?

Then she looks at the stuff piled at the entry hall's far end. The briefcase is still there.

Galina's beat-up blue duffel is gone. The car is gone.

The *icon* is gone.

There's a note written in loopy Cyrillic script: *It belongs in a church.*

◎

When she asks a neighbor where the closest church is, he points Carson toward Saint Nikolai on the south side of town. It's about half a block east of Viktoriia, where she and Galina had supper last night.

The kilometer-plus walk helps turn on her brain and unkink her body. She broods about this new fresh hell on the way.

Saint Nikolai is a large, white building with a pair of tall columns flanking the red front doors. No dome. A gilt Orthodox cross and a large icon-like portrait of Jesus loom over her.

Carson's been in Russian Orthodox churches—a couple of weddings (which lasted freaking *forever*, standing up the whole time), a baptism, a funeral—but never as a customer. Her parents were good Soviet nonbelievers, as were most of their friends in Canada. Her mother dredged up her vestigial, long-ignored Jewish heritage to get a rabbi in Kharkiv to vouch for her. It was enough for them to leave the USSR in the '70s when Soviet Jews were allowed to emigrate. Carson sometimes wonders what she'd be like (if she existed at all) had they gone to Tel Aviv instead of Edmonton.

She ties on the navy-blue kerchief she bought as she walked through the market on her way to the church. Then she climbs the four steps, passes between the columns, and pushes through the doors.

She paces through a roomy, softly lit vestibule and a pair of wrought-iron gates into the nave. The space she enters reminds her of cathedrals she's been in: wide, tall, long, lit from above through windows near the ceiling. Like the one in Milan that Matt dragged her into last year, except that one was full of pews and this one has enough empty floor for a hockey rink. Chandeliers full of electric candles hang overhead.

An icon is propped on an ornate wood-and-gilt stand a few steps past the gate. It's the one Heitmann unwrapped at the chicken farm. *That was easy.*

Too easy?

A woman shaped like Galina stands alone at the front of the nave's north half. A simple white scarf covers her head. To the right, near the raised dais at the room's east end, stands a bearded priest in a long, black cassock. There's nobody else in sight.

Carson works her way to Galina. Her black eye and bruised

cheek have colored up since last night. The white headscarf isn't so simple; it's densely tatted lace. Even Carson can tell it's old. Carson hisses, "You stole the icon."

Galina's hands are clasped in front of her. She doesn't look up. "It belongs in a church."

"It belongs in a museum in Bonn. It's their money I'm paying you with." That gets her a scorching look from Galina. "Look, I get it. It means something to you. But the museum's spent a ton of money to get it back. They won't want to hear I left it on the prairie."

"You're too late. I gave it to the church."

"It's not yours—"

"Hush! I'm trying to listen to God." Galina returns to praying, if that's what she's been doing.

Wonderful. Carson watches her for a few moments. What'd she say yesterday? *You always have to do the right thing.* Must be nice to have that kind of certainty. It's nothing Carson's ever had since she crashed into adulthood early and discovered how complicated everything is. "You mad at me?"

"Yes."

"Why? Is it about last night?"

"You want to get rid of me." Galina shoots Carson a wounded look. "All I want to do is help."

"All I want to do is keep you alive."

Galina resumes listening to God.

The priest gives Carson a sour look. Because she's talking? Because he can tell she doesn't belong here? She tries to figure out what to do as she glances around the sanctuary. Broken windows, empty spaces on the icon screen, fraying carpet on the dais. The tiled floor is gently glossy, but that takes muscle, not money.

She passes behind Galina and marches toward the priest. Up close, he's younger than she imagined. There's no gray in his full, heather-brown hair and beard, and his face shows less mileage than hers or Galina's. He watches her like she's a species of animal he hasn't seen before and he wants to figure out if she's dangerous.

"*Otets.*" One of many Russian words for *father.* She has no idea if it's the right one.

He nods. "My child."

Child? "You're not older than me." Should she have said that?

Too late to take it back. "Maybe younger."

An almost-smile. "All the members of this church are my children, just as we are all children of God." He has a good voice for a priest: smooth, gentle, warm.

Here goes. "My friend over there"—she nods toward Galina, who's watching them—"says she gave you that icon back there. Did she?"

The priest solemnly nods once. "Yes, she did. It is a very generous thing to do. It's very old and precious. I imagine you already know that."

"I do. She gets…*confused* sometimes. It doesn't belong to her. Doesn't belong to me, either. It's stolen. I'm taking it back where it belongs." *I hope.*

"I see." He frowns. His palms scrub each other in front of his hips. "If I may ask, where does it belong if not in the house of God?"

This is another time she wishes Matt was here. He'd spin a big line of bullshit and the priest would just hand over the icon and be happy about it. Talking was never her strong suit, and persuading people with words rather than a headlock is way outside her skill set. "An art museum in Germany. Bonn. Somebody stole it seven years ago. They've been looking for it since."

"I see." The priest glances at Galina, then toward the icon, then settles on Carson again. "Tell me…do you think an art museum in Germany is an appropriate home for that precious object? You know what it represents, yes?"

"It's an Annunciation." Good thing she listened to Heitmann.

"Yes. It shows the moment when the Archangel Gavriil tells the *Theotokos* that—"

"The what?"

"The Blessed Virgin. This is when she learns that she will give birth to the Son of God. Can you imagine her reaction? Can you imagine the courage she must have had to accept her part in the most important event in history?"

Carson knows exactly how Mary reacted to waking up pregnant. And did Mary have any choice? Could she say 'no' to the God who destroyed cities and turned people into pillars of salt? This is what she'd been afraid of: that they'd end up arguing theology rather than the real world.

The priest smiles gently. "It is overwhelming, yes? Icons help us focus on the people and events they depict so we can revere them. The icon your friend brought to us will help every member of this church to contemplate the awe and the power of that moment, and the Blessed Virgin's strength and courage then and throughout her life. The people who see the icon in that museum—will they do this? Will they understand what it means? Or will it be a pretty picture to them?"

She knows where this is going. Once they get into philosophy, she's sunk. She needs to keep them rooted in reality. "Doesn't matter if it's appropriate. The museum owns it. If I decide to leave it here, they'll send somebody else to get it. You don't get to keep it."

The priest frowns. Maybe he's not used to people telling him *no*. "Is it right? Is it just? How did the museum come to have this–"

"Doesn't matter. It's theirs. Even if it somehow becomes yours, you know you can't keep it." She points to the screen across the dais. "The gaps up there used to have icons?"

He follows her finger, then nods sadly. "Yes."

"Where'd they go?"

After a few moments, his hands resume scrubbing each other. "There was fighting here two years ago. There were soldiers. Some damage you see happened then."

"Men with guns took them."

"Yes."

Just what she'd figured. "You have any idea how much that icon is worth? How old it is?"

"It is priceless to us."

"Maybe to you. Other people put a price on it." She's going on pure instinct now. Her plan ran out a few minutes ago. "What makes you think more men with guns won't take this one? Want to figure the odds on whether it'll still be here Sunday after next?"

Carson turns when the priest glances over her shoulder. Galina's drifting toward them, looking grim. He turns his attention to the icon screen. "You have a very dark view of the world."

"I've earned it. You take confessions, right? Between that and what happened here, tell me you don't have a 'dark view.'"

"Do you intend to take away the icon?"

"I'm leaving with it. Either you give it to me or I take it, but it's not staying." This probably qualifies as threatening a priest. She ought to feel worse about it than she does. Another reason for God to smite her if She's still in that business.

He turns to her. His eyes have hardened in the past minute. "What do you want from me, then? My *blessing?*"

Galina lands next to Carson. "What are you doing?" She speaks Russian, probably so the priest can understand.

"Trying to fix what you did." Carson stumbles over an idea. She knows bribery; she understands it. Apparently, the people here do, too. She says to the priest, "You said the damage happened two years ago?"

"Yes."

"Why haven't you fixed it yet?" She's pretty sure she knows, but wants him to say it.

"We have made...*some* repairs. The things we had to do, like patching the roof. There's no money for the rest."

Score. "How much would it take to fix everything?"

"Everything?" The idea startles him. He glances around helplessly, then shrugs. "I don't know exactly. Tens of thousands of rubles, I expect. Why?"

Carson slides her fingers into her left pants pocket. They brush one of her wads of cash. "How far would you get with, say, five thousand euros?"

The priest's jaw drops. So does Galina's. She gasps. "That's...375,000 rubles?" Then she whispers into Carson's ear in Ukrainian, "That's not my money, is it?"

"Don't worry," Carson whispers. Now she's about to bribe a priest. Is that better or worse than threatening him? She pulls the sheaf of euros and counts them out so he can see every note. "Will five thousand cover it?"

He watches the euros flash by like it's breakfast and he hasn't eaten in a week. "Why would you do this?"

He's gotta know already. Carson holds the stack of twenty-five €200 notes at eye level. "I give you this so you can make your church nice again. Then I thank you for keeping the icon safe until I could pick it up. Then—"

"No." Disgust crawls all over Galina's face. "You can't do this. It's wrong."

"Yeah?" Carson turns to the priest. "Then I walk out with the icon and take it back to its owners. You lose it a week earlier than you would. Big deal. You get something out of it other than a rifle butt to your head." She fans out the notes so he gets the full picture. "Deal?"

Galina folds her arms hard, grimacing. "I'm not watching this." She grumps away toward where she was before.

The priest tries to keep from staring at the money but can't help himself. "This is…about…more than worldly things." His voice isn't as certain as his words.

She doesn't believe he believes this, or at least that he's not as convinced as he'd like her to think. Still, he's steering them back to philosophy, where she loses. What does she do with that?

Then it hits her: Rodievsky. The Russian *mafiya* boss who owns her soul. She works for him when she isn't working for Allyson (and often when she is). She recalls the things she's seen in his offices and dachas, and in the ones his buddies own.

She tries to run through what she wants to say, but as usual, there's no time. If she doesn't get this right, she may have to take the icon at gunpoint. She doesn't want that; too much can go wrong, and a whole different bunch of people will start chasing her.

"You asked if a museum's the right place for the icon. We could argue about that all day. Here's something I think we agree on. Oligarchs? *Mafiya pakhani?* They love religious sh—stuff. They give money to the church to clean their sins. You know this place's infested with them, right?"

"Yes." The sadness and resignation written on his face show that he knows all too well.

"So word gets out there's a six-hundred-year-old icon here. Some thug gets it. I know these people, I know how they work. You try to stop them, you die. Then it goes on a wall behind some predator's desk. Only people who'll ever see it are other crooks and predators. Think they give a shit about the Annunciation?" *Oops. Too late.* "No. They see millions of euros on the boss's wall. I say that's not the right place for it. Do you?"

The priest shakes his head like it's made of lead. "You have no respect, do you?"

"Neither do they. Difference is, I won't kill you if you get in my way." She holds out the money to him. "Fix your church. Make it nice for your people. Stay alive for their baptisms and weddings and funerals. They need you more than they need that thing." She thumbs toward the icon.

He stares at the money for a long time. He stares toward the icon. He focuses on a window near the ceiling that's partly covered with cardboard. He sighs. "Render unto Germany that which belongs to the Germans." He slides the money out of Carson's hand. "Render unto God that which belongs to God. Take it. Keep it safe." He looks like a kicked puppy.

Should she feel happy or dirty? She'll have time on the road to work that out and probably beat herself up for it. "Good decision." Carson glances at Galina—praying intensely, it looks like—and her gut twists again. "One more thing. Explain to her why this is the right call. She won't listen to me. Take care."

CHAPTER 18

Carson sits on the top step of the stairs leading to the church, enjoying the warmth of the first sun she's seen since she landed in Dnipro on Tuesday.

She feels like a real shit—leaning on a priest so she can take away the most valuable thing in his whole church, maybe the whole town. Even if it isn't his. Even if she doesn't believe in the church thing. It still feels slimy. That's saying something, given the things she's done for Rodievsky.

The icon's wrapped in an old gray blanket. It leans against the wrought-iron railing around the landing. While she knows hardly anything about art, she's aware this isn't the best way to keep the icon safe. She's been staring at Heitmann's phone for the past ten minutes, a call all set up, just waiting for her thumb to start it. Finally, her thumb makes the decision for her.

"Hello?"

She wishes she'd rehearsed this better or longer. "Matt? Carson."

"Um…hi."

"Too late to call?" A ten-hour time difference; it's midnight where he is.

"Usually, but I just got back to my hotel. Where are you? The connection's crappy."

"Ukraine. Where are you?"

"San Francisco. What're you doing there?"

"Working. You?"

"The same." A pause. "Are you okay?"

Meaning, *why are you calling in the middle of the night? Especially when you never call me?* That's why it took ten minutes for her thumb to make a decision. "I have an art question."

"Oooh-kay."

What was that in his voice? Irritation? Disappointment? And why do I care? "Got an icon. It's really old. It's—"

"How old is 'really old'?"

"Six hundred years or so. It's wrapped in a blanket. How do I not ruin it?"

She can hear him sit and sigh. "Wood panel?"

"A slab. It's heavy."

"How did you get it?"

"Never mind. I gotta carry it around. What do I do?"

Another pause. His breathing whispers over the connection. For some reason, that settles her a little. It's a relief to use English again; she didn't realize how tiring it is to speak Ukrainian almost nonstop. Russian's easier for her. More recent practice.

Matt says, "Are you sure you're okay? You sound...I don't know. Down."

He noticed? "Bad situation. I'm tired. Took a round."

"You got shot?" *Shock? Concern?* "Have you seen a doctor? How bad—?"

"Had a vest on. It just hurts. What about the icon?"

"Jesus. You need to worry about taking care of *you*, not *it*."

He sounds like he actually cares. They've been on two agency projects together; they got along pretty okay by the end of the second one. She didn't expect this kind of reaction from him. She'll have to think about what it means, if anything. "When I'm done. For now, what do I do?"

"Okay, okay. This blanket—is it soft? Rough? Dirty? Tell me about it."

"It's old. Clean. Pretty soft. Think it's been washed a lot."

"That's good. It'll help pad the surface. Can you get a plastic trash bag, like one of the big green ones?"

"I guess. Why?"

"Put the whole thing in the bag and tape it shut. Two bags if you can manage it. You need to keep the piece dry—a board that old can warp if it gets wet. The same can happen with big swings in temperature. Does that help?"

The red door opens behind her, revealing a grumpy-looking Galina. *She'll keep.* "Yeah, that's good. Anything else?"

"Don't bang it around. The paint surface will be fragile. How did you get this thing?"

"Long story. I'll tell you later. Um...how're you doing?"

"Okay." It sounds like a shrug. "Just a bunch of things to sort out. I've got a week to renovate a house. It's gonna be intense."

Try getting shot. That's not fair; she'd panic if she had to renovate a house. At least he knows how to do it. "For Allyson?"

"Yeah."

Galina stands on the second-to-the-top step's far end, leans back against the handrail, and folds her arms tight. Her expression's about sucking lemons.

Carson says, "Look, I gotta go. Thanks for the help."

"Call. Check in. So I know you're okay. Okay?"

She hesitates for a moment. He's always been nicer to her than she deserves, though he hasn't hesitated to read her out when she's needed it. This level of concern is something new, though. Not unpleasant, just…different. "Sure. I'll try, but…I gotta go."

"Take care of yourself."

Carson glances at Galina. Whatever she has to say, it won't be nice. Should she try to hold onto the friendly voice a few minutes more? Not without figuring out what she's been hearing the last few minutes. "Thanks. You too." She disconnects, then sighs.

Silence except for the breeze kicking around leaves. Galina's eyes burn holes in her hair. The thing is, Carson doesn't want to fight with this woman. It's pretty inevitable given what happened last night and this morning. *Might as well get it over with.* She wrestles on her poker face and turns to meet Galina's stare.

Galina asks, "Boyfriend?"

Is that what it sounded like? Back to Ukrainian. "No. A guy I know. A…friend."

"I won't apologize."

"Won't ask you to. You did what you thought was right. Wish you'd talked to me first. We could've avoided the whole thing."

Galina watches her feet shuffle. "I still think I'm right."

"Yeah. Well. You lost this one. Move on."

More pickle face. "Last night, you said this isn't my fight. You are wrong. It is."

"Even if it is, I still can't ask you to risk your life for me. It's not fair to you."

"*Fair?*" Galina lunges away from the railing and crosses half the step's length before she pulls up. "*Fair?* Who are you to say that? Is it fair that over a million people had to leave the Donbass because of *kolorady* like those men who attacked us? You come in from the outside, you don't know how anything works around here, and you tell me this doesn't have anything to do with me? You try to throw me away?" There's more heat in her voice than Carson's heard since they met...including when Galina had a shotgun aimed at her head. Galina stabs her own chest with a finger. "*I* get to decide. This is *my* place. *My* home. Besides, I am not doing it for *you*. Yes, I want you to stay alive long enough to pay me. But this is for *me*. Those Makiivka *tarhany*? They owe me, and I'm going to collect. Taking those paintings and that money from them will make them hurt. I want that...for *me*."

Carson sits stunned. She hadn't expected this much raw emotion from Galina. Even harder to take: she's mostly right. Carson never thought Galina's in this for anything except the money. She never asked, either. She's so used to mercenaries that she hardly knows what to do with a crusader.

Galina, yesterday: *You always have to do the right thing.*

She's an idealist. Maybe the most dangerous thing in the world...because you can't change their minds, but they can change yours.

"I'm sorry," Carson says as quietly as she can. All they need is for both of them to get spun up. "Having danger come to you is one thing. Going looking for it is something else. Ask how I know."

"It won't be the first time."

"You need to tell me about that someday." Carson meets Galina's stare. She's never had to work this hard to keep someone from being a bonehead. "You have a husband. You have somebody to live for. What happens to him if you run out of luck?"

"Don't patronize me." Galina glares at Carson. "We both took risks. He's where he is because of it. I am here doing this because of what I did." She aims a determined look at Carson as she points at the icon. "You don't want that to be here? Okay. The priest says it's the best thing. But I will make sure it goes to where you say it belongs. No bandits will get it. I promise that to you. Yes?"

Carson's had a lot of experience with other people's promises. *I promise I'll be home for your championship game. I won't drink a drop before your graduation, I promise! I promise I'll pull out in time. I promise you, I'll treat you the same as the rest of the cadets. Being a woman won't hurt your chances with the promotion board, I promise.*

Yeah. Right.

That's why she decided a long time ago that if she made a promise, she'd keep it, no matter how bad it got for her. Because if she didn't, what was the point? Why say those words?

Can she trust Galina? Will she keep her promise? Will she bug out when things get hard? The stone in her face makes Carson believe she means every word. Galina didn't need to be told what to do last night; she just did it. She could be useful even if she might be a zealot. "If I have anything to say about it, I promise."

Galina edges a couple steps closer, then stops just out of reach. "I still say it belongs here."

"Noted. If you pull a stunt like this again, you're not even getting gas money." Carson slings the icon under her arm. "Might not have far to go. My people say Stepaniak's been stopped just outside town for over eight hours. Let's go find him."

CHAPTER 19

Rogozhkin watches through his binoculars as the Makiivka Brigade's patrol approaches the highway bridge across the Kalmius River. It's not close enough yet for him to hear the vehicles—a BMP-2 and two ancient Zil six-wheel cargo lorries—but for once the weather's reasonably dry and the morning mist burned off nearly an hour ago.

Syrov, the bearded lieutenant in charge of the *spetsnaz* section sent by the 45th Guards, lounges against the tree next to where Rogozhkin stands. "No casualties, sir?"

"If you can avoid it."

"We can." Syrov shrugs. "It takes longer, that's all."

"We're not that pressed for time. We let them go when I'm done with them. Their militia will come looking for them if they disappear."

The BMP's low rumble finally overcomes the river's burbling at the foot of the grove screening Rogozhkin and Syrov. The lieutenant pushes off from his tree and raises his compact binoculars. Then he taps his radio earpiece. "Ready."

Rogozhkin can find only two of Syrov's ten men when he scans the area. The mark of a well-trained team. The lieutenant and his section drove in from Russia through Amvrosiivka last night, took an hour's rest and meal break, and are now ready to capture the patrol without having slept for over twenty-four hours. *Ah, to be young and immortal again...*

The BMP noses past the gravel road about fifty meters east of the bridge.

Syrov touches his earpiece again. "Execute."

Two *spetsnazovtsi* step onto the road shoulders about fifty meters west of the bridge. Each has an olive-drab Klyukva antitank missile launcher perched on his shoulder; both point at the BMP. They're ten meters apart. If the BMP's gunner decides to be a hero, he can shoot only one before the other blows the armored fighting vehicle to bits.

The driver's no fool. He stops in the middle of the bridge, exactly as planned.

In an instant, the other eight *spetsnazovtsi* materialize seemingly out of thin air to surround the lorries. Moments later, the drivers are face-down on the road with their wrists bound by zip ties. The men in the lorries aren't stupid enough to run or fight.

No matter how many hundreds of times Rogozhkin has seen this, it never fails to impress him. *I used to be able to do that.* He still could if his jeep hadn't run over a Serb landmine in Kosovo sixteen years ago.

He steps onto the bridge's west end just as Syrov and one of his men march a militia captain from the BMP to meet him. The captain looks younger than Syrov and his eyes threaten to burst out of his face. His head jerks back and forth as he stares at his three captors. Waiting for someone to cut his throat, no doubt.

Rogozhkin glances at the name tape on the captain's chest, then gives him a paternal smile. "Captain Monya. You've left your neighborhood. What brings you here?" He keeps his voice calm, almost gentle. So many men think yelling shows strength. To him, it shows fear.

Monya swallows and works his jaw a few times until sounds come out. "Ehm, Colonel, I…Colonel Mashkov told me our mission is…secret. Sir."

"I'm sure he did. You *do* know who I am, yes?"

"Yes, sir. I…I've seen you. At the base." The pitch of his voice climbs with every word. At least his Russian is decent.

"Then you should know that Colonel Mashkov has no secrets from me." Rogozhkin steps to within two hands' breadth of the trembling captain. "You being here causes a problem. You're in another militia's area. Did you know that? I'm here to get this sorted before things become complicated. So." He tries another smile, this one cooler. "Tell me why you're here."

"Y…yes, sir. We're hunting a bandit."

"All this"—Rogozhkin waves over the column—"for one bandit?"

"Well, ehm…it's two. Sir. Maybe three."

"Still."

Monya swallows again. "They're…they're the ones who killed

our people in Amvrosiivka."

Finally, something that makes sense about this whole circus. Rogozhkin waits for Monya to give details, but none arrive. "Why did they do that?"

The captain glances at Syrov to his left, then up at the man on his right—the trooper is a good ten or twelve centimeters taller than Monya—then back to Rogozhkin. "Sir…that's the part that's secret. Could we…?"

"Of course. Lieutenant, fall back."

"Sir." Syrov catches the other soldier's eye, then jerks his head toward the BMP.

When both are a few meters away, Rogozhkin says, "We're alone now, Captain. Why did the bandits kill your men?"

"Colonel Mashkov didn't tell you?"

"He gave me an incomplete report. I believe the investigation is still underway."

"Yes, sir." Monya doesn't seem quite as terrified now that the other two *spetsnazovtsi* are gone. *Perhaps he doesn't fear an old man? He should.* "The bandits stole our money, sir. The money for our pay."

Money? That's what this is about? Rogozhkin works hard to mask his sudden flash of anger. *What in hell are they selling to bandits? Weapons? Drugs?* "Go on."

"Ehm…Colonel Mashkov must have told you about the paintings. Yes?"

"Of course." *Paintings? What the…?*

"One of the bandits—Stepaniak, Abram Stepaniak—he was supposed to arrange the swap. The paintings for, I guess, ransom. A lot of money." Monya leans in a bit and lowers his voice. "Two million euros. The colonel was going…"

Two. Million. Euros. Half of Rogozhkin's brain listens to the captain rattle on while the other half turns this figure over and over. The man's right—it's a lot of money to be in the hands of bandits with no accountability.

A *lot* of money.

"Wait. Did you say 'a woman'?"

Monya stops hard. "Ehm…yes, sir. We don't know if she was part of Stepaniak's plan. She came to the meeting with him, but he shot her first. She shot one of his men, the one we captured?

Colonel Mashkov wants to talk to her."

"But she has half the money?"

"Yes, sir. Stepaniak has the other half."

Now this story doesn't make sense again. This woman was shot, but managed to take down a bandit and get away with the money? Unless... *Was she wearing a ballistic vest?* A million euros could be worth getting kicked in the ribs by a mule. Was shooting Stepaniak's man self-defense or eliminating someone she'd have to share the money with?

He's learned a lot from spending so much time in *mafiya* states like Chechnya and Moldova. Double-crosses, gangster politics, ruses, confidence games. A warped and evil world, but a perfectly understandable one. A world that pulls the puppet strings in Moscow now.

"Sir?"

Rogozhkin kicks himself out of his own head. There'll soon be time to consider this. "How do you know where this Stepaniak is?"

"Colonel Mashkov had our comms section put a GLONASS bug in the headliner of his Range Rover. You know what that is, right? Like the American GPS—"

"Yes, I know." A Range Rover. How subtle. No one would ever notice that in a place free-falling into the nineteenth century. "You have a tracker, of course."

"Yes, sir. On my mobile. It's hard to keep up with him—he can travel so much faster."

"And this woman's with him?"

"We don't know yet, sir. She may be."

"I understand." He does, mostly. That much money can cause no end of extreme behavior in an impoverished backwater such as this. It already has. "How many people know about this?"

Monya frowns. "Ehm...I do. Now you." He holds out a hand toward his stalled convoy. "They don't. They think this is for revenge. The money's a rumor back at the base. Why do you ask, sir?"

Rogozhkin's instantly ashamed of how automatically a plan had come to him: kill the captain, send the rest back to base, then take the money himself. He swats it down. *I'm not a gangster yet.* "The more people who know the secret, the more who'll be out looking for the bandits. You don't need more competition."

"No, sir."

What should he do now? The first priority is to stave off more squabbling between militias; they do enough of that without any good reason. "You need to return to your unit's operations area. You can't be found this far into another militia's zone. You surely can't explain to them why you're here. Do you understand?"

The captain looks dubious. "I don't know, sir. I have to talk to Colonel Mash—"

"Of course you do, but not from here. Go back to your own neighborhood, then ring him." Another idea disrupts Rogozhkin's train of thought. It's less toxic than the last one, even somewhat constructive. "I'll need that tracker. My men and I can travel with no restrictions. We'll find your bandits for you."

And the money. *We'll definitely find the money.*

CHAPTER 20

Mashkov desperately wants to kick a chair across the crowded Operations Center. It would be *so* satisfying. But it would also be the talk of the brigade for the next week.

He un-mutes his telephone headset. "Monya. Repeat that. Slowly."

"Yes, sir. The colonel's men disabled our radios. That's why I'm using my *mobilka*." Monya sounds shaken, his voice wavering. Completely reasonable after having been captured by ten Russian *spetsnaz* assassins.

It's good that only he and Vasilenko can hear what Monya's saying. Mashkov might have a rebellion on his hands if the other men in the Ops Center knew what had happened. "Understand. Where are you now?"

"We're on the southern edge of Novokaterynivka, beyond their visual range, I think. What should we do, sir?"

Bloody Rogozhkin. Where does he get the idea he can do this to my *men? I don't care if the bastard's our overseer from Moscovia. This is* my *country,* my *brigade.*

But he holds the purse strings.

No, this is too much. Here, he can interfere all he wants. But in the field…

The other men are watching him. Vasilenko's throttling the other phone receiver. He's heard both sides of the conversation; his face is red and his lips are white. The senior sergeant gets to be openly emotional that way. Mashkov has to channel his rage into orders.

He scans the map of Monya's area on the plotting table in front of him. "Do you still have the target's location?"

"Yes, sir. He's been stationary in central Starobesheve for over eight hours."

"Right." Mashkov traces the local roads with his forefinger. "Continue to the target. Go south on the highway to Petrivske, then west to the T0508 highway, then north to Starobesheve. If the hostile unit interferes with you again, engage. You outnumber them three-to-one. Understand?"

Monya's gulp is clear even on the patchy phone connection. "Yes, sir."

Mashkov disconnects and keeps concentrating on the map so he doesn't accidentally fry the other men with a glance. There's a better-than-even chance that Rogozhkin's thugs can wipe out Monya's troops despite their numbers. If they do, Mashkov will have a clear case for getting Rogozhkin kicked out of the DNR. A costly gambit, but worth it in the end.

"Sir? What do you want to do?" Lieutenant Colonel Shatilov, Mashkov's chief of staff, braces his palms on the table. A good man, and the only Ukrainian left in his senior staff.

Mashkov draws a deep breath. "Send the rest of Monya's company to support him."

"Second Battalion's still preparing for Monday's operation."

"I understand. Get that company ready and on the road. Who's in Starobesheve now?"

"Lev Brigade, sir."

Those lunatics. "Get their commander on the phone for me. Not the radio. It's time we had a talk. The last thing Monya needs is to tangle with our own people."

And they may be as tired of the "guests" as Mashkov is.

Rogozhkin watches through his binoculars as a steady stream of locals come and go through the double glass doors of the blank-faced clinic building a block away.

For all he knows, the bandit's one of them.

They'd found the black Range Rover within a few meters of where the tracker said it would be. The blood on the passenger's seat, the hole in the windscreen, and the ragged rear window confirm it's the right one, not that they had any doubts—fancy Western vehicles aren't exactly common here. Unfortunately, the ute's in such a public place that Syrov's men can't disable it safely. A flat tire will have to do for now.

Two *spetsnazovtsi* in civilian clothes circle outside the clinic, looking for signs of a patient with a gunshot wound. The militia captain's description—black hair and beard, hip-length blue leather coat, and a tall, very thin accomplice—isn't especially helpful.

Rogozhkin's Hunter is parked across the street from some kind of shopping plaza in the heart of Starobesheve, a busy place in late morning. Too busy. He doesn't like being this exposed, having people walk by eyeing the Hunter's Russian military registration plates and wondering why it's here. His kind are used to operating in the dark.

I'll be in the light permanently soon enough.

Rogozhkin sets the binoculars on the dashboard and slumps into the Hunter's front passenger's seat.

He'll be fifty-two in five months. That's like four hundred years old for a *spetsnazovets*. Some days the wear-and-tear makes him feel it. Bullet wounds, knife wounds, that goddamned Serb mine. God knows how many hundreds of jumps out of aircraft. (He remembers a joke an American Ranger told him during an exchange visit: *What three things fall out of the sky? Water, bird shit, and idiots.* So true.) The fights, the falls, the broken bones. Humping full packs up the sides of mountains. Those ungodly winters in Chechnya, miserable even for someone like him who grew up in Siberia. Fighting the endless ranks of Moscow's enemies.

The younger men look at him like he's a dinosaur and wonder why a crippled old man gets to keep wearing the blue beret. Sometimes one will get out of line and Rogozhkin has to show him why it's not yet time for the wolf pack to turn on that crippled old man.

Every time he sees the general, the man says to him, "Edik! I've got a young major, he needs a good command position. Have you thought about retiring yet?"

Yes, he thinks about it. It scares him in a way combat never did.

Now, watching the clinic, another thought runs a circle in his head: *that money.*

A lieutenant colonel's pension isn't what it was after twenty years of budget cuts. Hardly enough to go "home" to Minusinsk, as if he'd ever wanted to see that place again. Nothing close to what he'd need to live in a big city. Certainly not enough to attract a wife. He'd end up alone in a farm town like this with nothing to do except drink himself to death, like so many other old, washed-up soldiers.

That money.

Rogozhkin's mobile vibrates in his chest pocket. It's Yartsev. "Yes?"

"Sir, the situation's getting worse. Mashkov's sending the rest of Anna Company to support the patrol."

He sighs. "We'll watch for them. They'll be hard to miss."

"That's not all. He told Monya to push into Starobesheve. He's doing an end run—he'll be coming up T0508. And...he told them to engage if you stop him again."

"He *what?*" Rogozhkin takes a couple of deep breaths to calm himself. "He's gone too far. Get the Russian staff together. It's time for Mashkov to go. Have Proskurin prepare to take over as brigade commander and get Rostov to send another 'volunteer' to run First Battalion. This insanity has to stop. Understand?"

"Yes, sir. Will you return soon?"

He should. Mashkov's removal would be easier to direct from there. But... "Not yet. We need to stop that patrol before it links up with the rest of its company. And we still have that bandit to dispose of. I'll be back as soon as I can. Just get everything lined up, then hold in place, understand?"

"Yes, sir. I'll have Colonel Proskurin ring you this evening."

"You do that. Keep me posted."

Rogozhkin considers the Range Rover through his binoculars. They should wait for the bandit to appear, take him down, and recover the money. But they need to deal with the patrol, and that will take preparation if it's not to turn into a bloodbath.

The tracker still works.

He takes one more look at the clinic.

That money.

CHAPTER 21

Carson's phone is somewhere inside a two-hundred-meter-radius circle west of Petrivske. According to Olivia, Stepaniak turned it on right before he dumped it. The one building inside the circle—a ramshackle metal warehouse—holds only moldy hay and dead rats.

They stand on the road shoulder near the warehouse, thinking. The two eastbound trucks that pass by don't seem to notice a pair of women hanging out with their weapons.

Carson does a slow 360 scan. Fields to the south and north. A line of trees follows the road's north edge to the western horizon.

Think. Westbound. He's wounded, not driving. Won't leave the SUV. Can't throw far.

She says, "It's under the trees. See the hydro pole down there?" She points to a wooden utility pole about a hundred meters west.

Galina's cradling her shotgun like a baby. "Yes."

"We start there. Walk along the north side of the road in different directions. I'll call my phone. One of us should hear it."

Galina walks west; Carson goes east. She calls her phone every minute or so. There's hardly any traffic; it's just her and the crows and the leftover ringing in her ears from last night.

A fucking grenade? *Why do that?* Wait six hours and she would've handed over the money (well, most of it) in a hot minute.

Unless Stepaniak needs the paintings, too. Maybe the price for the club went up. Maybe he needs to buy a better class of hookers. Whatever. If he's the one she shot, she hopes he's bleeding out somewhere and that it hurts like hell.

A sound makes her stop. Electric guitars, a long way away. Then Bowie singing "Strangers When We Meet."

Her ringtone for an unknown caller.

She charges through the trees toward the sound until it rolls to voicemail. She calls again. It's coming from a broad swath of weeds a hundred meters wide and stretching over two hundred meters north. It's close to the road, though. She might be able to see it.

When the ringtone dies again, Carson calls Galina. "Found it. North of the warehouse."

"Okay."

Carson stalks back and forth along a ten-meter stretch of weeds, trying to locate where the sound is the strongest. Finally she finds it: a flash of blue at the edge of a rough clearing six or seven meters from where she's standing. She's about to plunge into the weeds when Galina's voice shrieks, "Stop! Stop!"

"What?"

Galina pounds toward her like she's being chased, waving her arms. "It's a minefield!" She grabs Carson's shirt and drags her onto the dirt surrounding the trees.

Carson shrugs her off. "How do you know?"

"There wouldn't be weeds if it wasn't mined. And this." She grabs a wood post sticking out of the weeds, revealing a faded triangular red sign on one end. White letters above a white skull and crossbones:

СТОП МІНИ!
DANGER MINES!

Galina pushes the signpost into the damp dirt, then faces Carson with a fist on her hip. "Forget your mobile. We should go."

"Most of my life is on that thing. I want it back."

Galina sighs. "Where is it? Show me." Carson aims her in the right direction and points. "The blue? I see it. Do you see the silver thing next to it?"

It looks like a dull-silver beer can with black lettering. Three black fins on the bottom grab Carson's attention. "What is it?"

"It comes from a *Uragan* rocket. They put many of these on the rocket, then shoot it over here and drop them everywhere. When they explode, they send out metal..." She makes a bomb burst with her hands and fingers. "Russia, Ukraine, both have *Uragans*."

Carson had her fill of fragmentation grenades last night. But her phone's *right there*... "So I won't touch it."

"That's the one you see. They never are alone."

Wonderful. "How do I get from here to there and back?"

Galina wanders off, muttering. She returns with a tree branch that's nearly two meters long, stripping the leaves and twigs. "Use this. Watch." Galina steps to the edge of the meter-tall weeds, grabs the pole's end with both hands, then brushes it through the tops of the plants to bend them out of the way. She points. "See?"

Another silver beer can, wedged nose-down into the ground. "Yeah."

Galina tosses the pole to Carson. "I will be behind the trees."

Do I really need that phone? She wasn't kidding when she told Galina that most of her life is on it. Other than Rodievsky, who calls her on a burner he changes out randomly, everybody she knows calls her agency cell. Hundreds of contacts, more hundreds of photos, her four different payment apps, her banking data, airline tickets, boarding passes, apps for most everything she does. Plus the agency extras: Olivia can find it anywhere, and her call and browsing history gets wiped automatically. Yes, she has a semi-recent backup on her work laptop in Volnovakha (might as well be in Australia), but anyone who picks up the phone will own her. No *way* is she leaving it here for some random asshole to hack.

She gently pushes the weeds back and forth, then steps carefully into the clear areas she finds. The first bomblet she uncovers—right in front of her, half a meter away—makes her jump like she saw a rattlesnake. She edges around it. The morning's still cool, but she's sweating a waterfall. She has to stop every other step to wipe her hands on her jeans.

It takes her almost ten minutes to reach the little clearing. It seems like a year and a half. She stops, catches her breath, then uses the pole to push her phone away from the bomblet it shares air with. One more step. She slowly squats, braces a hand against the ground, then with the other hand scoops up her phone.

The return trip is no easier. The path she took has disappeared. Comb the weeds, check for bomblets, step, repeat.

She uncovers another bomblet on its nose. It wavers, then starts to slide. She screws her eyes shut, waiting for the flash and thunder and the shrapnel tearing through her body.

Nothing.

She peels open an eye. The bomblet rests on a twig an inch above the ground. The twig bends slowly.

Maybe three meters to the minefield's edge. She picks the most open path, takes a deep breath, then sprints. When she hits bare dirt, she throws herself face-down on the ground, panting like she's just run a 10K.

Wham. Fragments cut through the weeds, zip over her head, and knock bark off the treetrunks.

Galina eventually slips out from between the trees and stands watching her, arms folded. "That was the most dumb thing I have ever seen."

"Fuck you very much." Carson staggers off toward the car. She paces a wide circle around the Slavuta while she slams a bottle of water and tries to make her hands stop shaking. Galina's right: it was a dumb thing to do. But now that it's done, she's sure she can run up a mountain…at least, once she catches her breath.

"I found this." Galina drops another cell on the hood on her way to the driver's door.

It's another agency phone, this one in a black case. The glass is cracked. Stepaniak's? Olivia can tell her. That's not her biggest problem right now.

Galina reappears on the car's other side, nipping at a water bottle. They stare at each other for a while. "You must be the most brave person I know, or the most crazy. Maybe both."

"Thanks. I think."

"What do we do now?"

That's Carson's biggest problem. She holds up her phone. "This is how we tracked Stepaniak."

"I know."

"It was here almost nine hours. How far can he get in that time?"

Galina shrugs. "Anywhere. He could be in the West, or near it." She watches the water she's swirling in her bottle. "You shot one. Maybe they're hiding, or in hospital."

"Maybe. Where's the nearest town with a hospital or clinic?"

"Not in Komsomolske?" Galina stares west down the road like she's looking for the answer in the haze. "Starobesheve. Less than ten kilometers from here."

Standing still means losing. Carson hates losing. "Let's go there."

CHAPTER 22

Carson settles into the passenger's seat and closes her eyes once they're on the road again. The thumping in her head has fallen into rhythm with the pulsing ache in her ribs. She can tolerate being a passenger for a change.

Galina's words echo in her head: *he could be in the West.* They'll never catch up to Stepaniak in civilization. The Cranach may be lost to her and probably the museum for God knows how many more years.

She still has the icon and half the money. Is that good enough?

They're close enough to town to get semi-decent cell service. Carson opens WhatsApp to text Olivia. `Need to ask allyson a question.`

`I will relay it.` Olivia never texts contractions and always punctuates.

`Cant get cranach can bring home icon + half cash ok?`

`Please stand by.`

`A says, "I will not pay her for half a project. Make it work."`

Shit. `She really say that?`

`I edited for content and clarity. Have you a reply?`

Does she? Carson's gotten into these wrangles with Allyson before and hasn't won yet. She's always been able to "make it work." Now that she can't track Stepaniak anymore, she doesn't see any way to work it out short of dumb luck or a miracle. That thought makes her headache even more miserable.

After a couple of minutes, Galina squawks and yanks the car onto the rough shoulder.

Carson's head bounces off the headrest. Lightning flashes behind her eyes. "What? What's wrong?" Galina twists to stare out the rear window; Carson follows her lead. A BMP—an olive-drab doorstop on tank treads with a hump of a turret on top—rumbles toward them faster than she thought they could go. Two six-wheeled trucks with canvas cargo-bed covers follow. No wonder Galina got them off the road.

"Are they chasing us?" Galina asks.

"No idea." The BMP swells in the missing rear window. The car shudders. If these guys *are* looking for them, there's no chance of an escape this time.

The BMP roars by in a clatter of track links and squeaking bogies. The Slavuta rocks as it passes, then again when the trucks sweep past. The car fills with exhaust stink.

Carson says, "Guess they're not looking for us. You saw the crests?"

"Yes. Makiivka Brigade." Galina makes it sound like *genital herpes.*

Dumb luck...or a miracle? "Follow them."

"Why?"

"They can track Stepaniak. I think they have a bug on the SUV."

Galina stares at her with a *now you tell me* look on her face. She shakes her head, then jams the car in gear and sets out to catch the militia patrol. The road was rough before, but now it's like driving over a rockslide. Galina waves out the windshield. "This is another reason I hate them. Their tanks tear up our roads."

The vibration's driving long metal spikes into Carson's temples. She drags the first-aid kit from the back seat into her lap while Galina swerves to avoid the worst road damage. She dry-swallows two Zitramon—like Tylenol—hoping they'll kick in before her skull splits open.

Soon they're on the T0508 highway, trailing the convoy by about two hundred meters amid huge, plowed fields. The car's front end shimmies like a hula dancer on speed. Carson's head pounds harder every minute. *Why's the militia in such a hurry? What's changed?*

Galina stomps the brakes, throwing Carson against her seatbelt. The Slavuta fishtails and squeals until it settles with a groan.

The patrol's trucks are herringboned across the highway about a hundred fifty meters ahead. Carson yanks her binoculars from the door pocket and focuses while Galina rolls the car onto the shoulder.

Three men in current Russian camouflage cluster around the end of the last truck, aiming their rifles into the open cargo area. Scared-looking militia troops tumble onto the road with their hands up. The armed men force the militia onto the road face-down, their fingers interlaced behind their heads.

Carson concentrates on the three gunmen: green balaclavas, body armor, Russian load-bearing gear, no patches. Each has two long weapons, a standard AK-74 slung behind his back and the pipe-like barrel of an AS Val suppressed carbine pointing at the militia troops. "Shit. *Spetsnaz*. Russian *spetsnaz*."

"What?" Galina's eyes go round.

Carson can't see much of the lead truck, but it looks like the same thing's going on there. Russians are shoving militia troops off the top of the BMP onto the road. "They're rousting the militia guys. Can't tell if this is an arrest or an execution."

"This makes no sense. Why—"

A trooper from the last truck tries to run. All the Russians turn to shout at him. He makes it to the other side of the road before a Russian, shaking his head, raises his carbine and puts three rounds in the man's back in what looks like one smooth movement. The runner staggers through a few more steps, then falls face-first into the grass along the road shoulder.

Carson peeks at Galina. She looks confused rather than shocked or horrified. *Not the first time she's seen that,* Carson guesses. Not the first time Carson has, either. It always leaves her with a hollow, slightly sick feeling that takes hours to go away.

The *spetsnaz* operators force two prisoners to toss the body into the back of the truck. Then a Russian hurls an olive cylinder bigger than a beer can into the cargo bed; another does the same with the cab. An instant later, twin white flashes pump out a ridiculous amount of white smoke. Within seconds, a fierce white-hot fire swallows the truck.

Carson barks, "Get us out of here. *Now.*"

CHAPTER 23

"Your bitch is coming for you."

Stepaniak, stretched out on a stainless-steel exam table with his shirt off, slews his head more or less in Stas's direction. The pain meds make focusing a chore but somehow don't stop the burning agony in his shoulder wound or the pounding in his chest where Carson's bullet slammed into his body armor. "What...are you...talking about?"

"That Carson bitch. She's on her way here. She's off the highway, probably on farm roads." Stas tosses the phone on Stepaniak's belly.

Stepaniak can barely figure out the phone's screen. A fuzzy red dot crawls over a blurry map. He peers at Stas, who's perched on a stool, looking like a vulture waiting for roadkill. Carson shot Stas in the back last night; now the man moves like he's made of rusted gears. "Your grenade...didn't work."

"Felt fucking great."

He would've objected had Stas told him ahead of time. They already had what they'd come for—trying to kill Carson was unnecessary. "Dear Stas." Stepaniak's voice is like soap bubbles on a breeze. "You have to...end this."

"Fuck that. You should've put one in her brain at the exchange. You made this mess, you deal with it."

"I would. Except..." Stepaniak flutters his hand over the IV tube in his arm, the bandages caking his left shoulder, his wrapped ribs, and his non-focusing eyes. The effort wears him out.

Stas takes a swig from his unlabeled bottle of *malynivka*, Ukrainian home-brewed liquor spiked with raspberries. "How do I get to her? Getting cute doesn't work."

"True." Stepaniak tries to shift, winces, then settles where he was. "You've complained...about my plans. Make one of your own. We...can't use the...Range Rover anymore. The militia...knows it. Try...something else."

Stas grows a predator's smile. "Yeah. I'll get it done. But I want half. I'm picking up your shit, I get paid for it. Understand?"

A surge of heat manages to burn through the fog in Stepaniak's eyes. "Do it first. Succeed first. Then we talk." He glares as best he can. "*Dear Stas.*"

CHAPTER 24

Carson asks, "Should the car make this noise?"

This noise is something like a washing machine spinning an off-balance load of wet towels. It had started this morning on the way out of town but faded away. Carson wrote it off as just another version of the Slavuta's endless racket.

Galina growls "no" through clenched teeth. She returns to urging the car to stay alive. "Come on, baby, just a little farther, you can do it…"

They'd backtracked almost two klicks from the burning patrol before veering off on a farm road that led them deep into dead-flat fields. Luckily, the past couple of rainless days had let the dirt-and-gravel paths dry out. The noise returned after a few minutes of jouncing and hasn't gone away since.

The southern outskirts of Starobesheve are growing large in the windshield when the car starts to buck. The sharp jolting has no rhythm to get used to. Galina switches from baby talk to prayer.

They turn right onto a semi-paved road and hiccup their way through what looks like some kind of industrial farm. Carson's pressed herself against her seatback so she doesn't get whiplash. "Where are you going?"

"To a petrol station. It's less than a kilometer." She pats the dashboard. "Come on, just a few more minutes…"

The Slavuta manages a couple turns while it chokes its guts out. It inches past some kind of truck yard. Then, *bang*. The engine stops instantly. Galina murmurs "no no no no no" as the car coasts another few meters, then creaks to a halt.

They both sit for a few moments, disoriented by the sudden quiet. Galina tries turning the key, but all the starter does is click. She sighs, then rests her forehead on the steering wheel's rim.

Carson looks around. Two red canopies on mustard-yellow columns appear off to their two o'clock about a hundred meters away. "Is that the station?" Galina nods. "Let's push."

Luckily, the Slavuta doesn't weigh a lot. Carson does most of the pushing while Galina steers. They eventually roll into the gas station's forecourt and stop near the minimart. Like most stations back home, it doesn't have a service bay. The car's going to stay broken.

Carson and Galina stand staring into the engine compartment, not expecting to see anything they can fix. Carson asks, "Anyplace you can get this towed?"

Galina shrugs. "There must be. I have to ask."

"Sorry the car died."

"It's a surprise she lasted so long." She sounds resigned, like she's talking about a 95-year-old aunt.

She? "How long have you had her?"

"Years and years." Galina needs a couple of tries to latch the hood shut. She blows out a long breath and runs her fingers through her hair. "Do you have a plan?"

Do I? The original plan had been to get here and follow the militia to Stepaniak. Carson glances south; the plume of black smoke over the patrol is finally thinning. *So much for plans.* "Fix this one, or get another."

Galina's eyes get big. "You would *buy* another car?"

"Why not? We got money. Not getting you a Beemer, though."

"A *pykap?*" The hope in her voice doesn't even try to hide.

"Whatever." Will Olivia let her expense it, or should she use the museum's cash? Or both? Carson lives off her expense account; nearly all her agency pay goes straight to Rodievsky to service her dad's debt. "Where do people here go to buy cars?"

"I will ask." Galina lays a hand on the Slavuta's hood for a few moments, maybe saying goodbye. Then she sets off for the station's minimart.

Carson leans her butt against the fender and scans the highway east of the station. There's not much traffic. A truck lot sits across the highway from the gas station, a handful of flatbeds parked randomly around a scattering of ratty single-story buildings. Just south of that is some kind of farm compound, judging from the barn-looking thing on the north end.

The barn doesn't interest her. The two men in camo standing in the driveway do.

Rogozhkin peers at the sad little blue car through his binoculars. "You're sure this is the one they saw?"

Syrov says, "Reasonably sure, sir. A blue ZAZ Slavuta with body damage and a missing side mirror. Two passengers."

"Two women?"

"They couldn't tell. The car ran south when my men lit up the lorries."

"I see." After burning the militia's lorries and blowing the tracks off the BMP, Rogozhkin and Syrov's men had regrouped in this farmyard. The owners knew better than to object. His Hunter and the team's two Tigrs are parked behind the barn so they won't be too obvious. Syrov had been monitoring the two troops he'd left watching the clinic until one of his men told him about the civilian vehicle that had witnessed the patrol's end.

Rogozhkin focuses on the woman leaning against the little car's front wing with her ankles crossed. Short brown hair, broad shoulders. Big. Not fat, but tall and built for work. Her black jeans fit well. The pushed-up sleeves of her blue polo shirt show off strong, chiseled forearms. A fine physical specimen. But something looks off. He passes the binoculars to Syrov. "Does it look like she's wearing body armor under that shirt?"

Syrov examines her for almost a minute. "Hard to tell, sir. The shirt's loose. I'd expect a woman like that to have bigger tits, but that could be the vest." He hands Rogozhkin the binoculars. "Should I send a couple of men to check her out?"

"Not yet." He scopes her again. Not hard to look at. "There may be a woman mixed up with this Stepaniak. She may be with him or against him. She shot one of his men." He waves the binoculars toward the petrol station. "She looks like she could do that. Keep an eye on her and the other one. Let's see if we need to worry about them."

Carson concentrates so hard on the two Russian troops that she doesn't hear Galina walk up until she says, "There may be a place."

"Where?" The shorter Russian hands binoculars to the other one, then paces into the compound. Carson wants to get her own field glasses but knows these guys might think that's sketchy.

Galina doesn't notice. "On Radianska *vulytsya*. There are two petrol stations next to each other. People with cars to sell sometimes leave them there. The man says it's about eight hundred meters from here."

"Uh-huh." Carson turns her back on the farm to face Galina. "Remember the Russians who burned that militia convoy? I think a couple are in that farm down there."

"Doing what?"

"Watching us. Maybe because we're witnesses."

"If that's so, they will have come to take us by now." Galina's voice is wound tight. She's trying not to look toward the farm but keeps peeking at it. "They may want to see what we do. If the police come here, maybe the *Kacápskyi* will try to kill us so we can't talk."

Carson grumbles, "You're just a ray of sunshine."

A silver four-door sedan turns into the station and pulls up three meters from them. A middle-aged guy with three or four days of shadow opens the passenger's side window from the driver's seat. "Can you help me? I think I'm lost." Russian. Nervous-sounding. Sweating more than the weather can explain.

Galina paces toward the car. "Where are you going?"

The driver licks his lips. "Um… Dokuchajevsk."

"Oh, that's easy." Galina bends and braces her hands on her knees so she can look in the open window. "Go out on the highway going that way, then turn left…on…"

Silence. Then, "Where's your shotgun, bitch?"

Stas's raspy voice.

Carson sidesteps to her left so she can see around Galina. Her hand goes automatically for the pistol stashed in her back waistband.

Stas's head and shoulders take up the bottom half of the open passenger-side rear window. His pistol points at Galina's forehead. He laughs at Carson's move. "Not so fast, bitch. Hands where I can see them."

You piece of shit. She can't draw fast enough to keep him from shooting Galina. Carson holds her hands at hip height, palms down. "Where's Stepaniak?"

"He couldn't come. You fucked him up. Disappointed?"

"Disappointed I didn't fuck *you* up." She could handle Stepaniak; she has no idea what to do with this freak. Her neck and face grow hot. She desperately wants to put a round between this asshole's eyes, but she can't risk a move as long as he's got a no-miss shot at Galina's brain. "Who's your friend?"

"The driver? Some *pizda*. Came with the car." Stas shifts to get a better angle on Galina, who's frozen. "Shut up and listen. The boot's gonna open. Put the money and the icon in there. Try anything, your girlfriend's brains are on the ground."

That's gonna happen anyway. He'll kill us when he gets the swag.

The trunk thunks open.

Carson swaps stares with Stas for a few seconds, then turns on her heel and forces herself to stroll to the dead Slavuta. She needs time to plan how to take out Stas without getting Galina killed.

The briefcase and the icon are buried under all the crap packed in the back. Digging them out will take a while, by design—they want any casual searchers to get tired and give up before they find the valuable stuff. She wants to slow-roll this, not only so she has time to think but also so Stas will get impatient and maybe make a mistake that doesn't involve shooting Galina.

She rummages through the Slavuta's cargo area. "You okay, Galina?"

"Yes." Her voice is almost an octave higher than normal.

"Hang in there. Shit-for-brains there knows if he shoots you, he's dead too."

Stas snarls, "Shut the fuck up. Do what I told you."

"Fuck you, dickless." Carson hopes goading the asshole will make him go after her instead of Galina. She just hopes Galina can move fast. "The grenade was whose idea?"

"Mine. Like it?"

Just what she figured. "I like that it didn't work. Typical."

She shovels the sleeping bags and Galina's duffel into the back seat. The camping gear is next. She hates that Galina's so vulnerable; this is exactly why Carson didn't want her to come along. *Keep him talking. Probably can't talk and think at the same time.* "Hey Stas. You going in on Abram's nightclub deal? Or is he gonna grease your palm and kick you out the door?"

Stas barks a laugh. "When I get this shit you got? The deal's gonna change. I already told him."

That's what you think. Carson finally uncovers the briefcase and the icon. Once she puts them in the sedan's trunk, she loses any leverage she has. She slips a strap of cash—another €20,000—from the Halliburton into the spare tire well, then locks and hauls the briefcase out into the open. "Here's Abram's money."

Stas's eyes zoom in on the case. *"My* money, bitch. That's—"

The driver kicks open his door and throws himself outside.

Stas yells something not-Russian. He swivels and shoots the driver three times in the back.

Galina bolts for the sedan's nose, then dives to the ground.

At least Galina's safe. Carson drops the Halliburton, draws, fires into the back door where Stas's ass should be, then works her way up as she edges toward the sedan from its right rear.

He screams in anger and pain. Shoots wildly out the window.

Carson ducks. He might get lucky. A car door opens on the other side with more cursing from Stas. Then *bangclank.* Gasoline fumes scour her nose. A peek past the trunk lid reveals a stream of gas pouring from the far pump a dozen meters away.

Oh, shit.

The second shot comes as she drops on her face next to the sedan.

Rogozhkin's standing in the courtyard, listening to the gunfire, when the explosion rattles the ground under him. He dashes to the driveway as fast as his leg allows. A fireball stabs thirty meters into the sky.

Syrov's crouched in the open, watching a piece of metal clang onto the road a few meters away. He then turns his binoculars toward a man running—no, more like staggering—from behind a silver sedan toward the petrol station's shop. Someone—a woman, maybe—is curled up in front of the car, covering her head with her arms. A body lies a few meters off its driver's side.

Rogozhkin drops to one knee next to Syrov. "What happened?"

"Someone inside the car shot the driver. The big woman started shooting at whoever did that, probably the guy who just ran.

Then the pump cooked off."

The big woman appears on the sedan's passenger side and chases the man in the camo trousers and black tee. A long, powerful stride, like a bull. *She can run.* Rogozhkin lowers his binoculars. "Secure the area. Take charge of anyone who's still alive. We need to own this place before the locals get here."

Carson clambers over a wrecked, rusty pickup behind the station's minimart and crashes into the waist-high weeds covering the field behind it. Stas is about thirty meters off, hop-running toward the truck yard over a hundred meters away. She finds blood on the ground along the path he's bulldozed through the weeds.

She gains on him quickly. She has only two rounds left in this magazine; the rest of her ammo's in the Slavuta. When she fires, she needs to make sure it counts.

The explosion still roars in her ears, shutting out all other sounds. It's almost as bad as after the grenade last night. If she goes deaf in a few years, she'll know what caused it.

Stas twists and shoots twice in her general direction. She drops on her face. When she does, she comes eyeball-to-eyeball with what looks like an olive-drab hubcap.

Galina, this morning: *There wouldn't be weeds if it wasn't mined. Oh, shit.*

Her heart needs a few moments to restart. She carefully edges away from the mine, stands, then picks her way to the beaten-down weeds where Stas has been. *He hasn't blown up yet. Safe enough.*

Stas gained a few meters, but he's slowing and his stride is getting choppier. He fires one more time at Carson. His pistol's slide locks back: out of ammo. He'll have more in the patch pockets on his trousers. She needs to end this before he reloads.

She closes to within fifteen meters. Stops. Aims. Puts one round between his shoulder blades, dead center. He's wearing a vest, but that's gonna Hurt. Like. Hell. He flops forward into the weeds. It takes only a few seconds to catch up with him.

Stas is trying to turn over: knees braced, one hand on the ground, his gun hand swinging toward her. His face and hands look like he has world's worst sunburn, probably from the gas pump explosion. Carson kicks the Grach like a rugby up-and-under, sending it arcing into the distance. Stas crashes onto his back with a yelp. A green hubcap nestles against Stas's side.

Carson says, "You were on a mine."

His grimace becomes a smirk. "Antitank mine." The pain mangles his voice. "Not heavy enough…to set it off."

Good to know. She lets Stas waste energy trying to sit up, then plants a foot on his sternum and shoves him down. "Where's Stepaniak?"

"Fuck you."

She squares her pistol's sights on the center of his forehead. "Those your last words?"

He chokes out a "heh," then spends some time failing to catch his breath. "Why do you care?" His Russian's disintegrating; she can barely dig the words out from under his accent.

"He's got something of mine. Also, the bastard tried to kill me. Where is he?"

"Gone."

"Fucking *where?*"

Stas stares at her through a scrim of pain. "Why should I tell you?"

"Because I'm taking him off the board. What you were gonna do. What he's gonna do to you when you bring him the swag. Want him to win? Keep jerking me around."

They glare at each other for a few moments. He pants, "You gonna…let me go?"

"Sure. As long as you go back wherever the fuck you came from." She can't tell if he believes her and doesn't really care. It's not like he has any options.

More glaring. "Stole a car for him…UAZ Patriot, green…He's going to Donetsk. Get lost in the city…then cross over."

"Where in Donetsk?"

"Didn't say. Friend of his."

"When'd he leave?"

"Hour ago."

If this is true, Stepaniak's got a head-start on her that'll be hard to make up even if she had a car. She'll never find him once he hits the city.

Stas grunts. "Get off me. You shot me…in the ass."

Carson removes her foot from his chest. "Could be worse. Could've shot you in the balls." She watches him fail to get comfortable. "After the grenade, why didn't you finish me off?"

He manages to laugh. "Thought the…the grenade got you. We had…better things…to do."

Not mercy. She'd been debating what to do with him. His answer helps her decide. "Remember when I said I'd let you go?"

"Yeah."

"I lied."

CHAPTER 25

Carson searches Stas's body for anything useful. She tries to avoid looking at his head. On her two wet jobs for Rodievsky, she'd used a suppressed .22: a small *pop*, a neat round hole, no exit wound, little mess. This time was...different.

Pulling the trigger felt powerful. He'd tried to kill her; he got what was coming. That feeling lasted about five seconds. Now her stomach's tying itself into elaborate knots and a sour taste coats her mouth.

She finds two extra magazines for Stas's Grach, now lost in the weeds. She loads the cartridges from one into her pistol's empty magazine and slips the other in her hip pocket. Then there's the nearly five hundred euros Stas doesn't need anymore, and the brand-new iPhone. A telltale big, juicy thumbprint on the screen makes her try pressing his thumbs in the same place until the left one opens the phone. She quickly resets the password and TouchID, then rummages.

An open app shows an OpenStreetMap view of the gas station and highway behind her. A red dot pulses over the gas station. That clinches it: the bug is in the icon. She'll dig it out as soon as she gets back to the petrol station.

When she zooms out, she finds another red dot on a highway leading to Donetsk.

She plots her next moves as she follows the trail of crushed weeds to the station, keeping her eyes glued on the ground to spot mines. When the weeds thin out and she can walk with some confidence, she looks ahead.

Two men in Russian camo stand at the asphalt's edge, watching her from about ten meters away. She stops a few meters from them. The one on the right is nobody—a standard-issue *spetsnaz* grunt with a helmet, tactical vest, and a suppressed carbine aiming her way.

The one on the left is shorter, older, quieter. Swarthy, Asian eyes, bristly black hair graying fast. No field gear. His pistol's holstered and his thumbs are hooked on either side of his belt buckle. Rolled-up sleeves show ropy forearms. His shoulder loops say he's a lieutenant colonel, but even without that clue, she'd have bet he's the one in charge.

They stand staring at each other for some moments. She finally says, "*Shto?*" Russian for *what?*

The colonel's eyes finish one more up-and-down scan of her. "Do you know an Abram Stepaniak?" His voice has as much mileage as the rest of him.

She could lie. But if they have Galina, she may have already told them: not a good way to start. Whose side are they on? They're obviously not backing the militia. But who knows what that means? Anything she says could get her killed.

Carson settles on, "Unfortunately." *Which one will shoot me?*

The colonel nods. "We should talk."

"You're...*who* exactly?"

"This is a conversation best done sitting." No heat on it, just a fact.

The grunt searches her roughly, takes her pistol and the knife strapped to her calf—she knows better than to fight him for them—then zip-ties her wrists behind her. The moment the plastic tightens, a familiar bolt of panic streaks out of Carson's gut into her ape brain. She hates—*hates*—not being in control, not being able to act, not being able to fight back.

The grunt pushes her along behind the colonel to a pumped-up brick of a vehicle wearing mustard-olive-and-black camouflage parked next to the silver sedan. A GAZ Tigr, the Russian Army's answer to the Humvee. At least half a dozen *spetsnaz* troops hold down the gas station's perimeter, ready for action. The pump fire's out, but a billow of smoke still blows across the highway. The stench of burned plastic makes her stomach even angrier with her than it was.

She checks the minimart. Galina sits on the curb next to two guys Carson had seen inside, their hands tied behind their backs. A Russian covers all three with his AS Val. Galina and Carson exchange a glance, then Galina looks away.

The colonel opens the Tigr's left-hand rear door. The grunt essentially throws Carson into the cargo compartment. She struggles onto her knees, fighting hard to control her breathing and to avoid grinding her teeth into dust. Then she levers herself into the middle of three tan jump seats lining the Tigr's side behind the driver's seat. The colonel takes the middle one on the facing side. The grunt slams the door shut.

"I am Rogozhkin." He leans forward, folding his hands between his knees. "What do I call you?"

Names are hard. If she uses her cover—Lisa Carson—she sets herself up to be accused of being a foreign spy. She can't pass for a local. If she uses her real name, she'll have a hard time playing the talk-to-my-embassy game if she needs to later. Also, a local name might tag her as a fascist spy from Kyiv and get her buried. Nothing has a clear upside.

She covers her hesitation by trying to find a not-painful way to sit. With her hands and arms behind her, she has to perch bolt upright on the seat's front edge. That's their whole point—keep her awkward and off-balance. She still doesn't know whose team this guy's playing for.

Finally, she picks the least bad answer. "Tarasenko."

"Who did you kill in that field?" Rogozhkin says it like, *Why did you wear that shirt today?* His Russian carries a provincial accent that Carson can't place.

What Yurik taught her about *spetsnaz* interrogation techniques makes her decide to be cooperative without considering whether she has any other options. Having made that decision, she's not as scared as she probably ought to be. "One of Stepaniak's goons. Stas."

"Why?"

"He tried to kill me last night."

He nods. "Why?"

"I had something he wanted."

"I see." It's busy behind his eyes. "How do you know this Stepaniak?"

"We work for the same company."

Rogozhkin's eyebrows shoot up. She must've surprised him. "Company?"

Carson explains the money-for-art deal with as little detail as she can get away with.

The Russian grinds this over for a moment. "This Stepaniak

killed everyone except you."

"He shot me, but I'm wearing a vest. Ever take a round while you're wearing ballistic armor?"

"Yes. It's very painful."

"Got that right. I took down Vadim to find out about Stepaniak's plan. Left him for the militia. I took the other picture and the rest of the money."

"Why did you take the money? It belongs to the Makiivka Brigade."

"Thought I might need it to buy the picture from Stepaniak. I don't care who gets the cash"—not entirely true; she's still trying to work out a way to keep it—"but I need to get the pictures back to the museum. It's why they're paying my company."

The colonel leans back into his seat and crosses his arms. He peers at her, pursing his lips. Maybe trying to figure out if she's telling the truth. Then he opens the rear door, murmurs to the grunt standing guard outside, and watches the man jog toward the Hunter blocking the south driveway.

In a movie, Carson would saw through the zip tie with a car key, whack Rogozhkin over the head, take his sidearm, rescue Galina, and fight her way out. In real life, she'd never make it out of the Tigr. She sits and watches the grunt haul the silver Halliburton from the Hunter and bring it to the colonel.

Rogozhkin sets it on his lap. "Is this the money?"

"If that's the same briefcase I've been hauling around, yeah."

He tries to flip the latches, but can't. "The combination?"

She'd locked it before she pulled it out of the Slavuta, just to pull Stas's chain. How much does Rogozhkin know about what happened at the chicken farm? Some things she'd told him surprised him. Maybe the kid she'd patched up died. Maybe the Russian hasn't talked to the kid, or to Vadim if he's still alive.

Holding out is a risk. But she has no leverage if he opens that case now. "Sorry. The German from the museum? He had the combo. I just carried the things. Security."

Rogozhkin frowns. He sets the case on the floor between them. "I don't believe you. How would you pay Stepaniak if you can't open it?"

"Don't know. Crack it with a pry bar or something. Then carrying it is his problem."

More peering. She can picture him with readers when he's alone. Then he rocks out of his seat and quietly sits next to her.

His nearness startles Carson. He's been civilized up to now, but how long will that last? Her hands are tied, Rogozhkin's armed, and the grunt's right outside; she's way closer to defenseless than her ape brain can tolerate.

Suddenly his elbow's on the back of her neck. He shoves her face between her knees, grabs her wrists, and pushes her arms almost straight up behind her. He growls, "Make me believe you."

Fuck! She stifles the half-scream fighting to get past her throat. The pain in her shoulders shoots straight into her brain. She'd expected a pistol muzzle in her ear, not this, even though Yurik had taught her this very move.

Don't show weakness. Don't show fear. They smell fear.

"Don't make me wait." Rogozhkin's voice has gone low and quiet.

Carson tries to take a deep breath, but being bent double makes that impossible. She wrestles with her rising fear while she tries to steady her voice. "Twist my arms off if you want. Answer doesn't change."

He pushes forward on her wrists a touch farther. She tries to relax as many muscles as she can so her own resistance doesn't add to the pain. It's hard when her shoulders are spasming.

Then he lets her go.

The end to the pain is almost erotic. Carson slowly sits up, then tries to roll out her shoulders. It only sort-of works. She glares at him. "Why'd you do that? I'm being straight with you. I'm cooperating." She hates how thin and wobbly her voice has become. At least she's not screaming.

Rogozhkin stares deep into her eyes. As close as they are, in other circumstances they could end up kissing. Now he's trying to open locked doors in her head. "Our prisoners are usually terrified of us, but you're not. Why is that?"

For once, Carson takes a moment to put together an answer she hopes won't have him use more stress positions on her. "I understand you. You're pros. You have a job to do. So do I. Don't make it complicated."

The colonel considers this. After a very long few seconds, he calmly returns to his seat. "What was your plan for coming here?"

"Follow the militia patrol. They can track Stepaniak's SUV. Could. What's your beef with the militia? Thought you own those guys now."

Another smile, one cold enough to make her suppress a shiver. "We can track him, too. He's in a clinic in the center of town."

Except he isn't. Should I tell him? "Who are you? Where do you figure?"

His dark-brown eyes resume rifling through her brain. "The woman out there, by the market." He waves toward the minimart. "Who is she to you?"

Nice dodge. "You first."

Rogozhkin's eyes get a few degrees colder. "We asked her, but she wouldn't say anything except her name. We can apply more pressure. It would be unpleasant for her, but we're good at getting information."

Carson's surprised it took so long for him to drag Galina into this. "I answered your questions, right?"

"Have you?"

"Sounds like it to me. We don't have a problem, you and me. You know why I'm here. I'm confused about why you are. If I know, maybe I can tell you things that'll help you."

"Such as?" An eyebrow arches.

"I don't know. I don't know what you want. Help me help you." Yurik had told her that even though *spetsnaz* operators learn torture, they'd mostly rather have captives tell them intel without it. Torture wastes time and isn't always effective. He also said some guys get off on it. She hopes this Rogozhkin isn't that way.

Rogozhkin stares at her the way a statue would. He doesn't move or blink or even breathe hard. Just the look makes her shoulders twinge. This goes on way longer than Carson likes. She fights hard to not blink or shift in her seat, but soon all she can think of is how dry her eyes are getting and how uncomfortable the seat is.

Then the colonel chuckles and shakes his head. "Fine. I belong to a liaison group. We're a conduit between the local militias and my army. We also have to keep peace between the militias. That patrol was outside its assigned area—we had to make an example of them. Does that tell you what you need to know?"

What he described sounds bureaucratic enough to be truth-adjacent. Carson's also pretty sure that's the best she'll get from him. "Galina's my guide. I'm paying her. That's her car." She nods toward the little dead Slavuta. "She knows just enough to be helpful. She doesn't like Russians much."

"That's not unusual."

She pushes the puck down the ice a bit more. "I get the part about keeping peace between militias. What do you want with Stepaniak?"

"As you said, he killed several Makiivka Brigade members. They want…closure. We can do that more efficiently and without causing as much trouble." He sits straight and plants his palms on his knees. "So. How can you help me?"

Decision time. Carson gazes out the rear window at Galina while she thinks. Given what she knows about the *spetsnaz* in general and their doings here in particular, she won't underestimate them. Rogozhkin won't let her or Galina go unless it benefits him. She doesn't know what happens to Russian prisoners here and doesn't want to find out.

That means doing a deal with Rogozhkin.

She doesn't like that option. She'd have even less control than she does now. She and Galina could still end up face-down in a ditch once the Russians get what they want, whatever that is. But if she tells them to fuck off, that's what'll happen anyway, just sooner. Probably after a lot of pain.

It's not the first time she's had to make a decision like this. Not that that helps.

She turns to Rogozhkin. "Untie me. Let's talk like grownups."

CHAPTER 26

Carson isn't surprised by the disgusted look on Galina's face.

"You want to do *what?*"

"It's not about *want.*" Carson pulls her closer to the Slavuta. "It's about not ending up like that poor bastard they shot on the road back there."

Galina gets in Carson's face. She has to go up on tiptoes to do it. "No. No deals with the *Kacápskyi*. Those people caused all this. They tried to take my country away. *No.*"

"Keep your voice down!" Carson hisses. "I went out on a limb for you. Know what happens when you say 'no'? They take you and those two guys and shoot you all in the back of the head. Then you go in that dumpster over there. *Then* they throw in a phosphorus grenade. There won't be enough left to fill a shopping bag. This is *not* a deal we get to say 'no' to. Understand?"

Galina stands there shaking, her face glowing red, her folded arms threatening to crush her ribcage. "How dare you do this without asking me?"

For fuck's sake... Carson takes a few breaths before she accidentally removes Galina's head. She leans in to stab Galina's collarbone with an index finger. "You notice me getting shoved into that fucking jeep over there? See me with my arms bent backward? These assholes aren't good about taking prisoners. They're not set up for it. Before they take off, they're gonna clean up this mess. That includes killing *you* if you're not with me. Got it? Questions?"

They stand like reflections, arms crossed, grimacing, staring daggers at each other. Galina says, "Sometimes you make me hate you."

"Join the club."

"We need a car."

Carson thumbs toward the silver sedan. "The Škoda."

They transfer the Slavuta's load into the Škoda Octavia. The taillights and rear window are cracked from the explosion. Carson wipes Stas's blood off the back seat. The entire operation takes less than ten minutes and happens without either of them saying a thing to the other.

Rogozhkin finishes with a *spetsnaz* lieutenant and stands by to watch the women work. He catches Carson's arm. "You understand that if you break our deal, my men will eliminate you. Yes?"

Carson stares at his hand on her bicep until he removes it. Then she stands straight—she's two inches taller than he is—and glares down at him. "If you break our deal, we're gonna have a problem. Yes?"

He gives her an iceberg smile. "Of course."

The Octavia is newer and nicer than the Slavuta. Plusher seats. Other than the wind whistling through the bullet holes Carson punched through the right-rear door and window, it's a lot quieter.

Still, Galina keeps fiddling with the mirrors and driver's seat, grumbling while she fiddles. She steers like she's still driving the Slavuta even though the new car handles much better. They veer across the road whenever she tries to avoid a pothole or impact crater on the T0509 highway. There are a lot of them.

Carson keeps her eyes on the pulsing red dot over Stepaniak's location on the tracker. He's approaching Mospyne, a city that looks about the same size as Starobesheve. From there it's only around fifteen klicks to the eastern suburbs of Donetsk.

Carson and Galina are supposed to lead Rogozhkin and his cutthroats to Stepaniak. Carson will use the money to lure him out of whatever hole he's in. When he's in the open, the Russians will kill him. She gets the painting he's carrying and a day to get across the contact line. Galina gets to go home…if she still wants to.

The icon's resting face-down on Carson's lap, padded by the folded blanket. She probes the back for the tracker chip using the tip of the tactical knife she'd taken from Vadim.

Galina glances at her, then smashes her lips in irritation. "Do you *have* to do that now?"

"Tired of being a target. You?"

"You'll ruin it."

"Learn to steer." It's been like this since they left the gas station. Galina's been winding up tighter with each klick they cover. Carson hates this, but it's something Galina's got to work out for herself.

She checks the tracker. "We should be coming up on Osykove."

"I know."

Carson glances outside. The last village had featured a number of ruined buildings and a lot of pockmarked walls. Now the road's flanked by trees, many of them stumps or splintered trunks. The trees give way to fields and a rusted, burned-out Russian tank near the road.

They pass a blue-and-white sign: "Осикове." Houses appear on either side of the highway. More ruins, more punctured metal gates, more gouges in the brickwork and concrete block. The scorched hulk of a civilian car lies half-buried under a collapsed carport next to a gutted house.

Carson says, "Take the next left."

"*I. Know.*" It's a low growl. Galina's face has turned to weapons-grade steel.

Carson expected anger, silence, snapped-off words; now she's got them. "Look, Galina, I'm sorry. I know you hate this deal, but—"

"Not that."

"Then…what's wrong?"

"You don't understand."

"No, I don't. Tell me, what's wrong?"

Galina stomps the brakes. They squeal to a stop. Her eyes are locked straight ahead. "This is where I died."

CHAPTER 27

Galina squinted through the smoke and haze from her foxhole in a knot of trees on the southern end of Chervonosilske. She had the PKM machinegun's sights lined up on the closest dark figure heading toward her from about a hundred fifty meters away.

Valya, sharing the foxhole with her, fired his AK at these new enemies, trying to keep their heads down. That worked with the *kolorady*, but not with these people. His eyes were red and his hands shook when he reloaded. Galina wasn't in any better shape. Like the rest of the battalion, they'd been awake for over three days and under fire for almost all of it.

The enemy started shooting at them, little pops like firecrackers. Their bullets zinged overhead or sprayed dirt in their faces. Galina wiped her eyes, sighted in on the lead figure, then squeezed the trigger for an instant, just as Valya had taught her in about thirty seconds when she arrived the night before. The figure folded in on itself and fell.

She pivoted to the next enemy. This burst missed. She fought the temptation to mash down the trigger and try to saw the *Kacáps* in half. Fire too long and the barrel overheats.

Someone thudded into the foxhole between them, jostling them both. Valya swore and shoved the person into Galina, spoiling her aim. She rounded on the intruder. "Who do you—"

"Galya?" It's Lyudmilla, a fellow lorry driver. "Where have you been? Why are you here? Bohdan's going crazy looking for you."

Galina stared into her friend's dirty face for what seemed like an eternity before finally trying to crush Lyuda in a hug. "Why are *you* here?"

Lyuda tried to hand her a full canteen and a slice of stale bread. Breakfast. Galina turned her toward Valya. "He needs it more."

She took a few more shots at the *Kacáps* while Lyuda tried to force Valya to take the food. When Galina reloaded, her hands trembled like she was eighty.

Another shell landed thirty meters or so behind them. The artillery and mortar fire hadn't stopped since the column got bogged down here midday yesterday. Burning houses, burning vehicles. What was left of Kostya, the man whose machinegun she used, sprawled on his back two meters to her left. He was starting to bloat.

Lyuda slapped Galina's helmet. "Get out of here! The battalion's moving out! Bohdan needs you to drive!"

She should go, but she didn't want to. True, she was a driver, not a soldier. *But we need soldiers...* "Cover me!"

She scrambled out of the foxhole and sprinted, zig-zagging, back into town, holding her helmet tight on her head. Another shell jolted the ground under her. She fell, then curled into a ball and covered her head as shrapnel slapped through the sheet-iron fence above her. It sounded like rain. *O, Bozhe. O, Bozhe. Budlaska, Bozhe...* She heaved herself onto her feet, then dashed north faster than she'd ever run before.

Not yet six. The sunrise scoured the horizon. The glare would be in the Russians' eyes. That may be why the small-arms fire was still thin and ineffective, and why the snipers hadn't had a go at her.

She stumbled into the small grove of trees at the road's north end. The command tent was to her left. The major, haggard, his head wrapped with a bandage, argued with his platoon commanders at a table dragged from the nearby farmhouse. She hurried past to the lorry carrying their last supplies.

Anton tossed empty crates out the back of the cargo cover while two other men—not from the battalion—heaved them to the side.

Galina stopped, pulled off her helmet, then caught her breath. "Anton! Where's Bohdan?" He waved vaguely to the east. "Thanks."

She trotted down the line of lorries—their last—until she found a knot of ragged men huddled in the trees. They were dirty, bloody, exhausted. She knew over half of them. *This is what's left of our army.* Her heart broke for the fiftieth time since yesterday.

So much had changed in two weeks. Her unit, the Donbass

Battalion, had fought its way into Ilovaisk on the 19th, part of the big offensive that was supposed to surround Donetsk and cut the terrorists off from Luhansk. They took the city. The terrorist militias were falling apart. Their men were dropping their weapons and leaving their uniforms in the streets. The patriots had *won*. Ukraine had *won*.

Then the Russian Army came.

Her husband directed the troops loading the wounded onto a lorry. *Bozhe. More wounded.* Her lorry, as it turned out, a big, snorting, six-wheeled Zil that cornered like a train engine on rails. Her tractor was more maneuverable.

She watched him work. Her handsome husband. Well, *she* thought he was handsome. Then again, he thought she was pretty. Maybe they were both crazy. He looked so confident, barking orders, pointing, urging the men on. She was so proud of the two chevrons on his shoulder straps. A junior sergeant, and after only three months!

Gunfire sputtered to the east: the woodpecker chatter of rifles, the thumping of heavy machineguns. Russian paratroopers trying to cut them off from the road home. She ran to Bohdan and threw her arms around him.

He squawked, then crushed her against him. "Where have you been? I was so worried…"

"I was taking food to the men on the line. One of the gunners was dead. I jumped in just for a few minutes until someone else could come and they never—"

His eyes got big, showing her how bloodshot they were. "That's dangerous! You could've been hurt."

Another shell screamed in. This one would be close. Everyone standing crouched. She dragged Bohdan next to the lorry's big rear wheels and pulled him down just as the ground jolted with the explosion. Something clanged into the lorry's cab. Galina grabbed the front of Bohdan's shirt and hauled him close to her. "What did you say? Too dangerous?"

He smiled and kissed her hard. His four days of black beard scraped her face, but she didn't mind; she was filthy and her mouth tasted like pig slop. Then he jumped back to work.

She listened helplessly as the gunfire grew louder and closer. She tried to help with the wounded but couldn't do much more than hold their hands and wipe the blood out of their eyes. Then Bohdan had two men swing the tailgate closed. She heard his voice crackle over the radio clipped to her shoulder. "Loading's done. Head out." Lorry engines roared awake up the line.

Bohdan met her halfway to her cab. They fell into another hug. She said, "Come with me."

"I can't. We have to hold them back so the convoy can get out."

"No!" She pulled away to glare at him. "You can't! You have to come, too!"

"No." He pulled her close. "You have to get out of this mess. Get on the road, drive like hell. Their artillery can't target you if you keep moving." He kissed her. "I love you."

"I love you!" She kissed him desperately. He boosted her into the lorry's cab. She roused the beast, then leaned out the window toward him. "You come back to me!"

The last time she saw him, he was waving in her side-view mirror.

The Russians shot at them the moment they cleared the village. The BTR escorting the convoy fired almost nonstop until a rocket blew off its turret. She watched, horrified, as burning men tumbled out and writhed on the ground. Bullets thudded into the sides of her lorry.

They crashed through Volodarskoho while the Dnipro-2 Battalion streamed fire into a treeline a few hundred meters to the south. Mortar bombs burst on either side of her. She screamed at each explosion until her voice guttered out. A smoky finger reached out from the trees and slammed into the lorry three places ahead of her. It disappeared in a flash and a billow of orange flame. She swerved around the wreck. The driver flailed in the cab, burning. Misha, a friend. She prayed harder than she ever had before and kept the gas pedal flat against the firewall.

Smoke scoured her lungs, watered her eyes. Her shoulders screamed.

The reservoir at Osykove's eastern end slid by on her right. She glanced to her left: Russian armor streamed west half a kilometer away. Trying to cut them off. Trying to kill them.

Please, God. Help me get these poor men home. Please don't leave us out here to die...

Houses to her left hid her from the Russian tanks. She was safe for a moment.

The lorry ahead of her suddenly veered to the left, blasted through a block wall, skimmed a massive tree and flipped on its side. Wounded men spilled out the back like sacks of wheat as she flashed by.

Then with a burst of searing agony, her world went black.

CHAPTER 28

Carson holds Galina, patting her back, repeating "Let it out, let it out" as Galina bawls into her shoulder. Carson's never been good at dealing with crying people. When she was substitute mom for her three younger brothers, they rarely if ever let anyone see them cry. She never could. It was more a wolf pack than a family.

So she rocks Galina and feels her back spasm with each sob and tries to dredge up something to say that isn't impossibly sappy or cliché or stupid. Nothing comes to her.

Galina eventually pulls away. Her face's red and puckered, her tears running down her lips and chin. She grabs a rag she'd transferred from the Slavuta to the Octavia's glove box, wipes her face, blows. Her shoulders still shudder. "Sorry." Her voice is tiny, almost lost.

"Don't be. You needed that."

She huddles in on herself, her hands squeezed between her thighs. She stares across the highway at a big, leafy tree in front of a quiet farm compound, unremarkable except for the huge barkless gouge on the eastern side of its trunk. "I ran into that tree."

"You were hit?"

"Yes. There was a sniper. His bullet went through my helmet and cut across here." She runs her right index finger from front to back along the right side of her head above her ear. "Just a little bit over and..." A mammoth sob hits her so hard, Carson's afraid it's the prelude to a barf. "I fell over on the seat. He checked on me. Or someone did. I guess he thought I was dead. There was so much blood." Her face dissolves again. "They were with the Makiivka Brigade. They shot...shot the wounded men...in my lorry..."

Carson collects her and lends her an absorbent shoulder again. She'd been through some bad times, but nothing like this. *How would I make it through this? Would I be a drunk by now? Eat a bullet?*

She strokes Galina's hair. *Who'd pat my back?* Bo, maybe—her older brother Boris—but even he's a little scared of her.

Galina cries herself out. She slumps in the driver's seat, staring at the green winged-arrow logo in the steering wheel's hub, looking like she shrank in the wash.

"How'd you get away?"

"I woke up and wandered." Galina snuffles. "A nice older couple found me and took me to their home. He used to be an animal doctor. He sewed my head together. When the 'authorities' came–"

"'Authorities'?"

"The DNR so-called *government*." She sneers the word. "Criminals. Always with their hands out. They make Kyiv look honest. The people who rescued me, they told the gangsters I was their daughter and I was sick. I stayed with them for a month. Then they took me back to our farm."

Carson waits in case there's more, but there isn't. "Want to visit them? Since we're here?"

"I would like to." She points back the way they'd come. "They live back there. They said it's too dangerous to come. People talk. Maybe someday…"

"What about Bohdan?"

A wince. "For a year and a half, I thought he was dead. Then I learned he was captured." Her voice's small and airless again.

"By the Russians?"

"By the militia. He was healthy, so they didn't shoot him." Galina looks around them. *Is she seeing it the way it is or the way it was?* "They gave him to the 'authorities.' *They* sold him and the other prisoners to a gangster who runs a labor camp in Shakhtarsk. A man came to our farm in February with a picture of Bohdan. He looked so thin, so old. The man said I have to pay two hundred hryvnia every month if I want them to feed him. I can have him back for five thousand euro." For the first time since she stomped the brakes, Galina focuses on Carson. She looks as lost as she sounds. "Where do I get that much money? I thought about selling the farm. But who would buy it? And then what would we do?"

"Then I came along." That explains why she took the job: desperation. "So, five thousand gets him out. What's the other six thousand for?"

Galina looks away. Her hands twist and tangle in her lap. "To leave." It's almost a whisper. "Bohdan has a cousin in Krakow. He says it's very nice. There's work. Their language is like ours."

"That's the first sensible thing you've said since we met."

Galina lets out a snuffle that could be a laugh. "I hate the idea. I hate letting these *tarhany* win. I hate"—she waves out the windshield—"that all this was for nothing." Her voice hardens. "We did the hard fighting in Ilovaisk. Us, not the army. We won. They didn't support us, they didn't follow up. They left us to the Russians, us and the other National Guard units. It was...*zrada*."

"What?"

"*Zrada*. Um...*izmena*." The Russian word for *betrayal*. "Just like what this Stepaniak did to you. What the 'authorities' do to us. What the Russians and the gangsters do to Donbass. What Kyiv does to Ukraine." She hurls a radioactive glare at Carson. "What you did when you made a deal with the people who killed my friends. All...*zrada*."

Shit. Carson had tried to be clever, using the Russians for top cover. Of course she ended up pouring battery acid into Galina's biggest open sore.

"I get it. I know what you're feeling." *All too well.*

Galina snorts. "How could *you* know?"

"I lost friends. I lost my career." She hesitates. She hadn't expected to get into this, but she wants Galina to know that she's not alone in this boat. "Corruption. Russians, even."

"Was there a war? People dying?" Galina makes a rude noise. "You have no idea. Don't talk foolishness."

That launches a bolt of anger into Carson's gut. She fumes for a moment. "Told you I used to be a cop, right?" Galina sniffs and nods. "Didn't tell you why I'm not now. I listened to your story; now you listen to mine." She doesn't bother to soften her words.

Galina shifts in her seat and stares out her window again.

It pisses off Carson even more. "I was in Organized Crime Enforcement. I got in because I speak Russian." No reaction. "We were after a guy, Gennady Rodievsky. *Pakhan* of the local *Solntsevskaya Bratva*. Know what they are?"

"Yes. Gangsters."

"Yeah. Probably a branch down here now. Some of those 'authorities' you told me about. We spent two years building a case on him. Finally got enough to bring him in on righteous charges. Did this big op, Special Weapons Teams, the whole thing. He was *gone*. Somebody tipped him.

"Lots of pressure from upstairs to find the snitch. So we did the usual—stand in a circle, point at each other. Then everybody pointed at the Russian chick." She finger-stabs herself. "No proof, totally convenient. Didn't help that I was the only woman on the task force. I'd busted up with Ron, who was popular. So they flushed me. Got my name in the news. I was the crooked cop. Lost almost all my friends. Goddamn landlord kicked me out, said he didn't want my kind there."

Galina's watching her now, frowning. Carson can't tell if it's because of the train wreck or because she's looking for a lie.

"Turns out it was a senior superintendent who had a jones for nose candy. Rodievsky owned him. *He* got to retire quietly. Nobody said to me, 'Gee, we're sorry, want your job back?' TPS dropped its case against me and slammed the door. Now I work for people I hate"—Rodievsky, not Allyson, though sometimes..."to keep them from killing my dad for welching on a debt." She matches Galina's stare. "How's that for *zrada?* Good enough?"

Galina's eyes examine the hands she has clasped on her lap. She nods once.

With that, all the heat sluices out of Carson. She hesitates, then caresses Galina's shoulder. "Look. I don't wanna harsh on you. You had a shitty time here. You did things I can't imagine. Just saying…well, I know what it's like to have the world turn to shit on you. That you can talk about it and I'll get it. Okay?"

Galina swallows, then nods again.

Carson glances through the rear window. The Tigrs' silhouettes are almost lost in the distance. "Unless you're gonna visit those people who saved you, we need to take off or Rogozhkin will sic his goons on us. Are you okay to drive?"

After a deep breath, Galina says, "Yes." She starts the car and pulls off the dirt shoulder.

"Turn left up here. Stepaniak's still in Mospyne."

About twenty minutes of stony silence later, Galina aims a basset-hound look at Carson. "I am sorry."

Carson gives her a half-smile. "Me too."

CHAPTER 29

Mashkov trudges to his office from the mess tent, carefully balancing his aluminum bowl of rice porridge and the plated Doktorskaya sausage sandwich so neither ends up on the gravel. He usually enjoys eating with the men. But today he's still dealing with the patrol disaster, as well as planning to deploy west to support Monday's operation near Dokuchajevsk...*if* the Russians let them join it. That damned Proskurin, the Russian in charge of First Battalion, also asked for an urgent meeting. Coincidence? Mashkov has no interest in going through *that* on an empty stomach.

Vasilenko jogs to intercept him. He's toting a serious expression and a mess tin brimming with *varenyky*, which seems to be all the man ever eats. "Sir, may I have a word?"

"Of course." There's been another disaster, judging from the look on the senior sergeant's face. "What's gone wrong now, Lenya?"

Vasilenko falls into step beside Mashkov. He glances over his shoulder, then drops his voice. "The Russians are up to something."

"They're always up to something."

"More than usual. I saw them come out of the training block next to the Ops Center about a half-hour ago. All the Russian officers together."

They're usually not that organized. Mashkov tries to dissect this news as they approach the command building. "Where's Second Battalion?"

"Anna Company just reached where the patrol was attacked. They'll rescue what's left of it. Vasily Company's following the GLONASS beacon eastbound on T0509 near Novokaterynivka."

"No sign of Rogozhkin and his cutthroats?"

"Not yet, sir."

They stop at the command building's weathered steel front door. Mashkov watches the setting sun hover over the trees west of the camp. "I have a meeting with Proskurin in twenty minutes. The more I hear, the less I like the timing." Puzzle pieces in his mind come together to make an ugly picture. "Come in with me. We need to make plans."

Mashkov sits back in his swiveling desk chair, holding the phone receiver to his ear, trying to be the image of calm even though he's seething inside.

He's more or less prepared for Proskurin. The man has no use for him or any other Ukrainian; the Russian barely hides his contempt at staff meetings or operations briefings.

Mashkov hadn't expected a whole delegation. Every ranking Russian in the brigade follows Proskurin into Mashkov's office, along with two soldiers Mashkov knows are Russian "volunteers." The last one in shuts the door.

The plan he'd made with Vasilenko is already in trouble. Proskurin wasn't supposed to come with a pack of jackals. *No way to go but forward.* Mashkov says into the phone, "Yes, sergeant, that sounds appropriate. Initiate Measure Alfa." As if they'd been having a long conversation about it.

"Yes, sir. We're standing by." Vasilenko carefully disconnects.

As he hangs up the phone, Mashkov scans the six men who now fill his office. Arrogance, contempt, and distaste are on every face except for the common soldiers, who look a little scared. Two officers even wear their ribbons, the cocky thugs. *Do they think that will impress me?*

He levels a cold stare at Proskurin. "Colonel, I thought you asked for a meeting, not a formation."

Proskurin's square face twists into a smile with no warmth or humor in it. Not that the man has any to spare. "Dima Artemovich, I know you like to come to the point quickly, so here it is: you're relieved of your command. I'm taking over."

Mashkov's surprised by how unsurprised he is. He'd heard of this happening in the other militias. Last year, several DNR commanders were assassinated, and the Russians didn't even try to deny they were behind it. Well, he'll be harder to get rid of. He pulls his blank face on tighter and folds his hands on the desktop. "On whose authority?"

"Colonel-General Kishovsky of the Southern Military District." Proskurin's voice says he thinks that's the last word.

Mashkov wills himself to chuckle instead of throwing the desk lamp at the blockhead. "The last time I checked, he's not in my chain of command. I answer to the commander of the First Army Corps, who reports to the Defense Minister of the Donetsk People's Republic. This Kishovsky means nothing to me."

Two Russian officers snicker. Proskurin's face turns pink. "You're a fool if you believe that. This"—he waves his hand toward the window—"so-called 'brigade' exists because we say it does. And you keep your shoulder boards because we say you do. And now we say, 'No more.'"

Each of the four officers aims his best glare at Mashkov. He stares back. He'll be damned if he'll let these thugs think he's scared of them. "What are the charges against me?"

Proskurin swaps a sly glance with Kuzmin, Third Battalion's commander and a true pain in the ass. "You ordered your men to attack a Russian military unit deployed in the field."

You bastard. Mashkov stands slowly, resting his fingertips on the desktop. "That would be the Russian military unit that attacked one of my patrols, destroyed three vehicles, and killed *two of my men?*"

"In self-defense."

The smugness on Proskurin's face makes Mashkov want to throttle the man. "'Self-defense' means shooting back *after* you've been shot at, not staging an ambush." He's pushing harder than he'd planned. He didn't expect this kind of abuse. He should have, though; he'd been taking shit from these people ever since they appeared from out of nowhere. Add to that the slow-rolling disaster surrounding that godforsaken money-for-art scheme and it won't take much to let his anger get the best of him. Mashkov hopes Vasilenko is where he's supposed to be.

Mashkov lets his voice go hard. "You people have different definitions for these matters. 'Advice' seems to mean giving orders, and 'assistance' means getting in the way."

"Enough." Proskurin's face slowly darkens. He draws his sidearm but lets it hang by his hip. Maybe he believes the sight of a weapon will make Mashkov break down. He holds out his left hand, palm up. "Give me your pistol, you *hohol* moron."

The slur throws more petrol on Mashkov's mounting anger. He again glances from face to face. Their superiority turns his stomach. Is their plan to shoot him here in the office, or take him outside and do it in front of the troops? Either way, he won't survive if he does what they want. Neither will the brigade.

Mashkov unsnaps his olive-drab holster, then slowly pulls his pistol. He holds it up for the Russians to see. "A Makarov. A Soviet copy of a Walther PP." He gives Proskurin his best feral smile. "You people never were very original. Like your performance just now."

Proskurin's face turns cherry red. He starts to swing up his pistol. "You—"

Mashkov's inner volcano finally erupts. He shifts his grip on his Makarov and shoots Proskurin through his open mouth from less than two meters away. Then he swings right and puts a bullet into Kuzmin's forehead.

His office door slams open. Half a dozen of his troops rush in, weapons ready, Vasilenko in the lead. The two Russian privates are face-down on the floor in an instant with rifle muzzles pressed into their skulls. The two surviving Russian officers turn to fight, scrabbling at their holsters, but Mashkov's men beat them to the ground with their rifle butts.

It's over in a few moments.

Vasilenko steps out of the scrum to the front edge of Mashkov's desk. "What do you want us to do with these bastards, sir?"

I just shot two men at point-blank range. Mashkov watches the blood pool around Proskurin's head. Bozhe, *what have I done?* All his insides congeal into stone. He's never killed anyone until now, at least not by himself. *I'm a businessman. I'm a logistics officer. I'm not—*

"Sir?"

Mashkov shakes his head hard, trying to rattle his brain into thinking mode. "Put the two privates in the cells. They were just doing what they were told, but I don't want them running free. The officers..." He doesn't know. He hasn't thought that far ahead. He hadn't planned to kill anyone; he was supposed to say *Yakov* at the right time and Vasilenko—who had been listening at the door—would burst in with his men and arrest the Russian.

This action was supposed to be about relieving an insubordinate underling...not a full-on rebellion.

Well, he's committed now. All the Russians were in on this. Unless he pushes back hard and fast, the captains and lieutenants will finish what the majors and colonels couldn't. And he's not about to let that happen to his brigade.

Mashkov wishes that now, more than ever, he had the ransom money for those paintings. The Russian purse is going to slam shut. Two million euros can keep the brigade fed and equipped long enough to fight next week. After that...

He takes in a long, deliberate breath, then holsters his pistol. "Hold the officers in the washroom for now. Have the men fall in. I need to tell them what just happened. And arrest the Russian company and platoon commanders. Be polite about it if you can, but get control of them. We don't know how far this goes."

Vasilenko's eyes pop wide. "We don't have enough local officers to replace them all."

"I'm aware of that." He hears himself bark and pulls back. "Sorry. I know. Find Colonel Shatilov. Tell him it's time to change leadership of the units with Russian officers. We'll be using lieutenants and senior sergeants until we can get it sorted. At least they'll be loyal." *What am I forgetting?* "Where's Yartsev?" Rogozhkin's pet sergeant.

"In the Ops Center, where he's been since yesterday."

"Arrest him, too. He's probably how Rogozhkin found the patrol. Careful around him—he's one of those *spetsnaz* thugs, too."

Vasilenko gets his men to work cleaning up the mess. When they leave the office, he returns to the front edge of Mashkov's desk. "If I may, sir?"

Mashkov's desperately trying to work out what he'll say to the men in the next few minutes. "Go ahead."

"I know this isn't what we'd planned. Now that it's happened, we can't go back. We have to take it all the way. If we don't, the *Kacápskyi* will finish us off the way you did Proskurin. We have to be as hard as they are."

"Thank you, Lenya." Mashkov works hard to keep the doom out of his voice. "I know."

◎

Mashkov stands before the assembled brigade in "the plaza," the semi-ironic name they use for the gravel former parking lot in the middle of the former grain mill that's now their base.

Over a thousand troops are packed into tight formation by battalion and company with their officers—now all local Ukrainians—standing in front of them. All are watching Mashkov.

All these troops, waiting for him to tell them what to do. Ready to kill or die for him. It's the most impressive thing he's ever seen—and it's scaring the living hell out of him. Nothing in his business career prepared him for this. He was never supposed to be out here.

Yevgeny Brusilov, who founded what had at first been the Makiivka Battalion, was supposed to lead. He'd had military experience; he was the one who could make grand speeches and get the men charged up for battle. Mashkov had been content to be the logistics officer, trying to keep the men fed and armed. He was good at that. But then Brusilov got himself and the chief of staff killed in a completely unnecessary frontal assault on that damned airport outside Donetsk. Mashkov was the only officer who knew the brigade well enough to take over.

He read books to learn how to be a military officer. He read books to learn how to make speeches. But reading books about leadership can't make anyone a leader.

And now he's here...about to lead his people into a war on Russia.

He sucks in one more lungful of air, then raises the bullhorn. *Use your command voice. Be strong.* "Battalion commanders, put your battalions at parade rest."

The battalion and company commanders echo his order. Over a thousand troops step into parade rest, their feet shoulder-width apart, their hands clasped behind their backs. The rumble of that many people moving the same way at the same time makes him shiver.

Mashkov scans the faces of the troops in the front ranks. Their plainness and honesty give him the strength to force out his first words. "Men and women of the Makiivka Brigade! It is my responsibility to tell you about two important events that occurred in the past three hours. As you may be aware, a patrol from Second Battalion has been pursuing the bandits who killed our men in

Amvrosiivka. They are now near Starobesheve. Lieutenant Colonel Rogozhkin, our Russian advisor, took it on himself to stop the patrol. He and several Russian special forces personnel attacked the patrol, destroyed its vehicles, and killed two of our men."

Even though the troops are supposed to stay silent in parade rest, a rumble of anger rolls through the ranks.

Good. I need them mad. "About forty minutes ago, Lieutenant Colonel Proskurin, the ranking Russian officer in the brigade, and a group of other senior Russian officers tried to seize command of this brigade from me." More rumbling. "Fast work on the part of loyal troops stopped this mutiny. Two rebels are dead, and the rest are in custody."

He lets the growling in the ranks rise and fall like a wave. "The *Kacápskyi* have promised much and delivered much less in the past two years. They've stopped us from fighting for our freedom, the cause many of us have been dedicated to from the beginning. Moscovia thinks it can use us as pawns in its political games with the West. It thinks it can kill our leadership when we no longer dance to the Kremlin's tune." He hesitates. This is his throw of the fatal die. "For us, this ends today."

This time, the rustle of sound is more disbelief than anger.

Mashkov waves to Vasilenko, who escorts the two surviving officers from Proskurin's retinue—each guided by two troopers—from the command building to the middle of the plaza. When they stop, the soldiers knock the captives onto their knees, facing the formation.

Mashkov steps behind the two Russian majors, takes another deep breath, then raises the bullhorn. "We've relieved all the Russian nationals from command. We've taken back the brigade from the *Kacápskyi*. We're finished with the sneers and insults and distrust they show us in their arrogance. From today, the Makiivka Brigade answers only to our leaders in Donetsk, not to the foreign generals in Rostov-on-Don or the new tsar in Moscow."

Mashkov stabs his arm toward the two Russians. "The penalty for mutiny is death in any army, anywhere. These men led a mutiny against the rightful leadership of this brigade. They wanted to put that leadership in the hands of foreigners. They failed. We have to show anyone else with the same idea what will happen to them." Before he can think about what he's doing, he draws his pistol and shoots each man in the back of his head.

The troops fall silent. A few look away.

He holsters his weapon as calmly as he can make his shaking hand do it. "If you can't fight for the interests of the Donbass and its peoples instead of those of Moscovia…if you can't serve under officers who were born here, grew up here, have lives and families here, and fought here for our independence, then please turn in your equipment and leave now."

The troops start shouting, a few at first, then more and more as they urge each other on. "DNR!" "Down with Kyiv!" "Freedom for Donbass!"

Yes! That's what I need to hear. Now bring them home. "We are the Makiivka Brigade! We are strong! And you and I together will lead our people to freedom!"

CHAPTER 30

Stepaniak hunkers in the twilight of the abandoned building, waiting for sunset and for the pain to fade. If he drives after taking the painkillers the doctor gave him, he'll crash into a tree within ten minutes. If he doesn't take them, the grinding, throbbing torture radiating from his shoulder and chest and invading the rest of his body will blind him to everything else.

He's amazed he's made it to this little dusthole. Byryuky was to be simply a place he drove through on his way into Donetsk. It's another hick town like Komsomolske, just fields and crumbling Soviet-era farms. The pain changed that plan. Now he's stuck here. Donetsk is so close but out of reach.

The tracker shows that the icon's stopped on the highway about four kilometers south of here. He's been trying to call Stas, but the idiot doesn't answer. Stas's little reptile brain is no doubt trying to work out how to end up with all the money, though God alone knows what he'd do with it. Well, let him dream. His usefulness to Stepaniak is over once he brings in the icon and the money. *I hope Carson didn't suffer too much…*

By the time Carson tells Galina to stop, the pulsing red dot on the tracker has almost merged with the crosshairs that show her location. They're surrounded by plowed fields. A low-slung farm complex is about three hundred meters to their four o'clock; the southern fringe of what the GPS calls Byryuky hunkers about half a click to their ten o'clock. The only structure close to where they're stopped is a shot-to-shit concrete building with a corrugated iron roof forty meters to their one o'clock, surrounded by wildflowers and waist-high weeds.

Carson squeezes her eyes shut to fix her focus, but the world's still a little blurred when she opens them. She points to the two-story-tall target. "I think that's it. What is that thing?"

"A grain dryer." Galina cocks an eyebrow at her. "You know what that is?"

"We had them in Alberta. They look a lot different. I'm used to storage bins and towers."

"This one is small, for the local farmers." She waves toward it. "It got in the way of the war."

"Do a slow drive-by. I want to see if Stepaniak's Patriot is here."

The Octavia rolls past at a slow jogging rate, revealing two rusty, slightly out-of-focus hoppers on the first floor, a stubby smokestack for the dryer, and a concrete control shack. No green SUV. *Did Stas lie to me?* There's no Range Rover or any other kind of car, either.

The tracker shows the fuzzy red dot very slightly behind the crosshairs. The painting's in the grain dryer. "Go back and pull into the driveway. That looks like the place."

They exit the car fully armed. Carson points from Galina to the front of the ruin, then to herself and the back of it. Galina nods.

Carson recalls how Yurik taught her to clear large spaces. Stay near walls; use cover; look for tripwires and snares; move quietly; listen for sharp sounds; watch for shadows that aren't straight lines. On top of this, she has to search for the painting.

The grain dryer's back end is an open bay with a dusting of rotting wheat and the broken remains of a screw conveyor the operators must've used to load trucks with dried grain. There's not much cover, but there's not much light anymore, either. Carson moves through the area as fast as she can without tripping over debris, trying to be as poor a target as possible. Getting shot and having a grenade thrown at her have made her jumpy.

Nothing. No Stepaniak, no painting.

Galina appears in a doorway so suddenly, Carson almost shoots her. Both women startle. Carson has to let her heart slow down before she can speak. "Jesus, say something next time. Find anything?"

"I don't know. Come."

Carson follows her to the control shack. The door's missing and its windows coat the floor as crunchy glitter. A rusted and stained steel counter runs the room's three-meter width. Gutted control panels dot the wall above the counter. "No wonder they didn't reopen. What did you find?"

Galina points to a spot on the counter near the far left-hand wall. "It's the only thing that doesn't belong."

It's a microchip the size of a dime, a watch battery, and some fresh sawdust. It looks like the tracker she dug out of the icon and tossed out the window a few klicks ago.

Carson braces her hands on the counter and blows out a long plume of air. Her shoulders sag. "Stepaniak took this out of the picture. We've lost him."

Rogozhkin watches through his binoculars as the Tarasenko woman and her friend trudge to their sedan. So different from a few minutes ago: they went in like warriors, their weapons ready, their movements brisk and efficient. Tarasenko moves well. He likes that in a woman.

Neither carries anything that looks like a painting or like Stepaniak's head. He'd see something that size even at a hundred meters' range. When they slump against the car's nose, he lowers his binoculars and calls Tarasenko's mobile.

She answers, "*Shto?*" It's a growl, not a greeting.

"What did you find?"

"Stepaniak dumped the tracker chip."

Not a huge surprise. "How long ago?"

"Not long. He left blood on the chip. It's not quite dry. If he's bleeding that much, he won't go far."

"Agreed." Bad luck, but not yet fatally bad. Rogozhkin surveys Syrov's troops, stretched along the treeline between two fields south of the derelict grain oven. As he watches, the two men they'd left behind in Starobesheve pull Rogozhkin's Hunter into the grove behind him. It gives him an idea. "I'll send men into Byryuky to look for the bandit's vehicle. Our friends in the Starobesheve police told us a green UAZ Patriot was reported stolen two hours ago. We have a registration plate number."

"Wonderful." Tarasenko's voice says, *not wonderful.*

He can always tell when a soldier needs a bit of encouragement. "You found an important clue. Well done. Please join us while the search is underway. We're in the trees about a hundred twenty meters south of your position. I believe we have some food and water to share."

No answer for a moment. "Is that an invite or an order?"

"It's an invitation now. If you say 'no,' it'll be an order."

Another pause. "Be there in a few minutes."

Rogozhkin hopes he can get Tarasenko to talk about herself when she arrives. He's curious about how she came to be the way she is. He'd heard about what she did to Stepaniak's accomplice at Amvrosiivka and watched her end that other bandit without a qualm. Impressive.

A voicemail waits on his mobile. It's from Yartsev.

It's a disaster.

That idiot Proskurin jumped the gun and moved against Mashkov before the lower-level commands were secured. Proskurin's dead. Kuzmin's dead. Mashkov—*Mashkov!*—executed Arsenkin and Sidorov in front of the *whole fucking brigade.* When did he grow the balls to do that? Rogozhkin grows angrier and more incredulous as the bad news piles up.

"And...V Company...Second Battalion." Yartsev's running, out of breath. *What the...?* "They're..." Loud gunshots. A distant, muffled scream. "They're in your area. They're—" Distant automatic fire. A sharp cry from Yartsev. A *thud.* Something scrapes at the phone. Shouts, running feet. A jumble of voices.

The recording ends.

Goddamn it!

CHAPTER 31

Carson paces across the heavy layer of mulch between the trees to where Rogozhkin and the *spetsnaz* lieutenant are talking by a Tigr. Here and there, she passes a *spetsnaz* troop cooking a can from his Individual Ration Pack on the tiny, folding tin stove that comes in the IRP's shiny green blister pack. It's twilight beyond the grove. The flickering blue lights from the burning hexamine tablets look like grounded stars.

Rogozhkin nods at something the lieutenant tells him, then steps to meet Carson a couple meters from the Tigr. He gives her a smile that's more worried than pleasant. "Tarasenko. I know better than to ask if you liked your supper. Are you at least fed?"

He's being awfully nice to her this time around. He hasn't once tried to twist her arms backward. Whatever that's about, Carson's okay with it. "At least. It reminded me of dog food."

"You've eaten dog food?"

"Yeah." It's what happens when you're eight years old, your mother's too drunk to shop, your father's working on the other side of the province, and it's twenty miles to the nearest grocery store.

"Better or worse than the IRP?"

"Depends on the brand."

He chuckles. "And your friend? Is she satisfied with her meal?"

Galina's hunkered down in the car with her shotgun across her lap. "She won't touch it. Your people killed her people around here in 2014. Don't turn your back on her."

"There's a lot of that here. We thought we were helping, but…" Rogozhkin shrugs.

Bullshit. Okay, maybe you guys did. But the assholes who sent you? No way. Carson pushes that thought away from her brain's speech center. "We should be looking for Stepaniak."

"No need." He smiles. He has surprisingly good teeth. "We think we found his vehicle. We have a man checking the registration plates now."

"Sir?" They both look toward the lieutenant. He gives Rogozhkin the thumbs-up sign, then disappears behind the Tigr again.

Rogozhkin turns to Carson. "We found him. He's not so far away." He pulls his phone from a thigh pocket and brings up Yandex Maps, the Russian version of Google Maps. The glowing screen lights his chest and face in pale blue. He shifts so he's more than just Russian close to Carson's side. "We're here. That's the grain dryer you searched. And this…" he switches to satellite view "…is where we find Stepaniak."

Two long, narrow buildings run northwest-southeast in parallel in an overgrown compound next to a field about a klick south-southeast of the grain dryer. When Rogozhkin zooms in, Carson can just make out a third building, squarish with a brown roof, between the others. "Which one?"

"We don't know. There are no lights. The Patriot's parked between these two, here." He points to a spot on the square building's east side.

Stepaniak must've watched her and Galina waste their time on the grain dryer. "Have fun flushing him out."

"Oh, no." Rogozhkin steps back. "That's for you to do. Find him, lure him outside. We'll have snipers covering all three buildings. When he's in the clear, we'll eliminate him. That won't distress you, will it?"

"Asshole tried to kill me last night. What do you think?" What *will* distress her is when the sniper takes his next shot at her. She needs to figure out how to make that not happen. "I don't get why you want me in your way out there."

"Very simple. Yes, we could find him and eliminate him. He'd resist. It would cause a firefight and probably scare the poor people living nearby. Some of my men might be wounded. If you bring him into the open, we'll need only one shot. Much cleaner and safer for everyone."

Except me. Does his explanation sound reasonable? Yes. Does she trust it? Not a bit. What they talk about here and what she does over there don't have to be the same things. "Okay. I'll take Galina to back me up. I also need the money."

Rogozhkin's eyebrows jump. "You really think I'll let you walk off with all that money?"

Just what she expected. "I need something to bait the hook. If you don't want me to take it all, then give me a couple straps and the case. I can bluff him. You keep the rest." She remembers she's not supposed to have the combinations. "We'll have to open the case first."

"That's been done." He turns and calls out, "Syrov! Bring the briefcase."

A minute later, the lieutenant plunks down the Halliburton between Carson and Rogozhkin. The colonel shines a small flashlight on the top. "Open it."

She does. They all admire the cash. Then Rogozhkin says, "Lieutenant, get us something to put that in."

Once Syrov disappears, Carson asks, "What're you gonna do with it?"

"The money belongs to the militia."

"Not what I asked."

He waggles an index finger at her. "You should start convincing your friend to join you when you go to talk to Stepaniak."

Carson nods. As she heads for the car, she cranes over her shoulder toward Rogozhkin. "You should start telling your men to not shoot me."

Carson marches into the field on the treeline's south edge to get away from eavesdroppers. That so-called supper probably won't last her until midnight, far less until breakfast tomorrow. When she got to Dnipro (*how long now? five days?*), she found a good döner kebab place that was open until nine. Out here in the sticks, she'd be lucky to find a grocery store open past five or six.

Whatever. She punches the contact for "Mom" on her agency phone.

Olivia answers on the first ring. "One-Two-Six! I've been frantic."

Just hearing Olivia's voice makes everything at least fifty percent better. "I can't imagine you frantic."

"In my way. I see you're near Mospyne." She butchers the pronunciation. "What are you about now?"

Carson gives her a report on everything that's happened since they talked on Thursday. It takes her a while to realize that's yesterday; so much has happened since. Olivia listens and makes sympathetic noises until Carson runs out of steam. She's been babbling.

"This *Russian* person." Olivia puts a disapproving spin on the word. "Do you trust him?"

"No. I don't trust anybody in this fucking country, including me. You called the SAS?"

"No."

"You promised."

"I...suggested."

"Should've known. Look, I'm gonna kill One-Thirteen tonight."

"Oh, dear. I know the two of you have had your differences, but I'm certain we can—"

"I'm serious. When we go into that farm tonight, when I see him, I'm gonna shoot the asshole dead. And I'll smile when I do it."

Olivia sighs. "Of course. Given what you've told me, I can't say I disagree. However, he may be a villain, but he's also an associate. I need to inform Allyson."

"You do that."

Olivia's end of the line is all about typing for a while. As she types, she asks, "Is there anything you need that I can get for you?"

A new body. Two days of sleep. Three decent meals in a row. "Nothing you can get me."

"Pity." More clacking. "Allyson would like a word."

"Do I...?" *...have to?* She swallows the question. "Do you know where I am?" It comes out wistful, not challenging.

"It appears you're in the countryside. Other than—"

"I'm sitting in a field." She looks around her, hating how lost she sounds. "Stars are coming out. The sky's so damn *big* here. Like back home. Ever since I got here, it's been...well, it's alien here. Like going back in time. But it's also a lot like home. It's fucking with my head. I'm remembering shit I never think about. So I don't have any brainspace for Allyson's bullshit, okay?"

Olivia lets a few silent seconds go by. "May I offer a bit of advice?"

"Sure." It's never good to ignore Olivia's advice.

"Talk to her. I know you're not in the mood for her just now. I know how the two of you are. But please listen to what she has to say. If you don't, the next time you *do* speak, she'll be angry, and you'll not want that." She pauses. "Shall I connect her?"

Shit. Carson sighs. "What does she want? If she's not sending a chopper, she's got nothing I need."

"One-Two-Six..." Disappointed voice. "She wants to tell you why you're there."

"A little late." Carson chews on that for a beat. "You know, right? You tell me."

"Right." Olivia sighs. "We suspected One-One-Three may be working on two or more sides of this situ—"

"Shit. You didn't bother telling me?"

"She feared you'd enter the project with a preconceived notion and that One-One-Three would sense your suspicion. Allyson chose you not only because of your familiarity with this sort of thing but also because she trusted you to take charge of the situation and bring it to closure."

"So I'm cleaning up her mess."

"If you wish to see it that way...yes."

Carson would love to scream at somebody now, but not at Olivia. It's just as well she's not talking to Allyson. "Tell Allyson to go fuck herself. She dumped me in this shit—she doesn't get to second-guess me. Now I need to go shoot a tree or something."

"Save your anger for when you need it." Olivia's voice has turned confidential, like a murmured conversation in the dark should be. "Whatever you need to do, be quick and discreet about it. One-One-Three is a liability for us all. Solve our problem tonight."

CHAPTER 32

Carson and Galina huddle behind a low rubble heap about two hundred meters west of Stepaniak's hide. The half-moon—visible for once in the partly cloudy sky—splashes filmy light over the completely open ground between them and the farm buildings.

Carson sweeps the compound with her binoculars. "Nothing. Not even a lit cigarette." No matter how she shifts, the corners of broken concrete blocks dig into Carson's ribs where Stepaniak shot her. "No windows on the end of the two long buildings, just the doors. Trees masking the south side of the north building. If he's in there, he won't see anything."

A red light flashes twice from the square building's roof. It's the signal that Rogozhkin's three snipers are in place on the roofs.

Galina sighs. "I hate this. Helping the *Kacápskyi*."

It's not Carson's favorite thing either, but she's used to it. "Look at it as them helping us. Ready?"

They scurry single-file across the field between the rubble and the south building. Now and then, Carson's left knee slams into the briefcase. At least the damn thing isn't full anymore.

Carson slows when she reaches the concrete pad at the west end of the south building. She steps lightly toward the door, then glides her back onto the latch-side wall and silently sets down the briefcase. Galina does the same on the hinge side, holding her shotgun across her chest with the muzzle pointing downward.

Carson angles her Fenix tactical light at waist height and flashes the rusting metal door. The knob's gone. She pushes the door with one finger; it swings a couple of inches with a creak the Russians can hear across the highway. Carson flattens her back against the wall again in case someone decides to shoot the noise. No gunfire. She pulls her phone from her hip pocket, brings up WhatsApp, and passes it to Galina. "Send yourself a text."

"Why?"

"So we can communicate."

Galina's thumbs dance over the screen. A moment later, a tiny *ping* comes out of her sweatshirt's pouch pocket. She hands back Carson's phone. "What's your plan?"

"You go to the other end. There's no windows on the south side." She thumbs to her left. "Text when you're there. On 'go,' enter and work your way to the center."

Galina nods several times. The dark hides her expression. "Okay. What if I find him?"

Rogozhkin's plan has them "luring" Stepaniak into the open for the snipers to deal with. It's a bullshit plan. "Got a problem with shooting him?"

Galina stares out into the dark for a while. "No." Her voice barely carries past the door.

"It's okay if you do."

"No." Louder this time.

Carson's still not sure Galina's serious. "Okay. He's wounded. Don't know how bad. Stas said I fucked him up, but who knows what that means. Ready?"

"Yes."

Is it good or bad that Galina's stopped scolding me for swearing? "Go."

While she waits, Carson peeks around the corner at the building's north wall. Long, narrow windows along the top, just like on the other side. Every minute, this looks more like the chicken coops at Amvrosiivka. *How many damn chickens do these people need?*

Her phone screen lights up with a text in Ukrainian from Galina: `Ready`.

It's time. `Go`.

Carson kicks open the door, then rolls through the opening until she hits a heavy industrial steel shelf unit loaded on both sides with empty cages. No chickens anymore, but the stench makes her eyes tear. No footsteps or gunshots. No moonlight makes it inside; she'll have to use her flashlight. No chance of surprising anybody.

She surveys the situation using brief pulses from her flashlight. There are four of these shelf units across the building, each ten meters long with two-meter aisles between them. The floor's covered with leaves, dirt, and feathers. If she wanted to switch her flashlight to full power, she could light up the far wall a hundred meters away.

Carson brings the Halliburton inside. She won't need it, but she'd hate to have somebody swipe it with €40,000 still inside. Then she fast-walks to the south wall, turns, and shines her flashlight down the aisle just long enough to confirm it's empty. Light off; slide to the next aisle; light on. Repeat until she hits the north wall. Turn again, ghost down a random aisle in the dark, head back to the north wall. Repeat. Galina's flashlight beam occasionally flares in the distance. Their lights pick out a couple of rats and a marten looking for a meal.

She doesn't see Stepaniak or any evidence he's ever been here.

Carson and Galina meet almost exactly in the building's center. Galina says, "I found nothing."

"Same here. Let's check out the square building." Carson hesitates. "Stay in the shadows. Snipers don't need to know where we are."

It's one story, flat-roofed, about thirty meters to a side. All the windows were boarded over long ago. Once they force open a door, Carson and Galina find a warren of what were offices or storerooms. Now they're just empty rooms full of graffiti, rotten insulation, broken beer bottles, and the occasional rat.

The women emerge into the shadows along the building's east side on the edge of what's left of a gravel parking area. The Patriot's a few meters away, lonely in the middle of all the empty space. They duck behind the rusty hulk of a roll-off garbage bin.

Carson peers at the north building through her binoculars. It's the same size as the south building, but it appears to be split in half. The west end is another oversized chicken coop; the east end has a number of roll-up cargo or shop doors crusted with peeling paint and sprayed-on tags. A standard entry door stands partly open about twenty-five meters from the far end.

Galina whispers, "If he's here, he must be in there."

"Yeah." Carson doesn't like the idea of a single point of entry. It's too easy to shoot anything that comes through. *Is there a door on the east end? On the north side? Booby traps? Tripwires?* She hates this shit—she's a cop, not a soldier.

Galina watches her, waiting. *What's the right play here?* When in doubt, get more information. Carson grabs Galina's arm to pull her close. "Go around there"—she points to the west end—"and about halfway down. Tell me what the wall looks like on this part." The east end. "Doors? Windows? Signs of life? I'll see if there's a door on the east end. Then we'll make a plan. Got it?"

Galina half-stands to look past the bin to the north building. "Yes. I understand."

"Come here." Once Galina crouches next to her again, Carson opens the briefcase to pull a strap of euros. She holds it out to Galina. "Take this."

"Why?"

"In case something happens to me."

"Nothing will happen to you."

"Just…for fuck's sake." Carson grabs the neck of Galina's tee, pulls, then dumps the bundle of cash into her shirt. Galina yelps and tries to push Carson's hands away, but it's too late. "I don't trust the Russians and I don't trust Stepaniak. If things go south, take off. Try to get to the car and go home. That's more than enough money to get your husband out of that camp and get you both to Poland. No, don't argue. Say 'yes.'"

Galina grumbles and takes more time than necessary to straighten her tee and sweatshirt. She finally mutters, "Yes, fine. Nothing will happen to you. I will see you inside." Then she sprints toward the north building.

Rogozhkin lies prone in a knot of trees roughly two hundred fifty meters west of the derelict farm, watching the action through his binoculars. At least, trying to watch; the women are staying under cover so effectively that ever since they entered the southernmost building, he's hardly seen them.

He sets down his field glasses and uses a handkerchief to wipe his eyes. It's been a long day, and it'll be a longer night.

What did Yartsev mean by, "V Company is in your area"? How close? What are they doing? Rogozhkin's hoping against hope that Yartsev's still alive. He was—*is*—a good man. But Rogozhkin also mourns the loss of that inside line he had into the brigade's movements. Being blind is always bad, especially in the field.

How can the militia know where I am?

Something tickles the inside of his skull. He brings up the

tracker on his phone. The return from the GLONASS beacon should still be in Starobesheve.

It isn't. It's across the highway. *What the...?*

He hisses, "Syrov! To me!"

The lieutenant materializes from the shadows and drops next to Rogozhkin. "Sir?"

"The men who came back from Starobesheve. Did they bring the beacon with them?"

"Yes, sir. We installed it on the women's car. If they try to get away, we can track them. So can the militia. They won't get far."

Shit. He can't even get mad at Syrov—it's a good idea. They'd eliminated the militia patrol's ability to move; they should have the field to themselves now. It should've taken half a day at best for the militia to get that company ready to move out. And yet...

"Destroy the beacon immediately."

"But—"

"Just do it. *Now.* Is anyone left over there?"

"One man, but he didn't install it. I'll have my sergeant tell him where it is. What's happening?"

Rogozhkin aims his binoculars across the field to his ten o'clock, toward where they left the women's car. *Oh, shit.*

Carson's guess was right; there's a door in the building's east end. Its knob is also missing, and the door's cracked a few inches. It's dark on the other side.

She makes a slow 360-degree survey of the area. Mostly scrub weeds and a salting of shrubs, backed by a black wall of trees along a road. The bulky front end of a Tigr shows through a gap in the trees. Rogozhkin's men are over there someplace. Are they to stop leakers or clean up any mess she makes? She hopes she won't find out the wrong way.

Her phone vibrates in her hand. A text from Galina: windows behind trees next to wall door in middle.

Gap in the trees?

yes near center.

Will door open?

Pause. no blocked.

Two ways in: the door next to Carson, and the one in the south wall. She doubts Stepaniak would hole up anyplace he can't see out of. He must be near the center of the building. Go to south door enter on go.

Carson pockets her phone, clutches her Ksyukha to her chest, then rolls through the door. A glow in the distance outlines a doorway. She ends up crouched off to the north side, out of any line of fire.

She risks a brief pulse from her flashlight to get oriented. A vehicle service bay: workbenches, a floor jack, a roll-up door. Small noises amplified by hard surfaces fill the space. She edges to the doorway into the next room. The distant glow is gone; whoever owns it must've heard her.

It's almost completely black in here. She has to feel her way to the opposite wall, past the door, through the next room. If she takes full steps, she crunches debris; if she shuffles, the grinding of dirt and dead leaves on concrete gives her location away. If whoever's down there has infrared goggles, she's done.

Her phone vibrates, startling her. From Galina: at the door.

Go im to your right.

Carson stands absolutely still, breathing through her mouth to cut down on the noise in her head. She hears the squeak of a door and the soft brushing of careful footsteps. The steps pause, replaced by post-run breathing. Then the scrape of a pivot. Slow, receding steps.

Carson texts Galina: Im behind you now.

A brief light bloom from a phone screen reveals Galina's position, four meters ahead.

Two suppressed gunshots echo down the hall: *phutphut*. The muzzle flash sears afterimages on Carson's eyes. The nearly instant *clangclang* tells her the bullets punched through the door she'd come through a short while ago.

Carson and Galina carefully work their way toward the source of the shots, sliding almost silently around doorframes, then breaking toward the outside walls for cover. Galina's to the left; Carson's creeping forward to the right, almost doubled over. As she crabs through another doorway, Stepaniak (because it has to be him) puts a round through the soft wood doorframe above her head, spraying her with splinters.

Her phone vibrates. `stopped make a noise.`

Carson slams the Ksyukha's folding metal stock into the slab. The *clunk* rings off the walls.

Phut.

Boom. The shotgun blast sounds like a cannon.

Carson dashes through the doorway, barks "Coming in!" to warn Galina, then crosses their now-shared room in a few steps. She dives through the next door, lands in a crouch, falls back into a flip, then comes up with her carbine ready. "Light!"

Galina's flashlight beam plows like a searchlight through the dusty air and turns the north wall into daytime.

Stepaniak leans against a workbench leg on the right edge of the circle of light. The right side of his shirt is shredded and shiny from his armpit to his belt. Carson, squinting against the sudden glare, finds his suppressed MP-5 about a meter from his right hand. She scrambles closer, kicks it away, then backpedals, letting her Ksyukha fall loose on its sling. She draws her pistol and Fenix, aims both at Stepaniak's head, and barks, "Sidearm?"

His head slews toward her. "Don't worry...dear Carson. I'm...in no condition...to fight."

The light circle shudders. Galina steps into the room slowly, flashlight in her left hand, shotgun wedged in the crook of her right arm.

He shifts his focus to Galina. His smile looks more like a grimace. "Ah. You. We meet at last. Well done." Back to Carson. "Well. What now?"

Carson can barely hear him, and what she hears is slurred. This isn't how she'd pictured this scene and isn't sure she likes it. Wanting this moment and having it are two very different things. "You dumb asshole. Why didn't you just do the deal we made?"

Stepaniak tries to laugh but chokes instead. "Stas reminded me...we needed...more money. Had to have...the art." He leans to his left to drag his right hand and arm closer. The effort makes him grimace. "Stas is dead?"

"Yeah."

"You...you did it?"

"Yeah."

He nods slowly. "I hoped...hoped he wouldn't kill you."

"Then why'd you send him after me?"

"So you could end him." He tries another unsuccessful smile. "It worked, dear Carson. Now we can deal...you and me. And her? You will...will introduce me...to your friend?"

Carson can't help but laugh. "Galina, this is Stepaniak. The bandit."

"Hmpf. Not pleased to meet you."

"Hah." Stepaniak peers up at Carson. "This one has...spirit. Like you did...when we met. I...always admired that. I...do still."

"Where's the picture?" Carson won't let Stepaniak try his bullshit on her again.

"Here." He waves his left hand upward. "You have...have the money?"

"Not anymore. Some Russians want your head on a stick. They have it."

He frowns. "Not the militia?"

"They want your ass, too. Russians got to me first." The slab vibrates through the soles of her boots. *What's that about?* "Where's your money?"

Stepaniak scowls at the floor. Then he tilts his head to his right. "There."

Carson swings her light in that direction. It lands on the rucksack Galina gave her about a hundred years ago.

Rifle fire crackles outside. Carson and Galina exchange glances. Spetsnaz *doesn't have anything to shoot at...do they?*

"Dear Carson. Did your Russian friends...bring company?"

The thumping of a heavy machinegun bounces through the building.

Carson's pretty sure what's happening. If she's right, they're all out of time. "Galina, get out of here. *Now.*" She jerks her light to the room's west wall, picking out another door. "Where's that go, Stepaniak?"

"To the chicken shed...Full circle, yes?"

An explosion outside. The rafters creak and shake.

Carson shines her light on Galina, then sweeps it to the door. "You heard him. Get out. Hide where you can. They're looking for him and me, not you." Galina looks pinned in place, shock all over her face. "Fucking *move!*"

"Yes. Yes." Galina stumbles toward the door, but pauses as she passes Carson. "I will find you."

"Go. Be safe."

Stepaniak groans as he tries to rearrange himself. "It's the militia, yes?"

"Yeah." *What do I do? How do I get out of this?*

"Dear Carson...please don't let them take me."

Carson's about to lunge for the knapsack when she hears him wheeze his plea. She stops, moves her light to his face. She never expected him to give up like this. She'd always figured he'd talk or shoot his way out of everything. But there's no fight left in his eyes.

She steps in front of him. His head is a bit slow to follow her movement. He looks up at her with a dazed but not unpleasant expression. "Be safe, dear Carson."

Before she can second-guess herself, she puts two rounds into his heart.

Doors break open. The clatter of running boots fills her ears. Shouts.

A tsunami of soldiers crashes over her.

CHAPTER 33

SATURDAY, 14 MAY

Galina steps out of the farm building into a war.

Armored vehicles roar everywhere, their heavy machineguns thumping. Militia soldiers swarm the area from the west and east. Shooting, yelling, grenades.

She slips between the building's north wall and the screen of trees next to it and makes herself as small as she can. All the pictures from Ilovaisk stream through her mind—the Russians closing in on her foxhole, the burning lorries, Misha contorting as the flames devoured him… She curls in a ball, sobbing, "No no no God please no not again no…"

A few minutes later, the assault ends as suddenly as it began. Galina's all cried out. She wipes her eyes and nose on her sleeve, then crawls to the building's end to see what's happening. Militiamen carry or help their wounded to a collection point somewhere in the dark. A pair of militiamen dump a Russian's body off the square building's roof like it's trash. Officers shout commands and try to collect their men.

Then two soldiers carry Tarasenko toward a BTR with extra antennas on it. A command vehicle.

Is she alive? Galina can't tell. She's covered with blood and her shirt's half ripped off. Galina's first reaction is to attack, to shoot the men and try to get her to safety someplace. But there are too many militia *tarhany* to try anything rash like that.

Other than the dead man from the square building's roof, she doesn't see any *Kacápskyi*. *Did they get away? Are they hiding? Are they all dead?* She hopes they're all dead; serves them right. Not that she wants the militia to win. Maybe if the militia killed the Russians, other Russians will come destroy the militia. They both lose. She wins; Ukraine wins.

One by one, the armor and lorries snort themselves alive and stampede off to the south. She knows exactly where they're going: Kuteinykove, their home base, less than twenty kilometers south and east.

The dead farm goes quiet. Only the wind rustles the trees and whistles through the gaps between the buildings. She sits with her back against a tree trunk, hugging the knapsack. Trying not to cry and struggling to decide what to do next. She hears Tarasenko's voice from an hour ago: *If things go south, take off. Try to get to the car and go home.*

She walks carefully to where the militia left the dead *Kacáps*. They took his rifle, field gear, and boots. He's now just another broken corpse in a nation full of them. She stares at him for a long while. The dead don't scare her anymore; she pities them. Except dead *Kacápskyi*.

Galina spits on him, then trudges toward the highway and the Octavia.

She risks taking the highway that skirts Kuteinykove, but the *kolorady* at the militia checkpoint just wave her through even though it's well past midnight and nothing except Russian convoys are supposed to be moving. Maybe it's a sign.

I should stop and look for Tarasenko.

She's dead. They want her body for a trophy.

Is she dead? I saw her head move. She's strong, hard to kill.

Even if she is alive, what can you do for her? She told you to go home. Listen.

Galina reluctantly keeps driving.

She pulls into her farm's driveway at the cusp of sunrise. Everything looks the same. Of course it does; she's been gone, what, two days? It just seems like forever. Friday lasted a month.

Galina steps into the morning chill without her sweatshirt. She hoped it would wake her up, but all it does is make her cold and distracted. She starts to unlock the side door into her house, but stops—she doesn't want to go inside yet. She doesn't know what she wants to do.

So she drifts across her back yard to her field. Little green spikes poke out of the ridges, encouraged by the last few days of rain. She automatically squats, pinches dirt from the nearest furrow, then sniffs it. Moist, rich, strong. It's not the soil's fault that she can't make a living farming, that she had to cook in the Dontsement company cafeteria in Amvrosiivka to make ends meet. The soil's kept her alive (but only just) since the cement factory fired her when she wouldn't sign that stupid declaration supporting the rebellion.

There's no future here for her or for Bohdan. They made their decisions, but it didn't work out. Now it's time to start over. If they can. If this place will let them go.

Two hours later, Galina's washed, changed clothes, and packed her things and Bohdan's into the new car along with what little else is worth taking to their new lives.

The car idles at the junction of the road leading north from Olhynske and the T0507 highway at the south edge of Amvrosiivka. If she turns right, she goes to Russia (nothing she'd ever do). If she turns left, Kuteinykove is the next town. Her plan is to go straight and stop at the grocery store next to the Amvrosiivka bus station. There she can buy food and drinks for the long drive ahead to Shakhtarsk to free Bohdan, then west to free them both.

She can't force herself to go forward.

Galina can still see the money in the knapsack she hid under the luggage, the pile of yellow notes with the fancy glass door on the front and the bridge on the back. More money than she's ever seen at one time. Certainly more money than she's ever had in her hands. Far, far more than she needs to free Bohdan. Many times more than they need for the trip to Krakow, to get a flat, to live until they find jobs. They don't even *need* jobs with all that.

The money Tarasenko gave her is already too much. But it's at least *real*, not some fairy story, not a number she can't comprehend. She focuses on that single bundle of yellow notes.

Why did she give me so much?

Galina remembers the argument they had on the church steps in Komsomolske. How they promised each other they'd keep going until the icon and the painting are where they belong. That hasn't happened yet. The icon's gone; she'd checked when she got to the car. The *Kacápskyi* must've taken it before the militia attacked, just like they took the other money.

She hasn't kept her promise. Neither has Tarasenko. *She's got an excuse. What's mine?*

What happened to Tarasenko? Does she need my help?

Does she want *my help?*

Galina wipes her eyes on the tail of her sweatshirt, then fishes the stack of cash out from under the seat. She holds it up to remind herself it's real.

I have the money. It's mine. No one can take it from me.

She looks both ways on the highway.

Which way do I go?

CHAPTER 34

The first time Carson comes to, the entire world is shaking. The noise is worse than a metal band in a small bar. Her wrists and ankles are tied. Every square inch of her hurts like hell. When she finally pries open her eyes, the red-lit interior of some kind of armored vehicle surrounds her. Half a dozen militia troops fill the space.

One says, "Hey, this one's awake."

Another says, "Not for long."

Something hard whacks her on top of her head.

The next time she comes to, everything's black.

Am I blind?

The idea slices through the jumble of pain and memory fragments clogging her brain. Someone's been using her head for drum practice. She tries to see her hand in front of her face (her wrists are untied—bonus), but can't.

She rolls onto her back. It takes a lot of effort and shoots fireworks into her eyes. The floor beneath her is cool, slimy, and rough. Slimy and rough?

She's naked. *Aw, fuck.*

Okay. They beat the shit out of me and stripped me. What else did they do?

Her crotch doesn't hurt any worse than the rest of her, which isn't saying much. She can't check for blood if she can't see. *Don't go there. Don't. Go. There. Deal with it later.*

She lies there, letting her brain drift. Not that she can stop it.

After however long, she manages to roll onto her hands and knees without blacking out. Some time later, she works up enough courage to try to stand. Bad idea; she stays upright only because she's next to a ribbed steel wall rough with rust. Her groan echoes.

When the blind whirlies pass, she works her way around the room, estimating dimensions with her armspan. It's two meters wide, two meters and change deep, with a steel door grafted onto one side. The air's cool and damp. A shipping container? The floor feels like dirty plywood. A plastic bucket sits in a foul-smelling corner near the door.

Getting up and moving around partly clears her head and settles her stomach. Everything still hurts, but it's under control...sort of. Carson starts stretching and bending slowly, probing for any bone or joint damage. Her balance is off and her head throbs when she touches her toes, but everything still seems to work. Knee lifts are excruciating. Bicycles are okay in short spurts, but getting vertical again is tough. Doing wall sits is like rubbing forty-grit sandpaper on her back.

Her attempted warmup doesn't last long. Once she keels over a couple times and wades through several waves of pain, she settles on walking for now.

While she paces circles around the room, her own brain becomes her worst enemy. *You failed*, it tells her. *You failed the museum, you failed Allyson, you failed Heitmann, you failed Galina. You failed. You failed.*

Her brain doesn't stop there. *You're blind. A hit you took broke something. You're useless if you can't see.* The anxiety mixes with the hunger from last night's small, crappy dinner to tie her stomach into a bow.

I'm getting too old for this shit.

Is Galina okay? Did she get away? Do they have her too? Is she here? The militia shouldn't know about her unless Rogozhkin told them, which she doubts. Somebody was shooting at somebody at the ex-farm, and the only people around to do it were the *spetsnaz* and the militia. That's a big clue that the two aren't on speaking terms. So unless Galina got caught in the crossfire, she should be okay.

There was a lot of crossfire. Lots of soldiers. Lots of ways to get hurt. *Please don't let her be hurt. Galina doesn't deserve that.*

Carson will survive. She won't enjoy it, but she'll make it.

Where am I, anyway?

◎

The caged light in the ceiling is a miserable yellowish compact fluorescent bulb, but when it blinks on, it's like a supernova exploding above Carson's head. Her pupils are as dilated as they'll ever be; the sudden light's physically painful. She slams shut her eyelids and braces herself against the wall opposite the door.

She can definitely see light and dark. When she pries one eyelid open a fraction of an inch, she can make out the rust stains on the walls through the glare. The relief almost buckles her knees.

The door squeals open.

She cracks both eyelids. A militiaman stands in the doorway, his hands in his pockets, staring at her.

Carson doesn't even consider covering herself. That's what this tool wants—for her to be ashamed or frightened or both. *Fuck him.* She's been naked in front of guys almost since she can remember. Small apartments, single-wide trailers, shared bedrooms, tiny bathrooms, a steadily growing number of brothers, European parents…naked's no big deal. Even though she's dirty, covered with bruises and scrapes, starving, still woozy from what may be multiple thumpings, and feels like absolute shit, she will *not* let this chirp see her defeated.

Carson leans into the far corner, crosses her ankles, crosses her arms (making sure she doesn't cover her nipples), and stares right back, hoping her squint looks like attitude. The trooper's eyes sweep up and down between her throat and her knees, pausing at strategic points.

Some seconds later, she says in Russian, "I won't dance until you put in a pole." It comes out as a feral growl; she hasn't said a word in hours and hasn't had anything to drink for longer.

The trooper snorts and shakes his head. He drags in a short three-legged wooden stool and sets up a regular-sized ladder-back wooden chair just outside the door. Then he stands aside so another man can stop in the doorway.

Carson recognizes this one. He's the officer who showed up at the chicken farm after Stepaniak's stunt. His older-pattern Russian camo is clean and fits well. He stands straight, like he had in Amvrosiivka a decade ago. She gives him credit—his eyes don't go too far below her collarbones.

She rasps, "Go ahead and look. Everybody else has."

His eyebrows arch. "You speak Russian?"

"Among other things."

"Just so you know, you're not getting special treatment. We strip all our prisoners. It makes them more...cooperative."

"Especially in January."

He gives her a pale smile. "They become very cooperative in January." He waves toward the stool. "Please, sit. We need to talk."

The stool's built for a six-year-old and is next to the bucket. No way is she sitting on the damn thing. "I'll stand for now. Standing feels good."

"Suit yourself." He settles on the chair and crosses his legs. "I am Mashkov, Dima Artemovich. Colonel in command of the Makiivka Brigade. What do I call you?"

This again. Big parts of her brain are still mush. Pushing ideas around is hard, tiring work, and so is maintaining an attitude. A name? She eventually goes for simple, about all she can handle right now. "Tarasenko."

Mashkov nods. "Are you sure you don't want to sit? You look...unsteady."

She feels it, too. Maybe pacing for however long wasn't such a good idea. "Only if I get the chair."

"Sorry, no. You put two of my men in the hospital and another three on light duty. You're not popular here."

I did that? She can't remember much that happened after she shot Stepaniak. "They probably deserved it."

He frowns and shifts in his chair. "You were found in a room with Abram Stepaniak. Do you know him?"

"Yes."

"He was dead. He'd been shot at least four times by at least two different weapons. Do you know how that happened?"

"Yes." Glowing static creeps into her vision. She tries to breathe slow and deep, but it isn't working.

He waits for her to go on. "Would you care to inform me?"

"He attacked me twice in the past couple of days. The chest shots? That was me."

"You killed him?"

"Yes."

"How do you know him?"

Carson reuses what she can remember of the summary she gave Rogozhkin. It takes a while; her tongue isn't behaving. She tries to blink away the static but it won't leave her alone. *Maybe the stool isn't such a bad idea…*

Mashkov taps his knee idly while he considers her. Whatever he's doing, he's not letching on her; it's cooler, more abstract, like he's looking at a picture that doesn't make any sense. Not how men usually look at her when she's naked.

"This Stepaniak took half the ransom from the Amvrosiivka massacre. *Our* money. Do you know where he put it?"

She can picture the knapsack at the farm. She was going to pick it up when Stepaniak asked her to kill him. *They don't have it?*

Carson's head floats like it's full of helium. She tries to squeeze the stars out of her vision with her eyelids, but it doesn't work. "Stepaniak…had…" She's collapsing into a hunch. That won't do. She tries to stand straight.

Her knees turn to jelly.

She doesn't feel herself hit the floor.

CHAPTER 35

Carson wakes up to a woman's voice speaking Russian.

"...*thinking?* Look at her! She's been beaten half to death."

Mashkov's voice, defensive. "She was standing a few minutes ago."

"And she's not now. You should've called me as soon as she got here." The woman's voice is closer to Carson than Mashkov's. "And, *naked?* You put a woman in a cell that these men can get into, and you take away all her defenses? You know—"

"Remember the five men you looked at a few hours ago?" Mashkov sounds like he's had enough of being read out. "*She* did that to them. She's hardly defenseless. What's wrong with her?"

Carson wants to be unconscious again. She hasn't even bothered to open her eyes. But someone's near her: a latex-covered hand rocks her onto her back, then another latex hand gently pats her cheek. She fights her eyelids open.

A pretty young brunette with a kind-but-worried face looks down at her. "Hi. How do you feel?" Russian, but gentle, like she's talking to a hurt kid.

It takes a while for Carson to work up enough spit to say anything. "Like shit."

The brunette smiles a little. "I bet. I'm Dunya. I'm the brigade's chief medic. What's your name?"

That again. The answer's no easier than last time, though this time it's about not being able to think. "Lisa."

"Okay, Lisa. I'm going to take you to the clinic—"

Mashkov: "You are *not*—"

"—so I can examine you and patch you up—"

"A guard's going with you, then."

"—with a guard, but don't worry about him. I'll take care of you. You'll be *safe*." Dunya points at the guard in the doorway. "You. Give me your blouse. Now." Nothing gentle about that.

The guard looks to Mashkov for help. The colonel gives him a whatever-makes-her-happy wave. The guard reluctantly hands Dunya—a senior lieutenant, according to the shoulder boards on her baggy uniform top—his hip-length camo field tunic.

The medic manages to wrestle the blouse onto Carson and get her on her feet. Carson has a good four inches on her. Dunya helps her stagger toward the door.

Mashkov retreats to give them room. He doesn't look happy. "She's your responsibility now, Lieutenant."

Dunya stops. "Sir. If I can fix her up enough for her to start making trouble, you can do whatever you want to me…because I'll be a miracle worker. We'll be in the clinic."

The clinic's a small, white box of a building close to the front gate, about twenty meters from the makeshift prison. It must've been a clinic longer than this complex has been a military base; there's a lot of wear on the powder-blue ceramic tile lining the walls in the three rooms, and the scratches and dings on the stainless-steel examination table are rusted.

Dunya shoos away the guard, gets Carson seated on the table, then peels the tunic off her. She tsks. "What did they do to you?"

"Don't remember."

"Well, the first thing we need to do is clean you up. Between the blood and the dirt, I can't see a thing. Come on."

Carson sags against the tile of a small shower cubicle in the back of the exam room while Dunya gives her a thorough top-to-toe scrubbing with sturdy rags, bottled water (the tap isn't working), and soap that smells like it'll kill any living organism it touches. Then Carson melts onto the table and lets her mind wander as Dunya does a workup on her, including a pelvic exam.

"You are a very lucky woman. I don't see any labial or vaginal trauma. There's bruising, but you've got bruises all over you, so…"

Carson drains two full water bottles in less than two minutes as she sits slumped on the table's edge, her legs dangling. For the first time, she can take stock of what's happened to her. All the dark welts make her look more like a leopard than a woman.

She watches a slightly blurry Dunya fill out a chart at the stainless-steel counter along the opposite wall. Rescue? Carson's not fond of being rescued; it makes her feel weak. She'd rather work out her own problems. In this case, though, she wasn't getting out of that tin box without help. Maybe Dunya will be an ally, something she needs here while she's so messed up. "There was a kid at the chicken farm in Amvrosiivka. Did he make it?"

Dunya turns, a slim eyebrow up. "Did you patch him up?"

"Yeah. Is he okay?"

"Hardly." Dunya rests her rear against the counter's edge. "He's alive...thanks to you."

At least I did something right.

Dunya's cute little nose scrunches. "What are you? You're not from here."

"How do you know?"

"You're healthy."

It took Carson almost two years of working for Rodievsky and Allyson to figure out how to explain what she does without inviting a lot of unwanted questions. "I fix things."

"Okay." She waits a few beats. "What kinds of things?"

"Things that need fixing."

More waiting. Dunya sighs and rubs the back of her neck. "Okay. It looks like you were hit on the head hard enough to break the skin at least three times. I'm about ninety-nine percent sure you have a concussion. It's amazing you don't have any broken bones. I'll give you something for the pain, and you're going to lie down on that table and rest for a while. Your body needs time to heal. I'd let you sleep in my cot, but you need more support than that. While you're resting, I'll try to find your clothes and get some food for you. Please don't try to leave—you're in no shape to go anywhere. Understand?"

Carson's not sure she can walk, far less escape. "Why are you doing this?"

"What, my job?"

"No. Being nice. You saw what I did to your guys. I'm the enemy or something, right?"

Dunya gazes at her for what seems like a long time. The action behind her eyes tells Carson she's trying to figure it out herself. Then she steps to a glass-fronted cabinet and rummages through medicine bottles. "Yes, I saw what you did to those men. But I also saw what you did for the boy, Artem. You didn't have to. Stopping to do it probably put you in danger. So I think you're probably a good person who I don't want to make mad." She drops two white capsules into her left palm, then brings them to Carson. "Take these. You know, I see a lot of abused women when I go out in the villages on calls. I never see them hit back. So maybe…maybe I see you and think, someone's finally hitting back."

CHAPTER 36

Mashkov enters the Ops Center and crosses to Vasilenko, who's frowning at the plotting table in the room's center. "What do you have for me, Lenya?"

The senior sergeant concentrates on his radio headset. He holds up his left hand, palm out: *wait a moment.* Then he murmurs, "Understand. Makiivka Ops out." He pushes away the microphone stalk and shifts his focus to Mashkov. "Did you get anything out of the woman?"

"She passed out before she said much. Lieutenant Fetisova is patching her up enough for questioning."

Vasilenko frowns. "Why are we even bothering with her? She was part of that massacre in Amvrosiivka. Why not—"

"We don't know what part." On his way here, Mashkov had to answer several versions of the question, *when are you going to shoot the woman?* At least he's had a chance to practice an answer. "Frankly, the only reason she's still alive is because she saved that boy's life. There's more to it than what's in the rumors going around. She's tied up with Rogozhkin somehow, we know that. Maybe she'll be useful for getting our money back from him. We'll see. You called for me?"

"Yes, sir. Remember the beacon on the bandit's Range Rover?"

An odd question. "Of course. Except it moved to a Škoda saloon. That's how we found him in Byryuky. Why?"

"It's moving."

Rogozhkin asks nobody in particular, "Who's driving that car?"

He's sitting on a collapsible sling chair on a concrete pad outside the warehouse sheltering his Hunter and Syrov's two Tigrs. The storage yard is less than three kilometers from last night's debacle at the ruined farm, but the militia didn't bother to chase him or Syrov's men. He finds that curious.

"What car?" Syrov grumbles. He plunks onto an upended plastic bucket, slurping tea from a tin cup. His mirrored sunglasses reflect the two warehouses across the hundred-meter stretch of concrete and dirt from where they sit.

"The one the women were driving."

Syrov shrugs. "Maybe it's the women."

"Mashkov's people got Tarasenko. I don't know what happened to the short one."

"Maybe she's driving it."

"Could be. She's heading north. Maybe she has enough sense to get out of this mess. How are your men?"

Once the scale of the militia assault became obvious, the section broke off its defensive fire and withdrew. God alone knows what the militia was shooting at after that—itself? Two snipers managed to melt into the night, but the third was trapped and killed. Syrov personally led a sortie to recover the man's body. Rogozhkin told them all to stand down and get some rest, though he doubts they did much sleeping.

Syrov drains his cup. "They're angry. I don't blame them. Vitya was a good man. Fucking militia got lucky." He leans his elbows on his knees. "What now, sir?"

What now, indeed? They took the icon from the Octavia and almost a million euros from Tarasenko. The militia must have the rest.

He knows what he *should* do. He *should* turn over the money to the militia, then find Tarasenko and give her the icon, as they'd agreed.

But that doesn't solve his retirement problem. It's also complicated by Proskurin's aborted coup attempt against Mashkov. Rogozhkin knows he won't get a warm welcome in Kuteinykove.

He *could* spirit the money off to a numbered account in Cyprus. He *could* contact certain Moldovans he met years ago who can sell the icon for a substantial sum of money. True, it's a gangster move. Then again, he's been enriching other gangsters and warlords for years. This way, he could put in his papers and find a little place to settle down in Crimea, where it never gets too cold. He remembers it from his time helping rip the peninsula away from Kyiv's greedy fingers. Green grass and sunshine in February: no secret why

Moscow wants it so badly.

Neither solution requires Syrov or his men.

When in doubt, rely on old habits. "I'm waiting for instructions from Rostov."

Syrov nods knowingly. "Sir...the men were wondering if we could send some money to Vitya's family. You know how low the death benefits are, even if the army admits he was killed in action."

"I know. How much?"

"Fifty thousand?"

The least he can do for a fallen soldier. "That's fair." He makes a quick calculation. "Take another fifty for yourself and the men. It's the only reward they'll get. And...ask them to keep quiet about it. *All* of it. Nobody else needs to know."

"Thank you, sir." Syrov grunts off the bucket and shakes out his legs. "Do you need us anymore?"

Rogozhkin hates to let them go until he knows what he's going to do. "I'll tell you in a few hours."

"When you hear from Rostov." Something in Syrov's voice implies he may not completely believe Rogozhkin's waiting for orders.

"Of course."

Rogozhkin watches Syrov disappear into the warehouse. He settles into his chair, massaging his leg.

Then his satellite phone rings. General Tulantyev. *Now what?* "Rogozhkin here."

"Edik. Good morning." Tulantyev sounds expansive. It seems too early for him to be drinking already, though. "Or is it? Perhaps you should tell me."

He knows. But how *does he know?* "Sir, I'm not sure I follow."

"Don't play the innocent with me." His voice turns hard. "The coup at your pet militia? Or should I say, *attempted* coup? Surely you're aware of it, if you didn't actually organize it."

Rogozhkin takes a moment to calibrate how he should handle this. "Sir, I'm in the field. All I've heard are rumors that Proskurin tried to arrest the local commander and died doing it. I won't know more until I get back to the base."

"So this isn't your doing?" Skepticism lies heavy in his voice. "It's not like you haven't done this before."

"True, when it's been necessary. I don't mean to boast, but if

I'd organized this action, it wouldn't have failed. You know that from my record."

The general grumbles, "Yes, yes, I know. I also know that two of our colonels and two majors are dead and the *hohol* commander's declared war on us. What in hell is happening out there? Why are you in the field?"

Rogozhkin explains in very rough terms the bandit problem and how he's trying to keep the militias from butting heads. He leaves out the parts about the patrol, the money, the women, and the stolen artworks; there's only so much complexity that Tulantyev can deal with.

"So what happened?"

"I don't know, sir. Proskurin's a bigot and an egomaniac. The local commander, Mashkov, is a Donbass patriot and a pain in the ass. They've been butting heads for over a year. Proskurin may have taken advantage of my absence to do something rash. Now that the bandit's dead, I can look into this matter and report my findings."

Tulantyev's line goes silent for an unusually long time. *Who else has been listening? Who's Tulantyev talking to now? What intel hasn't he shared? How much trouble am I in?*

"Edik Gregorivich."

"Sir?"

"You've let things get out of hand. The locals are killing our officers, for God's sake. You're supposed to keep them in line. I'm relieving you. Don't go to the militia base—God alone knows what they'll do to you. Report back here with that *spetsnaz* section we sent you. We'll discuss this matter and decide what we're going to do with you."

No. Oh, no. "But, sir—"

"No buts. Your time in the field is done. I expect to see you in my office on Monday morning. Understand?"

Rogozhkin understands. His world is ending.

CHAPTER 37

Carson sits as straight as she can on the exam table and glares at Mashkov.

He raises an eyebrow. "Was that a difficult question, Miss Tarasenko?" He'd asked, *Are you feeling better?*

"I want my shit."

She'd still be naked if Dunya hadn't scraped up some extra-large utilities for her. Carson's clothes and gear are still missing. If Dunya hadn't fed her after she woke up after lunchtime, she'd be good and pissed off.

"Lieutenant Fetisova is dealing with that." Mashkov settles into the ancient rolling office chair. "But before you get it, we need to establish exactly what part you play in this situation. You understand that, of course."

Carson glances toward Dunya, who's leaning into the corner formed by two legs of the countertop lining the opposite walls. The nurse's eyes switch between her and Mashkov like she's watching a tennis match. She'd insisted on sticking around, making Carson marginally happier. "Whatever. Let's get it done."

"Right. The money. Where is it?"

"Stepaniak had it. I never got it." She stares at the wall for a moment. "Any of your guys go missing? Maybe they took it."

"None of my men are missing. If you *had* taken it, what would you have done with it?"

"Give it to Rogozhkin."

Mashkov leans back and frowns. That must be a surprise. They really aren't working together. "What did he intend to do with it?"

"Give it to you." Shrugging hurts, like everything else. "That's what he said."

"Where did you meet Colonel Rogozhkin?"

"Outside Starobesheve. I shot Stas—Stepaniak's goon—and Rogozhkin and his people grabbed me. I didn't get much choice about helping them."

Mashkov prods her through a step-by-step recitation of everything she did from the massacre at the chicken factory to the moment she killed Stepaniak. She tells it straight. Lying gets her nowhere, and she's in no condition to keep track of lies anyway.

Carson rolls out her neck and shoulders, blinking away the stars creeping into her vision. "Look. All I want is the pictures. The money can go wherever. But the pictures go to Bonn with me or there's gonna be a problem."

"I believe we've seen what you mean by a 'problem.'" He flashes a grim smile. "We confiscated the Cranach from the room where we found you. Where is the icon?"

"I had it. If you don't have it now, then Rogozhkin does."

"He also has half of our money."

"Welcome to my world. It's been going this way since Wednesday." She scowls. "What's going on between you two? Thought you were on the same side."

He hesitates, clearly sorting out what to tell her. "Not all our Russian brothers have our best interests at heart."

"No shit? I could've told you that."

Mashkov gives her a hard look. "Lieutenant, I need to have a private conversation with Miss Tarasenko."

Dunya says, "You know I can keep secrets, sir."

Carson thumbs toward Dunya. "She gave me a pelvic exam. I don't have many secrets with her anymore."

Mashkov winces, then composes himself. "As you wish. Have you any idea where Colonel Rogozhkin is now?"

"No. Thought Rogozhkin was coming back here. Since you're asking, I guess he didn't."

"He hasn't. We lost contact with him yesterday."

"Around the time you shot the Russians?"

Mashkov's cheeks warm a few degrees. "You're well informed." He aims a scolding eyebrow at Dunya.

Carson says, "You have a history of that. Shooting prisoners. Like at Ilovaisk?"

Mashkov snaps, "I wasn't commander then." His ears turn pale red. "The situation here is very...*fluid* just now. Yes, we've broken with our Russian minders. That means we've also broken with their supplies and funds. We need the money Rogozhkin has to make up the troops' back pay and to fill our petrol storage before we begin an operation next week. You say you're anxious to recover the icon and return to the West. This makes me think we have a certain…shall we say, commonality of interests. Would you agree?"

For once, Carson thinks about her answer before she says a word. Moving anything through the sludge in her head is like walking through Jell-O.

Mashkov's right: she has unfinished business with Rogozhkin. But saying that will lead to Mashkov asking her to get the money from the Russian, something she's not so keen to do. "You know he's got ten *spetsnaz* operators with him, right?"

"I'm aware of that. I believe there are nine, now."

"Losing one will piss him off." Carson turns toward Dunya. "How many in the brigade?"

"One thousand one hundred eighty-six, not counting prisoners and patients."

"Let's see…" Carson taps her lips with an index finger. "Twelve hundred of you against ten of them. That's almost a fair fight."

Mashkov's face turns stony. "Your point?"

"If you take him on—*seriously* do it, not just trip over him like last night—prepare to lose a lot of troops. I've seen what ex-*spetsnaz* can do. I can imagine what the real deal can do with an army behind them."

"Your *point?*"

"He'll maybe give me the icon. I did him a solid by killing Stepaniak. But he won't give up the money unless he feels like it. What can you offer him?"

Dunya raises a hand. "Since I'm here… Lisa shouldn't be going anywhere. She was beaten. She has a concussion. She needs to recover before she goes running around out there."

Lisa? Oh, yeah, that's me. "What'll you give Rogozhkin if he hands over the money?"

Mashkov crosses his arms and rocks in the chair. "I have Rogozhkin's *starshina*, a man named Yartsev. He's in hospital in Amvrosiivka with two bullet wounds. The lieutenant tells me that he'll survive. I know how I feel about my senior sergeant and I expect Colonel Rogozhkin feels the same about his. The question is whether this Yartsev is worth a million euros to him."

Good play. Hostages usually get people's attention. But it's never a good idea to expect sentimentality in a special operator of any kind. Rogozhkin doesn't strike Carson as someone who'll trade away a big advantage for a small return. Mashkov may know something about Rogozhkin that she doesn't.

"Miss Tarasenko." Mashkov leaves the chair and paces toward the now-useless sink. "If I set you free, won't you go directly to Rogozhkin to collect the icon?"

"I would if I knew where he is. Which I don't."

"He may know where you are."

"How?"

Mashkov leans back against the sink and faces Carson again. "According to what you told me, he seems to be able to find you."

"The first time was about an explosion. Then he followed me from Starobesheve to Byryuky."

"Was he always in visual range?"

"Well, his guys…"

"Are you certain?"

Maybe it's the headache or the pain pills, but Carson's confused. "What are you saying?"

Mashkov lets a satisfied smile spread across his mouth. "I have reason to think he can follow you. I won't go into more detail. If you leave, I expect he can find you again."

That sounds like Mashkov thinks Rogozhkin has a tracker on her. But how would he have managed that? Yeah, he stood real close to her before she and Galina went to the farm, but she'd have noticed if he'd planted something…wouldn't she? "Did you find something in my clothes?"

"Perhaps." Mashkov considers her for a while, though Carson's not sure he's actually seeing her. Finally, he nods once. "I propose this: I release you and provide a vehicle. You drive toward Mospyne."

"It's not safe for her to drive." Dunya leans toward Mashkov while pointing at Carson. "She gets dizzy. It's a symptom of concussion. If that happens while she's driving—"

"Yes, Lieutenant, I understand." Mashkov waves her off. "I would be very surprised if Colonel Rogozhkin doesn't come to you, either to pay his debt or to get intelligence about what's happening here. You relay my offer—the money for Yartsev."

"So I'm delivering a message?"

"Yes."

Carson braces her palms on the tabletop so she can stretch her back and buy some thinking time. This scheme gets her close to the icon—assuming Rogozhkin comes out of whatever hole he went into—and all she has to do is pass on Mashkov's demand before she takes the painting and icon and makes a run for the contact line. It could end this gong show real fast.

It's too easy.

She glances at Dunya—watching Carson with the expression of a worried mother—then focuses on Mashkov. "Let's see if I got this straight. You give me the picture and let me go. I let Rogozhkin find me. I tell him your deal, take the icon, and disappear. Did I miss anything?"

"Yes, you did." Mashkov gives her a meaningless smile. "I let you go, but I keep the Cranach for now to make certain you do as you're told. It appears that isn't something you do well. If you refuse, I put you in a cell and leave you there until the brigade returns from next week's operation. If you don't return by tomorrow at sunset, the painting will go into secure storage and you won't see it until we return, if then. The only way you can take it away it is to buy it with the money Colonel Rogozhkin took from us. Do you understand now?"

CHAPTER 38

Carson's clothes appear about thirty minutes after she and Dunya finish dinner. It doesn't take long to sort through them. When she's done, she tosses her blood-caked jeans on the pile in disgust. "Fuck." English.

Dunya pokes her head out of the storeroom and says in clear, lightly accented English, "Do you speak English?"

"Uh, yeah. Do you?"

"Yes." Dunya leans against the doorjamb. She's taken off her baggy uniform blouse, exposing a semi-tight olive-drab tee shirt. She's petite and fine-boned, though her tanned arms have a fair amount of definition. "Mama and Papa hired for me a tutor. I do not get to speak as often as I want. Is it easier for you than speaking Russian?"

"Yeah."

Dunya smiles. "Can we speak in English? I like to practice. You can right me when I am wrong."

"Correct you." This is unexpected, but welcome. Carson's brain hurts enough without adding the constant translation strain. "Okay. You're doing fine."

"Thank you. What is wrong with your things?" She frowns. "Are wrong?"

"Is wrong. Everything's bloody."

Dunya raises an eyebrow.

"Okay, my fault. Both my shirts are torn to shit. And *this...*" She holds what's left of her Cheata bra. "They cut this off me. I paid a hundred bucks for this thing and they *destroyed* it."

Dunya's perky little nose wrinkles as she peers at what Carson's waving at her. "What is that ugly thing?"

"Compression bra. And yeah, it's ugly, but it's to keep me alive, not get me laid." She gets back a blank expression. "You wear body armor in the field?"

"You mean the bullet vest?" Dunya waves her hands over her

torso like she has one on. "Yes, sometimes."

"Ever have a problem when you run or move around a lot, and your tits move, and your vest shifts out of place?"

"Tits?"

"Breasts."

"No." Dunya cups her breasts through her shirt. "They are small. I wear two sport bras and it is good."

"Yeah, well, you saw mine. Sports bras don't cut it. This squashes everything together so they don't move at all." Carson glares at what's left of her very expensive bra. *They couldn't take a minute to figure out how to unzip it? Assholes.* She tosses it in the nearest garbage can. "And my baton, knife, and sidearm are still gone." *On the black market already?* She wouldn't be surprised, but she'd be pissed. At least she got her watch back. Good thing she left her money in the car.

Dunya sorts through the messy pile Carson left on the exam table. She holds up the jeans. "You can wash this in the sink. Use the water bottles. The rest...?" She shrugs.

Carson grabs the jeans, her underwear, and her socks, and stalks to the battered porcelain sink. "Please *please* find me a shirt. This thing's scraping the shit out of my nipples. The more that happens, the more pissed off I get. You won't like me when I'm mad. Okay?"

Dunya's mouth twists. "Okay. I will lock the door when I go. If you run away, the guard will shoot you. It will make me very sad."

While Dunya's gone, Carson searches the storeroom, which is also Dunya's bedroom. She finds a rumpled cot, a clothesline crowded with underwear, two jumbled shelves of uniforms and clothes, and miscellaneous supplies. As she scrubs the blood out of her jeans, she tries to figure out what to do next.

There's no way she's leaving the Cranach behind when she walks out of here. She's done with chasing the damn thing all over. But Mashkov isn't going to change his mind. She'll have to take the painting, then leave before he notices. *Good luck with that.*

Where does he keep it? He's got to have a secure place to store valuables, like money and codebooks. It'll be someplace he can keep an eye on. The command staff must have offices around here. But where?

Dunya would know. She probably won't just blab it out,

though. Carson could beat it out of a guy, but not another woman. Men do more than enough of that shit; she doesn't need to add to it. Certainly not with Dunya.

Once she gets the painting, she has to get out. Carson saw a tiny sliver of the base on her way from the cells to the clinic while she was concentrating on not tripping over her own feet. The only window in the clinic is obscure glass. How many guards are at the front gate? How far is it from the command offices?

Again, Dunya would know. All Carson has to do is get her to talk.

Forty minutes later, when Dunya returns with a large olive-drab tee shirt, Carson's head throbs from too much thinking...and she still doesn't have a plan.

She slips on the tee—*so* much better than the camo top's rough stitching—and perches on the exam table. "Thanks. You're a lifesaver. Hope it wasn't a lot of trouble."

"It is no problem to find." Still speaking English. Dunya hangs her uniform blouse on the back of the desk chair, steps out of her runners, then curls up in the chair. "I must lie to the supply sergeant to get it. He will not give it to me if it is for you." She sighs. "I wish I have your body. I feel so small and weak next to the men."

Carson gets that a lot from other women. "It's a lot of work to keep up. Don't worry; you're fine. I wish I had your face." *Get to it...* "So...what's Mashkov's story?"

Dunya thinks for a few moments. A soft little smile touches her lips. "He is a very good man. A good commander. He loves the brigade and he loves the people in it. He was with the brigade from the beginning, do you know? He is usually very fair. That is why he disappoints me today. What he asks of you is unfair." She swivels until she can stare at the ancient refrigerator grumbling across the room. After some consideration, she raids it for a bottle of yellowish liquid and two shot glasses that she sets up on the exam table. She pours shots and hands one to Carson.

It smells like lemons and cloves. "What is this?"

"*Spotykach*." Dunya belts her drink. Her eyes flare, and she blows out a sharp breath.

Carson chugs the shot. There's sugar and coriander, too. It's an eye-opener. "Vodka?"

"Yes." Dunya refills the glasses. This round, she sips.

There's more than one way to get information…

Vodka isn't Carson's favorite—she prefers single-malt whiskey and the occasional Manhattan—but at least this tastes like something. "So. Mashkov."

Dunya lets out a big sigh. "This week has been very difficult for him. He tries so much and he expects much of self."

"Himself."

"Yes. Sorry. I think he feels very alone."

Carson notes the concern, even sadness, in Dunya's voice, and the semi-dreamy look on her face. "Does he know you have a crush on him?"

Dunya gives her a puzzled frown. "A crush?"

"You're in love with him."

Dunya's cheeks pink up. "I think he does not notice. If he does, he says nothing."

He can't be that clueless. "Ever just lay it out for him? Tell him?"

"I cannot do that!" Dunya's cheeks shift from pink to red. "He is very married."

"So?"

"He rings his wife every night if he can." Dunya's talking to the floor now. "Or he writes the email. He loves her very much."

It's almost cute, watching the nurse turn fifteen again. But it's also maddening. Carson's known so many smart, accomplished women who were still tangled up in that high-school waiting-for-the-cute-guy-to-notice-her bullshit. "She's not here. He's a guy. And you're pretty."

"No!" Dunya almost throws herself from the chair but catches herself in time. "He could make me leave. I could not. No."

This isn't the talk Carson wanted, but it's the one she's got. A little girl-bonding might help when she segues to what she wants to know—the painting—so she might as well push this talk down the ice. She refills their glasses, then sips while Dunya downs hers in two goes.

The conversation's level degenerates as the booze level sinks in the bottle: brigade gossip, Dunya's nonexistent sex life, men. Over an hour trickles by. Dunya, overheating, kicks off her uniform trousers and flaps the hem of her shirt, exposing seriously functional black underwear and a figure that would be cute if her ribs weren't so visible.

Carson does her best to nurse the shot glass. She can't afford to get pissed drunk—like Dunya is doing—if she expects to get out of here. She also has to keep Dunya from getting so blitzed that she passes out before she gives Carson the info she needs.

She hates doing this to the nurse. Dunya's been nice to her, took care of her. Wants to be friends. Carson knows what it's like to be a woman in an all-male organization—the harassment, the groping, the isolation, the insults and slander, pinups or dildos in her locker. It's gotta be harder for Dunya; she's small and cute and she's held onto her femininity. At least Carson could try to be one of the guys, not that it helped.

Dunya wraps her arms around her shins and rests her chin on her knees. "What will you do?" She's back to speaking Russian.

"About what?"

"About your painting. About Rogozhkin. About…" She shrugs. "You told the colonel you will think about what he asks. What will you tell him?"

Carson had meant to steer them to that topic in a while. She figured she'd need to ease into it. Maybe not. "Why ask now?"

"Because I'm very, very drunk." Dunya's over-careful with the words, like a good drunk should be. "If you ask me something or ask me to do something…I probably will."

Carson's brain isn't foggy yet—misty, maybe—but she takes a moment to herd her words together so she doesn't blow the mood. "I won't do it. I can't stay here. Mashkov may throw me in a cell just because. And I'm not leaving without the picture. Understand?"

Dunya gives her a slow, over-broad nod.

Carson refills Dunya's glass. "Let's talk about that picture."

CHAPTER 39

Carson leaves the shadows in front of the clinic, edging around the bluish pool of light surrounding the gate. She can't avoid the crunch of her boots on gravel, but at least she can be a dark shape rather than an identifiable person.

The gate guards pay no attention to her. Carson takes in a few lungfuls of cool-but-damp air. It burns off some of the mist in her head. She hopes she can do this next part without getting dizzy.

She feels like absolute scum for leaving Dunya passed out and duct-taped to her chair. That poor girl's going to be in *so* much trouble. She'll probably get bounced from the brigade. But as Dunya poured out her heart, even Carson could tell the nurse's lonely and desperately unhappy. *Leaving's the best thing for her.* The thought doesn't help Carson ignore the slime all over her.

She unlocks the command building's main door with the key she stole from Dunya's abandoned trousers. Carson ghosts down a dim hallway until she reaches Mashkov's door, then turns ninety degrees. The pay office has a steel door with a serious lock on it. Dunya said the painting would be in there or Mashkov's office. Carson's lockpicks are with her laptop in Volnovakha. *Figures.*

Next stop: Mashkov's office.

It's unlocked. She carefully slides inside, using the hall light glowing through the door's obscure glass to silently pick her way across the room. Short stabs of light from the penlight she got from Dunya's desk help her get oriented. It's just as Dunya described it: a steel desk and credenza; a thick wooden conference table to her right with eight wood side chairs; a table next to the door behind her. To her left, a steel bookcase and the door leading to Mashkov's room. No sound from in there—he must still be sleeping.

Wham. The building rattles. Seconds later, what sounds like an air raid siren moans to life nearby.

What the hell?

The gap under the door to Mashkov's bunkroom lights up.

Carson dashes out the office door on tiptoes, eases it closed, then scans the hallway. The pay office is locked. The office across the hall is, too.

The lights snap on in Mashkov's office.

Someone pounds on the building's main door. She'd left it unlocked.

Carson spots a door marked "ТУАЛЕТИ" and shoulders through it an instant before the front door flies open. A sink, a urinal, and a stall. She bolts into the stall as running boots charge up the hallway. She climbs on the toilet, plants her feet on the seat, and sits on the tank. Her heart hammers her ribs. Fuzz creeps into the corners of her vision. The black-and-white tiled floor looks cool and clean and inviting. *What if I just fall off now?*

Wham. The building shakes again.

The washroom door slams open. The overhead light blinks on. Mashkov's voice: "—protects the other lorries. Get drivers to move the ones that aren't burning. I'll be there in a minute."

"Yes, sir!"

Carson's hand fumbles for her collapsible baton. It's not there; she never got it back. Then she reaches for her pistol but comes up empty. She never got that back, either.

Mashkov coughs. There's pissing in the urinal. A water bottle cracks open. A splash; hand washing. Paper towels. Then the door bangs open again, followed by trotting boot soles.

Quiet. Carson blows out the breath she's been holding. She carefully climbs off the toilet, then braces herself against the wall as her brain spins.

When she can see and stand straight, Carson hustles to Mashkov's office and starts a fast search for the painting. She scans the credenza's top and under tables, all while listening for doors opening or boots on linoleum. Nothing. Keys to the pay office? On a hunch, she checks Mashkov's desk drawers. She finds no loose keys, but her pistol's in the second drawer on the left with a full magazine loaded and a spare. Her baton and knife are next to it.

Where's the picture?

The door to Mashkov's bunkroom stands open. The room's a bit larger than Dunya's storage closet, but not by much. Industrial steel shelves line the wall to her right; to her left, three overhead cabinets are set above a cot just like Dunya's. Wall hooks hold uniforms and a blue vinyl suit bag. No painting.

The command building's front door bangs open. Boots hurry up the hallway toward her.

Carson slips inside the bunkroom, draws her pistol, and presses her back against the latch-side wall. Someone—probably male—tromps into the office. The desk chair rattles. Metal slides on metal. The credenza? The someone mutters something Carson can't make out. She checks her watch: twelve minutes since she walked into the building. Every minute more is a gift she can't count on.

The searcher says "Aha!" Boots trot out of the office, down the hall, and end with a door slam.

Carson stows her pistol and takes another look around Mashkov's roost. Nothing here looks like the painting as it was when she had it. There aren't any obvious hiding places, either; the room's not large enough for that. Except...

She drops to all fours and shines the penlight under the cot. Behind the spare pair of boots and the shower sandals she sees dust bunnies and a button. No painting.

The front door opens and closes. Boots scrape on the hall's linoleum.

Again? Carson draws her pistol. She'd rather not shoot anyone, but she'd rather not spend any more time here, either.

The boots pace toward Mashkov's office. They stop somewhere around the open door.

In one move, Carson steps into the office, pivots, and levels her pistol, ready to fire.

Her sights are lined up on Galina's forehead.

She's alive. She's free. She came back...for me?

Galina sticks her fists on her hips. She's wearing a camo uniform shirt over a black tee with the DNR flag on it. "*There* you are. I went to the clinic first."

Carson unwinds and sticks the pistol in her back waistband. "Took you long enough."

They hug in the doorway. Carson usually has to think about hugging, but not this time. They say "You didn't die on me" (Galina) and "I'm so glad you made it" (Carson) simultaneously, then laugh.

Carson asks, "How'd you know I was still alive?"

"I was watching the gate. A man took clothes to the clinic. I recognized Bohdan's shirt. Dead people don't need clothes."

"Good catch." *Wham.* Carson thumbs toward the sound. "That your work?"

Galina puts on a sly smile. "Could be."

If the painting's in the pay office, Carson can't get to it. For all she knows, it's in some hole Dunya doesn't know about. She also can't stay here to search, not with Galina's fireworks show going on. "Let's take off before somebody else shows up."

She lost. *So close…*

A large, loud fire east of the command building throws an orange glow on everything around the plaza. Shouts and water spray fill the air. The plaza was empty fifteen minutes ago; now it's filling with growling trucks and running drivers. It's easy for Carson and Galina to lose themselves in the chaos. The two guards at the gate are more interested in the fire than the two women who hurry by.

Carson wants to go back to the clinic to check on Dunya, to make sure she's okay, that she's not panicking or choking on her own puke. But she can't; there's no time, and it would put Galina in danger. "Does your plan have a way to get us out of here?"

Galina sweeps an arm across the plaza. "You see all these lorries? I know how to drive them all."

CHAPTER 40

Mashkov slumps on a plastic armchair outside the mess hall. Past one a.m. and it's still busier than daytime. He grinds the smoke grit out of his eyes well enough to make out Vasilenko pacing toward him out of the murk.

They exchange salutes. Vasilenko says, "The fire's out, sir."

"Finally. What's the damage?"

Vasilenko coughs. "Four lorries destroyed, five more damaged."

Forty-five thousand kilos of supplies that'll need another way to get to Monday's fight. "Casualties?"

"Nothing major. A couple of burns, some smoke inhalation. But..." The sergeant shuffles. "We're short a chief medic."

"Where's Lieutenant Fetisova?"

Vasilenko looks like he swallowed a rock. "She's...ehm...drunk and tied to a chair. Sir."

Mashkov leans his face into his hands. *Does it never stop?* "Show me."

Dunya had been cut loose by the time they reach the clinic, but the discarded strips of duct tape tell the story well enough. She huddles in the chair, her trousers on the floor, crying into her knees.

Mashkov sighs and massages his temples. "Leave us," he tells Vasilenko. Once the sergeant's gone, Mashkov slowly sinks into a crouch and watches the medic blubber for a few moments. "What happened, Dunya?" His keeps his voice kind.

Snuffle, snuffle. "Lisa got me drunk." Her words are slow and slurred.

"How did she know where you keep the *spotykach*?"

"I...I brought it out. To be friendly."

"Anything else?"

Dunya backhands the tears from her eyes. "She got my...my

key to the command building."

That goes right past Mashkov for a moment. When he puts the pieces together, a rock drops into his heart. "Did she want the painting?"

"Yes. So she can go home."

Dunya's key doesn't open the pay office. But if Tarasenko found the spare keys... "Did she tell you where she's going?"

"No."

Mashkov stands, shaking his head. "You'll have to go."

"I know." He can barely hear her. "I'm sorry."

"I am, too." He starts to turn away, then stops. "Why, Dunya? Why did you do this?"

Dunya looks up for the first time, squinting straight into his eyes. "She paid attention to me."

Again, he doesn't catch her meaning the first time. Then he thinks about it, and how she's acted around him for almost two years, things she's said in passing, and it all becomes clear. He should've seen it. Perhaps he could have prevented tonight's disaster. "Goodbye, Dunya. I hope you find what you want."

Mashkov charges to the pay office. The painting's still between the desk and the safe. He can breathe deeply for the first time since he saw Dunya in the clinic.

Well, to hell with Tarasenko. They're all better off without her here. With any luck, she'll be in the West long before the brigade needs to begin its movement west this morning. As for Rogozhkin and the other million? They'll never see him or it again. A bad ending. Mashkov has no idea how he'll keep fuel in his brigade's vehicles without that money.

Mashkov pours another glass of tea from the samovar in the corner of the Operations Center when he notices Vasilenko waving to him from the plotting table. The tea here has hardly enough kick to jump-start his brain on his way to the room's center. Mashkov's head is full of fuel burn rates and cargo load management from spending the past three hours huddled with the brigade's acting logistics officer. "Yes, what is it, Lenya?"

Vasilenko's eyes are bloodshot and droopy. His entire body

sags. "I didn't want to bother you with this—I know you're busy with the movement orders—but you need to know about it."

"What?"

"Remember the Škoda with the tracker beacon? It started moving around midnight."

"Škoda…? Oh, yes. Where did it go?"

Vasilenko stabs a forefinger at the end of a red pencil line snaking along roads to the west and north of the base. Mashkov bends and squints at the tiny print next to the fingertip: *Byryuky.*

The sun rises in Mashkov's head, burning off the fog. *Tarasenko's back at the farm. With Rogozhkin…?*

"How long has it been there?" His voice is stronger and clearer than it's been since the first explosion.

"About ninety minutes, sir."

Mashkov sweeps the room until he finds his chief of staff. "Shatilov! To me! Now!"

There's still time to save the plan. We can still get the money…and deal with that damned Tarasenko and the Russian.

CHAPTER 41

Rogozhkin paces the cracked-asphalt schoolyard, stretching his legs after sitting in the Hunter for longer than was good for him. The long, narrow school building is a fine place to hide from Syrov's men in case Command tells them to drag Rogozhkin with them to Rostov-on-Don. Buried in the southern fringe of Mospyne less than a kilometer and a half from Syrov's bivouac, set back from the road, nobody around until Monday morning—they'd have to be very lucky indeed to find him if they actually tried. Not that they'd be likely to do that. Five thousand euros each with another fifty thousand for the dead sniper's family should buy a little gratitude.

The eastern sky slowly takes on a low violet glow. The first stirrings of dawn. Soon it'll be his favorite time of day, that fraction of time when the sun nears the horizon but hasn't yet peeked above it, when the wind calms and the mists pool and night becomes twilight. The promise of a new day without the actuality of it spoiling things.

What do I do now?

Tomorrow morning, he's supposed to report to Tulantyev and submit to being the scapegoat for the Makiivka Brigade going rogue. The coup against Mashkov wouldn't have failed if he'd been there to provide adult supervision; he'd engineered enough changes in the command of local units to know how to do it right. *Fucking Proskurin...*

With any luck, that damned militia will get itself wiped out in tomorrow's push against Kyiv's army near Dokuchajevsk and the whole issue will be moot. They rebelled, they failed, end of story. But even if that helps Rostov or Moscow to sweep the whole thing under the rug, his career is still over.

Is it too late to retire?

Rogozhkin checks his watch: four-fifteen. He can't call Tulantyev until after five. Until then he'll have to try to snatch a few minutes of sleep while his brain tortures him with possibilities and alternatives, each worse than the last.

"Where are you, Edik Gregorivich?"

Rogozhkin's gut sours. *Tulantyev's using my patronymic. He must be annoyed.* "In Mospyne, sir. There are a couple of things I need to clean up before I head back to base. Syrov's section should already be on its way there."

"You were supposed to go with them." The general sounds grumpier than usual at this hour.

"I understand, sir. If I may…I'd like to retire. Now. I can go to the military assistance group in Donetsk and—"

"You *what?*" Tulantyev sounds like he just woke up all at once. "It's too late for that. Moscow's involved now. God alone knows how they found out so soon. They want to make an example of someone so this doesn't happen again. Proskurin's dead, so they're looking at you. You should've put in your papers yesterday or Friday."

Rogozhkin mutes his phone and grumbles a string of curses. Of course Moscow's involved. They're involved in everything except the actual conditions in the field, the ones that make all the difference. He lets his anger settle before he un-mutes. "Why not Proskurin? Being dead makes him the perfect scapegoat. They've done it before. No trial needed, nobody to object. On top of it all, it's really his fault anyway. Why not—"

"You want to try that? Go ahead. Maybe they'll buy it. More likely, they want a live body they can send to a gulag, just to get their point across. You grew up in Siberia, didn't you? Maybe it won't be so bad for you."

"There's nothing good about a military prison, sir. Not for a man my age. It's a death sentence. You know it as well as I do."

"Yes, yes, I know it." The general sighs. "Look, Edik, if it was up to me, I'd let you retire right now, go run a tavern in Sevastopol or whatever. But it's out of my hands. Some inspector-general is coming down here from the Defense Ministry. He'll arrive tomorrow. You're to be here when he arrives. Do you understand?"

It's worse than he'd thought. They've already decided to hang him out to dry. "Yes, sir. I understand perfectly." *Better than you think.*

Rogozhkin's still brooding by the time the sun crests the horizon and floods the land with light.

In his thirty-three-year career, he's never disobeyed a direct order. He'd grumbled about the more boneheaded ones, even complained a few times to his superiors, but never refused to do as he was told. That kind of behavior wasn't tolerated by the Soviet Army nor by its Russian successor. More important, it went against his sense of honor. In the First Chechen War, he'd seen the damage that insubordinate troops could do and vowed he'd never let that happen under his command.

But now he has to choose between two ugly alternatives:

Follow orders and be sent to a hellhole of a military prison he'd never leave alive.

Save his life but destroy his honor and reputation by becoming a deserter.

He weighed the alternatives nonstop from the time he ended his call to Tulantyev to this moment. The first rays of morning sun are like disinfectant, pure and strong and capable of killing the disease inside him, whatever it is.

He can disappear. He knows how. The army trained him to be invisible.

His honor? Nobody cares about his honor except himself. There's no such thing as "honor" in today's Russia. Everyone's a gangster now, working the angles, grasping for whatever he can get, however he can get it. This so-called "war" here is nothing but another grab for power, for resources, for advantage. A cynical game played by the suits in the Kremlin and the gilded epaulets in the Ministry of Defense.

All he has to do is get out of this backwater, reach the West, and reinvent himself. That's the promise of the West, isn't it? Second chances?

He groans into the Hunter—too much pacing on his bad leg—and checks his phone for email. There's one waiting from the 45th Guards legal office; he already knows what that says. He starts shutting down the active apps, a bit of housekeeping he still does even though it's no longer necessary.

He finds the tracker app. Brings it up out of curiosity.

The red dot's at the farm in Byryuky, two kilometers from here.

He knows where his first stop will be.

CHAPTER 42

A loud *clank* kicks Carson out of her restless sleep.

She pries open her eyes. The sky's brightening, but the sun's not quite up. She's on a concrete slab, propped against the opening for a roll-up door. No idea how she got this way. Every part of her body hurts.

She's at the entrance to a vehicle maintenance bay at the Byryuky farm. The Octavia's a meter from her, its nose resting on a wheeled floor jack. A booted foot sticks out behind the left-front tire.

Carson tries to say something, but nothing comes out. Her mouth and throat are deserts. Looking around, she discovers a half-full water bottle near her knees. Draining it revives her voice, sort of. She rasps in Ukrainian, "Why are you under the car?"

"Something was loose." Galina sounds like she's talking into a bucket.

Okay. The top edge of the sun crests the horizon, flooding the area with golden light. Carson lets herself drift. She should get up and walk around, but she knows how that'll feel. She'd rather ache in place. Some Pepsi or lemonade would be nice to cut through the funk Dunya's Ukrainian rotgut left in her mouth. Then again, that rotgut and the pain meds made for pretty good anesthetic last night.

Galina squirms out from under the car, a sour look on her face, wiping her hands on a rag that's seen a lot of that lately. She gives Carson a once-over. "How do you feel?"

"Shitty."

"Need more water?"

"Yeah."

Galina hands her a bottle, then carefully kneels facing the sun, closing her eyes to bask for a few moments.

Carson watches Galina's shoulders wilt with every breath. "Get any sleep?"

"No."

"Sorry."

Galina shrugs her face. "It's like harvest time. I work eighteen or twenty hours a day to bring in the crops, then more hours to get them to the market."

Carson had seen that at home. It made her glad she isn't a farmer. "Have I thanked you yet for getting me out of that place?" No response. "Thank you."

This time, Galina shrugs her shoulders.

"Why did you come back for me? You had your money."

"You gave me too much." Her voice is flat. "I had to earn it."

"I'm glad you did." *Say it now.* Carson thought a lot about this in that cell. "I want to help you get Bohdan back. Whatever you need."

Galina studies her lap. After a few moments, she holds out her left hand open and flat. Carson glances between Galina's face and hand. Then she slowly wraps the fingers of her right hand around Galina's left.

"I have been alone for twenty months." Galina's voice is so low, it barely carries to Carson's ears. "I haven't spent so much time with a person since..." Her eyes blink open. "I am sorry if I am not very good at it anymore."

Carson wishes she knew what to say.

They quietly sit holding hands, watching the sun climb into the sky until they both sigh and squeeze at the same time.

Galina labors to her feet, then shakes out her legs. "Now what do we do?"

"Eat, then pack up." The pain's put her off her feed to some extent, but she'll need breakfast sometime soon. "Mashkov thinks Rogozhkin will try to find us."

Galina's lip curls. "How? Why?"

"Not sure on either. Mashkov thinks Rogozhkin's got a way to track me. Why? Maybe to give me the icon or get intel on the militia. Not so sure about that, but whatever. I need to get that icon back to the museum. But if Rogozhkin's got it and doesn't want to be found..." It's too depressing to think about. She wants this whole mess to mean something. It keeps resisting.

Galina folds her arms grumpily. "I don't want to wait long. As soon as you are in the West, I need to free Bohdan. I do *not* want him in that camp one day more than he has to be. He's been there too long."

"Yes, he has. Remember, I'm coming with you. Let's give Rogozhkin an hour to find us, then we'll go."

Carson drags herself off the slab and clumps around outside until she can move most of her joints again. She pulls up the hem of her tee to reveal a nearly solid field of black and blue across her abs, and the green blob where Stepaniak's bullet hit her about an eon ago.

Once she's ambulatory, she shuffles down the building's central corridor until she reaches the room where she killed Stepaniak. It looks smaller in daylight. Dried blood is splattered across the concrete floor and on the walls. She stares at the rusty stain in the corner where Stepaniak leaned against the workbench leg. "You stupid bastard. Why'd you do it?"

Nobody answers. Carson shakes her head, then drifts back to the maintenance bay.

They burn off the rest of the next hour with housekeeping— nibbling on road food, emptying trash from the car, cleaning the windshield. Carson brushes her teeth and hair. Galina changes clothes, including her underwear (*so* jealous…Carson would kill for clean underwear). She also tosses Carson another well-washed flannel shirt. "You need something to cover your chest."

As they repack the car, Carson gets a glimpse of what might be the knapsack. She's about to ask Galina if she has the lost money but hesitates. *What if she says* no*? Do I check? So much for trusting each other…*

But she needs to know. She might have to help keep the secret. She might need that money. "Um, Galina. When you left here last night, did you—"

Galina abruptly pulls a pistol from her waistband and aims past Carson's right shoulder.

What the…? Carson swivels to look out the bay entrance.

Rogozhkin stands centered in the doorway, his feet shoulder-width apart, hands folded in front of his hips. "Good morning, ladies. Care for a chat?"

And here he is, Carson thinks. She carefully presses Galina's Makarov down until it's aiming at the floor, then steps toward the Russian. "Figured you'd forgotten us."

"I would never." He flashes an almost covert smile. "We should talk."

"Sure. Start by telling me where the icon is."

"It's in the back of my vehicle, along with the money I took under my safekeeping." He nods toward Galina. "Good morning to you, Galina. Or is it Galya?"

Galina sneers at him. "To you? Demchuk." She spins and stomps to the car's trunk.

Rogozhkin turns to Carson, shrugging. "She's still angry with me, I see."

"You're still Russian."

"True." He sweeps a hand toward the spotty ankle-high grass outside. "Let's walk."

It's good to get away from the mold and dust and residual chicken stink in the farm building. Rogozhkin walks with his hands behind his back; Carson keeps her arms folded to stop her breasts from swaying. She hates going braless. "I need the icon. You promised I could have it if I led you to Stepaniak."

"Yes, I did, and you'll get it. I keep my promises." He studies her face. "What happened to you?"

"Got in a fight."

"Did you win?"

"No."

"That's disappointing."

"Was for me, too."

"I can imagine. You should put something on your knuckles so they don't get infected."

"Thanks, Mom. How did you find us?"

"Remember the beacon in Stepaniak's Range Rover? It's in your car now. Syrov put it there."

Carson halts and glares at Rogozhkin. "And you didn't tell him to do that?"

"No. I learned of it during the attack. There was no time."

So *that's* what Mashkov was hinting about. They knew the Octavia was hanging around the base. Galina's very, very lucky...or really good. "Mashkov said you'd find me. Now I know how."

Rogozhkin chuckles. "I imagine Mashkov's like a child at Christmas with Stepaniak's money."

Carson parses his question. *Is that why he wants to talk?* "He didn't get it."

His eyes widen. "Really? Who did?"

Careful. "Don't know. There were a lot of people in that room. What do you want?"

Rogozhkin's face turns thoughtful. He watches a nearby scrum of early birds hunting for worms. "You want to go to the West. You know that's not straightforward, yes?"

"That's what Galina tells me."

"I can get you across the line of contact."

"So can Galina."

"Perhaps. Using the legal ways. Unless she's an accomplished smuggler, she may not know the others. You'll need those to get past tomorrow's offensive."

Carson stares at him. *What the hell?* She lets the unasked question—*can I come with you?*—simmer on her brain's hot plate for a few steps. "Why would you do this?"

They reach the chicken coop's western end. Rogozhkin's Hunter rests on the gravel road just past it. He turns to her. "My time here is…done. Mashkov's militia may be hunting me."

"Not the 'why' I meant. You can get across borders better than any of us. Why do you need us?"

He nods sadly. "You're right. I can cross the contact line. I can't get past Kyiv's army alone and I have no need to spend time in a PW camp. I want to get out of Ukraine into a neutral third nation. Did you come here on a commercial flight or by private aircraft?"

"Commercial to Bonn, private jet to Dnipro. Why?"

"Did you have to go through passport controls in Dnipro?"

"No."

"As I thought. I have a Russian military passport. You can imagine what Kyiv's border police will make of that." He smiles. "As I said, I can help you and your friend Galina go over the contact line. In return, your company's jet can take me out of Ukraine with you. Bonn is fine, though if you could arrange a stop in Cyprus, that would be ideal."

Carson has to unbury what Rogozhkin isn't saying. "Why not go home?"

"To Russia?" He almost automatically shifts his focus east. "Did Mashkov tell you what happened yesterday?"

"You mean, your Russian friends trying to take him out and blowing it? He didn't, but somebody else did."

"That wasn't Moscow's desired outcome."

Meaning, he's in the shit with his own people. "Speaking of Mashkov: he wants that money. He says he'll give you a guy named Yartsev if you hand it over."

His eyebrows leap for his hairline. "Yartsev's *alive?*"

"I guess. I didn't see him. Mashkov says he's in a hospital in Amvrosiivka."

"Will he live?" His voice is tight, but hopeful.

Must be close to this guy. "Mashkov thinks so."

He sighs in relief. "Good." Rogozhkin's jaw sets. "So now Mashkov's a kidnapper. Well, he won't get his ransom. I'll tell Command where Sergeant Yartsev is and they'll deal with it."

"Why not Syrov and his men? They're closer."

"They've already left the country."

"That was fast." Almost like they're running away. That's not her problem right now...probably. "So, you promise you'll get us out of the Donbass if I promise to get you out of Ukraine?"

The Russian puts his friendly face back on. "That sums it up well. But there's something else." He points toward the maintenance bay. "That tracking beacon on your car? I know where it is. Help me and I'll tell you. Or don't and the militia can follow you. Did you leave with their permission?"

He's got her there. "It's not just my call."

Rogozhkin peaks an eyebrow. "Who else gets a say?"

"The woman who hates you."

"Why do you keep making deals with this *tarhany?*"

Carson knew Galina would ask that, so for once she has an answer ready. "Because we can help each other. And I understand him. There's a lot to say for that."

Galina walks away with her fists on her hips, muttering. When she finally stalks back, her face is hot pink. "We can't trust a *Kacáps.* I say we kill him." Galina doesn't even try to hide the exasperation in her voice. "Then you can take the icon and we can finish with this."

At least she's consistent. "You don't think he'd be useful?"

"Hmpf. For what?"

"Backup, if we need it. Someone else who's good in a fight. And, what if we can't use a regular crossing? He probably knows every back-door way across the line."

"If he does, why doesn't he go by himself and leave us alone?"

Carson hadn't told her this part, hoping she wouldn't have to. So much for hoping. "Because I can help get him out of Ukraine."

Galina's jaw goes hard. "*What?* You would help him *escape?* He wouldn't have to pay for what he's done? Why?"

"You should be happy about this. One of their senior officers is deserting. Don't you want that?"

"Remember the story I told you? The Russians shooting at me?" She thrusts a finger toward the roll-up door. "They were like *him*, with the striped shirts. They shelled us and shot rockets at us. They helped the militia attack us and kill our wounded. Why should he go free?"

"If you'd been up against *spetsnaz*, you wouldn't be here now. Their airborne troops wear the *telmyashka*. So do their marines. Rogozhkin may not even have been here when—"

"*Why are you defending him?*" Galina's face is bright red now. "Are you on his—"

"No!" Somehow, Carson ends up looming over Galina, using her command voice. She steps back and dials down her volume. "I know guys like him. At least, guys who used to be like him. They're a rough crowd." Especially the ones who work for the *mafiya.* "Special forces are like that everywhere. They don't trust civilians easy. Kind of like cops. But once they trust you—once you earn it—they will kill for you. And they'll die for you."

Galina advances on Carson. "Not good enough. Not if we have to put up—"

Rogozhkin appears in the doorway. "Ladies, if you haven't already, you need to decide *now*. The militia is here."

CHAPTER 43

The lead BTR opens fire as soon as Rogozhkin slews his Hunter onto the road into Byryuky. He's exposed for only a few seconds before the farm compounds on both sides hide him from the gunners. By the time the women get in the clear, the militia will be waiting for them. He hopes Tarasenko drives as well as she runs.

He glances in the rear-view mirror. The Octavia skids around the corner onto his road. An instant later, dirt erupts on either side of it while the car swerves frantically.

Tarasenko has a hard nose, but she seems to listen to reason. To mutual interest. She doesn't strike him as someone who makes an elephant out of a fly, as so many women do. He really should find out more about her.

Another glance in the mirror. The women are in town, about two hundred meters behind him, temporarily safe. *Good work.*

They left the farm before they could dispose of the tracking beacon. That's okay for now. He doesn't want to lose the militia quite yet. He saw the two Hunters leading the column: scouts, most likely. It'll be easy to lose the armor, but the utes can move as fast as he can. That's useful. He still needs to disappear from the army.

Those militia fools will help him do it.

Carson floors the Octavia's gas pedal once she stops zig-zagging. Rogozhkin's Hunter is a couple hundred meters ahead, but the Škoda should be faster. So far, militia gunnery hasn't improved.

Galina's slumped in the passenger's seat, her arms folded tight, her mouth set in stone. Carson had to pick her up and throw her into the car before they could leave that farm. Another few seconds and the BTRs knifing across the plowed field would've been too close to escape. At least she's stopped arguing, though sulking isn't much better.

She glances at the rear-view. A militia Hunter's about three hundred meters behind her, with the bulk of a BTR behind that. Rogozhkin's Hunter is closer now. She can't afford to lose him; they didn't talk about the route, and he still has the icon.

They approach a three-way intersection. Just as the Octavia enters the crossroads, another Hunter screeches off the north-south road into the intersection. Carson cranks the wheel to the left, hits loose gravel, and starts to spin toward what looks like a grocery store. Behind her, the Hunter skids sideways into the front of the building next door.

The store swells in her side window. Carson centers the wheel and punches the gas, hoping the front-wheel drive will pull them out of the spin before they go through the store's front windows. Gravel spews behind them. Just before the car pancakes into the wall, the front wheels hit something solid and the Octavia lunges forward toward the road...and the other Hunter.

Its driver's eyes are huge with terror.

Oh fuck... Carson pulls the parking brake, cranks the wheel to the left. The Octavia spins again, engine roaring, tires shrieking.

The Hunter leaps off the road and crashes through a fence.

Carson catches the spin in time to slingshot west on the road and race toward Rogozhkin's Hunter, stopped about three hundred meters ahead.

"Please don't wreck this car." Galina's voice, small and muffled. Her arms are wrapped around her head. "I need this car. Everything we own is in this car."

"I'll do my best." Carson keeps both hands clamped on the wheel so they don't shake. Her heart hammers as fast as a hummingbird's wings. Her shoulders and sides throb.

They follow Rogozhkin on a winding path out of Byryuky, through the southern fringe of Mospyne, then across open fields. Carson's rear-view mirror is empty for a while. As they approach Horbachevo, she glimpses a now-familiar blocky silhouette far behind her. Too much to hope they'd give up.

Rogozhkin's Hunter veers right, into the village, instead of following the main road.

Where's he going? Carson wants to keep running like hell. Getting bottled up in some podunk little town sounds like a bad way to die. But there's no choice: she goes where the icon goes. No matter what.

Rogozhkin cruises half a kilometer to where the paved street makes a sharp left, then turns right onto a sixty-meter dirt path that ends in a stand of trees. He weaves his Hunter to the back of the grove, slings his AS Val, then jogs a couple dozen meters toward the street, stopping at a second, smaller copse. He hopes Tarasenko isn't too far behind; what they need to do has to happen quickly if it's going to work.

The Octavia pulls in a very long minute later. It's coated with dust—he'd watched Tarasenko's spectacular bit of stunt driving from the far end of Byryuky—but there are no obvious bullet holes or other damage. The driver's door bursts open and Tarasenko bolts out, glowering. "Why are we stopping?"

"The beacon is in the right taillight assembly. Get it out now."

While Galina digs through the car's boot, Rogozhkin paces far enough away to avoid being overheard. He rings his counterpart with the Lev Brigade, which owns the territory he and the women are about to enter.

"Zagitov. Is that you, Edik?"

"Yes, it is. Does your gang of *bandity* still run a checkpoint outside Novyi Svit?"

"Yeah, last I checked. What's this I hear about you trying to dump the commander of your bunch of idiots?"

Word travels fast. "I was trying to work out an orderly transition. One of our guys jumped the gun and botched it. Suddenly I'm to blame."

"Typical. What's your interest in Novyi Svit?"

They discuss the checkpoint situation while Rogozhkin watches the women. Galina sits in the boot with her legs sticking out, bent away from him, her shoulders and biceps moving like she's working on something. *She'd better step it up.* Tarasenko's at the end of the path, her pistol out and ready, watching the road.

He finishes with Zagitov at the same time Galina holds up a

small black plastic housing trailing a pair of wires. She glares at him. "Is this it?"

"Yes."

She stalks to him and shoves the beacon into his breastbone. "Here."

At least she didn't try to beat him to death with it. "Thank you. Please take the car into that grove at the end of the path. Go as far in as you can."

Galina stomps back to the car, then drives toward the trees.

"They're coming!"

Rogozhkin spins toward the voice. Tarasenko's jogging down the path toward him. He waves her into the nearby trees.

By the time she crashes through the underbrush to join him, he's buried the beacon under some fallen leaves. She pants, "What's your plan?"

"Is it just the scouts or the full platoon?"

"All I saw were Hunters."

"Good." Standing up to almost thirty men with heavy weapons would be suicidal. He points to the leaves. "They're following this. There should be four of them, two in each vehicle. They'll dismount to enter here. We let them gather, then eliminate all four. Then we drive away before the rest of the platoon arrives. Questions?"

Tarasenko squints into his eyes. "Why haven't we driven off already?"

Because it doesn't solve my problem. "We need to blind them. With the scouts gone, the platoon will take longer to move. That's the margin we need to get across the Kalmius and lose ourselves in another militia's territory." The sound of engines creeps into the trees. "It's time. Cover over there. Watch for crossfire."

Carson doesn't like ambushes, but she understands them. The whole Wild West thing of walking down an empty street and trying to draw faster than the other guy is fundamentally stupid. If you have to get rid of your enemies, you do what's safest and most effective for yourself.

She gets what Rogozhkin's doing, and why. She doesn't have

to like it.

The engines grow close—sounding more like VW Beetles than military vehicles—then stop. Doors clunk open. Boots hit the ground. Carson, prone, squirms farther into the deadfall and leaf litter, wipes her hands one-by-one on her jeans, then tries to pump herself up to shoot men in the back.

Twigs snap and brush rattles as the soldiers advance toward the tracker bug. Carson can follow where the men are by how their little noises move left-to-right in her sound picture. After a few seconds, one of them passes no more than two meters in front of her. He joins a second three meters from her. It's closer than she likes. She's glad Galina's at the end of the road with the car; she doesn't need to be involved in this mess.

A militiaman says in Russian, "It should be here."

Another says, "It's in a car. We'd see a car. This isn't a forest."

A third grumps, "No shit. Where is it?"

Phut.

A body hits the ground. An unmistakable sound.

A man's voice: "What the…?"

Phut.

The more distant of the two troops she can see pitches forward, chasing the spurt of blood jetting from his mouth.

Rogozhkin. The AS Val. It's suppressed.

The soldier in front of Carson swings around wildly, his carbine raised, searching for a target.

Phut.

Another body falls to Carson's ten o'clock. The last soldier standing—the one in front of her—pivots toward the sound, rocking back and forth on his feet (wasted energy). An odd keening sound leaks out of him. He may not even hear it. Terror does strange things to people.

No fourth shot. This one's hers. Carson sighs. She sidearms a small rock straight out to her right. It clacks off a tree trunk. The soldier spins, shoots twice. Carson takes her time, lines up her shot on the center of his body armor, then fires one round. The soldier snaps backward and falls, his arms spreading on his way down.

When she steps into the tiny clearing around the hidden tracker, she sees three bodies splayed out in a semicircle, two with head wounds. The third man—the one she shot—gasps and whimpers, clutching his chest.

Rogozhkin steps out of his hide, checks the two dead men nearest him, then paces to the soldier who's still alive. He watches the man for a moment, then shoots him in the head.

Carson flinches. She didn't need to see that up close.

When she opens her eyes again, Rogozhkin's giving her a sort-of disappointed look. "Always finish your enemies. You don't get rewarded for mercy."

She hates the thought, but he's right. Stas didn't finish her off when he could have, and she killed him for it.

By the time they get the vehicles arranged nearby and move the patrol's Hunters just off the trail, Rogozhkin has three dead militiamen lined up at the grove's edge. "Load those in the nearer militia vehicle," he says. "I'll be out in a few minutes."

Carson says, "Fewer's better. The rest of the platoon could show up anytime."

He nods. "Noted. I'll be quick."

Only one of the three bodies is unusually heavy. Galina sacrifices an old towel to wrap their heads to reduce the blood transfer. Carson and Galina each take an AK-74, six spare magazines, and a wound kit, and pack them in the Octavia.

Carson checks her watch. They've been here for over twenty minutes. *What's Rogozhkin doing? Where's the rest of the patrol?*

Rogozhkin backs out of the trees, dragging a corpse by its armpits. He's now wearing a militia lance corporal's uniform and field gear. The body's dressed as a *spetsnaz* lieutenant colonel.

Carson growls, "What. The *fuck?*"

"I'll explain later. Help me put this in my driver's seat."

Together they wrestle the body into place. Galina watches the process with her arms folded, shaking her head. Rogozhkin tosses his AS Val into the passenger footwell, hauls his bags and the icon from the Hunter to the Octavia, then jogs into the trees again.

Galina helps make room in the Octavia's trunk for the icon. "What's the *Kacáps* doing?"

"No idea." Whatever it is, she wishes he'd hurry.

Rogozhkin returns in a minute with an AK slung across his back and a grenade in each hand. He offers one to Carson. "Have you ever used a grenade?"

She waves it away. "Once. Scared the shit out of me."

"No shame in that. It's good to respect the weapon." He hooks the spoons on his gear belt, shrugs the AK into his hands, then without any warning, empties an entire magazine—thirty rounds—into his Hunter's front and sides. Carson shelters at the Octavia's nose so she doesn't have to watch the dead soldier behind the wheel jerk and jolt under the barrage. A muffled blast ends a few seconds of relative silence, causing a small rainstorm of broken safety glass.

He has two grenades. Carson plugs her ears and opens her mouth to limit the damage the next explosion will do. First comes the grenade's heavy *thud*, then the roar of twin explosions that toss pieces of the Hunter into the road and through the trees. She peeks over the Octavia's roof. The Hunter's remains burn so hot that they warm her face even though the fire's several meters away.

Galina draws up next to her. She watches the SUV blaze for a few beats, then smiles. "I like to see Russian things burn."

Rogozhkin waves Carson toward him. "I need you to take a picture with your phone," he tells her. "Make sure you include the front registration plate."

"Why?"

"Just do it now before the plate melts."

Carson squats, snaps four photos of the cooking Hunter from different angles—she pretends she doesn't see the dead soldier burning behind the steering wheel—then shows them to Rogozhkin, who chooses one. He holds up his phone. "Send it here. Tell them where it is so they can follow up. Make sure you mention it's Russian."

The email address ends in "osce.org." The Organization for Security and Cooperation in Europe runs the monitoring mission in the Donbass. She's seen their white Toyota SUVs a couple times since she got here.

When Carson gets back to the Octavia, Galina cocks her head and peers at her. "Did the *Kacáps* pretend to kill himself?"

"Yeah. I just told the OSCE about it." She watches the burning Hunter slowly collapse on itself. "You want to drive dead bodies or everything you own?"

"You drive the dead men." Galina's smile is almost a snarl. "You helped kill them."

CHAPTER 44

Carson and Rogozhkin watch the militia Hunter with the crushed side slowly sink into the little reservoir outside Horbachevo with its load of three dead men. Galina stands a couple of meters away from them. She doesn't want to be anywhere near Rogozhkin.

"So, are you dead now?" Carson asks.

Rogozhkin gives her a sly smile. "Let's not talk about that yet. I'm still adjusting to my demotion."

Must be in deep shit with his people to do all this. "The militia will notice it's lost its scouts."

"Oh, but it hasn't yet. I've been speaking for them on the radio. You bandits abandoned your car in town and must have stolen another one. We engaged that nasty Russian and killed him. We're looking for the money."

"They're buying that?"

"Enough. So far. They'll be concerned when they arrive in town and all they find is a burned-out vehicle. That may be a while, though, since one of their BTRs broke down. I hope we'll be through Novyi Svit by then."

"Their mechanics suck that bad?"

He chuckles. "No. They're actually quite good. The BTRs are that old. You don't think we give them our best equipment, do you?"

Carson's starting to understand why Mashkov's so pissed at the Russians. "So now what? There's gotta be a checkpoint going into Novyi Svit."

"There is." The Hunter's death throes seem to have stalled. The rear sticks almost straight up with perhaps half a meter still above water. Rogozhkin shakes his head, pulls his Makarov, then shoots two holes in the rear window. Air whistles out until the SUV disappears in a cloud of spray and bubbles.

Pro tip: always punch out the rear window. "Should we care about the checkpoint?"

"Of course we should." Rogozhkin stashes his pistol and heads for the surviving Hunter. Carson follows. "*If* we were going to cross it. We're not. They're expecting us there one way or another, so we'll avoid it. I know another way to get from here to the causeway across the Starobeshevska Reservoir. The roads are crap and it works only if the area's bone dry, which it is now. Galina's car should be able to make it." He opens the driver's door, then turns to peer at Carson. "You hesitated before you shot that *militsioner*. Why? Did you lose your nerve?"

She returns his look with her death stare. "No. I don't like killing people who don't need it. Guess I'm still part human."

Their eyes stay locked together several seconds. Then he nods. "You still have a conscience. I hope that doesn't get you killed. It would be a sad waste." He climbs behind the wheel. "There's nothing obvious about the route. Try to keep up."

He wasn't kidding.

Carson and Galina take turns wrestling the Octavia along the seemingly endless network of dirt tracks, tractor paths, and railway maintenance trails Rogozhkin leads them through. The ceaseless jouncing and jolting keeps slamming the armrest and seat harness against Carson's bruises and aggravates her headache. The GPS says the straight-line distance is just shy of five klicks; she doubts they travel in a straight line more than a hundred meters at a time. The only silver lining: the sedan has decent suspension. If they were still driving Galina's old car, either it would be dead or she and Galina would be crippled.

They finally graduate from a rutted dirt path to a gravel road as they cross into the northern fringe of Novyi Svit. Rogozhkin pulls over at a place that offers a stunning view of an active rail yard. None of them move without a lot of groaning and gimping. Carson can hardly lever herself out of the car.

Rogozhkin tells them, "The next part is easier. The roads are paved up ahead. We can stop at a café I know about two kilometers from here. It's not much—it's in the bus station—but it hasn't killed me yet. Then we go over the reservoir, turn left twice, and we're on the T0508 to Starobesheve. Any questions?"

Carson's back cracks like a breaking tree branch when she stands straight. "Yeah. Am I shorter?"

Rogozhkin holds up a thumb and forefinger held about an inch apart. Deadpan until a little smile creeps out. Galina rolls her eyes.

They stop at the café to tank up on Russian and Ukrainian comfort food, then drive past the industrial hellscape of a major powerplant on their way south to the causeway. The T0508 heading southeast to Starobesheve is blessedly boring for almost five klicks. The fields on either side are flat in a way that makes pancakes look like the Alps. The powerplant at Novyi Svit dominates the landscape even from several kilometers away.

Then everything stops for a checkpoint. After over fifteen minutes in line, they cut into a gas station to fill up. A cop wanders by looking for graft opportunities, takes one look at Rogozhkin, and scurries away.

A rutted dirt track runs south from the gas station for about three-quarters of a klick. Carson slows the Octavia so it stays out of the cloud of dust Rogozhkin's Hunter throws up. It's rough, but it's better than twisting their way through Starobesheve. Fewer cops.

When they reach the highway, the Hunter slides to a stop. The Octavia joins it a few seconds later.

The highway's jammed with armored fighting vehicles and military trucks, all trundling southwest toward the line of contact. The rumble and the exhaust fumes overpower everything else, even inside closed cars.

Every one bears the shield of the Makiivka Brigade.

CHAPTER 45

Mashkov pinches the bridge of his nose. If the constant clatter and vibration inside the command BTR wasn't bad enough, now he has to deal with *this* mess. He un-mutes his radio headset. "Pioneer, Makiivka One. How long have you been out of contact with your scouts?"

"Makiivka One, Pioneer. Ehm…forty-five minutes or so." Lots of static on the transmission. Of course; a clear signal would be too easy.

"Pioneer, Makiivka One. Was there anything unusual about their last communications?"

"Makiivka One, Pioneer. No sir. They said they killed the Russian and abandoned the Škoda. They're following the women to Novyi Svit. We can't find the Škoda here, so…"

So what happened to them? "Pioneer, you found the Russian's vehicle, yes?"

"Makiivka One, that's affirmative. It's burned to the axles, but there's definitely a dead man in it."

"Do you recognize him?"

"Negative, Makiivka One. He…well, *it* looks like a half-eaten roasted pig, sir."

God, what a picture. Mashkov mutes his mic, then sighs. Is Rogozhkin dead? He wouldn't have expected four privates could take down one of the vaunted *spetsnaz*, far less trap him in his vehicle. But Rogozhkin was getting on in years and had that bad leg, so maybe he just couldn't fight hard enough anymore.

But what about the money? Do those damned women have it now? Or…did the *scouts* find it? They kill the Russian, search his Hunter, and find a bag full of euros. Even a four-way split would make them all well-situated to bolt to the West and set themselves up anywhere. That could easily explain the radio silence.

Mashkov tells Pioneer to join up with the brigade in Styla, then waves Vasilenko out of his seat in the rear of the AFV.

The senior sergeant squats next to Mashkov's seat and braces against a bulkhead. "Yes, sir?" He has to yell to be heard.

Mashkov tells him the short version of the patrol's situation. "I need you to write a message for me. Have MOD pass it through to the police in every town in the region. Include the Škoda's registration plate number and descriptions for Rogozhkin and the two women." He pauses to weigh his options. "Send the plates for the two scout Hunters with Pioneer, too."

Vasilenko's eyebrows levitate. "Sir?"

Mashkov gives him a go-with-it wave. "Identify and detain. Spread the info through the brigade while you're at it. The more eyes we have looking, the better."

The sergeant concentrates on finishing the notes in his battered spiral-bound pad. "Are we assuming Rogozhkin is still alive?"

"I wouldn't be surprised, Lenya." Mashkov shakes his head. "These people are hard to kill. Like *tarakany*." Russian for *cockroaches*. "They may have our money. If they do, we can't let them hide under the kitchen cabinets. I'll be damned if we take our positions and can't leave them because we're out of petrol."

Rogozhkin paces around the militia Hunter with his satellite phone clamped to his ear. "What do you mean you can't help us, Dmitri?"

Zagitov makes an exasperated sound on the other end of the connection. "I didn't say that exactly. I can't be *seen* helping you. Rostov sent out a message a couple of hours ago. Any *spetsnaz* unit that sees you is supposed to report directly to Command. I'm wondering if fixing the Novyi Svit checkpoint for you will bite me in the ass now. And you didn't even go through!"

He'd never intended to. It does put Zagitov in a bad situation, though. "Sorry about that. We had to change plans on the fly. It was too much exposure. I appreciate the effort."

"Hope so. What's your plan now?"

Rogozhkin leans against the Hunter's front-left door, conveniently covering the worn Makiivka Brigade crest. The column of militia vehicles endlessly rumbles west. *At least they can do movement well.* "We're on the T0509 westbound. Anything we should look out for?"

Zagitov rummages through some papers. "Styla. It's the staging area for the second-line reserves. It's also a huge fucking mess now they're routing all the westbound military traffic through it. I swear, if this place had a decent road network…"

"A big mess sounds perfect for us. Lots to get lost in."

"Normally, yeah. But there's a battalion from the 45th Guards bivouacking there. People who know what you look like. If you transit the place, be careful as hell." Zagitov's hand scrapes against his phone's mic for a good twenty seconds. "Look, Edik, I gotta go. Good luck to you."

"Thanks, Dmitri. Be careful out there." The line goes dead.

Syrov and his men must've made it over the border into Russia. That would explain why Rostov-on-Don sent the alarm to all the field units. Rogozhkin's officially a fugitive now.

Tarasenko better have a plan to get him out of Ukraine. He can't imagine anything worse than falling prisoner to his own people. There's nothing *spetsnazovtsi* hate more than disloyalty.

Carson and Galina sit in the Octavia with the windows open to catch the freshening breeze. The wind-ruffled surface of the vest-pocket reservoir before them is as gray as the sky. Three hundred meters away, the highway's still jammed with westbound military traffic. Rogozhkin used a gap in the otherwise endless convoy to get them here an hour ago; at least they no longer have to gag on the exhaust and feel the ground vibrate under them.

Carson watches Galina stare past the steering wheel to the water. "What will you do when you get to Krakow?"

"What docs it matter?"

"Just interested. I don't know much about you or Bohdan."

Galina busies herself with picking at the corner of her thumbnail. She glances at Carson, then looks away. "I used to be a cook. In restaurants."

"A chef?"

"No, that's too fancy. A cook. I could make *Babka* Yulia's recipes in big batches. People liked them. They said it reminded them of their *babkas'* cooking."

"Comfort food?"

Galina shrugs. "I suppose. I will try to do that in Poland. There are enough Ukrainians there who might like it. Maybe I can start my own place someday."

Somehow, Carson had never imagined Galina doing something so domestic. She'd expected to hear about factory work or something, like Carson's mother had done before she and her father had left for Alberta. "What's Bohdan do?"

"He's a water engineer. He fixes pipes and pumps. He worked for Vodokanal, the water company. The Poles should need someone to fix their water pipes, yes?"

"Guess so." Carson tries to find an emotion on Galina's closed-up face. "How long have you two been together?"

"Eleven years. Married for nine. Apart for a year and a half." She looks at Carson face-on for the first time in almost two hours. "I need my husband. He's half of me. This time when he's been gone, it's—" She turns away suddenly, a little broken sound leaking out of her throat.

Not more crying. Carson can understand why Galina would want to, but still doesn't know what to do about it (if anything). She reaches out gingerly and lays a wary hand on Galina's shoulder.

Galina tries not very hard to shake it off, then concentrates on choking back her sobs. She manages to stuff them down her throat much faster than she had yesterday in Osykove. "I cry too much," she mumbles.

"You probably don't cry enough." Like Carson should talk. "The past few days've been rough on you. It's way more than you signed up for." She gives Galina's shoulder a squeeze. "Thanks for sticking with me. You didn't have to. You got your money."

Galina sniffs, then nods. "I promised to get you to the West."

"Yeah. Still doing the right thing?"

"Following *him* around?" She tosses her head toward Rogozhkin, who's pacing around the Hunter. "No. If I leave you and you die, your ghost will haunt me. I don't want you butting into my dreams for the rest of my life."

Carson almost laughs. "Believe me, I don't want to spend my afterlife in this place."

Galina waves a finger at her. "Be more careful, then. She who licks knives will soon cut her tongue."

Time trickles by. The convoy gets spottier, with larger gaps appearing in the file of vehicles. *If I'm gonna ask, now's the time.* "When you left last night, did you take the knapsack?"

Galina shoots her an annoyed glance. "Do you think I did?"

"I don't know. A million euros don't just disappear. If you've got a secret, you may need me to help keep it. Don't want to find out the wrong way what's back there." She thumbs behind her seat.

A long, edgy silence drags by. "Yes."

At least she's honest. "What are you going to do with it? It's a lot of money. Life-changing money."

"I know." Galina nibbles her lower lip absently. "We can buy a house or a farm. Start a business. Have some savings." She shrugs. "I don't know. Bohdan will help decide."

"Good luck explaining how you got it." Carson's been brooding all day about this conversation. She already knows where she has to take it. "You know I need to get the other picture away from Mashkov. The easiest way to do that is to buy it from—"

"*No.*" It's like a punch. "I won't give you the money if you will give it to that *tarhany*. I will *burn* it first." Galina thrusts a finger toward Rogozhkin. "Why don't you ask him for the money *he* took? Why should he keep it? He's not leaving his life behind—"

"Actually, he is. That's not the point. He—"

"What *is* the point?"

"I'm almost certain that with him, it's either the money *or* the icon, not both. I need the icon more. I get too greedy, he dumps us and leaves."

"You don't think he will do that anyway?" Galina's voice is getting as hot as the flush in her face. "Why do you trust that *Kacáps*?"

Shit, this again. "Who says I do?"

"You let him take us who-knows-where. You do what he asks. You let him *flirt* with you."

"Flirting? Really?"

"You haven't noticed? Hmpf." She shakes her head. "He's a murderer. How do you know he won't murder us when he's tired of us?"

Maybe he is *flirting and he's just bad at it. Maybe I can't see it because it doesn't happen to me much.* "He's got no reason to kill us. He needs me to help him get out of the country. You? I think he

234 • LANCE CHARNES

tolerates you because he doesn't want to piss me off."

"You wait. He's planning something." Galina spends more time watching Rogozhkin pace. "What if he leads us into a trap?"

The same thought's been nagging at Carson. "The people looking for us are looking for him. Tough needle to thread." But not impossible; he's got connections she and Galina don't. "Look, we got the icon. If things get sketchy, we run. Okay?"

Galina snorts. "Finally, you talk sense." She leans forward and shoves a work-worn finger in Carson's face. "Don't make me choose between Bohdan and you. If you don't run when we should, I will leave you."

Carson feels her spine turning to dust as they drive to Styla. The ten kilometers of highway are nightmares of broken and rutted asphalt. The dozens—maybe hundreds—of tracked armor and heavy military vehicles that had rolled through in the past few hours left behind unending washboard and loose chunks of pavement.

Galina does her best to avoid the worst of it while she fumes. "These *laiky!* They destroy everything even just driving around!"

Carson doesn't know what *laiky* means and won't bother to ask. Most of the Ukrainian insults she knows she learned from eavesdropping on her parents. This isn't one they used.

They pass a BMP on the shoulder with militia troops staring into the open engine compartment, like it's a beater car that stalled. Galina snickers.

Carson, who's now driving, scams them past a Lev Brigade roadblock outside Styla. Rogozhkin leaves the women behind on the dirt road that skirts the town.

She glooms over Rogozhkin abandoning them. *Where'd he go? Did he leave us? Is he rigging a trap?* Every minute, Carson expects to turn a corner and find another roadblock, or see Rogozhkin face-down in the dirt with a pack of militiamen pointing rifles at him.

Thirty agonizing minutes later, they find Rogozhkin's Hunter parked in a treeline a bit over a hundred meters away from the highway on the town's west side. Carson pulls up behind the SUV on the dirt road's verge. Rogozhkin climbs out the driver's door in not-often-worn jeans and a pressed blue-gray button-down shirt with the sleeves rolled to his elbows.

Carson steps out of the car and gestures toward Rogozhkin's outfit. "New uniform?"

He nods toward the Hunter. "That's not useful anymore. Mashkov knows by now that his scouts are missing. I'll hide it in the trees and we'll continue in your car. Or is it Galina's?"

"It's hers."

"I hope she won't tie me to the bonnet like a dead deer. It's thirteen kilometers to Dokuchajevsk. There's still onward movement on this part of the highway, but nothing like what we saw in Starobesheve. We follow the highway through the city, get lost in the civilian traffic, then transit the line and go through the Novotroitske crossing. If everything works well, we may be in the West before sunset."

Carson's heard that too many times here. It never works that way.

CHAPTER 46

The closer they get to Dokuchajevsk, they closer they come to the war.

From the front passenger's seat, Carson watches the scars go by. Zig-zagging earthworks, now covered with grass. Abandoned, semi-sunken firing positions for tanks and artillery in groups of three or six abreast. Impact craters in fields. Burned-out hulks of trucks and armor near the road. Ruined buildings. The occasional dud Uragan canister sticking out of the earth. Twice they have to edge past unexploded mortar bombs embedded in the road, surrounded by broken concrete blocks.

By the time they skirt the sprawling spoil heap from the local quarry—a klick wide, six to fifteen meters high—and pass the wind-rippled reservoir on the city's eastern edge, Carson expects to see something like those pictures of Baghdad or Tripoli: ragged shards of buildings, piles of broken masonry, fallen wires, trash, roving skeletal dogs.

But Dokuchajevsk isn't like that. The first few blocks are the same kind of compounds as the ones she's seen in the larger towns—houses with flocks of outbuildings, surrounded by walls or fences, citified versions of farms in places like Olhynske. Those give way to larger buildings, two or three stories tall with significant street frontage. People scurry along the sidewalks, a mix of civilians and military, mostly looking like they know where they're going and when they need to get there.

Galina—in the back seat—says, "Everyone is stocking up on food and water before the fighting starts. Especially water. The water system always goes down when there's a battle."

Carson looks more closely at the people the Octavia passes. Their European string bags bulge with food. Little folding carts are stacked with flats of water. The car passes what looks like a market street packed with busy shoppers. "Are there that many battles here?"

"Enough." Rogozhkin waves toward the world beyond the windshield. He'd insisted on driving to keep up appearances: *This is Ukraine. The men drive.* "Kyiv claims the Minsk settlement gave the town to the West. There's—"

Galina grumps, "It did. You people won't give it up."

He glances over his shoulder. "The people who live here don't want to go back to being under Kyiv's thumb. They—"

"Disappear when they speak against you and your gangster friends in Donetsk?"

Carson holds up a palm to each of them and puts on her mom voice. "Children, stop it. No civil war inside the car, or you walk."

Rogozhkin points over the steering wheel at the large, flat-topped gray hills straight ahead. "Galina, you'll be glad to know that Kyiv's troops are on the tops of those slag piles."

"They are?" Galina leans forward, poking her head between the front seats. She watches the piles grow steadily larger for a few moments, then falls back into her seat and claps her hands, cackling. "Thank you, *Bozhe!*"

They turn right at an imposing school building, then head northwest along a commercial-verging-on-industrial strip. A steady stream of traffic rolls by in the opposite direction. Carson navigates Rogozhkin through a dog-leg onto the road west. Three hundred meters ahead, the westbound traffic stops.

"Let me guess," Carson says. "Another checkpoint."

Galina says, "Yes, near the line of contact. The local police make it for bribes."

"Is this normal?"

"It's normal to have a queue. The queue isn't usually this long."

"How far to the checkpoint?"

"Three kilometers, maybe."

Carson sighs. "We could be here 'til dark." She glances at Rogozhkin. "You're not saying much."

He turns up a hand. "I know this route, but I don't use it. We have other ways to get across."

"Why aren't we using those?"

"Because we'd have to walk. At night." Rogozhkin twists toward Galina. "I assume you want to keep this car?"

"Yes."

He turns to Carson. "So."

They sit in silence for a while. Galina broods in the back seat. She'd almost pitched a fit when Rogozhkin said he's driving, and they've had hardly anything to say to each other since. Carson senses that Rogozhkin would like to talk to her—the regular glances her way and the navigation questions he doesn't need give her clues. She figures he doesn't want to be too chummy with Galina chaperoning.

Carson's brain has been grinding over the Galina-money problem since before Styla. Now's the time to do something about it. She pushes open her door. "I gotta stretch my legs."

She drifts far enough ahead of the Octavia so that Galina and Rogozhkin can't eavesdrop, then pulls her phone. She'd gotten Mashkov's number from Rogozhkin when they met up west of Styla. He didn't ask why she wanted it, but his eyes told her he knew.

"This is Mashkov." Lots of background noise, big engines, muffled shouts.

"Tarasenko."

A long silence. "This is unexpected. How did you burn my lorries?"

"I didn't. I just took advantage of the distraction."

"That's not all you took advantage of. You cost me my senior medic."

Poor Dunya. Lucky Dunya. "She was unhappy. I'm not proud of what I did to her. But now she can go have a life and be happy again. She loved you, you know."

Mashkov sighs. "I know that now. What do you want?"

Carson heaves in a huge breath before diving into the shark-infested water. "It's about what you want. Stepaniak's money. I found it."

"You—" He breaks off. Carson figures she could hear him think if there wasn't so much noise behind him. "Did Rogozhkin have it? I know you're with him."

"I was. He's dead, as far as I can tell. Doesn't matter where it came from—I have it. I'll make you the same offer I gave Stepaniak: the cash for the picture." When he doesn't answer right away, she says, "Don't overthink this. Don't be stupid like Stepaniak was."

"Why should I trust you? Lieutenant Fetisova trusted you and you betrayed her."

Yeah, rub it in. "I did what you teach your troops to do if they're captured. I didn't hurt her. A year from now, she'll thank me. Anyway, I got something you want and you got something I want. We play this straight and we both come out ahead. We either both win or we both lose. How about it?"

Mashkov's end of the line goes silent. Carson checks; they're still connected. Is he thinking? Talking to somebody else? Can he find where she is? She glances back at the car, which hasn't moved since she got out. Galina's chair-dancing in the back seat. *How will I sell her on this? Will I have to fight her for the money?*

Mashkov's phone un-mutes. "What do you propose?"

"A swap in a public place. I bring the money; you bring the picture. I'll have one other person with me for security. You can, too."

"Wait—you want *me* to come personally?"

"Yeah. I'm—"

"That's ridiculous. I have to get the brigade ready for combat. I'll send—"

"If you want your money, you come get it. I'm tired of your people chasing me and shooting at me. How have middlemen been working for you so far, Mashkov?"

That may be a growl on his end of the line. Or maybe it's a diesel engine.

Slam it home. "We can finish this in ten minutes. Then you'll have your million euros and I can leave this fucking place forever. I promise you I'm on the level—no tricks, no ambush, no risk to you. You'll walk away safe. It doesn't get any better than this. Say 'yes'."

Mashkov breathes in loudly enough to drown out the noise. "I don't have the painting here."

"Get it."

"I can have someone bring it. It'll take at least two hours to get here. Where are you?"

"Dokuchajevsk. Same as you."

"Very good. The city administrative building is on Independence Street. There's a football pitch behind it. I suggest we use it. I can contact you when the painting is here." Carson likes hearing the urgency in his voice. He's bought in…maybe. "I'm entering into this in good faith. But I must warn you, Miss

Tarasenko—if you try to trick me, I'll shoot you where you stand."

"Same here. You try anything, I'll kill you. Send a photo of the picture when you have it." She cuts the call before things can get more complicated.

A bouncy pop tune Carson remembers from Thursday morning fills the inside of the car when she slides into her seat. She glances at Rogozhkin.

"Eurovision." He rolls his eyes, then rocks his head back toward Galina.

Carson's stiff from inactivity, achy from her injuries, and mentally drained. This supposed one-day-plus-travel, quick in-and-out project has turned into a slog. She's sick of this place—the bad roads, polluted water, poverty, lines, fighting, death—and wants to go home. She rarely wants to go home. Living in hotels suits her; they're usually clean and comfortable, and the staff is nice to her. There's no past in a hotel. "Home" is a crappy bachelor apartment in Rexdale with white noise provided by the airport. There's lots of past there.

This road may lead her home. The contact line is walking distance from here. She could get there in less than thirty minutes without trying hard. She's sure Galina and Rogozhkin are already thinking about what they'll do on the other side. But if she crosses now, she goes back home a failure.

She has to tell them they have to stay longer. *How do I do this?*

"Wait a minute!" Galina's head surges between the two front seats. "She won? Jamala *won?*" She whoops and thrusts her fists as high as she can without punching the headliner.

Galina's celebration kicks Carson out of her own head. Now that she's listening again, she recognizes the song on the radio and flashes back to that bar in Komsomolske: the pretty brunette in the blue gown on TV, the dramatic words that Carson couldn't figure out, Galina grinning and clapping, the Russian-speaking drunks grousing and throwing insults. Jamala was Ukraine's Eurovision entry.

Galina, now laughing, wraps her arms around Carson's neck from behind. Carson hopes it's a hug and not attempted murder. "She won!" Galina crows. "Ukraine won!" She plants a big, sloppy kiss on the top of Carson's head. Then she pokes Rogozhkin's shoulder with a finger. "*Your* guy lost."

He shakes his head sadly. "Politics."

Carson closes her eyes. *Galina's in a good mood. That just makes this harder.* To make the swap work, she's got to get the money Galina took from the farm at Byryuky. She can't see a way to do that except by lying to Galina or stealing from her. Carson doesn't want to do that.

It's not her money.

Not the point. If anyone deserves to get the cash, it's her.

Point is, you got a job to do. Do it half-assed, you don't get paid. Make it work.

Just as Galina settles down, Rogozhkin sticks his head outside his window. A bright blue Opel Astra hatchback approaches slowly in the opposite direction. Someone holds an oversized sheet of paper out of the sunroof with "Checkpoint closed" scrawled on it in Russian.

Rogozhkin mutters, "Damn."

A minute later, a slate-gray VW station wagon passes. A young woman in the back seat yells out her open window, "It's closed! The checkpoint's closed!"

Carson stifles a *whew* reaction. Now she doesn't have to pull them out of line.

Rogozhkin cranks the wheel and roars into a gap in the oncoming traffic. The distance they'd covered in almost an hour going west passes in less than ten minutes heading east.

Galina asks, "Where are we going?"

Rogozhkin doesn't answer until he's turned left on the highway that had brought them to this point. "North. The crossing at Olenivka may still be open."

Carson checks her GPS. Olenivka is an exurb of Donetsk about seven klicks north of here. It's split by the H20 motorway, the local version of a freeway. The road they're on now hits the H20 a few hundred meters west of the contact line. "If this checkpoint's closed, why would Olenivka be open?"

"You're in the Donbass." Rogozhkin flashes her a quick smile. "Don't expect logic."

This is how Carson can buy time. "Is there a hotel here?"

"Yes, in Dokuchajevsk center. Why?"

"We should go there and check in before they run out of rooms."

Galina leans forward between the front seats. "But what if we can get out through Olenivka? I can drop you where you want and—"

"What if we spend another hour in line and the checkpoint's already closed?" That comes out harsher than Carson intended. She turns her voice down a couple notches. "I'm not sleeping in the car or some abandoned house. Not again. I need a shower and a real bed. We all do. Okay?"

Rogozhkin says, "She has a point." Another sudden U-turn takes the Octavia south.

Galina sighs and flops back into her seat. "At least it's a nice hotel. It's more than I like to spend, but since you will pay…"

Carson feels a second or two of relief, followed by another lurch of guilt. She still has to get the money away from Galina. No matter how it goes, Galina's going to be pissed and resentful. This tentative friendship—or whatever it is—that they've built will go straight down the toilet. Carson knows all too well what that feels like…and it's already making her sick.

CHAPTER 47

The Hotel Mriya fills the southern edge of a plaza centered on a statue of Lenin on a black-marble pedestal. The hotel itself looks like it should be a university or government building—two stories tall with a grand central portico fronted by six tall columns and a broad staircase. A pack of cars is already parked on either side of the entry.

Carson and Galina end up in a room on the second floor overlooking the back courtyard and staff parking. There's a small sitting room with a desk, a mirror, and a couple wood-frame chairs. The separate bedroom has two low, single beds and—thank God!—a real washroom.

Galina turns on the sink's tap. Clearish water comes out. "There's water!" She says it like a kid says "There's a pony!" on Christmas morning.

Carson's already stripping. Dropping the body armor feels like losing a hundred pounds. "I need a real shower. Don't get in my way." By the time she drags off her underwear—the same ones she's been wearing since Wednesday—Galina's done peeing loudly and rattles open the washroom door.

She gasps. "The *kolorady* did *that* to you?"

It's the first time Carson's seen her own body in a day and a half. There's more black-and-purple than unblemished skin. Some bruises are nearly as dark as her body armor. The cuts and scrapes are now rust-colored accents to the green edges on her contusions, forming a weird camouflage all over her. "Yeah." She sweeps the thin white towel off the foot of her bed. "If you got something stronger than paracetamol in your first-aid kit, I'll pay you extra."

Carson's stretched out naked on her bed, drifting on whatever was in the big, white lozenges Galina gave her when she stepped out of the shower. It's wonderful to not have all that *stuff* on her, chafing her sores, irritating her bruises. Being rid of the body armor feels like a day at a spa.

Galina had gone all maternal on her, rubbing some kind of salve into her scrapes and cuts, even washing her tee, underwear, and socks (in real soap and water!) and hanging them in the shower. They drip noisily.

Another stomach-growl erupts as a masculine knock rattles the front door. Galina—freshly showered and changed, her hair still damp—sets down the book she's been reading at the sitting room's desk and crosses left out of Carson's sight. The door creaks open. "What do *you* want?" Galina hisses.

"I was wondering if you ladies would like to—" It's Rogozhkin.

"Keep your voice down. She's resting."

"Sorry." His volume decreases by about half. "Would you ladies like to join me for a walk in the park? It's becoming a nice evening, and we all need to work out the kinks from driving on these roads."

"You mean the ones you people destroy with your tanks?"

Oh, hell. So much for resting. Carson gathers stray bits of her voice. "Galina, play nice."

Rogozhkin calls out, "Miss Tarasenko?" The door squeaks, then rattles.

"No!" Galina snaps. "You stay outside! She's not decent."

Not decent? Carson last heard someone use that phrase in a CBC costume drama. She'd like to just keep drifting, but her gut's past *eating would be nice* and approaching *must have food.* Sitting up is harder than it should be; a good excuse for some exercise. "Rogozhkin? Give me ten minutes and I'll come with you. Galina, you want to come?"

"I would rather eat nails."

As Rogozhkin leads Tarasenko across the square to one of Miskyi Park's entrances, he notices she's moving stiffly, with a rather unbecoming half-frown on her face. "Do you feel any better?"

"No."

"I'm sorry to hear that."

"Me, too." She squares her shoulders. "Galina gave me something to sand off the sharp corners. That helps."

Late-afternoon gold washes the dramatic clouds overhead. They enter a paved walk under a canopy of tall, leafy green trees. Apparently, not everything is ruined in this part of the country. "Galina's been taking good care of you, then?"

"For the past couple of hours. She swings between hating me and wanting to mother me. I get it, but it keeps things interesting."

"I see." The damage to her face is painful to look at. She's rolled up the sleeves of her tatty plaid work shirt, exposing forearms that are just as abused. He knows about pain, and hers must be significant. Yet she's not complaining. "No body armor this evening?"

She shoots a stern eyebrow his way. "Can't. Galina washed my tee shirt. I got nothing to wear under the vest."

"No extra clothes?"

"The plan was, I'd be here for a few hours. Why would I pack more clothes?"

Rogozhkin chuckles. "I've known one or two women who'd carry several pairs of shoes to go to the market." He waves to the north. "It's too bad it's so late. The Old Market is a few blocks that way. You could get what you need there, but I'm sure the shops are closed by now."

"Oh, well. What's with the limp?"

He glances at her to check whether she's making fun of him. There's no smirk or sneer; it's just a question. "Kosovo. A land mine."

"*Kosovo?* How long have you been doing this?"

He weighs his answer. He doesn't want to hide his age, but he doesn't want to emphasize it. "When I was drafted, it was still the Soviet Army. My first foreign deployment was to Afghanistan."

Tarasenko nods thoughtfully. Then she peers at him for a few steps. "You said you're from Siberia. Are you Yakut?"

"Close. My mother was Khakas. Southwestern Siberia."

"Knowing how most Russians feel about non-Europeans, I'm surprised you got so far."

She knows about that? "When you win enough medals, kill enough enemies, and keep enough secrets, you're hard to ignore."

They emerge from the trees on the edge of a football pitch

behind a school. Several young women sit threading strips of green and brown cloth into a net spread across the patchy grass. Tarasenko stands next to him, not too close but not too far, with her arms folded tightly. "What are they doing out there?"

"Making a camouflage net. It's one of the touching things about this war—all the home-made effort on both sides. Hand-knit socks and mittens, home-cooked food, crowdsourced field gear. It reminds me of stories I've read about the Great Patriotic War." He watches the young women—schoolgirls, now that he's had time to look—expertly weave the colors together to make something that looks natural. "The question here is, which side will get it when it's done?"

"From what you told Galina, it should go to the local militia or something."

Once again, he needs to consider his answer. "That's what I told her. It's entertaining to wind her up—she reacts so predictably."

"You lied."

"I shaded the truth. There's some support for the DNR here; it's not hard to find the graffiti. But most of the people are loyal to Kyiv. I'm sure Kyiv's army gets almost real-time reporting on the location of every DNR asset in this city. If they ever seriously try to take it back, the locals will make sure there's no safe place for the DNR men or for us. And then Donetsk will be surrounded on three sides."

Tarasenko's eyes search his face. "Bet you weren't supposed to tell me that."

"Perhaps." Her examination makes him a bit uneasy. He turns away and crosses onto another tree-shaded walkway. The sprinkling of people sharing the area is thin and mostly distant. Tarasenko catches up and walks beside him, matching his stride.

"You seem to be an intelligent woman. I'm sure you know or suspected this already. Lying to you only diminishes me. I don't want to do that." He meets her sandy-brown eyes. "I also want you to know that I'm not a zealot like Galina. I came here with a job to do. I did it, now I'm done."

Why is he justifying himself to this woman? Because he finds her attractive? He's been attracted to other women over the years, but never felt a need to explain himself the way he does now.

Perhaps because he's facing the end of his career without a plan for what comes next? Because he's never until now met a woman who isn't afraid of him?

"I get it," she finally says. "Can we go by the football stadium?"

"Of course." He wants to ask why, but won't. He can tell it's not idle curiosity. "Did you call Mashkov?"

Long pause. "Yes."

"And?"

Tarasenko's face reflects the wrestling match inside her. "He'll swap the Cranach for cash."

Just as he'd expected. It's the only possible reason that she'd want the man's phone number. "You mean the cash Stepaniak had."

"Yes."

"So you do know where it is."

"Yes."

"Galina has it?"

She gives him a sharp look. "Why do you say that?"

"It's the only thing that makes sense. Mashkov doesn't have it, I don't have it, and I assume you don't. If you can get to it, that leaves her." He leads her to an open gate. "This is the stadium. Not exactly Luzhniki, but..."

Tarasenko surveys the grounds—a regulation football pitch, seating lining the long sides, a fieldhouse on the west, floodlight standards at either end. "What's 'DFDK'?"

"On the seats? It's for the dolomite mine. They sponsored it."

"Are these gates always open?"

"I don't know. Are they a problem if they're not?" The concrete walls on either side are only two meters high. "Is this where you'll meet Mashkov?"

She doesn't answer as she drifts toward the footpath again. That may be her answer.

"Be careful. Have you ever heard of Stearne's Law?"

"No. Who's Stearne?"

"A crazy American Ranger I met on an exchange tour. He said that paranoia isn't mental illness—it's the result of acute situational awareness."

Carson nods, pursing her lips. Her eyes are aimed someplace far away.

The gap in the conversation becomes uncomfortable. He nods toward her folded arms. "Are you cold?"

"No."

"Where's your home?"

"Canada."

"Ah. You're one of *those* Ukrainians." That explains a lot.

"Yeah."

"Your Russian is very good. Very current."

"I get to use it a lot."

"Working for this company you mentioned?"

"That and other reasons."

She's making him do all the hard work. *Is this a test?* "Do you have a man in Canada? Children?"

Tarasenko arches an eyebrow. "You have anybody?"

Is she asking because she cares, or to put off answering me? "I'm afraid I've never had the time, opportunity, and interest all at the same time to get a wife. A lot of men in my position can say that. I'm sure you've met a few."

"Yeah. The job's always more interesting than taking out the garbage." Another sharp look. "It's hard to find a woman who'll put up with being tied to a man she never sees." She lets a few steps go by. "Who isn't rich."

At least she's not afraid to have an opinion. "Quite so. Now I'll have the opposite problem—finding a woman who won't mind her man being home all the time."

"Get a hobby."

Rogozhkin chuckles. "I'll have time for that. There's a line from a poem I've always liked: 'Let there be spaces in your togetherness.'"

"'Fill each other's cup but drink not from one cup.'" She gets a faraway look in her eyes. "'Give one another of your bread but eat not from the same loaf. Sing and dance together and be joyous, but let each one of you be alone, even as the strings of a lute are alone, though they quiver with the same music.'" Tarasenko pulls her focus from the other side of the world. "Kahlil Gibran. I like that one, too. I know two poems by heart. That's one of them."

This, he hadn't expected. The woman can handle a weapon *and* quote poetry. "Did you ever have a chance to use that advice?"

"Sort of. That thing about the job being more interesting than chores? That was my ex." They emerge onto a paved plaza dominated by a Soviet war memorial. She stops to read the inscription. "Other women were also more interesting than chores."

"He was a fool."

"One way to put it." She nods toward the marker, a relief of a Soviet soldier in a flowing cape, carrying a flag that reads, *For the Homeland.* "I guess they're buried here."

"Yes." He steps back, comes to attention, then salutes the monument. Tarasenko watches him quietly. He returns to her side. "My grandfather died outside Minsk in 1944."

"My grandfather ran an antiaircraft battery near Kharkiv. He met my grandmother there." She paces west, toward another footpath. "You're not giving back the money, are you?"

The question surprises him; her directness doesn't. "Why do you say that?"

"The militia's hunting all of us. They want me and Galina because we screwed them. We can't fix that. Mashkov wants the million euros you still have in your backpack. Give him the money and he's gone."

There's no reproach in her voice. She's asking about a practical solution to a difficult problem. The more time Rogozhkin spends with her, the more he likes her. "Would you think less of me if I don't?"

"Depends on why you're doing it."

"Fair enough." He feels her eyes again. A pointed look, but not a hostile one. "My career's over. Tomorrow I'll officially be a deserter."

"There goes the pension."

"Exactly. I need something to live on in exile. All my career, I've followed official orders to help make gangsters and warlords rich and powerful. Now it's my turn."

Tarasenko's lips are pursed, her eyes thoughtful. "Well, that'll help with the 'finding a wife' thing."

"I hope so."

Another few quiet steps. "What's the plan for tomorrow?"

No scolding, no speeches, no appeals to duty or morality. *She understands.* "Well, the highway's out. The locals probably closed the western checkpoint early so they can fortify it. It wouldn't do to leave a road open to let Kyiv's armor go rolling through. The same very likely applies to the northbound route. The last time I saw the plan for tomorrow's operation, the main push is south of the city to eliminate the salient around Mykolaivka."

"And east is the wrong direction."

"True. If we can go by foot, I know several routes. Perhaps you could persuade Galina…?"

"Forget it. Everything she owns is in that car."

"Pity. I'd like to try the northern route to Olenivka. It may not be open, but there are a lot of meanings for 'closed' and some are porous. If that's how it is there, we can get out easily without having to deal with artillery fire. If it's closed, there's another way we may be able to use. It's much…*harder*, but still possible so long as it doesn't rain between now and then."

Tarasenko shakes her head. "No rain in the forecast."

He knows that. "We'll start at 0300. We have to wait for dark anyway, and by then any guards will be half-asleep." They reach the southeast corner of Lenin Square. "Would you like to walk more?" He hopes she'll say *yes*. He's enjoyed her company and this conversation.

Tarasenko's phone buzzes. She pulls it from her hip pocket, then turns the screen to show it to him. It's a photo of a very old depiction of the Annunciation. "Mashkov's got the picture. We're meeting in half an hour."

CHAPTER 48

Mashkov buttonholes Vasilenko as the senior sergeant bustles through the half-activated temporary command post. "I need a sniper section. Now."

Vasilenko wipes his forehead on his sleeve. "Yes, sir. Where are they going?"

"To the city administration building. High positions overlooking the football pitch. Send them in a civilian vehicle if you can."

"Okay…I'll see what I can do. What's the target?"

"Remember the Tarasenko woman? She's going to be there at 1915. So will I. When I light a cigarette, they take her down. Understand?"

Rogozhkin watches the clouds slowly turn red through his hotel room's window.

Tarasenko's deal with Mashkov may hold an opportunity for him.

Mashkov killed the brigade's senior Russian officers and started this rebellion. If he dies, the rebellion loses its leader and its momentum. It won't take much to impose another commander, one more…*acceptable* to Moscow.

And if Rogozhkin kills Mashkov, he'll have a powerful argument to clear his name. Proskurin and the rest failed; he cleaned up after them and brought matters under control. He'll be able to fight off the wolves and retire honorably.

He knows where Mashkov is going to be, and when. No matter where he sets up, he'll be no more than a hundred meters from the target. An easy shot with an AK.

Yes, Tarasenko said she'd promised Mashkov there'd be no tricks or traps. He's sure Mashkov promised her the same. But will he honor that?

Rogozhkin doubts it. The man holds grudges.

So he can both get rid of Mashkov and protect Tarasenko from her own scruples. A win for everybody.

Except Mashkov, of course.

"I told you before. No. I won't do it."

Carson clamps her mouth shut so she doesn't blurt out the first few things that roar into her head. "You know that isn't your money, right?"

Galina plants her fists on her hips. Her face is pink heading toward scarlet. "I know. It doesn't matter. I won't let you give all that money to *that man*." She pokes a fingertip into one of the many bruises around Carson's collarbones. "If you say you want it for yourself, I would say, 'Here, take it.' If you want to give it to the Red Cross or the church, I would give it to you in a minute. But *him?* Do you remember what I told you about Ilovaisk? Those creatures shooting the wounded men in my lorry? Maybe they shot *me?*" She jams her arms together over her chest. "No. Absolutely not."

So far, this has gone just as badly as Carson expected. Once again, she wishes Matt was here. He can sweet-talk people… "Galina, look. I wouldn't ask if I had any other option. I—"

"Why don't you take the *Kacáps's* money?" She jabs a finger toward the room's front door. "He shouldn't get it—"

"Because he'd kill me. You, too. Believe me, I thought about it a lot. I even thought about fucking him to—"

"Watch your language."

"Give it a rest. I gamed that out as far as I could. We end up in a bad way no matter what. So here we are." Carson forces herself to breathe slow. It helps her cool off and think. She'd like to sit on the bed but can't afford to give up her power position. "Do you think the museum's gonna forget about that picture?"

For the first time, Galina doesn't stomp on Carson's words. It's progress.

Carson makes an effort to calm her voice. "They won't, you know. They'll send somebody else with another suitcase full of money. Probably the same cash you have now. I told you all this about the icon. The situation hasn't changed."

Galina's face is holding on pink. The fire in her eyes has turned into glowing coals.

"You saying 'no' won't stop this. Mashkov's gonna get his money. Somebody else will walk into danger to finish it. And..." She didn't want to play this card, but she needs it. "I probably won't get paid for anything that's happened since Wednesday. That's what my boss says."

Galina's mouth slowly unclenches. The fire dies in her eyes. "They...won't pay you?"

Carson shrugs. "I spent a lot of the client's money and didn't get the job done. That's how it goes."

"That's not fair."

"Lots of things aren't fair. You know that first-hand. So do I." Carson holds out her hand, palm up. She gentles her voice as much as she can. "Come on, Galina. I don't want to fight you. I want to get us out of here and help you get Bohdan and send you off to your new lives. Can you help me do that?"

Galina stares at the hand, then her own feet, then out the window, then into Carson's eyes. "I have hated those people for two years. People like Mashkov, the *Kacápskyi*, all of them. They took my husband away from me."

Please don't. I know you've been hurt. I can't fix any of that. Please...

"Now all I want is to get Bohdan back. I will do *anything* to do that." Her eyes close for a moment, then reopen. "If that means I have to give you this money to give to that Mashkov person, I will even do that. Even if it makes everything inside me ache." She stomps to her bed, drags out the rucksack, then drops it into Carson's hands. "Take it."

Carson rummages through the bag, grabs a strap of cash, and hands it to Galina. "Here. This way, Mashkov won't get his full million."

Galina turns the bundle of €200 notes in her hand, then holds it out to Carson. "No."

"Take it. You've earned it."

Galina weighs the strap, sighs, then squats to hide it in her duffel. "Are you going by yourself?"

"I don't want to. Will you come with me? Watch my back?"

"Okay." Galina looks up, frowning. "I don't want you to haunt me if the *tarhany* kill you."

Carson almost smiles. "Thanks. After this, I'll stop licking knives."

Carson checks her watch. Five minutes to the swap. She thumbs Mashkov's number into Heitmann's phone, just to confuse things.

"This is Mashkov."

"Tarasenko. The plan's changed. I don't like the swap site. There are too many overlooks for snipers."

He sputters. "You can't change things this late. I—"

"The Avanhard football stadium in the park. I'll see you there in five…if you want your money."

The floodlights on the four tall standards—two at each end of the field—are lit by the time Carson and Galina approach the stadium from the south through the Soviet war memorial, even though there's nearly an hour of daylight left. A lot of people freak out at the thought of being in the middle of a couple dozen bright floods. When she steps onto the surprisingly well-kept sod, though, it's a flashback to Alberta.

Galina's eyes are wide, her jaw's stiff, and her head's on a swivel. She keeps wiping her palms on her jeans, alternating so she always has a grip on her AK. "We are so exposed," she mutters.

"He will be, too. Didn't you play sports in school?"

"Not in a place like this. Did you?"

"Yeah. This reminds me of my high-school rugby matches."

"I am not surprised that you play rugby."

Nobody ever is. Carson scans the stands. Nearly all the individual plastic-backed seats are empty. Most are white; blocks of blue seatbacks are interspersed with white ones that spell out "DFDK" in huge Cyrillic letters. There's a couple making out in one corner in the back row and a gaggle of girls smoking and giggling near the fieldhouse at midfield left. "This is like the crowd for our matches. Girls' rugby wasn't much of a draw."

Galina stands a couple of paces away, holding her rifle across her chest pointing down, looking like she's the one in the crosshairs. "Your parents didn't come?"

"Pops would when he was in town. My brothers would. Mostly they liked watching healthy girls in tight shorts jump on each other." When that line doesn't get the usual laugh, she glances at Galina. "It's okay. There's hardly anyplace to hide."

A figure in Russian camo appears in the fieldhouse door. He's almost fifty meters away, but he stands like Mashkov. After a few moments, he marches down the short stairs and onto the field, followed by a militiaman carrying a familiar dark-green rectangle in front of his chest.

Mashkov stops about five meters from Carson. "Good evening, Miss Tarasenko. I'm glad to see you're exactly on time. Shall we begin?"

Rogozhkin covers in the bushes a few meters from the stadium's northwest portal. He's been there for nearly half an hour, wondering where Tarasenko was. The militia sniper bustled in six minutes ago to take position behind the wrought-iron gate with the Olympic rings. This one knows what he's doing; he'd set up with economical movements and no noise. He's now prone with his Dragunov sniper rifle settled on a bipod near the gate's bottom rail.

The sniper knows that part of his job, but he didn't check the bushes for threats.

It's 18° C and humid. Rogozhkin's black wool turtleneck and balaclava were heavy and sticky twenty minutes ago; now they're frustrating the mosquitos even more than him. It's almost comfortable compared to doing this during a Chechen winter.

Rogozhkin checks his watch. 1917; time to start. He slowly edges out of the bushes, taking care with every step to not disturb the foliage. When he reaches the asphalt driveway, he draws his Vityaz tactical knife and ghosts the two meters to the sniper. Luckily, the man's watching the football pitch through his rifle's scope, not paying attention to his environment.

After two breaths, Rogozhkin drops a knee on the small of the man's back, then wraps a gloved hand around the sniper's mouth when his head rears back. Rogozhkin then rams the knife through the base of the man's skull into his brain. His body bucks twice, then goes limp.

Once he disposes of the corpse in the shrubs, Rogozhkin takes up the Dragunov to check the action in the stadium. Tarasenko and Mashkov are face-to-face in the center of the pitch, roughly five meters apart, her with her arms crossed, him with a hand resting on the top of his holster. Galina's three or four steps behind Tarasenko and to her left, an AK aimed at Mashkov, who has his own second a few paces to his right, holding a plastic-wrapped painting with both hands.

The brigade has four three-man sniper sections. Mashkov would use a full section. There may be two more hostiles here.

Rogozhkin starts hunting with the scope.

Mashkov tries to watch the rifle's muzzle with some measure of detachment. Difficult when it's aimed at his head.

Tarasenko growls, "Ease off, Galina."

The shorter woman—Galina, apparently—shifts her grip slightly but doesn't lose lock on his forehead. He's seen that kind of hatred before in other people's eyes, but not usually when they're also threatening to shoot him. He swallows. "Miss Tarasenko, I came here in good faith, as promised. Can you please…"

"*Ease off*, Galina." If Tarasenko wore a uniform, that tone of voice would've added *that's an order*. They may not have that kind of relationship, but Galina clearly heard it: she slowly lowers the barrel to point between him and Bulaev with the painting.

"Sorry about that," Tarasenko says, not sounding terribly sorry. "She's had bad experiences with your brigade."

"I understand. Do you have the money?"

Tarasenko pulls off an olive backpack, unzips the top, then tosses it on the ground halfway between them. She nods toward Bulaev. "That the picture? Open it up so I can see it."

Mashkov nods at Bulaev, who settles on one knee. They'd already undone the wrapping, so all the private needs to do is pull the painting from the outer bag and peel back the inner plastic sheet to expose the painting's face.

Mashkov gestures toward the bag. "May I?"

Tarasenko nods. She's obviously wearing body armor and is likely armed. Should he trust her? He knows better than to trust her friend Galina. But he still needs to check the money.

He squats next to the knapsack and gaps the top opening. The mound of yellow banknotes inside practically glows in the harsh light. He was usefully tense before, but now his heart starts galloping like a racehorse approaching the finish line. *So close...* "Is it all here?"

"As far as I know. Can't vouch for what Stepaniak did when he had it. It's about the right weight."

"I'm curious. How much do a million euros weigh?"

"Fifty straps of a hundred notes each? A bit over five kilos."

Mashkov's not surprised Tarasenko knows how much the money should weigh. She likely does this regularly. He hefts the bag with his right hand; it feels about right. He burrows his hand into the pile and pulls a bundle of notes from the bottom. Currency, not newsprint or butcher paper.

He stands, slings the knapsack over his shoulder, and takes another good look at Galina. If her eyes were cannon, he'd be erased from the Earth by now. His brain makes a few automatic connections. "Tell me, Miss Galina...did you burn my lorries?"

Her feral smile answers before she says a word. "Yes. I enjoyed it. At least no one was in them. Not like when you burned ours."

Tarasenko blows out a long breath. "Galina..."

Mashkov raises a *stop* gesture toward Tarasenko. "No, it's fine. Miss Galina, did you fight?"

"Yes. The Donbass Battalion." She stands straight and squares her shoulders.

Our past sins return to haunt us. Going any farther down this road could make things tricky. *Time to end it.* "You fought well. Miss Tarasenko, you have your painting, I have my money. Our business is done." Except it won't be as long as these two are still walking. He reaches into his left breast pocket. "Do you mind if I smoke?"

◎

Rogozhkin has a clear shot at Mashkov's head. The rangefinder in the rifle's sight says the distance is just shy of a hundred meters. The wind's out of the southwest at around ten kilometers per hour; a minor windage adjustment.

Do it now.

But he's found the other two members of the sniper section. The young man in the dark hoodie winding his way through the east stands isn't ready yet. The one who worries Rogozhkin most is the man at the southeast gate. Tarasenko's partly masking him; Rogozhkin can't get a good solution on him that lasts more than a few seconds.

He may be able to kill Mashkov, but the other snipers may get to Tarasenko before Rogozhkin can neutralize them. A poor outcome.

He swivels his sight back to Mashkov just as the man picks a cigarette pack from his breast pocket.

Mashkov doesn't smoke.

It's a signal.

Rogozhkin exhales, then brushes the pad of his index finger onto the Dragunov's trigger.

Mashkov fits a cigarette between his lips and positions the plastic lighter. He flicks down the little lever.

Click. Nothing.

He tries again. No flame.

He'd borrowed the cigarettes and lighter from Shatilov. The way the man smokes, it's no surprise the lighter's empty. *Damn it!*

Tarasenko says, "Can that wait? We're done. I'm taking the picture." She lunges forward, pulls the painting and its wrappings out of Bulaev's hands, then backpedals to stand next to Galina.

A gunshot, to his left.

Carson and Galina land on their faces together. "What the *fuck?*"

Mashkov and his helper are also face-down. The helper has his arms crossed over his helmet, like that'll stop a bullet.

The girls in the stands are scattering like sparrows, shrieking and climbing over each other.

Another shot, this one from the south end of the field. *Of course the bastard brought snipers!*

A third shot, from the north end. A *clang* of metal on metal south of her makes her look toward the closed gate. A man in a black track suit sags into a heap on the ground.

Carson picks up her head just enough to look over her shoulder. A guy in a hoodie in the east stands is pulling a rifle from what looks like a fishing-rod bag. Another shot from the north blows out the back of his head.

What the fuck?

Then it makes sense: Rogozhkin. *How could he know?*

He couldn't. *But why...?*

Another shot. A tuft of grass pops up an inch from Mashkov's head.

Her brain vomits up a whole scenario in an instant. She heaves herself onto her knees and screams, "Don't! Don't do it! Stop!"

Then she throws herself on Mashkov.

He grunts. "What are you doing?"

"Saving your fucking life. Keep your head down."

Galina's on one knee, firing single shots toward the north gate. Off in the distance, a police siren keens.

Mashkov growls, "Who is that? Did you bring someone?"

Carson repositions herself so her body shields all of Mashkov above his knees. She slaps the side of his head. "No. *You* sure did. Two snipers? I should let this asshole kill you."

He looks bewildered. "Why don't you?"

"Because I promised no tricks. I keep my promises...even when they suck. Shut up before I change my mind." She turns her head toward Galina. "*Stop shooting!*"

Galina stops shooting and stares at Carson. "What? Why?" She's bewildered, too.

"Because..." *God help me* "...he's friendly."

Galina and Mashkov look at her like she's nuts. Maybe she is.

Now all she has to do is keep Rogozhkin from killing Mashkov long enough to get out of this place.

What is she doing?

Rogozhkin sights in on where Mashkov's head should be and gets a scope full of Tarasenko's upper back instead. He was so close on that last round, but he'd overcompensated.

And now *this*...

Tarasenko hauls Mashkov upright and starts hustling him toward the fieldhouse. Rogozhkin tries to get a firing solution, but she's in the way.

Shoot her first, then him.

No. That's not me anymore. Besides, I need her to keep me out of Kyiv's PW camps.

They disappear inside. Galina scurries after them a few moments later, hauling the painting.

Shit.

He dumps his AK next to the dead sniper, cases the Dragunov, salvages as much ammo as he can from the body, then melts into the darkening shadows.

CHAPTER 49

Mashkov signs yet another sheaf of orders and hands them to the orderly. His hands are still shaking from that circus at the football stadium.

Tarasenko saved his life. Why? Especially when he tried to have her killed?

Why did he do *that?*

Fear. Frustration. She kept getting in the way. How many of his men had she shot? She disgraced poor Dunya. And her little friend destroyed or damaged nine of his lorries to help her escape.

Yet she saved his life. And the brigade has a million euros.

He stretches and yawns. The past hour on top of his lack of sleep last night has caught up with him. He'd like tea, but he couldn't bring his kettle from the base and the abandoned farmhouse that's now his headquarters has barely enough electricity to run their computers and radios. A junior lieutenant foolishly tried to use the antique microwave oven an hour ago and brought down the brigade's entire comm network.

He passes through the ramshackle kitchen for coffee—absolute swill, but effective—and enters the former-bedroom-now-plotting room. The topographic map spread out on a folding table in the center shows the brigade's progress as it deploys to its positions. Shatilov and a sergeant stand by the table, both wearing radio headsets. As Mashkov watches, the sergeant wipes a unit symbol off the plastic sheet and draws its replacement with a grease pencil. Crude and old-fashioned, but at least it doesn't need electricity.

Mashkov joins the men at the table. "What's our status, Evgeniy?"

Shatilov shoves a clipboard with a thick wad of paper—the combat order—under his right arm, then swivels the headset microphone away from his face. "Sir, we're about sixty percent bedded down." He draws a fingertip around the south end of a kilometer-wide topographic feature. "Third Battalion's taken its positions south and east of the quarry, here. They're digging in now. They're due to link their left flank with Lev Brigade's right in the next hour." He takes a hit from the cigarette burning between the middle and ring fingers of his left hand, then points to a spot between the quarry and a large, triangular mass just to its northeast. "Second Battalion's here, bridging the gap between the quarry and the spoil heap. They're emplaced and ranging their weapons." His finger stabs the top of the artificial butte. "UA infantry here."

Kyiv's army, so close? "How many?"

Shatilov turns up his left hand. "There's no good intel on that. Could be up to a company. They call their base up there 'Everest' because they can see for kilometers in every direction, or so I'm told." He mashes his finger onto a roughly trapezoidal tan blotch. "First Battalion's in reserve in this quarry here, just east of town. Kyiv's spotters can't see them, and the UA artillery will have a hell of a time placing ordnance on them. It's a steep drop-off. They're more likely to drop rounds into the lake at the bottom." He takes another drag, then chuckles. "Wouldn't that be a shame?"

Mashkov can't focus right now. "Yes. Yes, it would."

Shatilov dismisses the sergeant, then skirts the table. "Dima? What happened up there? You've been half here since you got back. Are you hurt?"

"No." He sags onto a folding metal chair. "I should be dead." He gives Shatilov a quick rundown of the action. "I don't understand what happened. She had every reason in the world to let me die…and she saved me."

Shatilov claps Mashkov's shoulder. "You're alive. You got the money for the brigade. Losing the three snipers is shit, but…" He shrugs. "You won. Win gracefully. Let it go."

"Let it go." Mashkov's head feels like stone when he shakes it. "Rogozhkin was there."

"Rogozhkin's dead. The Russians say so. Our scouts took his money and they're probably having a huge drunk in Kyiv right now."

"Then who else? Who could she get who can shoot like that?" He throws up his hands. "Who else would want to kill me?"

"The longer you're in this business, the longer that list gets." Shatilov ankles another chair in front of Mashkov and sits, bracing his elbows on his knees. "It doesn't matter. You got the money just in time. We can pay for supplies and petrol. We're in the hunt...because of *you*."

Mashkov knows all this, but can't feel it. Two near-death experiences in three days are too much. "Hooray for me. Remind me why you're not running this brigade?"

Shatilov snorts. "I'm just a broken-down old soldier. All I know how to do is fight. You know how to do the rest of it." He takes one last puff, then crushes the butt under his boot heel. "So do it. Forget Rogozhkin, forget the women. Lead us. We need that."

He's talking sense. Mashkov sighs and nods. *But if I ever get another shot at that bastard Rogozhkin, I'm throwing everything we've got at him.*

CHAPTER 50

Carson leans back against the rusted housing for a conveyor belt and stares out the empty window into the darkness. The almost-half-moon hovers over the horizon, about to set; the low angle stretches long, black shadows toward her from the four-story apartment blocks across the street. A stiff breeze rattles the weeds and blows bits of trash through the ruined grain dryer's open bays, sounding like people sneaking in to finish her off. All good reasons to not be able to stay asleep.

She checks her watch: 2:36 in the morning. Twenty minutes until they have to go.

Galina's sleeping in the car like a well-fed cat: curled up in the back seat, draped in a wash-weary blanket, her fists under her chin. Rogozhkin is…well, who cares where he is.

They'd bailed out of the hotel as soon as all three of them got back from the stadium. Between the cops and the militia, it was too dangerous to stay. When Rogozhkin poked his head into their room to see if she and Galina were ready, Carson sucker-punched him. She should've thanked him for saving her life and Galina's, but she was furious he'd almost screwed up her plan.

Now she's as far up in the weathered concrete building as she can get, feeling both mad and guilty, watching the northern part of the town sleep.

Bootsteps clunk on the scabby steel diamond-plate walkway. Carson raises the AK cradled in her lap and flips the safety, just in case it's not who she thinks it is. Or in case it is.

"It's me." Rogozhkin's voice, just loud enough to carry the three meters or so between them. He closes the distance, then grunts as he sits next to her. "Is it safe to sit here?"

"No." She safes the rifle and settles it across her thighs. "Maybe."

They sit silently for a while. Rogozhkin finally says, "I should've told you my plan."

"You think?" She keeps staring out the window, but doesn't see anything. "I promised him 'no tricks.' I promised he'd be safe. I told you that in the park."

"I didn't realize you took it so seriously."

"I keep my promises. Otherwise, what's the point of making them?" She chucks a broken lump of concrete out the window. "Now Galina's mad at me for not letting her kill Mashkov, *and* not letting you do it."

Another long pause. "I'm sorry."

Carson watches him watch her with a sad little frown on his lips. She grabs the front of his shirt, kisses him hard, then pushes him away. "Thanks for saving my ass."

"You're welcome." His eyes are wide and the frown's turned into a semi-smile. "Where did you get your training?"

She edits the story down to the least she can get away with. "A guy named Yurik in Vienna. Ex-FSB Alpha Group. You know that saying, 'what doesn't kill you makes you stronger'? It was like that." Rodievsky paid for the six grueling weeks she spent with Yurik Vasiliev so she'd stop acting like a cop and start doing things the *Bratva* way. She still goes back for refreshers.

Rogozhkin nods. "You could do worse." He squeezes her arm, then takes his hand away. "I woke Galina. She'll be ready in a few minutes."

"She didn't shoot you."

"I was careful. Did you eat?"

"Some." When they arrived at the grain dryer, Galina insisted on buying food at the ATB supermarket about half a klick away. Carson wanted to go with her, but Galina told her to keep an eye on "the *Kacáps*." Bread, sausage, and canned vegetables served cold didn't make for much of a meal, but they kept Carson's stomach from rebelling. "Are we still heading north?"

"Yes. It's always best to try the easiest option first." Rogozhkin hauls himself to his feet and shakes out his legs. "You should come down—"

Approaching engine noises bounce off the grimy, graffittied cast-concrete walls. Carson and Rogozhkin swap puzzled glances that become more alarmed as the noise gets louder. They scramble along the catwalk to the building's east side.

A dozen or more pairs of wide-set headlights swarm the open dirt field east of the grain dryer. The ones in front pull up due north of where Carson and Rogozhkin stand; the ones following glare off clouds of dust. There's just enough residual moonlight to highlight boxy cabs on eight-wheeled chassis, packing what look like bundles of sewer pipes.

Rogozhkin murmurs, "*Uragans.*"

"What?"

"BM-27s. Multiple rocket launchers."

"Yours or the DNR's?"

"Ours. We didn't give these to the DNR. We don't trust them that much."

The shadows of men leap out of the cabs. Glowing red and white cones—probably attached to flashlights—swing front to back as the men run ahead of the transporters, then stop to signal where each launcher should go. Within a couple of minutes, the entire five-hundred-meter-long field is covered with the rumble of engines and the whine of electric motors swinging the sewer pipes—launch tubes—into position.

Carson checks her watch. Five to three. "When's the battle supposed to start?"

"First light. 0430. There's preparatory artillery fires beforehand, but I thought that's supposed to start at T-minus-thirty."

"Why here?" Carson pokes her head out the window. Dull yellow streetlights surround the field. "There's houses over there, apartments back there. The New Market's down there." About a hundred meters south. "Won't the Ukrainian Army shoot back?"

Rogozhkin sighs and pushes his fingers through his hair. "Yes. That's exactly why this battery is here."

Her brain follows that idea down some very dark holes. "They *want* the army to shell houses?"

"Yes." He sighs. "These launchers will fire on the UA artillery's last-known locations. Our UAVs jam Kyiv's counter-battery radar. The UA will see incoming fires but won't be able to calculate accurate origins. Their spotters on the slag heaps will see the rockets coming from here and send coordinates to their fire-control centers. The UA artillery will respond and drop ordnance all over here. They'll hit houses, the market. Kill civilians." He points out the window using his whole hand. "These launchers will be long gone by then. I don't doubt that RT has camera crews standing by in the park to run up here and shoot video of Kyiv's latest atrocity."

Carson's no stranger to dirty dealing, but the sheer cynicism of this move takes the wind out of her. "Is this a regular thing?"

"Yes, just not at this scale." Rogozhkin lets out a bitter chuckle. "The final irony? When the UA responds, our UAVs will get fresh coordinates for their artillery. Then *our* artillery, about ten kilometers east of here, will have up-to-the-minute targeting intel. If they *don't* respond, we'll know they won't hit this area and we get a safe firing position that's almost on top of the contact line. It's lose-lose for them."

"You guys are real bastards. You know that, right?"

Rogozhkin nods. "I've known that for a long time."

A blinding-yellow billow of flame shoots out of the back of the nearest launcher. White thunderbolts of light streak toward the west with the shriek of the sky being torn open. Both Carson and Rogozhkin clap their palms to their ears.

Then another. And another.

Rogozhkin grabs Carson's arm and pushes her away from the window. "We have to go!" he yells in her ear. "The counterfire will be here in a few minutes!"

They storm down the steel staircase to the ground floor and dash to the open bays where they parked the Octavia the previous evening. They find the car but not Galina.

Carson circles the slab, peering into the dark shadows. She finds Galina sheltering behind a concrete pier on the east side, holding up her phone. "What are you doing?" Carson yells.

"Taking video. You know what they are doing, yes?"

"Yeah, Rogozhkin filled me in. Come on! This place's gonna get stomped to shit!"

Galina glares at Carson. "I have to get them driving away!"

Carson's lost track of how many launches have happened in the past couple of minutes. She's partly deaf and getting scared, waiting for shells to start pummeling the area—and this building. "We need to be in *front* of that! We'll be stuck here if we're not!"

The nearest launcher roars west to the road next to the field. Galina's phone follows its progress. Carson grabs her arm, drags her to the car, and stuffs her into the back seat while Galina sputters and flails at her.

Rogozhkin stomps the gas pedal, sending them rocketing out the west side of the grain dryer toward the road. The red taillights of at least four *Uragan* launchers speed northbound.

The Octavia swerves onto the road heading southbound and tears past the boxy apartment blocks to their right. Lights flick on in their windows. *Get down, people,* Carson tries to tell them telepathically. *Take cover. This is gonna be bad.*

Rogozhkin skids the car right at the first intersection. The shrill whistle of the first incoming shell leaks through Carson's half-open window.

A flash of light behind them.

Whump. A gout of flame and smoke shoots upward from behind the market grounds.

The car squeals right onto the highway, cutting off Carson's view. Galina sits rooted on the back seat, her eyes blown, clutching the headrest on Carson's seat. Carson closes the window so they don't have to listen to the shelling. The supermarket and bank flash past on the driver's side.

A hundred meters ahead of them, a gas station explodes.

CHAPTER 51

Galina screams.

It's Ilovaisk all over again. The whistles, the blasts, the ground shaking with each impact. Random death all around her.

The windscreen fills with fire.

The flashback hits her all at once: a burning lorry, flaming men leaping from the back, Misha's arms flailing.

Something metal clangs off the roof as the car swerves right, through a bus turnout, to avoid the inferno across the street.

Galina screams again.

"Galya! Stop!" Carson climbs halfway over the front seatbacks to grab Galina's hands before they open the car door. "Stop! It's okay! Fucking *stop!*"

Galina shrieks, "Let me out! I have to get out!"

Rogozhkin swats Carson's right leg. "Stop kicking me! Get her under control and sit your ass in the seat!"

Carson knees his shoulder. "Get off me! She's been through this before. Just—"

The car swerves. Tires rumble on gravel, then lurch over the blacktop's edge.

Carson lets go of one of Galina's hands to wrap her left arm around the headrest and keep from getting thrown into Rogozhkin's lap. Galina claws at the door lever. Pops it. The door gaps, showing the asphalt blurring by beneath them. The steady *whump, whump, whump* of shelling behind them and the thunder of heavy guns in the distance fill the car.

"...out! Let me *out!* Let me—"

Carson tumbles over the front seats, slamming a boot into the headliner on her way. She lands like a truckload of potatoes on Galina's back and uses her body weight to pin Galina in place. The car swerves to the left, slamming the door closed.

Galina sobs and scratches at the door, but not with any strength. Her cries wail like a siren that rises and falls in a semi-regular rhythm. Her body bucks against Carson's like she's being electrocuted.

Carson wrestles with Galina until they're both sitting and Galina's bawling into Carson's stomach, her arms tight around Carson's waist. Carson strokes her back and murmurs, "It's okay you're safe I'm with you we're safe it's okay…"

Rogozhkin watches them in the rear-view. "What happened to her?"

"Ilovaisk. She was in the retreat. Her unit got chewed up. A sniper shot her."

He blows out a long breath. "That will do it."

Minutes pass before Galina settles into hiccups and little grinding noises in her throat. She finally sits up enough to wrap her arms around Carson's neck and bury her face in Carson's shoulder. She whispers, "Is it over?"

Carson hugs her hard. "We're out of it."

For the first time since they fled the grain dryer, she can pay attention to the outside. The highway has turned into a two-lane country road over rolling terrain. Behind them, flashes of what looks like—but isn't—heat lighting bounce off the thickening clouds. She says to Rogozhkin, "We can't go back into that."

"We may have to if the checkpoint's closed."

"How far?"

"Two kilometers, more or less."

So close. Carson rocks Galina, cooing, "It's okay, girl. We'll be fine. I'll keep you safe."

Galina shudders, then pulls away. Her face is bright purple in the dashboard's blue glow and shiny with tears and snot. "I'm sorry."

Carson could barely hear her. "Rogozhkin, get me a rag out of the glove box." She takes it from him and gives it to Galina, who starts to mop up. "Don't be sorry. I'm sorry you had to go through that again."

"You told me to go. I should have listened."

"You were doing what you thought was right."

Rogozhkin asks, "What was she doing?"

"Taking video of those rocket launchers. Is that a problem?"

He shrugs. "They're not mine." His voice turns into a mutter. "Anymore." He glances at the women. "Galina, I know you don't want anything from me, but hear me out. I wasn't at Ilovaisk, but men I know were. It broke some of them. The intensity, the brutality. If you've made it until now without something triggering you, you're doing very well."

Galina stares at him for an uncomfortably long time. Then she nods once and looks away to continue drying her face. She glances at Carson. "You called me Galya." Her nickname.

"I figure we know each other well enough by now." Carson strokes Galina's hair. "Ready for the checkpoint?"

Galina closes her eyes, takes a shaky deep breath, then nods.

The black-and-white city limits sign says "Yasne," which consists of a few streets of housing to the west and a sprawling industrial complex to the east. The checkpoint's a hundred meters past the highway's intersection with the road that ties the two halves together. Rogozhkin panic-brakes the car a few meters short, shaking his head. "We're not getting through here."

Carson peeks past his shoulder. Three Jersey barriers stretch across the road and its shoulders, completely blocking the way forward. A BMP's parked alongside the barriers with its turret facing north. A top hatch swings open and a soldier in a tanker's helmet pokes out his head, squinting into the Octavia's headlights.

Rogozhkin shifts into reverse and floors it.

They reach the crossroads less than a minute later. Carson checks out the scene. To the right: dual railroad tracks and a dark street lined with darker trees and the hint of houses. To the left: a lit guard shack at the industrial complex's main gate. "Is there a way past the checkpoint in that plant?"

"If there was, we'd be using it right now." Rogozhkin nods to the right. "If we go down there, I know a road that will take us to within five hundred meters of the contact line."

"What's on the other side of the line?"

"Another half-kilometer walk through their side of the gray zone. Most of it is mined, though mostly with antitank mines. Then Kyiv's lines."

"What'll they do?"

"Take us prisoner."

"Mmm. Fun."

Rogozhkin glances at Carson, giving her a sour look. "You'll be fine. I won't enjoy it as much. I'm not certain what they'll do with her." He gestures toward Galina, who's watching the conversation bounce back and forth while clutching the rag to her mouth.

Carson asks, "Can we drive it?"

"No. Well, yes, if we have a tracked vehicle. Not in this."

"You should go." Galina's voice is rough, but stronger than it's been since the grain dryer. "Both of you. Get across while you can. I'll..."

She's right. It's quiet here. Maybe we can make it across the Ukrainian lines without getting caught. Carson's *so* ready to be done with all this, to get out of this shithole, to leave all the violence and death behind. She can taste that döner kebab in Dnipro. She'd kill for another pair of underwear.

But she'd promised to help Galina free Bohdan.

She'd promised to get Rogozhkin to the West so he can retire.

Carson says to Rogozhkin, "You said there's another way through. What is it?"

He stares out the windshield for a while, his right hand squeezing and releasing the steering wheel. "Do you remember that spoil heap I pointed out? The one with Kyiv's troops on it? There's a road between it and the quarry. It's a gravel road, huge ruts from the tipper lorries that haul the dolomite to the plant, but a road. It runs into a north-south road—more gravel—that leads to a dirt trail that eventually drops us into Novotroitske."

Galina mumbles, "Hmpf." Then she asks, "What about the *kolorady?*"

He twists to look at them. "They may have a screening force along the approach to the spoil heap. The shelling may force them to keep their heads down. Once we get between the spoil and the quarry, we're in Kyiv-held territory, only they don't usually have a presence in it. They rely on the observers to call in indirect fire on any DNR forces that wander into it."

"And the Ukrainian Army?" Carson asks.

"The last intel I saw said their line parallels the H20 between the motorway and that north-south gravel road I mentioned. The line's more a concept than a physical reality through town, though. If we can get into Novotroitske, we should be able to reach the

H20 without trouble."

"That sounds too easy."

"The way I described it, it is. The roads are miserable. There's no light. The fighting will be three to five kilometers southeast of there. That ought to distract any forces in the area, but that's a *may*, not a *will*. The road's periodically mined, sometimes even on purpose. But I've used the route, it works, and Galina here can probably get her car through it."

All three of them fall silent for a long time, thinking of all the ways each option can go bad. The number of *mays* and *probablys* and *mights* scares the shit out of Carson. She likes having a plan that isn't based on blind luck or divine intervention.

Maybe that's the best this place has to offer.

Galina speaks first. "You should cross here. It's easier, it's safer. Leave me here, get to the West. I'll manage."

Carson swivels toward her. "How will you get to Shakhtarsk if we leave you here? You have to get Bohdan out of that camp. You *have* to. He's relying on you."

Galina bows her head and snuffles. "You can't get hurt. You can't risk that...that *mess* the *Kacáps* just said. I won't have you die for me."

"I'm not dying today. Neither are you." Carson focuses on Rogozhkin. "This other way. Can you get us through it?"

He pushes his fingers back through his hair. "I did it once. But Galina's right—it's a lot easier here."

Carson glances between them. "You both agree on something."

Galina snarls at her. Rogozhkin says, "It won't last."

"This place is easier only if we leave Galina behind and you risk having the Ukrainian Army grab you. What happens when they find out who you are?" Carson shakes Galina's shoulder. "And you're gonna get halfway across the Donbass on your own? Really?"

She lets them think, mostly so *she* can think...and decide.

"Fuck it. We all go or we all stay. Rogozhkin, get us to this back door of yours."

"Did they plan this blackout," Carson asks, "or did it just happen?"

Except for the still-burning gas station, Dokuchajevsk is dark by the time they return. The northern streets are deserted; no streetlights or shop signs or even LEDs on vending machines break the shadows. The only light comes from the Octavia's headlights and the strobing reflections on the low-hanging clouds.

"A shell or rocket probably broke something." Galina squeezes Carson's hand. "If you don't like the dark, you shouldn't live here."

Rogozhkin cuts through neighborhoods of homes to avoid any civilian or military police on the main roads. He'd bypassed the area by the New Market to keep from distressing Galina. There are no living creatures in sight other than a few prowling dogs.

What's going through Rogozhkin's mind? He's been quiet and watchful since they left Yasne behind. *Second thoughts? Worrying the back door's been slammed shut and locked?* Carson could ask, but he probably wouldn't say much with Galina listening.

She rolls down her window partway. It's in the low teens (Celsius) and damp outside; the cool air sweeps the stale funk out of the car. The rumbling of nearby artillery is clear enough to make out individual guns. A more distant thunder to the east—Russian artillery?—is like an echo. The only other sound is the hum of the tires on asphalt.

Rogozhkin turns right, then pulls over to the white-painted curb. He twists to look at Carson. "I need you up here with your weapon." He checks his phone, then shows the screen to Galina. "If you want your video to do any good, send it to this email."

She peers at the screen without leaning forward. "OSCE?"

"They're the observers. You'd better send it now before we lose mobile service."

Galina frowns. "Why are you helping me?"

Rogozhkin pockets his phone and sighs. "What they did wasn't honorable. I've played tricks on my enemies, but I tried to never deliberately target civilians unless they targeted me. What you saw in that field? They did that to kill innocent civilians for propaganda. Send the video so someone will know the truth."

They sit staring at each other for some moments. Then Galina pounds her phone's virtual keyboard.

Carson slides into the front passenger's seat and checks her pistol and AK. "How far?"

"Not far. This takes us to the mine entrance."

They quickly pass out of the city into a small forest split by the road. Part of a three-story building with a pitched roof anchors the road's end. Behind it, the dark bulk of two spoil mounds masks the gun flashes of the Ukrainian Army artillery on the other side.

Rogozhkin slows a hundred meters from the road's end. A Jersey barrier blocks the right-hand lane just before the road tees into a three-way intersection by the building. As the car creeps closer, a man starts swinging a flashlight with an illuminated red cone on the end. By the time the Octavia is within thirty meters of the barrier, the headlights pick out two men, both in camouflage.

Carson grumbles, "Here we go again."

The car coasts to the soldier with the flashlight. Rogozhkin rolls down his window.

Another soldier stands at the road's edge, around five meters behind the barrier. His buddy with the flashlight skirts the car's nose and plods to the open window. "Road's clo—"

Rogozhkin shoots him with a black suppressed pistol Carson hasn't seen until now. The bullet goes under the guard's chin and out the top of his helmet. The soldier behind the barrier crumples with his rifle still pointing at the ground. Rogozhkin motions to Carson. "Help me get them off the road."

The bodies go into a nearby stand of trees; dust and gravel cover the bloodstains on the ground. Rogozhkin turns the Octavia left onto a gravel track. The headlights are off. "You saw who they belonged to, yes?"

Carson nods. "Makiivka Brigade." She checks on Galina, who's sitting straight with her shotgun across her thighs. A tight smile crinkles the corners of her eyes.

The forest closes in on the narrow road until it's little more than a slot lined with leaves. The lack of light means Rogozhkin has to roll forward at walking pace, constantly correcting.

Galina says, "Give me my flashlight."

She gets out, walks five meters ahead of the Octavia, then turns the light onto the road behind her. The moving pool of bright white is a beacon for the car to follow without blinding the people left in it. Rogozhkin says, "She's finally being useful."

"Leave her alone. She's had a rough time."

Galina stops shy of a set of well-used rails crossing the road. She flicks off the flashlight, then steps across the rails and disappears into the trees.

Rogozhkin: "Should I be worried?"

Carson: "No." *I hope.*

A few minutes later, Galina jogs back to rap on Carson's window. "You should see this."

Carson and Rogozhkin follow Galina over the tracks and around a corner to the edge of the trees. To their one o'clock, a string of BTRs lines the road past an electrical substation and over a hump at the foot of the southernmost pile. Cargo trucks are half-hidden in the trees that rim a large open area to their ten o'clock. The bright dots of flashlights drift between vehicles.

They stand, staring, for a couple of minutes. "Let me guess," Carson says. "That's our road."

Rogozhkin sighs. "Yes. Running through the middle of a motor rifle battalion."

Mashkov and Shatilov follow the beginnings of the offensive through their radios while the sergeant plots unit movements on the map.

Shatilov stares through his haze of cigarette smoke at the latest updates. "The 31st isn't moving very fast," he says to no one in particular. The 31st is a battalion tactical group, the pieced-together units the Russian Army uses to rotate manpower through the Donbass theater.

Mashkov measures with spread fingers the distance from the start line. "Half a kilometer since 0345." It's now 0420. "The 54th isn't doing much better." He smiles at Shatilov. "I thought they're supposed to be able to fight at night."

Shatilov chuckles. "They say they milk chickens."

The sergeant holds up his free hand. "Colonel Mashkov, I'm getting a report from the Lev Brigade's command net. A Russian armored company is moving north from the start line."

North? Mashkov shakes his head. "That can't be right. Where are they?"

"Still south of the Sukha Volnovakha, sir." The now-dry river that slices off the southernmost part of Dokuchajevsk from the rest.

"Keep an eye on that." Mashkov glances at Shatilov, who shrugs.

Damned Russians. It's typical—Rogozhkin kept telling Mashkov the brigade isn't ready to fight, but now two of their units are bogged down and a third is wandering lost. *First Corps may have to put us in early. Wouldn't that get the Russians' goat.*

"Sir?" The sergeant again. "First Battalion CP's reporting. They sent men to relieve the guards at the mine complex entrance." He gives Mashkov a confused look. "The guards are dead, sir."

Carson, Galina, and Rogozhkin hunker down behind trees near where the gravel road crosses the rail line. The Hunter that clattered past a few minutes ago had come out of almost nowhere; Galina had just enough time to move the car into the trees before the SUV passed through going north.

Carson checks her watch: 4:09. She isn't a tactical genius, but even she's smart enough to know they don't want to drive through all that hardware out there in daylight. They don't want to drive through it at all, but stopping isn't an option.

Galina says, "I have an idea."

Carson says, "We need ideas."

"They have their lorries in the trees. Maybe the soldiers on the hill didn't see them. What if we could get them to notice? They could tell the artillery to blow them up."

"And destroy Mashkov's supplies?" Carson's heard worse ideas. She's come up with worse. "How would you do it?"

"Burn some of the lorries." Galina's smile tells Carson she'd like to do this even if it was completely pointless, just to give Mashkov more shit to deal with.

It's not pointless now. "Getting shelled is a good distraction. Could be good cover."

Rogozhkin says, "Until a round falls short and takes us out." He leans his elbows on his knees. "It could work, though. Burn the lorries at both ends and the middle so the spotters know where the arc is and how deep it is."

Carson groans onto her feet and stretches. "Whatever we do, we do it now. We're running out of night."

"True." Rogozhkin stands and rearranges the Dragunov across his back. "I have a lighter in my bag. Do either of you?"

Galina says, "I do."

"Right. We do the arson while Tarasenko drives to that electrical station to pick us up."

Carson pulls her phone to examine the satellite image. The answer doesn't fill her with confidence. She grabs Rogozhkin's arm as he heads toward the car. "You know it's over half a klick to the other end of the treeline, right?"

He frowns. "Well, I need the workout."

"Can you even run that far? With your leg? If something pops halfway there, we can't get you out."

Rogozhkin stops to let Galina get out of earshot, then closes on Carson. He murmurs, "What do you propose?"

She takes one more look at the arc of trees. "I'm beat to shit, but my legs still work. Give me your lighter. I'll burn shit, you drive."

His frown becomes a scowl. "What if you get dizzy again?"

"I'll deal."

"If they catch you, they'll kill you this time. They'll do it slowly, too."

Like I don't know that already. "They won't buy you drinks, either."

The steady mechanical whine of small engines working hard grows quickly in the background. Carson and Rogozhkin plunge into the trees. An instant later, two GAZ jeeps slide around a turn and bounce over the railroad tracks, heading for the front gate. Once their noise fades, Carson says, "Bet they know we're here now."

CHAPTER 53

They're soon all ready. Carson and Galina have AKs, cigarette lighters, and two pairs of Galina's oldest socks each. Rogozhkin has his black PB suppressed pistol he used on the guards, the sniper rifle, and a Russian Vityaz tactical knife. Carson recognizes the Vityaz from the knife work Yurik dragged her through (which she loathed). They stand in an arc around the Octavia's open driver's door, glancing at each other, not knowing what to say.

"Get going," Rogozhkin almost barks. "Someone will get the bright idea to search the trees."

Carson tips her chin at Rogozhkin's pistol. "Sure that antique won't blow up in your hand?"

"Don't set yourself on fire. And don't lose my lighter—it was my father's."

Galina and Rogozhkin stare at each other for several beats. She says, "Don't leave us out there," then turns and melts into the trees.

Rogozhkin chuckles. "Progress. She's talking to me."

"Don't get a big head about it." Carson follows Galina into the dark.

They creep through the forest's edge carefully, trying not to snap branches or flush noisy birds on their way to the nearest trucks, perhaps thirty meters from the car. Galina whispers, "Tarasenko. What's your given name?"

Names again. "Why?"

"You call me 'Galya,' but I don't know what to call you. You said yourself, we have known each other long enough."

Carson usually doesn't tell anyone her real first name. It's too easy to look up the stories about her being the bent cop, the mole, the traitor, the gangster's pawn. TPS did a real job on her. But she's told Galina most of the stories by now. She considers *Lisa*, her main cover name, but she doesn't want to lie anymore, not to Galya. So she whispers her actual name.

Galina says, "That's pretty."

"Like I need a pretty name."

"It can't hurt." Galina glances at her as her mouth holds in a smile. "Larochka?"

A diminutive for her name. "Let's go with Lara." Another, less little-girl nickname.

They discover that what looks like a forest is actually a scrim of trees—no more than ten or twenty meters deep—along the rail line. Darkness makes it appear endless. That's useful; they can walk along the track ballast and not risk running into some soldier or truck driver taking a piss against a tree in the dark. The downside is that they can't see the trucks or anyone near them.

After what seems like enough walking, Carson turns into the trees again, then prowls toward the western edge with her rifle ready. She shuffles her feet slowly so she doesn't break any deadfall or rustle leaves. No lights, no voices, just the man-made thunder ahead of her and the sinister noises wind makes in the forest.

She steps between two trucks about five meters apart, giant square shadows against the murk of the forest and sky. A few moments later, a light brushing sound and a tap on her shoulder tell her Galina's arrived. Carson dips her head next to Galina's and murmurs in her ear. "Check for drivers, then light it up."

The truck to her left is full of cartons but empty of people. She unscrews the fuel filler cap and stuffs one of Galina's socks into the hole, then stands with Rogozhkin's heavy textured silver lighter clutched in her hand. *Here's where it gets real.* They've been under the radar until now; once she torches the sock, that's over.

She coaxes a flame out of the lighter—it takes three tries—and touches it to the sock's cuff.

Galina meets her near the train track. They jog south, trying to stay on weeds and dirt so they don't draw too much attention to themselves.

The sound of a very large door slamming at the end of a very long hallway breaks the still. Carson risks a glance behind her. A fireball rolls into the dark sky, lighting the tops of trees all around it. Seconds later, a second *crump* launches another fireball.

It's on.

Carson picks up speed, checking her GPS every few seconds to see if they've reached the halfway point in the arc of forest. The blip never seems to move. Men yell in the dark to her right; an engine coughs to life. *Don't leave yet. We're not done with you.*

A gunshot behind them. She pivots, runs backward a few steps. *Shooting at us? Shooting at shadows?* Galina's also checking behind them, though she has enough sense to watch where she's going. While it's easier to move out here, it's also awfully exposed. Carson's battered legs can just barely run faster than Galina's.

The GPS blip reaches the arc's midpoint. They swerve at the same time and plunge into the trees, glad for the cover. The first set of trucks Carson reaches brackets two militiamen nervously swinging their rifles toward every sound, real or imagined. She finds Galina—behind the next tree over—then waves her south.

Four trucks later, they stop at an unattended pair. Carson trots to the one farther south and hops onto the rear bumper to check the cargo bed for any sleepers. It's stuffed with wooden crates. She risks snapping on the lighter. Stenciling on the crates: 30mm cannon shells.

Oh, hell *yes. This one gets to burn.*

She jumps down and starts for the gas tank, but a harsh *psst* makes her turn and level her rifle. Galina's on the other truck's bumper, waving her over. Carson joins her and looks at the pool of flickering yellow cast by Galina's lighter.

More wooden crates, these about a meter and a half long. The first thing that catches Carson's eye is stenciling that reads "РПГ-26." "Rocket-propelled grenades?"

"Yes." Galina's eyes glitter in the flame. "We could use these."

"For what?"

"For that armor." She points toward the road. "I saw these at Ilovaisk. They cut right through the BTRs and BMPs. We need that to get to the other side."

Carson looks at her the way she would any other crazy person. "How do we haul these things around? The crates look heavy. We still have to blow up two more trucks."

"No crates." Galina hands Carson the lighter, then swings over the tailgate. She uses a small tactical knife to pry the top off the nearest crate; it sounds like she's torturing a peacock. Then she hoists two olive-drab tubes a bit less than a meter long by their skinny green shoulder straps. "Here, take these."

"We gotta get out of here! Those troopers'll hear us. Come—"

More squealing. Galina slings the next two launchers over her shoulder. "Okay, we burn the rest."

At least the RPGs weigh only about three kilos each. Carson slings hers over her neck and left shoulder, then jumps to the ground and hustles to the truck full of ammo. She bolts for the railroad tracks the moment she lights the sock in the gas tank—they don't want to be anywhere near here when this load goes off. The RPG tubes rattle against each other every time she even thinks about moving. *So much for stealth.*

It's awkward and loud to run, but Carson and Galina run. Carson keeps her eyes on her watch. Sixty seconds. Ninety seconds. *Bangs* like extra-large M80s crackle through the woods. A hundred twenty—

A volcano erupts behind them.

The ground jolts under them. Carson stumbles but doesn't fall. A fiery mushroom cloud boils thirty, forty, fifty meters into the night, lighting everything around them like a slow-motion flashbulb. Shells cook off in groups, sounding like a huge firefight all in one small area.

Then *bam. Bam. BAM. BAMBAMBAM.* Popcorn made of explosives. Is that what happens when a truckload of RPGs burns?

Carson doesn't want to find out. She grabs Galina's arm—she's been cackling and whooping like crazy—and drags her south as fast as they both can move. The noise doesn't fade; if anything, it gets louder. An entire battle's going on back there, loud enough to even drown out the artillery fire to the west.

They run out of forest.

Men and vehicles race across the open field, dragging their shadows behind them as they near the burning trucks and woods. Several Zils have pulled into the field; BMPs roar into position to guard the area. The electrical substation lies to Carson's nine o'clock. Firelight glints off its wires and transformers. As they watch, the truck with the RPGs cooks off in a blinding gout of yellow flame and the roar of a meteor strike. The concussion slaps them backward.

Glowing fuzz speckles Carson's vision. *No, not now. I can't do this now...*

"Come on!" she yells. No need to sneak around anymore. "That way! Let's get the last two!"

They charge across twenty meters of open ground toward the

last two trucks in line, which are mostly exposed by the thin trickle of trees.

The fuzz gets thicker. Carson's head fills with hot gas and butterflies. She waits for Galina to tear off toward the next-to-last Zil, then braces her palms on her knees and tries to shake the dizzy away. It won't leave, but it stops growing for a few moments.

She heads for the truck at the end. Its engine's running. She checks the cab and finds a militiaman behind the wheel, about to pull out. She automatically hauls herself onto the running board and clubs the man with her rifle butt. He goes face-first into the steering wheel, then sideways into his shoulder harness.

Carson grips the window frame and the driver's seatback to keep from ending up on her ass. Tries to breathe deep and slow. Nothing works. She fumbles open the driver's seatbelt latch, lets him tumble onto the ground. Ends up on her knees, gasping, her gut in a blender.

"What's wrong?" Galina's voice in her ear.

An arm wraps around Carson's shoulders. *Gotta get out. Gotta hide.* She tries to tell Galina but doesn't know how to say *dizzy* in Ukrainian, so she uses the godawful long Russian word.

Galina *tsks*, then leaves.

The crackling fires and yelling men and growling armor overwhelm Carson's few working senses. She finds herself bent double, her forehead pressed into the cool dirt, desperately trying to puke and not able to.

Galina returns after several hour-long seconds. She tries to drag Carson upright but can't. "Get up!" she shrieks. "We have to go! The lorries will explode any time!"

Yeah. Trucks. Explosions. Carson staggers onto her feet, then crashes to her knees. Tries again. Galina gets in front of her and takes Carson's whole weight on her left shoulder, wobbling but not falling. Left foot forward. Right. Tiny clear areas in her vision: the substation's a little closer. She manages a few more steps.

Wham. Yellow-white glare pastes their shadows to the ground ahead of them. The slap of a concussion knocks them both flat.

When Carson looks up, what little she can see is filled by a BMP clanking straight for her.

CHAPTER 54

Rogozhkin covers in the dark behind a tree a couple of meters from the Octavia. Which will come first: incoming fires behind him, or militia guards in front of him? Either way, things will get hot soon.

He follows the women's progress by the noise they cause: two explosions of the sort he expects from large petrol tanks igniting, then two cataclysms that vibrate the ground under his feet. Now men and vehicles fill the air behind him with their racket. It's good that the women stirred things up; it's bad that he can't hear the approach of the guards anymore.

Voices in front of him. Sounds, not words. *Three? No, four men.* Unless they're blind, they'll certainly see the Octavia when they get close enough.

There should be two more blasts. Where are they? What happened to the women?

The first intelligible words from the approaching guards: "Look over there."

Rogozhkin switches from long, deep breaths to shallow, silent ones. He'll have one chance to catch these *muzhlany* unaware. The last thing he wants is a firefight; he misses his ballistic vest like a lost lover.

He sees them before he can hear them, thanks to the racket beyond the trees. At least they can't hear any better. Two targets appear on each side of the car, rifles ready, uselessly sweeping the darkness in front of them. He'll deal with the two on the passenger's side first.

One stage-whispers, "Isn't this the car they told us about?"

"Yeah. The spies and the deserter."

Spies? Deserter? Technically he's only absent without leave now; he won't be a deserter until he crosses the contact line. Calling the women "spies" is a bit of a reach.

A target shines an unfiltered penlight into the driver's window.

Bad choice: it'll wreck his night vision. Rogozhkin shifts focus to the nearer two, whose heads swivel here and there as if they're looking for werewolves.

Here's your werewolf.

He aims the suppressed PB pistol past the target at the right-front tire, then fires one shot. *Phut.* The target near the right-rear door crumples, but his rifle clunks against the car on his way down. The other three instantly snap alert. *Damn.*

Crump. Crump. The last two lorries explode at the field's far end.

"What was that?" a target yelps.

The target by the right-front tire spins almost a full circle. "Yuri? Where are you?"

Phut. He's down.

The target by the car's nose watches his buddy collapse. He sprays the trees in front of him with his AK. The rattle of his rifle covers the *phut* of Rogozhkin's pistol and even the *clang* of the man's helmet hitting the car's bonnet as he falls.

The fourth target—previously near the driver's door—is now under cover. Rogozhkin curses silently as he scrambles in a crouch toward the Octavia's rear end. The last target's fixated on the trees ahead of the car; that's where the shots will have seemed to have come from. Rogozhkin's got two things in his favor: the outside noise has rendered them both essentially deaf; and, he's been fighting in the dark for years, while the brigade's occasional night maneuvers were more slapstick than skill.

The target fires bursts into the trees. First ahead of him, then across the bonnet.

Typical panic reaction. Rogozhkin covers behind some shrubs at the car's rear. *Train them not to, but they still do it.* Bullets spray him with bark and chunks of sapwood. While the target shreds the foliage off the driver's side of the car, Rogozhkin shifts to a position behind a tree that gives him a full view of the prone target. Aims. He'll wait until the kid gets into a crouch to fire across the bonnet again, which he's sure to do. They always go in a circle.

The target twists and riddles Rogozhkin's tree.

Rogozhkin's flat on his back, clutching his right hip, gritting his teeth so he doesn't make a sound. He lets his brain cycle through a long string of curses, just to get the trash out of the way so he can think. The mine in Kosovo didn't hurt as much initially—he was immediately unconscious after that—but this is up there with the round he took through his right lung in Afghanistan.

Inventory. He can breathe. He can move his right leg, though it doesn't feel good to do it. He can sit up. There's no arterial flow, so he won't bleed out quickly. *You won't die yet. Finish what you started.*

He leans against the shredded tree trunk, aims at the last target. *Phut.* The man bounces off the car's left-front wing, then collapses.

Rogozhkin takes a moment to catch his breath and blink away the tears from the pain. *Good thing I know where my wound kit is.*

High above him, a high-pitched whistle plummets from the sky.

The BMP's turret-mounted machinegun opens up. Its jackhammer rattle cuts through the growing chaos of noise.

Bullets whiz over Carson like demented, supersonic mosquitos. Her vision's slowly clearing, but her head is still mostly a vacuum. Someone's yanking her arm.

It's Galina. "Over there! Over there!" Her eyes are wild. She stabs a hand toward a lone tree, three or four meters away. Then she crawls away the way most people do—elbows and knees, torso up in the air.

Carson lunges at her and knocks her over. "Not like that! Your ass is a huge target! Like this." She automatically starts a low crawl the way Yurik taught her: flat on her belly, arms stretched forward, swing her right knee even with her hip, push with the leg and pull with her elbows, repeat with her left knee. Bullets splash dirt and rock fragments on her. It's slow and tiring and dirty, but she never gives the gunner more than a ten-inch-high target.

As soon as they reach the tree, it starts to dance like a clubber on meth. Leaves, branches, and wood fragments spatter them. Galina wrestles an RPG tube off her back while trying not to leave any air between her and the ground. She fiddles with sights and pins and *shoot the goddamn thing already!*

Whoosh. The BMP shudders. Black smoke rockets out firing ports and an open hatch on top. The AFV coasts to a stop.

Galina tosses the tube aside, then falls back next to Carson. She's breathing like she finished an ultra-marathon.

Carson says, "Nice shot."

"It was so close. I couldn't miss." She wipes her forehead with her sleeve. "I never used one of these. They trained us how, but we never had enough to actually shoot one for practice." Galina rolls her head to look at Carson. "Did you call my *dupu* huge?"

Carson flops a hand across Galina's stomach. "Girl, your *dupu* is perfect. Let's get next to that wall over there."

The concrete-block wall is part of the substation compound. The transformers buzz and crackle. Carson peeks around the corner at the field. Several Zils are out in the open, and men are disappearing into the trees to rescue more. The fires near the field's north end—where they'd destroyed the first two trucks—are dying down. Rifle fire pops in the woods. *What are they shooting at?*

A whistle falls out of the night.

The first artillery shell hits fifty meters away, about ten meters short of the trees.

Finally. "Get it right, you idiots," Carson mutters.

The next lands behind the woods near the field's north end. Some militiamen run faster, while others drop and cover their heads. A BMP grinds into position close to the dying fire near where the road plunges into the forest.

The road...

The next rounds blast holes in the treeline, throwing dirt and plants and parts of trucks into the air. *Whump. Whump. Whumpwhumpwhump.* Explosions walk down the woods from north to south. Some fall short, but even those often hit something. Men who were running to save trucks turn around and sprint to save themselves. Huge blasts tell where loads of ammunition used to be.

Galina prays loudly behind her.

Carson stares at the north end of the road, waiting for Rogozhkin to drive the car through this inferno to take them home.

◎

Rogozhkin's driven through artillery barrages before. It's not his favorite thing to do. Doing it in a civilian sedan is an even worse idea.

But the women are waiting for him. They've done the hard work so far. It's time for him to do his part.

He shifts to take as much weight as he can off his right hip, now bandaged and bloody beneath his shredded jeans. Turns the key, backs carefully onto the road, shifts into first, rolls slowly over the railroad tracks, then stops at the clearing.

The entire eastern side of the field is fenced by flame. It's like daylight out there. While a few BMPs and BTRs have drifted onto the field, most are still at their positions next to the road, though their turrets are turned to watch the carnage. At least ten of the beasts stand between him and the substation, where the women are (or are supposed to be). He'll have to drive right under their guns.

Adapt and overcome.

Rogozhkin revs the engine, then pops the clutch. The Octavia leaps out of cover and bolts past a BMP. He does what he can to make the car a bad target. A dirt plume spouts a few meters behind him. Small-arms fire winks from foxholes to his right.

Fifty meters ahead, a BTR pulls across the road. Its turret swings toward him.

"He's coming!" Carson yells. "He's on his way!"

The silver sedan perfectly reflects the wall of fire's intense yellow light as it slaloms across the road. Unfortunately, that same light shows how many armored fighting vehicles stand in Rogozhkin's way. Two are already shooting at him.

Galina presses against Carson's back and peeks over her shoulder. "Look! One's trying to block the road."

"Can you hit it?"

"I don't know. How far is that?"

The weird light and lack of landmarks gives Carson some trouble trying to estimate distance. "Couple hundred meters. What's that thing's range?"

"Two hundred fifty meters."

The Octavia swerves around a fountain of dirt. Rogozhkin's

covered maybe a hundred of the four hundred meters between the field's north end and where she and Galina are huddling, trying not to be noticed. Three football fields is a long way with so many guns aimed at him. "Better get to it, then."

Galina points to the substation compound's west end, a hundred meters away. "Let's go up there."

The shelling stopped sometime when Carson wasn't paying attention. The militiamen who were face-down on the ground trying to be too small to die are starting to raise their heads. The fires have erased the dark. Still, when Galina runs along the wall, Carson follows. At least her balance is steady enough that she doesn't bounce off the concrete.

Galina settles on her right knee, prepares the RPG, aims, then squeezes the trigger rod on the top of the tube. The grenade whooshes up the road. Carson tries to guide it telepathically into its target.

A cloud of dirt billows from the ground next to the BTR.

Galina hurls the empty launcher into the nearest crater. "I missed!" She swivels to Carson. "You try."

"Me? I've—"

"Go on, try it. Maybe you'll have more luck." She holds up her hands. They shake like Jell-O in an earthquake. "I can't hold it steady."

Carson peels an RPG launcher off her shoulder. Galina steps her through the setup: pull the pin at the top of the housing; flip up the sights; line up the peep sight with the bottom-most range indicator on the front sight. Carson's heart flutters almost as fast as Galina's hands. Dark haze halos the BTR's turret—it's shooting at Rogozhkin. She takes a deep breath, exhales, then presses the trigger rod. A wispy smoke trail arcs toward the BTR.

It lurches. Black smoke jets out from under the turret.

The Octavia skids around the now-dead beast, bounces back onto the road, and plunges forward.

"Yes!" Galina pounds an especially sore bruise on Carson's back. "You got it!"

Something blasts away part of the wall's corner above their heads. Jagged chunks of concrete rain on them. Heavy machinegun rounds churn the dirt and the wall's edge.

Whatever's shooting at them is on the compound's opposite

side and coming their way. *So much for celebrating.* Carson shoves the last launcher into Galina's hands. "Take it out!"

Mashkov can't keep up with the torrent of radio traffic being firehosed into his ear. He'd stepped outside briefly a few minutes ago during the bombardment's peak. It was perhaps the most terrifying experience of his life.

Now reports deluge the command net. Casualties, destroyed equipment, units forced from their positions. Mashkov, Shatilov, and the sergeant try to sort it all out with little success.

One message jumps out at Mashkov: "…silver car on the road heading south…"

What? "This is Makiivka One. Repeat that last transmission about the car."

"Sir, there's a silver car on the access road to the quarry. It's heading south. Some of our units have engaged but haven't stopped it. We have at least two vehicles hit by RPGs—"

"What? Not by shelling?"

"No sir. One just got hit. It's RPGs. Maybe the *banderovtsi* special forces are here?"

Mashkov tries to stop the madhouse in his head so he can think. "This is Makiivka One. Identify yourself."

"Vovchak Ops, sir."

The Second Battalion operations center. Probably some poor sergeant swimming in bedlam in an armored vehicle that seems more like a target than protection. "Vovchak Ops, Makiivka One. Stand by." Mashkov snaps his fingers to get Shatilov's attention. "Have you heard anything about civilians on the field?"

"Yes." He clamps his cigarette between his lips and flips through the pad of lined paper he's been using for notes. "Here. About…eight minutes ago. Vovchak Logs reported two women running toward the substation. They're seeing mermaids."

Two women. Silver sedan. Bozhe, you truly are great. "Vovchak Ops, Makiivka One. Do not—repeat, do *not*—destroy the silver car. Capture and hold. There may be two civilian women in it or near it. Capture these spies if you can, but if you can't, neutralize them. Do you copy?"

Shatilov stares at him, his cigarette hand turned up. "What?"

Mashkov lets himself laugh for the first time in days. "We've got them, Evgeniy. We've got Rogozhkin and the rest of that damned money."

Rogozhkin aims the car at the two militiamen who step onto the road a few meters ahead of him. They blow holes in the windscreen. He ducks behind the dash, steering with one hand, trying to keep the accelerator pressed flat. Rounds pass through the car's interior and leave through the rear window.

One militiaman steps back. Rogozhkin twitches the wheel and clips the other as he passes. The man pinwheels off the road into a nearby power pole.

Something's changed. The BMPs have stopped firing their 30mm cannon at him. The BTRs aren't using their heavy machineguns anymore, only the 7.62s. He hasn't had to dodge a grenade for a couple of minutes. *What's going on here?*

The substation's getting closer. Two figures are clumped together at its northwest corner, one tall and one short. *Tarasenko and Galina? Tarasenko made it?* He'd been hoping she'd survive, but he's surprised by the relief he feels at seeing her.

A dark shape hulks off the substation compound's west end: a BMP on the edge of the road that leads to the quarry. Its main gun is aimed straight at him.

Carson glances at Galina. "Why did they stop shooting?"

"No idea."

Carson peeks around the wall's pulverized corner. The BMP's still there, twenty meters away, sandwiched between a tree and the road's sweeping right turn that leads to the quarry and their path out of this jungle.

Rogozhkin's less than a hundred fifty meters from them. The heavy thumping of cannons has died out; now she hears only the chattering of machineguns and the fire's roar.

Galina sets the RPG launcher on her knee. "Should I kill it?"

Should she? Something's happening that Carson doesn't understand. Maybe her brain's still screwed up from the concussion and dizziness. For whatever reason, the BMP's stopped being a threat. But for how long? "Not yet. We might need that for something worse."

Carson's watch claims it's 4:48. They'd stepped off from the car at 4:14. *All this in thirty-four minutes?* Thirty-four hours she could believe.

She's So. Damn. *Tired.* The pain meds Galina gave her yesterday are long gone by now. The first glimmer of dawn fringes the eastern horizon, backlighting the smoke billowing from the flaming woods. Soon enough the night will be gone and with it, their cover, such as it is.

This isn't the best idea any of them have had.

The Octavia's a hundred meters away. Carson taps Galina's elbow and points toward the car. She checks the BMP—still there, still buttoned up. Then movement catches her eye.

Something's moving in an overgrown patch about fifty meters west of the road. The fires light up a dozen militia troops crawling through the bushes, three of them packing machineguns. One by one, they settle into the weeds and face the road.

Finally, she gets it: they don't want to blow up the car. They think the money's in it. (It is.) Maybe they think the paintings are in it, too. (They are.) *Us? They don't care about us.*

She huddles with Galina. "They're setting up an ambush."

"Over there?"

"Yeah. They'll open up when Rogozhkin stops to get us. They want to kill us so they can have the car."

Galina nods. She looks drained even in the firelight. "What do we do?"

Even if Carson can put down the men with the machineguns, the survivors will tear her apart. They have the only cover out here. As fast as Rogozhkin's traveling, there's not much time for a Plan B. Once he gets here, that BMP will be able to open up on him at point-blank range, and the troops in the bushes will mop up what's left. Close enough to use aimed fire and not worry about blowing up the car.

"I don't know what to do," Carson mutters. Words she hates to say.

"Okay." Galina grabs Carson's arm. "Lara…I promised I'd get you out of here."

"Yeah. You better keep it, too." She gives Galina a one-armed hug. "Stay alive."

"You, too." Galina's eyes get big. She almost clocks Carson when she throws her hand out to point. "Look!"

The Octavia's off the road and bouncing over the churned-up dirt toward the substation's east end. Here and there militiamen leap out of the way, but only a couple shoot at the car.

Carson pumps her fist. "Yes! Let's get down there. Stay close to the wall."

They run as fast as they can in a combat crouch along almost a hundred meters of whitewashed concrete block. Up ahead, the Octavia skids to a stop. Seconds later, a cluster of single shots cuts through the aural chaos from the car's direction. Carson readies her rifle. *Is he taking fire?*

Carson and Galina at last reach the car. Rogozhkin's crouched behind the open driver's door, mowing down the last of five militiamen who'd been sheltering against the substation's east wall. When Carson flops into the front passenger's seat, he glances her way, drops the magazine from his Dragunov, reloads, then thrusts it stock-first at her. "Take this."

There's blood on the driver's seat and all over Rogozhkin's right hip. Carson rasps, "What happened to you?"

"A guard got lucky. Hold on."

The car lurches past the substation and the five bodies splayed near it, then slews around the corner to regain the gravel road. Concrete utility poles go by like fenceposts. A scabby treeline grows large in the windshield.

Galina yells, "There's a BMP—"

"I know!" Rogozhkin cranks the wheel to the left. They arrow past a utility pylon toward a small gap that appears between two substantial trees.

Carson fumbles her seatbelt on and closes her eyes. The last thing Rogozhkin needs right now is her screaming about dying.

The car shudders and bounces, goes briefly sideways, then passes something that scrapes the doors on her side. The Octavia stops shimmying a few seconds later as the tires settle into the reassuring crunch of rubber on gravel.

Carson opens her eyes again. The Octavia's fighting the gravel to climb a short grade. They crest a rounded ridge and pitch downward. She peers past the bullet holes in the windshield. "Holy shit."

An enormous crater opens in front of them, ringed with gravel roads and ramps that spiral down into the murk the dawn hasn't yet reached. The west end fades into the darkness.

"Impressive, yes?" Rogozhkin swerves them onto a road that hugs the chasm's north rim. "Roughly two kilometers east-west by a kilometer north-south. You should see it in full daylight."

"No, thanks. I saw stuff like that back home, at the tar sands. They were always depressing to look at." She turns to Galina in the back seat. "Are you okay?"

They make a matched pair: filthy, bleary, drained. Galina tries for a smile that doesn't quite work. "Can we not do that again?"

"Sure."

The car slows. Rogozhkin steers it toward the road's right edge, the one farthest away from the endless drop to the bottom. "Miss Tarasenko, can you drive?"

"You fucking kidding? Not the way my head is. Why?"

"Ehm...I may have lost more blood than I thought." The car grinds to a halt.

Galina says, "She can't drive. She almost passed out back there."

Rogozhkin frowns at Carson. "Really? You weren't going to tell me?"

"For fuck's sake, Rogozhkin, why didn't you say you're bleeding out? Get out, I'm driving."

Galina yelps, "No! If you get dizzy, we'll end up down there!" She stabs a finger toward the massive pit on the other side of the road.

He leans his forearms on the steering wheel. "We may do that anyway if I go much farther."

"*I'll* drive!" Galina shoves open her door and bolts out. "I'm the only healthy one here. Besides, it's my car." She stomps to the driver's door while Rogozhkin drags himself outside. They both look back along the road at the same time. Galina says, "Lara?"

It takes a moment for Carson to react to the name, and another few seconds to follow Galina's pointing finger.

A BMP turns onto their road. Its tracks churn up a cloud of gravel and dust behind it.

They change seats in fast-forward, Rogozhkin in back, Galina driving, Carson next to her. The Octavia has only just restarted when flame and dirt spews up ahead of them.

Carson mumbles, "Not this shit again."

There's not much room to zig-zag, only a meter-wide shoulder on the right adjoining a steep upward slope, and a ragged, crumbling edge on the left that ends at what looks like a bottomless pit. Galina does what she can, jinking side to side, speeding up and slowing down.

Rogozhkin—who's been busy with Galina's first-aid kit—says, "You have an Aglen."

Galina glances in the rear-view mirror, then twitches the car to the right. "A what?"

"Aglen. RPG-26."

"It was in a lorry."

"Clearly. Stop the car."

"Are you *insane?*"

"Why are we running when we can fight back? Stop the car."

Galina mutters as she steers the car as far to the right as she can without blocking the right-rear door. Rogozhkin slides out with the RPG slung over his shoulder, then sticks his head inside. "Miss Tarasenko, I may need you. Can you step out?"

Need me for what? To take over if you keel over from blood loss? She crawls from the car, then ducks as a shell rips by and explodes a few meters ahead of them. "What?"

Rogozhkin slaps the car's roof. "Galina, drive fast. Keep him occupied. When he's gone, come get us."

Galina's face is wide-eyed shock. "What? Leave you both here? What if you can't kill that thing?"

"Then don't come back. Go to the West and save your husband. Turn left at the end of this road, then right onto the second dirt road. That will lead you to Novotroitske. Go." He slams shut the door.

Carson gets it. She'd have liked to have a say in this, but she sees what he's doing. She leans down to look through the window at Galina, who spreads her hands in the universal *what now?* gesture. Carson doesn't want to be stranded here, but the BMP's rapidly catching up and she doesn't have time to cook up something else. So she nods and points to the west.

Galina drives off, spraying them with loose gravel.

Rogozhkin's moved behind a shallow outcropping of rock and is preparing the RPG. Carson crowds in behind him. "Why do you need me here? You have way more experience—"

"So she'll come back. If it's just me, she won't." He peeks around the rocks, then pulls in his head almost instantly. "Ten seconds. I need you to make yourself flat against the slope. This has a backblast."

She does as she's told. The cannon's *boom* gets louder with every shot. The shells rip past, the heat crackling the air. Black bursts kick up around the Octavia as it shrinks in the distance.

Shoot the fucking thing! Shoot!

Rogozhkin shoulders the launcher. He goes still. Then his fingers press the trigger bar. The grenade's *whoosh* ends abruptly in a *bang*.

The BMP clatters past them. Black smoke streams out its top hatches. It slowly drifts to the left.

Thirty meters down the road, it flies off the edge of the quarry, somersaults, then disappears into the dark.

CHAPTER 55

The Ukrainian Army stops the Octavia just shy of the H20 highway in Novotroitske, west of the line of contact.

Carson finds their standardized, vivid green-and-brown camouflage comforting after six days of soldiers looking like they'd got their uniforms at yard sales. Not that she really cares at this point. As long as they don't throw her in jail, they can dress like Smurfs if they want.

A sergeant in full battle-rattle flags them down as they approach a line of water-filled orange-plastic barriers. Galina opens her window without being told and hands the soldier her ID book before he asks for it.

He shines a flashlight on the passport, then on Galina's face. "Where are you going?"

"Novotroitske Hospital."

"Where have you been?"

"Dokuchajevsk. We were stuck—they closed the roads because of this battle thing." She throws in a little extra attitude: *wars are so inconvenient!*

Carson glances toward Rogozhkin. He pretends to be asleep on the back seat, curled up on his left side so the sergeant can get a full view of the blood on his hip.

The sergeant flashes his light on Carson's face. "Your ID?"

Carson hands him her Canadian passport, hoping he won't notice there's no visa or stamp for her entry. *Will these guys search the car?* She and Galina had cleaned it out once they got to the quarry's western end, tossing all their long weapons (except for Galina's shotgun) into the pit and making sure the paintings and Rogozhkin's backpack of cash are well-buried. That doesn't stop her gut from developing a swarm of locusts.

The sergeant hands back Carson's passport, then pins Rogozhkin with his flashlight. "Who's he?"

"He works for my company." Carson lays a protective hand on

Rogozhkin's knee. "A militia took him prisoner on the other side. They stole all his papers and shot him when we were escaping. That's why we have to go to the hospital." The fatigue and emotional wear-and-tear in her voice are completely real. "He's lost a lot of blood. Please?" She hates pretending to be pathetic—too many women she knows do that to get their way—but it's the right play for now and she doesn't have to work too hard at it.

The sergeant's flashlight beam rests on Rogozhkin's blood-caked hip. The otherwise-new jeans and once-pressed shirt sell the story of a Westerner caught in a bad place. The sergeant shakes his head, then waves them through with his flashlight. "Stay off the highway. It's closed to civilian traffic."

"Thank you, sir," Galina says, her voice all sweetness. "And thank you for protecting us from the terrorists."

Mashkov slumps in his folding chair and massages his temples as the drumbeat of doom overwhelms his radio headset.

Third Battalion, south of the quarry, got hit hard by Kyiv's artillery. Then it collided with a counterattack by two full armored battalions that's stalled the Russian units that were supposed to break the enemy lines. So much for Moscovia's supposed military superiority.

Second Battalion lost almost ninety percent of its supplies, including nearly all its reserve ammunition. Between the shelling and Rogozhkin and his damned women, the battalion also lost fourteen fighting vehicles and dozens of men.

And the Second Battalion BMP that chased Rogozhkin along the quarry? Its comms suddenly went dark. Mashkov has no doubt what happened.

That damned Rogozhkin and his triple-damned women got away...with the brigade's money.

Mashkov sighs heavily and rocks out of the chair. As he stretches his back, he says, "Evgeniy, whatever happened to that Russian tank unit that wandered off the line?"

Shatilov leans his palms on the plotting table, looking like he's missing the last three pieces he needs to finish the puzzle. "No idea. It disappeared. Maybe it got caught in the barrage."

"That would be ironic." The offensive's less than two hours old and it's already in trouble. Kyiv's army knows its business now, not like two years ago when it could hardly get out of its own way. *Why are we sitting here? Why don't they let us fight? We need a maximum push, now!*

The sergeant's voice says, "Colonel, General Kedrin is on the phone for you."

Finally. The First Corps commander must be calling to put the brigade in the fight. *Better late than never.* Mashkov races to grab the receiver from the sergeant's outstretched hand. "This is Mashkov."

"Colonel Mashkov." A buzz of crosstalk in the background almost drowns Kedrin's normally soft voice. "I'm told you've been asking to be committed to the assault."

"Yes, sir." *This is it! He's going to let us fight!* "We're ready to help in any way we can. We've taken some losses from the shelling, but I still have one entirely uncommitted battalion and two others that are still mission-capable. The men are ready to go."

"I see." Kedrin sighs. "I'm afraid that won't be possible. The Minister has told me personally that your brigade is to stay in place. You won't be in this fight, Mashkov."

It's like Kedrin reached through the line and punched him. "Sir, I don't understand."

"I think you do. Our...*partners* won't have it. I trust you understand what that means."

The Russians. This is their revenge for him taking back the brigade. "You need everyone you can get, sir. The offensive's already slowing—"

"I'm well aware of the operation's progress, Colonel." His voice has turned hard. "If I commit your brigade, our partners may ensure the offensive fails. When the operation is over, we'll talk. There's a lot to talk about, Mashkov. Kedrin out." The line turns to static.

Dazed, Mashkov drifts to the open door to the farm's gravel driveway. The cool, damp air washes over his face and helps clear Shatilov's secondhand smoke out of his lungs.

Shatilov asks, "What was that about?"

The Makiivka Brigade's an outcast. Mashkov's men are shut out of the biggest operation likely to happen this year...because of *him.* If the operation fails, he doesn't doubt someone will find a way to blame the brigade...because of *him.*

What have I done?

When he blinks his eyes clear, he sees a tank crouching at the end of the driveway. A late-model T-72, olive with no markings. *No markings. Russian.*

The turret whines until its 125mm gun points straight at him.

Mashkov barely has the will to breathe. "*Zrada.*"

Carson checks Rogozhkin into the Volnovakha Central District Hospital's trauma center, then shuffles outside to slump on a bench under a pair of trees near the main entrance. If nothing else, the Russian has a high pain threshold—he'd ordered Galina to drive the half-hour south over back roads from Novotroitske to the "big city" of Volnovakha so he could get "proper care."

She stares at her phone for a long time. Then she thumbs the contact for "Mom."

Olivia answers on the first ring. "One-Two-Six, where have you been? We fretted."

"People still fret?"

"I do. Are you well? Are you safe? I understand there's fighting near your location."

Carson holds up the phone to capture the muttering of heavy weapons in the distance. "I'm west of the line. I'm still breathing. I'll be safe when I'm in Toronto."

"Yes, of course." Olivia clears her throat. "I've orders from Allyson to transfer you to her as soon as you make contact. Before I do, though, is there anything you need immediately?"

Clean clothes. Clean water. A week of sleep. Enough pain meds to make that actually work. Decent food whenever I want it. "Don't look too hard at my expenses." Speaking English is weird after spending almost a week using nonstop Ukrainian or Russian.

"I rarely do. Also, Nought-Nine-One landed in Kyiv last night. Do you know him?"

One of the Russian associates. "Yeah. What's his deal?"

"He's there to support you if you need him. Do you?"

Carson's about to say *a little late?* but reconsiders just in time.

"Maybe. There's some stuff I'll need soon. Should I ask you or Allyson?"

"What is it that you need?"

Carson tells her. It's a longish list.

Olivia's silent for a few beats. "I...*can* get those things for you. However, it's unlikely you'd keep them long once Allyson susses it. I fear you'll need to speak with her."

"Figures." Carson grinds the heel of her hand into her forehead. "Where is she?"

"Shanghai. She's desperately trying to solicit Chinese business." She sighs. "I'm rather aged to learn Mandarin, but needs must. Shall I connect you?"

Carson makes a mental note to someday ask Olivia how many languages she speaks. "Yeah."

Shanghai's five hours ahead of Donetsk, so Allyson's wide awake and full of questions when she picks up the line. Carson gives her a report covering Friday through an hour ago. Then the grilling starts. Carson knew this would happen and wants it out of the way before she asks the boss for things that are way out-of-scope.

Allyson ends the inquisition with, "Are you well?"

"No. Thanks for waiting 'til the end to ask."

Allyson *tsks*. "Olivia informs me you need certain resources to finish the project. What are they?"

Carson goes through the list again. It's better organized this time, but isn't any shorter. She describes in more detail what she intends to do with each item.

Allyson's end of the connection grows quiet, then frigid. "You expect to spend our entire profits from this project to end the project?"

Here we go. "They're expenses. Bill the client."

That starts another wrangle of the sort they usually have. Carson wishes she had a hundred euros for every time Allyson says she's mentoring Carson, but the relationship's been more like a controlling mother/rebellious daughter thing since the start. Today's no different. They argue over every item on Carson's wish list. Forty minutes later, Allyson's okayed all but two minor things.

"Do you do this with Mr. R?" Allyson's voice is all about exasperation.

"Yeah. I tell him I need something, he gives it to me. That's what he pays me for." Or pays himself; nearly all the money Rodievsky "pays" her comes off her father's debt.

"He has more resources than do I." Allyson's throat rumbles. "We'll speak about this when you reach Bonn."

"Not going there. Like I said…I got things to do here first."

Carson wakes up Galina—asleep in the Octavia—to drive about three kilometers south of the hospital to the nice-enough Comfort Hill Hotel near the city center. Her room is just as she left it.

As they unload, Galina stands with her fists on her hips and frowns. "My poor car." The bodywork is scratched, dented, and peppered with dozens of bullet holes; the windshield is nearly opaque and the rear window's mostly gone; the suspension's wrecked; blood stains the front and back seats; and the driver-side mirror is missing.

Carson squeezes her shoulder. "She did her job."

They each eat an enormous breakfast in the hotel restaurant, then walk a few blocks to the Central Market, another haphazard collection of permanent storefronts and cluttered market stalls under metal-roofed sheds. There Carson launches her version of a shopping spree: clothes, underwear, disposable razors.

Walking around more or less freely without body armor and without bracing for someone to shoot her is Carson's working definition of paradise. She's always liked street markets and bazaars for the people-watching and for the vibrant life they have. She needs this. She needs to decompress, to melt back into the real world.

Galina follows her around, looking like she's about to break out laughing. She'll hold up something to show Carson and say, "This is cute."

"Yeah, but it won't work with my capris." Which she doesn't own.

Then back to the hotel. A long, *long* shower with her own soap, shaving her legs and pits, washing her hair with her own shampoo. More ointment on the cuts and scrapes. Her bruises are approaching that always-attractive green-purple stage; she ignores everything below her neck as she brushes her hair. Normal is horribly underrated.

She stretches out on one of the twin beds and tells Galina, "Wake me in an hour."

Her stomach growls her awake at one in the afternoon. Galina's snoring on the bed next to hers.

Rogozhkin's sitting up in his single bed when Carson steals into the hospital's recovery ward to visit. He's washed, freshly shaved, and alert, draped in a cotton hospital gown sprinkled with tiny pink and blue flowers. The place is reasonably clean and doesn't smell bad; better than average for a hospital on the edge of the Third World.

He smiles at Carson. "Miss Tarasenko. I hardly recognize you dressed like a woman."

"Nice." Carson's a bit embarrassed about how long it took her to choose her outfit: black dress slacks and low-heeled pumps with a long-sleeved linen blouse in cobalt blue. She perches on the edge of Rogozhkin's bed. "How bad is it?"

"A grazing wound. Not bad, given my history, just messy and painful. They sewed it up and gave me some good German antibiotics. How are you?"

"Alive. Colorful. When can you leave here?"

"They want me overnight for observation. They keep calling me 'Mr. Stepaniak.' A little joke of yours?"

"I needed the name of a Ukrainian citizen to check you in. You don't look like a Galina Demchuk."

Another smile. "I'm glad you noticed." He settles into a pillow propped against the robin's-egg-blue wall. "You came back. I wondered if you would."

She had, too. "I made a promise. I'll keep it. What's next for you?"

He pours himself a cup of water from a plastic pitcher on the wooden stand next to his bed. "I originally wanted to retire to Crimea. Have you ever been there?"

Carson shakes her head.

"Too bad. It's quite nice. But now that I'm a dead deserter..."
He shrugs. "Now I think Cyprus might be interesting. Excellent
weather, the sea and beaches all around. Nice people, the Cypriots.
They're used to Russians by now—I'll blend in. And the banks
aren't too fussy about where their money comes from."

She knows about the last two parts. Cyprus is a favorite
destination for rich Russians trying to offshore their assets. The
Cypriots are very understanding about granting residence permits
and passports to visitors who contribute enough money to the local
kleptocracy. "That should be nice for you. Just don't let them know
that million's all you have. Make them think you're spreading it
around and they'll take you more seriously."

Rogozhkin's left eyebrow peaks. "You know how the system
works there?"

"I know people who know." Like Rodievsky. "After the bribes,
most of your money will go to your new house. What will you do?
Can't see you waiting tables."

He laughs. "Neither can I. But..." He spreads his hands. "All
I'm qualified to do is kill people."

"That doesn't limit your options. You're Russian."

"True." He leans toward her, bracing his hands on his knees.
"What about you? What's next for...Lara, is it?"

She smiles without meaning to. *Flirting's nice.* "Go home.
Heal. Get back in shape."

"I didn't notice that you're out of it."

"Nice. Spend a couple weeks with Yurik. I need some real
combat training if I'm gonna keep doing this shit." She waves
toward the window, taking in most of the Donbass.

Rogozhkin pats her hand on the thin bedspread. "You did fine.
Is there a man?" He pauses for a moment. "Or a woman?"

Totally flirting. "Nothing regular. And you? Will you go for
some nice grown-up Greek woman, or find a twenty-year-old
blonde to play with?" *If he can ask, so can I.*

He chuckles again. "I doubt a twenty-year-old blonde would
put up with me for long. She'd probably kill me if she didn't spend
all my money first. As for the mature woman..." His smile fades.
"It'll be hard to find someone who'll tolerate me explaining what
I've done over the past thirty years. Someone who won't run away
in disgust afterwards."

Carson knows exactly what he means. She's learned how much she can tell other people without driving them off immediately. It's why cops marry nurses or other cops—nobody else can deal with the crazy hours and the shitty world they work in.

This is nice. Just talking, no pressure, no race to bed. Wish I didn't have to end it. "While you're finding yourself, I've got a job for you." Both his eyebrows tick up. "Remember I told you I'm supposed to get those pictures back to their museum? That still needs to happen. There's something I need to do here, but I want those things gone. So you're taking them to Bonn."

Rogozhkin falls back against his pillow and crosses his arms. His mouth opens to say something, then closes.

"A guy who goes by 'Piotr' will get here around noon tomorrow. He's another associate with my company. He'll take you and the pictures to Dnipro. A private jet will fly you direct to Bonn. The two of you take the pictures to the museum. There's some other stuff I need you to give them, too." Heitmann's wallet, ring, and watch. "Then you get back on the jet and go straight to Cyprus. You'll get a passport for whoever you want to be. Tell Piotr the name and nationality tomorrow and the passport'll be waiting on the other end."

"Why are you doing this?" He doesn't bother to hide his confusion.

"You promised to get me and Galina across the line. You did. If you weren't there, we'd both be dead. I promised to get you out of here. This is how I keep my promise."

He nods slowly. Then he leans forward and wraps his hand around Carson's. "Come with me to Cyprus. I don't know you very well, but what I know impresses me. You handle yourself well. You keep your promises. You're healthy and strong. And…what was it you said to me when we met? You understand me? I believe you do. We both know what it is to do what we have to, whatever the price."

Carson watches their hands nestle together. *He wants me to run away with him? That's a new one. Not even Ron did that.* The men she finds are usually satisfied with a weekend of fun and a goodbye kiss. There hasn't been a serious proposal for more since her ex.

Don't lose your head. He wants you to come play, not marry him.

What would that be like? Yeah, he's over a decade older, but she's no girl anymore, either. He's not bad-looking, good shape, speaks well, a nice smile. He probably has a really complicated past. Then again, so does she.

A few weeks? A few months, until the sex gets old and they drive each other nuts?

It could be a mess. Or it could be fun.

"I promised Galina I'd help get her husband out of prison. I have to keep that promise, too." She squeezes his hand. "Thanks for asking."

"Thank you for not saying 'no' right away."

Carson gets halfway to the door before she stops to turn his way. "By the way, if a woman named Allyson shows up one day to talk to you, listen to her. She's my boss. She may give you a way to pay for your retirement."

"You'll give me a good reference?"

"We'll see." Carson smiles. "Take care of yourself, Edik Gregorivich."

He returns the smile. "Until we meet again. Which I hope is soon."

CHAPTER 56

Carson wraps an arm around Galina's shoulders and squeezes. "You'll recognize him. Don't worry."

Worrying is what Galina's done most since they left Volnovakha Wednesday morning. She worried about being turned back after the endless wait at the Marinka crossing into Donetsk. She worried through their drive across the surreal calm and normalcy of Donetsk itself—street-food vendors, visitors snapping selfies at statues and fountains, people crowding cafés and busy shops, as if the war was on a different continent. She worried at each of the four checkpoints they navigated, spilling money into pockets belonging to cops and militias and a civilian group they didn't try to identify. She couldn't wind down in the hostel they found in Shakhtarsk. "How can you sleep?" she demanded. "He's *here*. Right *here*. Just two kilometers away."

This morning, Galina tried on every piece of clothing she had with her until she settled on a simple white mid-calf cotton dress covered with tiny blue dots. She brushed her hair compulsively until Carson took the brush away. "You look fine. He's not gonna care what you look like. You're gonna be the most beautiful thing he's ever seen."

They've been standing for almost half an hour at the iron-barred gate into a run-down industrial compound on the eastern edge of Shakhtarsk. Two shabby office blocks to their right; two large, rust-stained workshops to their left; battered shipping containers on the cracked cement slab; armed guards by the doors; concrete-block walls and concertina wire all around.

"What if he's not here anymore? If they sold him again?" Galina's voice is shaky verging on broken.

"Then we'll go there. We're not leaving without your husband."

Carson's had more physical contact with Galina than she has

with any other woman in her adult life. Holding hands, hugging, letting Galina cry on her shoulder; it's a little uncomfortable, but she knows she needs to do it. She promised she'd help Galina get her husband back. If that means giving her someone to hold onto, Carson will do that.

Two figures appear from the larger of the two workshops. One wears a shiny gold track suit and polished Doc Martens; the other one's draped in a ragged, colorless smock, the remains of camouflaged trousers, and what look like shower scuffs. Track Suit saunters toward the gate while Smock shuffles behind him with zip-tied wrists.

Galina breaks away from Carson, grabs two of the bars across the gate, then presses her face against the metal mesh. As the two men come closer, her breathing sounds more like weeping. "Bohdan?" she whispers. "Oh no oh no oh no." She rattles the gate and screams, "Bohdan! Bohdan, it's me! Bohdan!"

Smock—Bohdan—seems to snap out of a coma. His nearly-bald head swings up and his eyes open wide. "Galya?" It's more a croak than a voice. "Galya?" Tears start pouring down his filthy cheeks, leaving tracks of cleaner skin behind.

Track Suit reaches the gate and pauses to light a cigarette. He shows Galina a big smile. "*Pani* Demchuk. This is the one you want?" His Ukrainian is so chunky, even Carson notices.

Galina struggles to breathe. "Yes. Yes."

"You are sure? I have others, not so worn out. Maybe—"

"No! This one. He's my husband. Please let me have my husband." The edge of hysteria on her voice worries Carson. They need to be well clear of here before Galina can lose it.

Track Suit unlocks and swings open the squeaky gate. He laughs. "Look at you. So pretty for your man. You must love him very much. Enough to take him as a scarecrow, yes?"

"Yes. I…I brought the money." She tears a bundle of bills from her purse and holds it up. When Track Suit reaches for it, Galina almost throws it to him.

Carson pushes off the car's nose and steps closer to the gate. She doesn't like handing over the money before the hostage is free. She takes a quick inventory of Track Suit: skinny (no bulk under the loose material); probably a pistol in his right jacket pocket; lots of chunky finger jewelry that'll tear her up if he gets in the first punch.

Track Suit riffles through the sheaf of €200 notes, then puts on a frown. "I am so sorry, *Pani* Demchuk. This is not *nearly* enough."

Oh, you bastard...

Galina looks like the wall kicked her. "But...but your man said five thousand. It's all there, every—"

"But that was so long ago." Track Suit gives her a fake-disappointed look. "We have spent so much more to keep him alive. We need you to reimburse all that money, you know. You must give us ten thousand."

"*What?*" Galina's shriek nearly shatters Carson's sunglasses. "You can't! It took until now to get it! Please, please don't do this!" She starts sobbing. "*Pleeeeeease.* I'll give you money, I'll—"

Bohdan rasps, "No! Please, no!" Track Suit backhands him onto the ground.

"Galya, shut up." Carson hates doing this, but the last thing they need is for Galina to shovel all her money at this little shit. She grabs Galina's hand as it dives for her purse.

Galina looks at her like Carson hit her, which she essentially did. "I have to!" she sobs. "I can't lose him, I can't, not now—"

Carson crushes Galina's face into her shoulder. She whispers, "Shhh. You won't lose him. I promise. I won't let that happen to you. You're...you're a friend. I don't have a lot of friends. People I can trust. I...don't do trust well. But I trust you. Do you trust me?" She gently peels Galina off her shoulder.

"I do."

"Okay. Let me deal with this *khui*. Stay here."

Track Suit's face twists like he just stepped in dog shit when Carson marches to the gate. He stabs a finger toward her. "*Pani* Demchuk, this is who?"

"She's...she's my friend."

"You should tell your friend to stay out—"

"*You.*" Carson steps in front of Galina and aims a loaded finger at Track Suit. "You want money, you talk to me."

Track Suit gives her an up-and-down scan. She knows he's seeing a woman, but only a woman. Her new long-sleeved blue tee covers her arms and is loose enough to hide her body armor, and her black crepe traveling slacks fit loose on her hips and thighs.

He snorts, then swaggers to within a couple hand's breadths.

"You have a name…*friend?*"

"Not one you need to know." She grabs the front of his track suit jacket, hauls him through the gate, then drives her forehead into the bridge of his nose. He yelps and staggers backward as blood spatters his jacket. While he's busy, Carson takes two quick steps forward, squats, wraps her arms around his knees, then yanks his legs out from under him. His head bounces off the slab with the sound of a sandbag falling.

In an instant she's on top of him, a knee in his diaphragm, yanking a tiny PSM pistol from his pocket. She racks the slide and jams the muzzle under his chin. "Are you listening?"

Track Suit moans. He tries to tilt his head back to get away from his own weapon, but Carson presses harder.

"*Are. You. Listening.*"

He pants, "Yes. Yes."

"Good." She cranes over her shoulder. "Galya, get Bohdan out here. Now." She turns to the skinny, squirming asshole under her. "Know what I like about these little pistols? They're great for close-in work. The little slug won't leave your skull. It bounces around and chews up what little brain you have. Did you know that? Shake or nod. Show me you're listening."

Track Suit shakes his head like he's being tased.

"Good. I work with people like you. You disgust me. I'd rather pull the trigger now and make the world a better place. But your people made a deal with my friend. A shitty deal, but a deal." Galina and Bohdan are murmuring to each other behind her, but she doesn't try to eavesdrop. "The best you get is to go with the original deal. Your other option—the *only* one—is that I drag your sorry ass with us. We go to the nearest field. My friend gets her shotgun and turns you into chopped pork because of what you and your asshole friends did to the man she loves. So, you want to live?"

His eyes have grown huge during her speech. If he's looking, he'll see in her eyes that Carson is dead serious—and she's hoping he'll go for the second option.

"Go," he gasps. "Go away. Don't come back."

She and Galina hustle a sobbing Bohdan into the cobalt-blue Suzuki Grand Vitara SUV parked a few steps away, facing the street. Galina follows him into the back seat while Carson climbs behind the wheel. The tires chirp when she stomps the gas pedal.

They're knifing westbound on the H21 motorway—here a glorified two-lane city street—by the time Galina and Bohdan pull themselves apart. Galina grips Carson's shoulder. "Bohdan, this is my friend, Lara. Lara, my husband."

A thin, dirty, calloused hand pushes between the front seats. "Lara...thank you for bringing my wife to me."

She shakes his hand with her left. "Glad I could." And she is. Watching them in the rear-view mirror, seeing the relief and love and yearning in their faces, how they cling together and try to catch up on almost two years of kisses all at once, nearly breaks her heart. *Nobody in the world would ever be that happy to see me.* Her own fault, she knows, not that it makes the thought any easier to take.

Bohdan blinks at the baggage piled behind him. "These are our things?"

Galina's still trying to stop the tears sluicing down her cheeks. "Yes. Yes, my darling. It's all we have left."

"But where's your car?"

She strokes his cheek. "*This* is my car. Lara gave it to me."

Actually, Olivia did. She found it in Dnipro on a used-car website. An all-cash offer in euros brought the price down considerably. Piotr bought it and drove it to Volnovakha. Galina cried when Carson handed her the key on Tuesday.

"If you're going to drive all the way to Krakow," Carson says, "you need something better than that tin can you had. New life, new car."

Bohdan gently squeezes her shoulder. "Thank you for our new life."

Carson takes a good look at him in the mirror. Under the dirt and sunken cheeks and red eyes and buzzed-off hair, she can just about see the smiling man in the photo at Galina's house.

After all the bad things I did here...I did something good. Made things better for someone. And I made a friend.

Is it enough?

It'll do for now.

Five hours later, once they'd crawled through the Marinka crossing again, Carson pulls over at a crossroads just outside of town and shuts off the engine.

Galina yelps, "What's wrong? Why are you stopping?"

"Relax. Nothing's wrong." Carson hauls a bottle of Bulgarian champagne from under the driver's seat. She opens her window, pops the cork outside, lets the overflow soak the spotty grass they're parked on, then hands the bottle to Galina. "Congratulations. You two are out of the Donbass. Back in Ukraine. Your new life starts now."

Galina takes a huge swig from the bottle, then passes it to Bohdan. Her grin takes over her face. "What about your life?"

Carson shrugs. "We go to Dnipro. You guys have a suite waiting for you at the best hotel in town. I've got a room there, too. I get some sleep, then get on a plane and go home." Or to her next project. Whichever comes first, or pays better.

Bohdan coughs after his drink of the sparkling wine. He holds out the bottle to Carson. "We will not forget you."

The wine's swill, but it's the best swill Carson's had for a long time. "And I won't forget you."

ABOUT THE AUTHOR

Lance Charnes has been an Air Force intelligence officer, information technology manager, computer-game artist, set designer, *Jeopardy!* contestant, and is now an emergency management specialist. He's had training in architectural rendering, terrorist incident response and maritime archaeology, but not all at the same time. Lance's Facebook author page features spies, archaeology and art crime.

LIKE WHAT YOU READ?

Share your experience with friends! **Leave a review** on your favorite online bookselling site, on a readers' social network (such as Goodreads) or promotion site (such as Bookbub), or just on your blog or Facebook wall. Someone told you about this book; please pass on the favor.

WANT TO KNOW MORE?

There are lots of ways to keep tabs on Lance and his novels, and to find additional material, reading group guides, deleted scenes and more.

Official Website
https://www.wombatgroup.com
Sign up for Lance's newsletter! Be the first to find out about new books, special deals, and the occasional giveaway.

Facebook Author Page
https://www.facebook.com/Lance.Charnes.Author

Goodreads
https://www.goodreads.com/lcharnes

Twitter
https://www.twitter.com/lcharnes

Jake Eldar's and Miriam Schaffer's names may kill them.

Jake manages a bookstore in Brooklyn. Miriam is a secretary at a Philadelphia law firm. Both grew up in Israel and emigrated to build new lives in America. Neither knows the other exists...until the Israeli intelligence agency Mossad uses their identities in an operation to assassinate a high-ranking Hezbollah commander in Doha, Qatar.

Now Hezbollah plans to kill them both.

Jake, Miriam and ten other innocents in five countries – the Doha 12 – awake to find their identities stolen and their lives caught between Mossad and Hezbollah in an international game of murder and reprisal. Jake stumbles upon Hezbollah's plot but can't convince the police it exists. When his wife is murdered in a botched hit meant for him, Jake and Miriam try desperately to outrun and outfight their pursuers while shielding Jake's young daughter from the killers on their trail.

Hezbollah, however, has a fallback plan: hundreds of people will die if Jake and Miriam survive.

> "*Doha 12* will have you riveted from beginning to end... be one of the first discoverers of an exceptional writer." – *Seeley James, author of* The Geneva Decision

> "*Doha 12* is an exciting and hard-to-put-down read of fiction, not to be overlooked." – *Midwest Book Review*

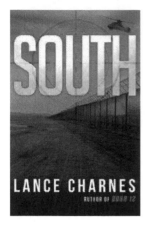

Luis Ojeda owes his life to the Pacifico Norte cartel. Literally. Now it's time to pay.

Luis led escaping American Muslims out of the U.S. during the ten years following a 2019 terrorist attack on Chicago. He retired after nearly being killed by a border guard. But now in 2032, the Nortes give Luis a choice: pay back the fortune they spent saving his life, or take on a special job.

The job: Nora Khaled – FBI agent, wife, mother of two, and Muslim. She claims her husband will be exiled to one of the nation's remote prison camps to rot with over 400,000 other Muslim Americans. Faced with her family's destruction, she's forced to turn to Luis – the kind of man she's spent her career bringing to justice.

But when the FBI publicly accuses Nora of terrorism, Luis learns Nora's real motive for heading south: she has proof that the nation's recent history is based on a lie – a lie that reaches to the government's highest levels.

Torn between self-preservation and the last shreds of his idealism, Luis guides Nora and her family toward refuge in civil war-wracked Mexico. The FBI, a dogged ICE agent, killer drones, bandits, and the fearsome Zeta cartel all plan to stop him. Success might free Luis from the Nortes... but failure means disappearing into a black-site prison, or a gruesome death for them all.

"*South* is a compelling futuristic thriller, as convincing a cautionary novel as Margaret Atwood's *The Handmaid's Tale* was in its day..." – *CriminalElement.com*

"*South* is a riveting work of action/adventure suspense that is a real page-turner... Lance Charnes demonstrates a truly impressive knack for deftly creating a complex and thoroughly engaging story..." – *Midwest Book Review*

Allyson DeWitt is the president of The DeWitt Agency. Its headquarters is a brass plate outside a discreet Luxembourgeois lawyer's office door. Its corporate treasury is in Vanuatu. Its directors are strangely untraceable. Its only other full-time employee is Olivia, who's able to arrange for the damnedest things when an Agency associate needs help.

Matt Friedrich is the Agency's newest employee. He has a certain useful set of skills that he learned while working in a crooked L.A. art gallery, and other knowledge that he gained while hanging out in federal prison with Wall Street types who had bad lawyers. He's out on supervised release and working for $10 an hour at Starbucks to pay off over half a million in debts and restitution.

When one of Allyson's clients has a need to fill that involves art in whatever form, Matt gets the project. He can knock down a chunk of his debt with each payoff... so long as he stays alive and out of jail. Sometimes he's paired with Carson, a disgraced Toronto cop who has her own debts, problems, and useful skills. Together they make a pretty good team – if they don't kill each other first.

Follow Matt as Allyson's projects drag him around the world, where he sees new places, meets new friends, avoids new enemies, and discovers (or pulls off) new scams. If he plays his cards right, he can make a lot of money, pay off his debts, and build a new life. All he has to do is not screw up... which is much harder than it sounds.

The DeWitt Agency Files series

Four years ago, what Matt Friedrich learned at work put him in prison. Yesterday, it earned him a job. Tomorrow, it may kill him.

Matt learned all the angles at his old Los Angeles gallery: how to sell stolen art, how to "enhance" a painting's history, how to help buyers hide their purchases from their spouses or the IRS. He made a load of money doing it – money he poured into the lawyer who worked a plea deal with the U.S. Attorney. Matt's out on parole and hopelessly in debt with no way out...until a shadowy woman from his past recruits him to find a cache of stolen art that could be worth millions.

Now Matt's in Milan, impersonating a rich collector looking for deals. He has twenty days to track down something that may not exist for a boss who knows a lot more than she's telling. He's saddled with a tough-talking partner who may be out to screw him and up against a shady gallerist whom Matt tried to send to prison. His parole officer doesn't know he's left the U.S. Worse yet, what Matt's looking for may belong to the Calabrian mafia.

Matt's always been good at being bad. If he's good enough now, he gets a big payday with the promise of more to come. But one slip in his cover, one wrong word from any of the sketchy characters surrounding him, could hand Matt a return trip to jail...or a long sleep in a shallow grave.

"The mystery has enough twists and turns – with the characters keeping plenty of secrets – to keep the reader guessing until the very end... A charming start to what promises to be an intriguing series." – *The BookLife Prize*

"*The Collection* is a breezy read in the way the very early Leslie Charteris' Saint novels were breezy: entertaining with an underlining of grit below the surface..." – *Criminal Element*

Dorotea DeVillardi is ninety-one years old, gorgeous, and worth a fortune. Matt Friedrich's going to steal her.

The Nazis seized Dorotea's portrait from her Viennese family, then the Soviets stole it from the Nazis. Now it's in the hands of a Russian oligarch. Dorotea's corporate-CEO grandson played by the legal rules to get her portrait back, but he struck out. He's hired the DeWitt Agency to get it for him – and he doesn't care how they do it.

Now Matt and his ex-cop partner Carson have to steal Dorotea's portrait from a museum in a way that nobody knows it's gone, and somehow launder its history so the client doesn't have to hide it forever. The client's saddled them with a babysitter: Dorotea's granddaughter Julie, who may have designs on Matt as well as the painting. As if this wasn't hard enough, it looks like someone else is gunning for the same museum – and he may know more about Matt and Carson's plans than he should.

Matt went to prison for the bad things he did at his L.A. art gallery. Now he has a chance to right an old wrong by doing a bad thing for the best of reasons. All he has to do is stay out of jail long enough to pull it off.

"Interlacing storylines give this series its charm... It's nice to have some modern *It Takes a Thief* escapism to slip away to in this world gone awry. Suffice it to say, I can't wait for The DeWitt Agency Files #3." – *Criminal Element*

"A brilliant heist story filled with fascinating art history reminiscent of Dan Brown or Steve Berry. Only better." – *Seeley James, author of the Sabel Security thriller series*

LANCE CHARNES

CHASING
CLAY

THE DEWITT AGENCY
FILES #3

It's pure white, deep blue... and dirty all over.

Nam Ton ware – centuries-old ceramics from Southeast Asia's Golden Triangle – captivated the DeWitt Agency's tech-tycoon client. Now Immigration and Customs Enforcement is on his case for buying smuggled antiquities. To get immunity, he's hired the agency to run an off-books investigation into Nam Ton's source.

Disgraced ex-L.A. gallerist and ex-con Matt Friedrich is in charge. If he finishes within sixty days, he'll earn an early end to his probation. If he doesn't, he may go back to prison for bending the federal criminal code into a pretzel.

Soon enough, Matt's in San Francisco, getting tight with Savannah, the client's beautiful art advisor, to scam his way into the smuggling operation. As the burglary, blackmail, tax evasion and customs fraud piles up and Matt finds himself sandwiched in a federal turf war, he realizes he's in *way* over his head with no good way out. And that's *before* he ends up in a real live jungle.

Matt's dealing with a type of art he knows nothing about from an area he's seen only in war movies. Now the fate of some trafficked pottery may decide whether Matt gets his freedom... or spends a long stretch in a concrete cell.

"[The] novel is fast-paced with strong tension and a well-constructed plot...Protagonist Matt Friedrich's voice is distinct and believable. Charnes's dialogue is gripping and easily moves the plot forward... *Chasing Clay* is an entertaining and fast-paced mystery, featuring an everyman hero thrust into a high-stakes spy world." – *The Booklife Prize*